I0597006

Rue Toulouse

By
Debby Grahl

First published by The Writer's Coffee Shop Publishing House
Australia, 2015

Paperback ISBN- 978-0-9994630-3-1
E-book ISBN- 978-0-9994630-4-8

A CIP catalogue record for this book is available from the US Congress Library.

Graphic Design – Niina Kokko
Cover Images - © IgorBorodin / Depositphotos, © Csaba Peterdi / Adobe Stock, © Adrian V. Allenstein / Adobe Stock

Interior Design – Jennifer McGuire | JEM Book Designs

Dedication

To my husband, David, with all my love.
Laissez les bons temps rouler.

Prologue

Caterine Doucette lay in the white canopy bed, her tears soaking the lace-edged pillowcase as she clutched a Raggedy Ann doll. Her *grandmère* and *grandpère* had told her Mommy and Daddy had gone to heaven and would be sitting on a star watching her. But Caterine didn't want them to be on a star. She wanted them to be with her. She loved Grandmère and Grandpère, but she wanted to go home.

Caterine buried her face in the pillow and began to sob.

"Don't cry, Cat. It'll be okay," Bobby Doucette said as he stood next to the bed and awkwardly patted Caterine's back. "I'm here. Look what I brought you."

Caterine buried her face further into the pillow. "Go away, Bobby. I don't care what you have."

"Please, Cat, I brought you Rex. He always makes me feel better when I'm sad."

Caterine hiccupped then turned her face to see her seven-year-old cousin Bobby holding out his favorite stuffed puppy. "I don't think even Rex can make me feel better. Bobby, I want my mommy and daddy, and I want to go home. But Grandmère says I have to live here now with all of you."

Bobby nodded. "That's right, Cat. Just think, we'll always be together and we'll have lots of fun."

Caterine sat up and rubbed her eyes. "I don't feel like having fun. Bobby, why did my mommy and daddy have to go away?"

Tears filled Bobby's eyes. "Grandmère said someone hit your car and ran away. She said your car hit a tree and your parents had to go to heaven."

"But I was in the car. Why didn't I go to heaven, too?"

Bobby sniffed. "I don't know, Cat, but I'm glad you didn't. Here." Bobby handed Rex to Caterine. "You'll be okay here with us. My daddy and Uncle Jules are going to fix up Raymond and Randal's old tree house for us to play in. And you can have tea parties with Paulette and Charlotte."

Tears again began to flow down Caterine's cheeks. "I don't want to have tea parties with them. Your sister Paulette pinches me every time she sees me and tells me if I'm bad I'll be taken to the swamp and left. And cousin Charlotte calls me 'Grandmère's spoiled brat.' "

Bobby frowned. "Don't pay any attention to them. They don't like me either. So it will be you and me against them. Just think, Cat, every time they're mean to us, there'll be two of us to fight back—not just one."

Caterine's lower lip trembled. "But, Bobby, I want them to like me. My mommy said they were mean to me because they were jealous that I was Grandmère's favorite granddaughter. But I don't want to be her favorite if it means no one likes me."

Bobby shrugged his thin shoulders. "I think Grandmère likes you more because you're nice, not mean like them." Bobby's eyes brightened. "You know what I think will make you feel better?"

"What?"

"A mug of hot chocolate with lots of marshmallows. I'll bet if we go down to the kitchen, Cook will fix us some."

Caterine rubbed her nose. "We're supposed to be sleeping. Will we get in trouble if Grandmère catches us?"

Bobby smiled. "Naw. I do it all the time. Now if my mommy or Aunt Frances sees us, well . . ."

"Well what?"

"Run."

Caterine followed Bobby as they crept along the dimly lit hallway, their footsteps muffled by the thick carpet.

"We'll use the back stairs," Bobby whispered. "I think everyone is still in the parlor."

As they turned the corner, Bobby reached out his hand, stopping Caterine.

"There's light coming from under my parents' bedroom door. Be really, really quiet."

They were almost past the door when Hyacinth Doucette's shrill nasal voice, coming from the other side, stopped them.

"I don't care what Miss Dauphine says, Markus. That child doesn't belong here. She should go live with her mother's people in Virginia."

"For God's sake, Hyacinth, keep your voice down. You know as well as I that Suzanne left Virginia to get away from her family. The last thing she'd want is for Caterine to be sent into that dysfunctional mess. Mother isn't going to send Caterine anywhere, and you'd just better get used to it. My God, she's a six-year-old little girl who just lost her parents. Have you no compassion? Do you not realize how losing Luke and Suzanne has shattered my own parents? The last thing Miss Dauphine needs now is for Caterine to go live somewhere else."

"That's just my point. Miss Dauphine already treats Caterine like she's a little princess. Can you just imagine how she'll coddle the girl now? Why, she'll turn her into more of a spoiled brat than she already is."

"That's enough, Hyacinth. Caterine isn't a little brat nor will she become one. If you want to talk about spoiled brats, you don't have to look any further than Paulette."

"Markus, what a thing to say about your daughter."

"Yes, well, I didn't make her like that. *You* did."

"Let me tell you something. My Paulette is just as good as Miss Dauphine's precious Caterine. And I'll be damned if I'll stand by and let Caterine grow up thinking otherwise."

Bobby tugged Caterine's hand and whispered, "Come on, Cat. Don't listen to her."

Caterine held back a sob and followed.

As they approached the central staircase, they paused. Aunt Frances' and Uncle Jules' voices could be heard below.

"Honestly, Jules, I can't believe Miss Dauphine is considering taking Caterine with her to Ma Chérie," Frances Doucette said. "The child should be kept in school."

"It will only be for a short time until Caterine gets adjusted," Jules replied. "Mother wants to keep her close, and Caterine loves going to Ma Chérie, so it will be fine."

"That's the problem. Since Caterine was old enough to walk, your mother has taken her to that store, treating her as if she were the granddaughter who will inherit. Miss Dauphine has always been a stickler for tradition, and our Charlotte is the oldest, and therefore should be next in line. It isn't fair to Caterine to have her believe something that can never be."

"The truth is that neither Charlotte nor Paulette has ever shown any interest in Ma Chérie, so I don't blame Mother for wanting to have Caterine at the shop with her. As young as she is, Caterine already shows a talent for drawing. Why, she's already making her own clothes for her cutout dolls. Who knows, Mother may break tradition and leave the store to Caterine."

"She can't do that," Frances stated indignantly.

Jules chuckled. "Ma Chérie belongs to Mother; she can do anything she wants. But aren't you jumping the gun? Hopefully, Mother will be around for many more years, and it will be a long time before we have to worry about who inherits."

Chapter One

Caterine sat in the morning sunshine at the Café Du Monde with her friend Elaine LaBeau. A mild February breeze blew off the Mississippi River, bringing with it the soulful notes of a saxophone.

"I can't believe I let you talk me into coming here," Caterine said as she bit into her hot beignet. "Do you have any idea how many calories are in these?"

"Oh, who cares?" Elaine replied. She wiped powdered sugar from her chin and sipped her café au lait. "Mardi Gras is only two weeks away. It's time to be a little crazy. Besides, a few calories won't hurt you."

In the distance, the sound of a marching band could be heard. Elaine pointed. "People are beginning to gather for the Krewe d'Écrevisse parade. We'd better go if we want to find a place."

They stepped from the cafe onto Decatur Street.

"Wow, there's already a crowd," Elaine said. "Let's try over this way."

They wove their way around families with small children, college students holding go cups from Pat O'Brien's, and a group of ladies wearing dental conference badges featuring smiling teeth.

"I really should call Grandmère and let her know I might be late," Caterine shouted over the noise as she reached in her Chanel bag for her cell phone.

"Will you please relax? It's not even ten o'clock. Ma Chérie doesn't open until then, does it?"

"No."

"Then you don't have anything to worry about."

Caterine rolled her eyes. "I'm still expected to be at work on time."

They passed a man, painted silver, juggling oranges and skirted around horse-drawn carriages lined up for French Quarter tours.

"This is about as close as we're going to get," Elaine said. The music of a high-stepping band and the singing and shouting of the second line grew louder as the parade approached Jackson Square. "And here they come." She stood on her toes to get a better view. "Oh my God," she gasped.

"What?" Caterine asked as she bounced up and down waving at a float on which hot peppers danced with crawfish in a gumbo pot.

"Nothing." Elaine took her arm. "Let's see if we can find a better spot."

"What's the matter with you? This is fine." Caterine laughed at the next float. "They must be red beans and rice." She reached up and caught a string of silver beads. The crowd shifted and the laughter died on her lips when she saw what Elaine had already seen.

Across the square, his arms around a redhead Caterine knew well, stood Jonathan Day, the man she'd been dating for more than five months and the one man she thought truly cared about her. Stunned, the beads slipping from her hand, she whispered, "He told me he had to go to Mobile, and that's why he couldn't take me to your party."

Elaine tugged her arm. "Come on, Cat, let's go."

Taking shallow breaths, Caterine swallowed back waves of nausea and stared in disbelief as Jonathan bent to give the woman a kiss more appropriate in the bedroom than a public street. Tears of anger and humiliation burned the back of her eyes at the memory of her own passionate night in his arms, and how terribly wrong it had gone.

Elaine took a step forward. "Bastard. Let's let him know we're here. I want to tell him to his face what a scumbag he is. I can't believe he's with her out in public. The jerk doesn't even care if you see him."

"He'd expect me to be at work, not here."

"Yes, but anyone who knows you could have seen them. The guy is scum." Elaine turned. "Are you all right? You look a little green."

With every ounce of willpower she possessed, Caterine fought to maintain her composure. *I will not cry, I will not cry,* she mentally recited.

She wanted nothing more than to do as Elaine suggested and confront Jonathan, but years of proper conduct drilled into her by her grandmère stopped her. "I'm fine, let's go. I'm not about to cause a scene on a public street, nor will I give that woman the opportunity to gloat."

"Too late, he's seen us," Elaine said.

Caterine's eyes locked briefly with Jonathan's before she quickly turned away, crying out as her stiletto heel caught in the uneven pavement. As she lost her balance, she felt a strong male arm tighten around her.

"*C'est bien, cher.* I've got you," he said in a smooth Cajun patois as he held her close.

"Oh!" Caterine gasped as she was pressed against his hard chest. For an instant, she forgot to breathe as she gazed into deep blue eyes set in a handsome, chiseled face. "Excuse me," she stammered as she righted herself.

With his arm still around her, he smiled, showing even, white teeth. "No problem. I'm glad I could help."

Time seemed to stand still as they stood staring into each other's eyes. Suddenly, Caterine wanted nothing more than to put her arms around this stranger's neck and bury her face in his chest. Appalled, she stepped from his embrace and whispered, "Thank you." Unnerved by the mental image, she hurried away.

"For heaven's sake, Caterine, slow down," Elaine called. "You'll break your neck in those heels."

When Elaine fell into step beside her, Caterine wiped away fresh tears and turned to her friend. "Do you think I'm cold and unfeeling?"

Elaine gave her a quick hug. "Of course not. You're one of the kindest, most warm-hearted people I know."

Caterine waved her arms in the air. "Then what's wrong with me? I'm twenty-five years old and can't keep a boyfriend."

"Cat, you need to calm down."

"I don't want to calm down. For once in my life, I want to have a screaming fit. Laurie Conway? What a slap in the face. I hope the bastard catches some kind of disease."

"Caterine, wait."

At the sound of Jonathan's voice, Caterine quickened her steps.

"Cat, please wait," he called again.

Knowing he'd follow her all the way to Ma Chérie, Caterine gritted her teeth and turned to face him.

"What do you want me to do?" Elaine asked.

"Stand right there. I may need you to keep me from killing him."

Elaine grinned. "Go for it."

An out-of-breath, slightly disheveled Jonathan stopped in front of Caterine and gave her a sheepish grin. "Cat, if we could speak in private, I can explain."

Caterine dug her nails into her palms to keep from slapping his face. "The only thing I have to say to you is go to hell." When she turned, Jonathan grabbed her arm.

Caterine narrowed her eyes. "Take your hand off me."

He squeezed her arm harder. "You're going to listen to me."

She tried to pull away. When he held tight, anger turned her voice to steel. "If you don't remove your hand from my arm immediately, I'm going to call the police."

"Let her go, you bastard," Elaine said.

"Elaine, this is none of your business, stay out of it," he demanded before turning his attention back to Caterine. "Cat, sweet, this is a total misunderstanding. Laurie and I are just friends, that's all."

Caterine snorted with derision. "Jonathan, you're not only a cheat, you're a liar as well. As far as I'm concerned, you and Laurie Conway are meant for each other."

Jonathan put his face inches from hers and growled, "You listen to me, you haughty little bitch. If you weren't such a frigid block of ice, I wouldn't have had to turn to another woman for pleasure. You and all the Doucettes act like you're better than everyone else, but I'd rather have a warm, willing woman in my bed than one who's incapable of showing emotion."

Each of his words cut Caterine to her core. How could she have ever let down her guard with this man? How could she have trusted him enough to open herself for more hurt? Hadn't she learned at a young age how easily love could be thrown back in her face? She'd encased herself in a protective shell, and she'd been foolish enough to allow Jonathan to crack it open. When he'd tried to make love to her, she had truly wanted to respond, but the passion wouldn't come.

I'm not cold and unfeeling, I'm not, I'm not, she repeated to herself. She wrenched her arm from his grasp. "You want emotion, how's this?" She swung back and slapped his face. "I hope you and that slut will be happy together."

"Is there a problem here, *cher*?"

Caterine turned in surprise to see the man from the parade who'd caught her when she'd tripped. Her cheeks burned with mortification as she opened her mouth to respond, but nothing came out.

His gaze went from Caterine to Jonathan, whose hand covered his reddening cheek, then back to Caterine. "I'm not trying to intrude, but you looked like you could use some help. If I'm wrong, tell me and I'll leave."

"Then leave." Jonathan sneered. "Because this is definitely none of your concern."

He ignored Jonathan and stared at Caterine. "That's for the lady to decide."

Caterine's heart was pounding so hard she didn't know if she could speak. The power and sex appeal emanating from this man both thrilled and terrified her. She swallowed hard and stammered, "Th-thank you. I appreciate your offer of help, but my conversation with this man is through." She turned to Elaine. "Come on, let's go."

"Oh my God!" Elaine exclaimed when she'd caught up with Caterine. "Do you believe what just happened? Your very own Cajun knight in shining armor came to your rescue."

Caterine shook her head. "I can't absorb any of it. I need to sit down. Here's a coffee shop. Let's go in."

Seated at a corner table, they ordered two cafés au lait.

Caterine sighed and rubbed her temples. "If anyone had told me when I got up this morning that my day would turn out like this, I wouldn't have believed them."

Elaine grinned. "I'd say things are going rather well. You actually slapped Jonathan the jerk while being rescued by a hunky guy." She leaned closer. "And he sure seemed interested in you. I'll bet he could make you forget all about the creep. You know what? I should go back and see if I can find him and invite him to my party tonight."

Horrified, Caterine shook her head. "Don't you dare. I was embarrassed enough having him witness that performance. Elaine, I've never lost my temper and hit someone."

"Jonathan was acting like an ass and deserved it. I wish that guy would have laid him out flat."

Caterine couldn't help but smile. Ever since they'd met on their first day at McGehee's, a private girls' school in the Garden District, Elaine had taken Caterine under her wing. Elaine had smooth chin-length auburn hair, expressive green eyes and, thanks to the influence of two older brothers, a don't-mess-with-me attitude. Caterine, on the other hand, had just lost her parents and gone to live with her grandparents. Not only had she been shy, she'd had the self-confidence of a mouse. As adults, Elaine retained that no-nonsense attitude, and Caterine's confidence had grown with her success as a fashion designer, but in relationships she was still that scared little mouse.

Elaine cocked her head. "Speaking of Jonathan, I want you to know I never cared for him. I always thought he was a little too arrogant and a lot in love with himself."

A mixture of surprise and confusion filled Caterine's face. "Why didn't you tell me this before?"

"Because I thought you were crazy about him, and I didn't want to interfere."

Her face crumpled as she fought back tears. "Perhaps I need some kind of counseling. Considering my severely dysfunctional family, it's no wonder I'm unable to have a normal relationship. The way I was treated after my parents died taught me that if you don't let people close, you can't get hurt." She lowered her voice. "But I'm tired of being alone. I want to be able to give my heart to a man, to let him hold me and make love to me. But when I do, it all goes wrong."

Elaine took her hand and squeezed. "First, you're as sane as I am and nothing like your hateful family. As soon as the right man comes along, you'll be able to shower him with so much love and affection you'll probably drown the poor guy."

As a tear trickled down her cheek, Caterine laughed. "Yeah, right."

Elaine glanced at her Rolex. "Damn, look at the time. The caterers will be at the house in a half hour. I have to run and catch the streetcar. Will you be all right?"

Caterine nodded and hugged Elaine. "I've survived this before and I'll

survive it again."

"I'll see you later," Elaine said. "I can't wait to see your costume. What will you be?"

Caterine smiled. "Why, an ice princess. What else?"

Intrigued, Remi Michaud watched the pretty, petite blonde and her friend hurry away. *Forget it, bro. The lady's out of your league. Besides, she's exactly the type you swore to stay away from.*

On his way home after his morning walk, he'd decided to grab a cup of coffee and watch the parade. He'd been standing behind the blonde, admiring how the silkiness of her dress emphasized her nice ass and great legs, when she'd suddenly turned and stumbled into his arms.

He'd reached out to break her fall and found himself looking into a beautiful heart-shaped face, her sky-blue eyes brimming with tears. Stunned by the protective urge that came over him, his arm had tightened around her, and he'd found himself not wanting to let her go.

As she'd regained her balance and walked away, he'd taken an involuntary step toward her. At that moment, sunlight had reflected off the glittering diamond fleur-de-lis clip holding back her hair and he'd realized that every inch of her screamed uptown money. He'd been down that road, and if there was one thing this bayou boy did, it was learn from his mistakes.

When the man brushed past him heading in the direction of the girl, his cop instincts told him the guy meant trouble while his common sense told him to stay out of it. "Damn," he'd cursed under his breath as he turned to follow. He'd never had any common sense anyway.

He'd caught up in time to see the bastard grab her arm. Before he'd had a chance to knock him on his ass, she'd given the jerk a good slap. Remi smiled to himself. *Good shot.* At that point, he should have walked away, but he hadn't.

Now, the two women had left, and here he stood facing off with some angry asshole he didn't even know. Considering the fire in the guy's eyes, if Remi couldn't defuse the situation, he still might have to straighten him out. "Buddy, I have no problem with you. My concern was with the lady.

She's gone, so it's over." Remi turned to leave. Then the fool grabbed his arm.

"No, this isn't over. You interfered in something you shouldn't have. Someone needs to teach you to mind your own damn business."

Remi smiled. "And are you that someone?"

He narrowed his eyes. "I could be."

Remi pushed the guy's hand from his arm and leaned close. "Listen to me, you uptown preppy asshole. I'll do more than slap your face. I'll pound the shit out of you. So I suggest you get the hell away from me." Remi could see the indecision in his eyes before he turned and walked away murmuring, "Fucking Cajun swamp rat."

Remi thought about going after him but decided it wasn't worth it and headed back the way he'd come. He made his way around the end of the parade, his eyes automatically scanning the crowd. Old habits die hard.

After Hurricane Katrina had brought to an end any illusions that the NOPD would clean up its reputation, Remi and his partner, Paul LaBeau, had quit and opened their own private security company. That was six months ago and things had been going fine, until now. He frowned.

Tonight Paul and his wife, Elaine, were throwing some fancy costume party and expected him to attend. Since the day they had partnered on a drug bust over in Algiers, Paul and Remi had hit it off, even though their backgrounds were as different as those of a lobster and a gator. But, compared to working the street busting lowlifes, a high-class Garden District party was a whole 'nother kettle of boiled crabs.

When he reached for his pack of cigarettes, his pocket was empty.

"Damn." Would the cravings ever quit? As he waved at a group of teenagers dressed as shrimp riding a large po-boy float, his cell phone rang.

"Michaud."

"Hey, Remi, it's Paul."

"Yeah, man, where y'at?"

"Awright. How about you?"

"Doing fine."

"Elaine insisted I call to make sure you were coming tonight. I still can't believe that, as long as we've been together, there was never an opportunity to introduce you two."

"I don't imagine she spent a lot of time hanging around the Eight District, but tell her I'm looking forward to meeting the one woman who can keep your sorry ass in line."

Paul laughed. "That she does." He hesitated. "By the way, I wanted you to know that, unless she comes with someone, Desiree wasn't invited to the party."

A familiar stab of humiliation shot through Remi at the mention of the woman he had once thought he loved. This boy from the bayou had been fun as a plaything, but not good enough to marry. The revulsion he had seen in her eyes still gnawed at his insides like the constant craving for a cigarette. Well, he could kick the craving for Desiree as well as for nicotine.

"I was over her a long time ago, but thanks for letting me know."

"I want you to have a good time," Paul continued. "As a matter a fact, there's someone I'd like to introduce you to. She's a friend of ours. She'll be here tonight and I could set it up."

Remi scowled. "You playing matchmaker now, *cher*?"

Paul chuckled. "Someone has to help you out."

Visions of the blonde automatically passed through Remi's mind, and he mentally shook it away. "Yeah, well, I'll do just fine on my own."

"Oh, come on. It's time you got back out among the living. It can't hurt to meet the lady." Without waiting for Remi to reply, he asked, "What are you dressing as?"

"I don't know. I haven't thought about it."

"Well, I'll be Bluebeard, so look for me."

"Later." Remi placed his phone back in his pocket and paused to catch a string of silver beads tossed his way. Paul's party was becoming more complicated by the minute. He'd make an appearance, meet Elaine, then leave. He knew Paul meant well, but the last thing he needed was to get involved with another uptown spoiled snob.

He slipped the beads over his head, tossed coins into a street musician's open guitar case, and headed toward Toulouse Street and home.

Chapter Two

Caterine paused on Royal Street in front of Ma Chérie. Pride and love filled her heart as she stared at the quaint nineteenth-century building. When her eyes fell on the arched display window, she blinked in disbelief. There among the elegant dresses was a mannequin wearing a dress of such vibrant yellow it hurt the eyes.

As she got closer, laughter bubbled up in her throat. The hideous dress had so many ruffles it reminded her of a giant puffball. Curious to discover what such an outlandish dress was doing there, she pushed open the heavy oak door and entered the store's main salon.

Amusement turned to dismay at the scene that greeted her. In the center of the Aubusson rug, her petite grandmother, Miss Dauphine Doucette, stood squared off against her two daughters-in-law and her granddaughters Charlotte and Paulette.

The stubborn set of her Aunt Frances' pinched mouth and the defiance in her Aunt Hyacinth's protuberant eyes told Caterine the storm that was about to break would make a hurricane seem like a gentle breeze. She hesitantly made her presence known.

"Good morning," she said into the heavy silence. "Is something wrong?"

"Yes, there is most definitely something wrong," her grandmother said, her dark eyes snapping with anger. "Pray tell me, Caterine, what is your opinion of that?" She flung out her arm indicating the yellow dress in the window.

Caterine bit her lip to keep from laughing. Before she could think of a response, her cousin Paulette replied in her usual whiney tone.

"I'll have you know, Caterine, I designed that dress, and it's as good as any you've done. Just because I didn't go to some fancy school in Paris doesn't mean I can't create beautiful dresses."

Short and plump, Paulette had curly brown hair, pale blue eyes, and a Cupid's bow shaped mouth. Pampered by her mother, Paulette was used to getting what she wanted.

Caterine opened her mouth to respond, but her grandmother cut her off.

"Paulette, if I had thought that sending you to Paris with Caterine would have improved your skills, I would have done so. But that . . ." Again Miss Dauphine pointed toward the mannequin. "That shows me no amount of schooling could have refined your idea of fashion."

"Mama, are you going to let Grandmère speak to me like that?" Paulette said, pouting.

Hyacinth's face flushed beneath its coating of makeup, and her voice rose high and shrill. "Now, Miss Dauphine, that was uncalled for. You've gone and hurt Paulette's feelings. She has as much fashion sense as Caterine. She just hasn't had a chance to express herself."

"Grandmère doesn't understand my designs because they're colorful and fun, not stuffy and boring like Caterine," Paulette said with a pout.

"Actually, Paulette, if my choices are to be boring or be like you, I'll take boring any day," Caterine replied.

When Paulette opened her mouth to respond, Miss Dauphine waved her to silence. "That's enough." She turned to address Hyacinth. "I don't care for Paulette's designs because they're not her ideas, they're yours. You have never allowed that girl to have a thought of her own. She's been influenced by you from day one, and as long as you've been in this family you have yet to acquire any decorum or taste."

Caterine inwardly winced. Her grandmother's words were harsh, but unfortunately they were the truth. Hyacinth's blond curls were piled high on her head and her voluptuous body had been squeezed into a dress that would have looked better on a much younger, and slimmer, woman.

"Re-eally, Miss Dauphine, that's be-neath you," Frances Doucette admonished in her slow southern drawl. With her perpetually sour expression, Frances always looked as if she'd just bitten into a lemon. Tall and thin, with thick light-brown hair and hazel eyes, she had once been an attractive woman. Time and a disagreeable temperament had carved deep furrows into her once smooth face.

"Hyacinth and Paulette have a valid point," Frances continued. "It's time Ma Chérie branched out to accommodate other tastes. Imagine how much income we could generate by the addition of another line of clothing. We could clear out the lingerie room and set up racks to display the new styles."

Charlotte nodded. "Mother's right. If expanding our stock will bring in more customers, then it's just poor management not to do so." A few years older than Caterine, Charlotte had a low husky voice. She was attractive with dark hair and a pixieish face. On her second divorce, she cared mostly about pampering her perfect body, wearing beautiful clothes, and jet-setting around the world.

Seeing her grandmother's cheeks flush with anger, Caterine reached for her arm.

"Grandmère, do you need to sit down?"

"No, Caterine, I do not." She glowered at Frances. "I would have thought you, at least, would show more sense. Do you honestly believe I would compromise Ma Chérie's reputation by offering our clientele clothing such as that disgrace on display? As for our silk lingerie, it's exquisite. I shudder to think what you'd have me replace it with."

Charlotte stiffened. "There's not a damn thing wrong with sexy underwear. In case you're not aware, Grandmère, lace bloomers went out a long time ago."

Caterine's own temper was beginning to rise. "Charlotte, I don't know how long it's been since you've seen our lingerie, but we haven't sold lace bloomers since our great grandmother owned this store."

The icy stare Frances gave Caterine could have frozen Lake Pontchartrain.

"Caterine, contrary to your belief, you do not own Ma Chérie. So I would ask you to keep your opinions to yourself."

Caterine glared back. "You don't own it either. That's the point."

"Now, Miss Dauphine," Frances continued, ignoring Caterine, "Charlotte's right. We can't reach out to young women with stale designs.

We wouldn't be compromising our regular clientele. We'll still be offering elegant clothing."

"That's right." Hyacinth nodded. "We'll just be adding a little pizzazz to the place."

"*Pizzazz?*" Miss Dauphine's posture became more erect, and she balled her hands into fists. "All of you hear me and hear me well. I will close Ma Chérie's doors before I allow greed or tastelessness to lower the quality or standards this establishment is known for. Now, I will hear no more of this." She pointed to the display window. "Remove that horror immediately."

"Caterine, I have a dreadful headache. I'm going to call for Thomas to drive me home." She turned to Frances and Hyacinth. "In my absence, Caterine is in charge." With one more disgusted look at the mannequin, she swept from the room.

The women's venomous scowls had Caterine bracing for what she knew was about to come. Charlotte didn't disappoint her.

"You may be in charge while Grandmère is still alive, but remember this, Caterine, someday I'll inherit Ma Chérie, not you. And when that happens, there will be some big changes around here."

Paulette walked toward Caterine until their faces were inches apart. "That's right, and after Charlotte comes me. And if she hasn't already done so, I'll throw your uppity little ass out on the street."

"Get out of my face, Paulette," Caterine said. "Trust me, if you were ever in charge of Ma Chérie, you wouldn't have to throw my uppity ass out. I'd leave."

"Yes, well, that might be sooner than you think, you little bitch," Paulette snarled.

"Stop it," Frances demanded, glowering at Caterine before turning her attention back to Hyacinth. "Your ideas make sound business sense. Miss Dauphine is still living in the nineteenth century, and it's time she moved into this one."

Hyacinth nodded. "I wonder if Markus would have any influence over his mother?"

"I don't know, but it's worth a try. I'll speak with Jules as well," Frances added. "Perhaps between the two of them, they'll get her to see reason."

"See reason in regard to what?" Caterine asked, no longer able to control her temper. "Don't you understand how much this shop means to her? If you think for one minute Grandmère is going to turn Ma Chérie into a 'Tacky R Us' department store, you've all lost your minds. She will fight you on this, and she will win. Nobody's influence, including her sons', will change her mind. And as long as I'm able, I will fight you as well."

"One of these days, Caterine, you're going to get your comeuppance and learn you aren't as important around here as you think," Charlotte said.

"I told Jules that after your parents were killed Miss Dauphine made a big mistake coddling you the way she did, and see what's come of it," Frances said.

Hyacinth crossed her arms over her well-endowed chest. "Frances is right. You've always been a spoiled brat and Miss Dauphine's little pet. Well, missy, if I have anything to say about it, there are going to be big changes around here whether you like it or not."

"As usual, Hyacinth, you've missed the point. It doesn't matter what you want or what I want. Grandmère owns Ma Chérie. And as long as she's alive, I will make sure it's run exactly as she wishes."

Paulette's mouth formed into a thin line. "We'll see about that." She walked over to the display window, removed the yellow dress, and headed for the street door. "Charlotte, are you coming?"

Giving Caterine a final scathing look, Charlotte followed Paulette.

"We were supposed to stay until six and close," Frances said. "But since you're in charge, you can do it yourself." Her two aunts turned on their heels and went out the door.

Alone, Caterine sighed. Could this day get any worse? She glanced around the one place she'd always felt at home. Oil paintings depicting nineteenth-century New Orleans hung on cream-colored walls. Delicate spindle-legged tables held Tiffany lamps. Brocaded loveseats awaited clients who could enjoy crystal flutes of champagne while being shown rich fabrics and silks. An archway with tied-back burgundy velvet drapes led to a world of exquisite lace-edged lingerie and Ma Chérie's signature Fleur-de-Lis lotions, bath oils, and perfumes.

There were days when she wondered how she could continue to put up with all this family drama. She'd inherited her grandmother's talent for design and her love of Ma Chérie. All she'd ever wanted to do was come to the job she loved and create beautiful clothing.

She knew the only reason her grandmother put up with the aunts working at the store was to appease her sons. This latest scheme of theirs might have pushed her grandmother too far. At the thought of an aunt-free Ma Chérie, Caterine smiled and headed for her office.

"Close the door behind you, Caterine," Miss Dauphine said, seated behind a mahogany Queen Anne desk in the office they shared. "I wish to speak with you in private before Thomas arrives."

The irritation in her grandmother's voice made it clear her temper hadn't cooled in the least. Before Caterine took her seat, Miss Dauphine asked, "Have you recently opened the safe?"

Surprised by the question, Caterine shook her head. "Why?"

"Have you had reason to go through the file cabinet?"

Again she shook her head. "I have everything on the computer. I only use the file cabinet for storing copies. What's wrong?"

"When I came into the office, I noticed one of the file drawers wasn't completely closed. Upon further investigation, I saw where a piece of paper had caught in the drawer. Then I noticed the painting covering the safe wasn't straight. No one but you, myself, Frances, or Hyacinth has access to this room."

Perplexed, Caterine shook her head. "Why would they snoop around? They could ask one of us for whatever it was they wanted."

Miss Dauphine folded her hands upon the desk and leaned closer. "I haven't the slightest idea, but they've both been acting peculiar lately."

Caterine suppressed a smile. As far as she was concerned, her aunts had always been more than peculiar. They'd been downright scary.

"What do you mean?" she asked.

Miss Dauphine waved her hand in irritation. "Little things. I've caught them in hushed conversation, which they immediately stop when I enter the room. Hyacinth has been asking me about the running of Ma Chérie, and Frances has been hinting that she'd like more responsibility."

"Don't you think all of that was leading up to what happened earlier?"

Miss Dauphine rubbed her temples. "I don't know. Perhaps I'm overreacting. God knows I've done my best to get along with those women, but as hard as I've tried I've never trusted or cared for either of them."

Caterine reached out her hand and took her grandmother's frail one in hers. "I know it's hard to like someone when they're greedy and self-centered."

"If I thought it would help, I'd suggest they open their own store."

Caterine smiled. "Grandmère, that's a great idea. Then Paulette and Charlotte could run it and fill it with Paulette's designs."

Miss Dauphine shuddered. "Though that is a tempting solution, owning their own shop is not what interests them. They covet the power and prestige of Ma Chérie itself." She slipped her hand from Caterine's. "And that they shall never have." She glanced at her thin diamond watch. "Thomas should be here any minute. Isn't Paul and Elaine LaBeau's party tonight?"

Surprised at the change of topic, Caterine nodded.

"Didn't I hear that now that Paul has quit the police department he's opened his own security business?"

"That's right. Elaine said he's doing rather well."

"Good. Tell him I wish to speak with him about installing a security system in Ma Chérie. That should put an end to whatever those women are up to." Her tone softened. "Your dress for tonight is beautiful. Did you design it?"

"Yes, thank you. Elaine wanted to kick off Carnival with a costume party."

Miss Dauphine cocked her head. "I assume Jonathan will be escorting you."

A lump filled Caterine's throat as she stared down at her hands.

"Caterine?"

Swallowing hard, she tried to look nonchalant as she met her grandmother's eyes. "No, I'll be going alone."

"Really? Why is that?"

Caterine hesitated. How could she tell her grandmother she'd seen Jonathan in another woman's arms? Or about the confrontation they'd had, the thought of which brought back stirring images of her handsome rescuer.

"Caterine, is something wrong?"

Startled from her thoughts, she jumped. "I'm sorry, Grandmère. What did you say?"

"I asked you if there was something wrong. I take it by the scowl on your face there's a problem between you and Jonathan."

Caterine took a deep breath. "Jonathan and I will no longer be seeing one another."

"Well, my dear, I hope you're not too disappointed. I won't pry by asking what happened, but to be honest, I can't say I'm sorry. I never truly thought he was the man for you."

Taken aback, Caterine stammered, "But I thought you liked Jonathan."

"Oh, he's nice enough, I suppose, though I fear he has a rather large ego, which in time would become tiresome."

Caterine shook her head. "That's what Elaine said. I don't know how I didn't see it."

"Sometimes it's hard to see what's right in front of our face. The right man is out there, you just haven't met him yet. Why, who knows, perhaps tonight you'll meet a handsome stranger who will sweep you off your feet."

Chapter Three

Remi leaned against the makeshift bar in the corner of the ballroom. Feeling as out of place as a mudbug in a bowtie, he sipped his cold Turbodog and studied the other guests. He'd take a smoky bar on the bayou with people clapping to a Cajun two-step over this glitz any day.

When he'd arrived, he'd spotted Paul and spoken to him briefly, then Paul had gone off to find Elaine and her friend. That had been quite a while ago. He reached in his pocket for his cigarettes. Finding it empty, he cursed.

"Can I help?"

He turned at the sound of the low sexy voice to see a red-haired Cleopatra standing next to him holding out a pack of cigarettes.

"Thanks, but I'm supposed to be quitting."

Her cherry lips parted, showing small white teeth. "Well, handsome, if I can't help you with a smoke, is there anything else you might need?"

He grinned. "I appreciate the offer, but I was about to leave."

"Now, why would you want to do that? The evening is young. You never know what delights you might uncover at a masquerade ball."

Why indeed? What the hell was wrong with him? A beautiful woman was practically throwing herself at him, and he was about to walk away. In the past, he wouldn't have thought twice about taking the lady up on her offer. They'd have a great night together then he'd be gone. That was until one lady had played him for a fool.

Perhaps Paul was right and it was time for him to have some fun. But as his eyes traveled over Cleopatra, he didn't feel any stirring of desire. Great. Had Desiree messed him up for life? Then he thought of sky-blue eyes, long blond hair, and the attraction he'd felt. He forced a smile. "I'm sure there are delights aplenty, *cher*, but not for me tonight."

She gave him a seductive pout and ran her fingers down the front of his shirt. "Oh, I'm sure you can handle anything that's thrown your way."

Remi lifted her hand and gave her fingers a light squeeze. "I appreciate your confidence, but I'll still have to decline. Besides, there's a knight coming this way and he doesn't seem pleased."

Cleopatra frowned. "Damn, that's Beauregard. *Boring ass*, more like. My friend Charlotte set me up with him, and I'm going to kill her next time I see her." She gave Remi a hopeful look. "I can tell him I'm feeling ill, and meet you somewhere later."

He shook his head. "Sorry."

"As they say, you can't blame a girl for trying." She gave him a sultry smile and turned away.

He finished his beer as he watched Cleopatra take the knight's arm. At the love-struck look on the man's face, Remi sighed. *The poor bastard hasn't a clue what he's in for*. He placed his empty glass on the bar. He'd stayed long enough. Paul must have been delayed by other guests. Gumbolaya was playing in the Quarter. If he hurried, he might be able to sit in on a set.

Remi started across the room and for the first time in his life was struck speechless. Incapable of movement, he couldn't take his eyes from the vision in silver.

Caterine paused at the entrance to the LaBeaus' glittering ballroom, adjusted the silver mask upon her nose, and shook out the folds of her gown. Hundreds of guests clustered around tables laden with hors d'oeuvres, rich desserts, and fountains flowing with champagne.

Good grief, Elaine and Paul must have invited half of New Orleans. She wove her way through the crowd. Fragrant canna lilies, dahlias, and irises filled tall vases and spilled from woven baskets. Elaborately carved white moldings adorned high teal-painted walls. Heavy cream silk draperies framed three opened French doors leading onto a third floor gallery. A floor-to-ceiling mirrored wall reflected costumed guests as they danced beneath two crystal chandeliers.

Caterine squeezed around Snow White and a scarecrow and still didn't see Elaine. Impatiently she stood on her toes to peer over Marie Laveau and Henry the Eighth. She felt a sharp tap on her shoulder and turned.

"Looking for me?"

Caterine curtseyed. "Well, hello, your majesty."

Elaine, as Marie Antoinette, snapped her lace fan shut and smiled.

"You look great," Caterine said.

"Thanks. I always wanted to be queen."

Caterine snorted. "Yes, well, just don't lose your head over it."

Elaine's green eyes sparkled with amusement. "There's always that risk. I was worried you wouldn't come. What took you so long?"

"If you can believe it, my day got even worse."

"Don't tell me you heard from Jonathan again?"

"No, but almost as bad. My aunts and cousins were at their hateful best today."

"Now what? No, wait." Elaine signaled a tuxedo-clad waiter carrying glasses of champagne. "Drink this." She handed Caterine a chilled flute. "And before you say anything I have to tell you your gown is absolutely stunning. Turn so I can get the full effect."

Caterine pirouetted. The light reflected off the silver gown, making it shimmer and sparkle. Hundreds of faceted crystals, glittering like ice, cascaded down the front of the flowing skirt.

"You can tell your grandmère, once again, hats off to Ma Chérie. You outshine us all."

Caterine narrowed her eyes. "She would appreciate hearing there are still those who don't think she should turn it into a fashion mart."

"I have a feeling that comment has something to do with the aunts from hell, so what have they done now?"

Caterine took a long sip of her champagne, then explained.

"They're crazy. Your grandmère would never give up control of Ma Chérie, or allow it to be cheapened that way."

"No, she would not. I've never seen Grandmère as angry as she was today. If they keep pushing her, I'm afraid she'll do something to cause more problems than we already have. This has the potential to turn into a colossal Doucette family blowup. God only knows what kind of retaliation my cousins might come up with. But enough of my drama." She gave a dismissive wave. "I want to forget about Jonathan and my family and have a good time." She accepted another crystal flute from a passing waiter. "And I apologize for going on about my problems and not mentioning how fabulous everything looks. I especially love what you've done here in the ballroom. You and Paul did a wonderful job restoring the house."

"Thanks. I thought we'd never get it finished."

Caterine glanced at all the guests. "How many people did you invite?"

Elaine chuckled. "Honestly, I lost track. Paul kept adding his cop friends and guys from his security company to my list, and I don't know half of them."

"But isn't that what's fun about a masked ball, not knowing who the mystery person is you're talking to? What's better yet, you can do and say things you'd never consider doing or saying because they also don't know who you are. As the saying goes, *laissez les bons temps rouler*."

Elaine coughed, almost choking on her champagne. "Wait a minute. Back up. Did I just hear you say, *let the good times roll?*"

Caterine nodded. "I can't get what happened with Jonathan out of my mind, and I've decided that tonight the old Caterine doesn't exist. Since I'm in disguise, this is the perfect opportunity to prove to myself that Jonathan and those other men are wrong."

Elaine cocked her head. "Okay, what exactly do you have in mind?"

Caterine grinned. "If I meet someone who makes my pulse quicken and my toes curl . . ." She shrugged. "Who knows? Tonight the ice princess may melt away."

A wide smile spread across Elaine's face. "Good for you. If I'm not mistaken, your chance might be coming this way. Good luck."

Chapter Four

Before Caterine could respond, Elaine disappeared into the crowd. She turned in the direction Elaine had been looking and caught her breath. The man dressed entirely in black coming toward her reminded her of a dangerous outlaw from a past century. Lean and muscular, he stood close to six foot. He wore a loose, long-sleeved, V-necked shirt, snug pants, and low boots. As he walked, his body language exuded confidence, power, and incredible sex appeal.

The closer he got, the harder her heart pounded. *Okay, take a deep breath. You can do this. He doesn't know who you are; if you make an idiot out of yourself, it won't matter.*

"Hello, Princess. I believe this dance is ours," he said, his bayou cadence low and sultry.

Bereft of speech, she could only stare into the thick-lashed, deep blue eyes behind the handsome stranger's black bandit mask.

He flashed white teeth in a sensuous grin. "I'm not mistaken am I, *cher*? You looked so beautiful standing there glittering, I assumed you must be a fairy princess."

She swallowed hard, hoping her voice was steady. "I'm sorry to disappoint you, *monsieur*, but I'm not a fairy princess. I'm known as an *ice* princess. But who knows, I still might be able to grant you a wish."

"No, *cher*." He stepped closer. Gently placing his fingers under her chin, he tilted her head back to gaze directly into her eyes. "Whoever said you were an ice princess wasn't man enough to release your heat. Grant me my wish and I'll do just that."

When the meaning of his words managed to pierce her addled brain, her face flushed with embarrassment. How was she supposed to respond? This kind of flirtatious banter was way out of her league.

As their eyes locked and held, a gasp lodged in her throat. It couldn't be. It had to be her imagination. But as a remembered thrill of excitement shot through her, she knew he was the same man who'd come to her rescue earlier. By the surprise in his eyes, clearly he'd recognized her as well. My God, had Elaine actually gone back and found him? Best friend or not, this was too much.

A slow smile spread across his face. "Well, it seems we meet again."

Mortified from her head to her toes, Caterine opened and closed her mouth but nothing came out.

He chuckled. "This is one helluva coincidence."

Caterine blinked. Could this truly be an incredible coincidence and Elaine had nothing to do with it? She had to know. She licked dry lips and asked, "Did you come on your own or did my friend from this morning invite you?" As she watched, confusion, then annoyance, filled his eyes.

"I'm not crashing the party, Princess. And I've never met your friend."

At that moment, she wished the floor would open and swallow her whole. Not knowing what else to do, she put her hand on his arm. "I'm so sorry. I didn't mean to offend you. You see it was my friend, she . . ."

He took her hand in his and the contact ignited a spark that left her body trembling. Never in her life had she experienced such a reaction to a man's touch. When his hand tightened over hers, she wondered if he could feel it as well.

"Come on, Princess, let's dance." Not waiting for her reply, he guided her onto the floor.

Her head spinning, Caterine wasn't aware the band was playing a waltz until he put his strong arm around her waist, guiding her into the dance. As he twirled and dipped her around the crowded room, she felt as if she were floating across the polished wood floor.

"That was wonderful. Thank you," she said when the dance came to an end.

"My pleasure, but we can't stop now." He held her tight against him as the band began to play a sexy blues number.

She wrapped her arms around his neck, losing herself in the music and the gentle sway of his body, banishing everyone else from the room. She laid her head against his chest, inhaling his spicy scent, wanting to bury her nose in the soft hair visible in the open collar of his shirt.

"You're so sweet, *ma petite*," he whispered into her ear as he held her tighter.

The sound of his voice and his warm breath sent a chill of delight dancing across her skin.

"I'm in luck. They're playing another slow one. I get to hold you close a little longer."

She smiled into his eyes. "I don't mind."

"I'm glad to hear that."

As their bodies touched, a kaleidoscope of emotions whirled through Caterine. The urge to abandon herself in this man's arms both thrilled and terrified her. As if with minds of their own, her fingers ran through the silky hair at the base of his neck.

"*Vous vous sentez si bien*," he murmured and lightly kissed the sensitive skin below her ear. "You feel so good."

She thought about devouring his sexy lips with hers, but thankfully, the music came to an end before she disgraced herself in the middle of the dance floor.

"They're picking up the tempo, and as much as I'd like to stand here with you in my arms, we'd better move or join in. Come on, Princess, let's do it."

"Wait. I'm not sure. I-I can't." Caterine squealed as he led her into a Cajun two-step.

Breathless as the music came to an end, she laughed delightedly. "You certainly dance well."

With a wicked grin, he whispered, "When it comes to pleasing a lovely lady, I try to do everything well."

Caterine couldn't hold back a smile. "Oh, I'll bet you do."

They had stepped away from the dancers and accepted glasses of water from a passing waiter. "Now, *monsieur*, shouldn't you introduce yourself?"

"My apologies for being so remiss." He stepped back and gave her a gallant bow. "Jean Lafitte at your service."

She grinned. "A pirate. I should have known."

"Do you not like pirates?"

"I can't say I've ever met one, but I've heard they can be rather dangerous."

A slow smile spread across his face. "A little danger can be exciting, Princess."

Again he was standing close, filling her senses with his seductive voice and spicy cologne. The heat from his body had Caterine imagining being held in his arms on a sun-drenched beach while turquoise water lapped around their feet. His mouth was now inches from hers.

"Come away with me and I'll show you."

Come away with him. Oh, yes, how she'd love to run away with this pirate. Caterine's fevered imagination now had them in each other's arms on the deck of a gently rocking ship under a star-strewn sky. When his lips brushed across hers, the image changed to show him lowering her onto a bed of soft down. At the sound of his low chuckle, she blinked rapidly to wipe away the erotic scene.

"I'm sorry, what did you say?"

He smiled at her as if he could read her mind. "I said you look a little flushed. Would you like to go out onto the gallery where it's cooler?"

She took a nervous step back. "It is rather warm in here, isn't it?"

His knowing smile widened. "Exceedingly so. Shall we?" He took her hand and led her through the nearest open door.

The sultry night, the perfume of flowers, and the soft light from the candles placed along the gallery all heightened Caterine's sense of fantasy. He led them away from the circle of light spilling from the open door and took her into his arms.

"I hope you won't mind, Princess, but I have to do something I've wanted to do since I first laid eyes on you."

When his lips touched hers, desire as she'd never imagined shot through her. Up on her toes, she clasped her arms tightly around his neck and kissed him back with all the passion she had buried deep inside. As his kiss became more demanding, she tried to keep her shaking knees from crumpling beneath her.

He gentled the kiss. "*Je te désirer.*" He placed soft kisses along her cheek. "I want you, Princess."

Caterine let out a low moan. The sound of his words sent liquid heat pooling between her thighs. When he reclaimed her lips, he slid his tongue deep into her welcoming mouth. She clutched the fabric of his shirt. She burned hotter and hotter with a need she yearned to release.

As he slid his hand down her back, her body tingled deliciously. When he cupped her bottom and pressed her against his hard arousal, she thought she'd come apart in his arms. With her pulse racing and her mind full of erotic fantasies of this incredibly sexy man, she ignored the nagging voice in her head telling her to slow down.

To hell with being proper Caterine Doucette. She didn't know where this side of her had come from, but she wasn't stopping now. There was something about her pirate that made it all seem right. She'd waited all her life for a night such as this, and by God she was going to prove she wasn't frigid. Entwining her fingers in the thick black hair at the base of his neck, Caterine tugged in frustration. She met his hot kisses stroke for stroke.

"No," she groaned as he broke their kiss.

"Princess, let me take you home where I can finish this properly."

Not wanting to break the spell this man had her under, she whispered, "I want you now, Pirate."

"Are you sure?" He ran his finger along her kiss-swollen lower lip.

She hesitated for only a second. "Oh yes, I'm sure."

His teeth flashed. "Your wish is my command, *mademoiselle*."

Caterine laughed and took his hand in hers. "Then come with me."

Hand-in-hand they hurried down the outer stairs and deep into the garden until they came upon a fragrant vine-covered arbor. He gathered her in his arms and lowered them both onto a padded bench.

The night was quiet except for the rustling of the trumpet vines which encircled them in their own world of fantasy and desire.

"*Ma jolie fille,* my pretty girl." He began to trail hot kisses along her neck. "*J'aime te faire l'amour avec toi.* I want to make love to you."

She guided her hands over the fabric covering his muscular shoulders and sighed. "That's exactly what I want you to do, Pirate."

His warm lips stopped when he reached the top of her full breasts showing above her gown. He ran his tongue across her taut nipple, which strained against the smooth silk.

"You're the most enchanting woman I've ever seen. I want to taste all of you."

His words washed over her like a gentle caress and she smiled. "Yes, please."

"I intend on pleasing you, *cher*." He fumbled with the gown's tiny satin buttons, before cupping her breasts.

Caterine shivered with delight as he licked and suckled first one tight nipple then the other. As his tongue flicked over the swollen peak, the throbbing ache between her legs grew until she squirmed beneath him. As the pressure built, any coherent thoughts she might have had fled. "Oh, sweet heaven," she cried as the first orgasm she'd ever experienced slammed through her body.

He gave her a wicked grin. "Like that, did you?"

"That was incredible," she said a little breathlessly.

"That's only the first one, Princess. I'm going to take my time and enjoy every inch of you."

The heat glowing in his eyes sent flames of desire soaring from the top of her head to her curled toes. "Oh my, yes."

His hand moved over her hip and down her leg. He lifted the hem of her gown and slowly ran his fingers along her inner thigh. "How's this, Princess?"

She moaned aloud when his talented fingers gently began to stroke her. Wave after wave of exquisite pleasure flowed through her body, leaving her panting, struggling to breathe. Mindless of what she was doing, her nails dug into his back while she writhed against his hand.

"Oh, God, I'm going to again."

"*Mais yeah.*" His mouth covered hers, muffling her scream as her next orgasm sent her spiraling into ecstasy.

"*Mon Dieu*, Princess, you're driving me crazy." Swiftly he removed the slip of lace she wore beneath her gown. "Give me a minute."

Through passion-glazed eyes, Caterine caught a glimpse of a silver packet before he positioned himself to enter her.

"Oh." She tried to hold back her gasp of discomfort as her body tried to adjust to his hard thrust.

He froze. "Princess, I'm sorry, I . . ."

Before he could continue, she pulled his face to hers and softly whispered, "I'm all right. If you stop now, Pirate, I'll see you hanged."

"Princess, I'm incapable of stopping," her pirate growled, claiming her mouth and her body, sending her into a realm of sexual fulfillment she'd never known.

His labored breathing was the first sound to penetrate Caterine's satiated thoughts. Her body aglow, she marveled at the myriad of sensations this man had made her feel. She ran her fingers through her pirate's thick hair.

"I take it, Princess, you've decided not to have me hanged?" He rose slightly and grinned.

"Oh no, Jean Lafitte, I would consider that to be a terrible waste of an incredibly virile man."

He gave her a lazy chuckle. "Princess, consider me at your disposal any time you wish." He bent his head, gently kissed her lips, and whispered, "Although I fear you can no longer be considered an ice princess."

Caterine smiled. It was true. In his arms, all her fears and insecurities melted away. She never wanted this moment to end. The first time she'd looked into his eyes, she'd felt an instant attraction to him, but in her wildest dreams she had never imagined it would be a total stranger who would so easily cause her to abandon all her inhibitions.

Her pirate nibbled on her ear. "Come home with me, Princess. I want to make love to you until dawn." He kissed his way across her cheek then ran his tongue gently across her bottom lip. "We'll watch the sun come up, and I'll make love to you again."

Caterine's body instantly reacted to his words and his caress. As the tantalizing thought of waking up in his bed played through her mind, she opened her mouth to tell him yes when the distant sound of muffled voices slammed her back from fantasy to reality. What if they were discovered?

The thought of her aunts' gloating faces when they heard she'd been caught having sex in Elaine's arbor made her ill. Not to mention her mortification when she had to face her grandmother. The entire scenario was too unbearable to contemplate. She winced as the full implications of her impulsive behavior flickered past her mind's eye like a nightmare. *Good God, what have I done?*

Caterine frantically pushed at his chest. "I hear someone. Please let me up. What if they're coming this way?" Practically throwing him off, she jumped to her feet and straightened her gown.

"Wait a minute, Princess," Remi called as she hurried from the arbor. "What's your real name? Damn it, wait for me." As he straightened his own clothes, he spotted something shiny lying on the ground. He picked up the object and headed after her.

Chapter Five

Caterine ran as quietly and quickly as she could along the winding paths leading through Elaine's dimly lit garden. She darted through the back door that led to a mud room and the kitchen. As she swept by the startled caterers, she acted as if it were perfectly normal for a disheveled princess to be hurrying past.

"So far so good," she murmured, dashing through the quiet lower rooms. *Thankfully the party is on the third floor. I have a better chance of escape. I'll get my cape and bag and get out of here.* When she reached the cloakroom, she sighed with relief. Other than the hired attendants, there wasn't anyone around. With cape and bag in hand, she slipped from the house and through the night to her car. Caterine had her cell phone out when she started the Mercedes. She said a prayer of thanks knowing that whenever Elaine left her boys with a sitter she kept her cell phone handy.

"Hello."

"Elaine, it's me."

"What? I'm sorry, I can't hear you."

Caterine's voice rose. "Elaine, it's me, Caterine."

"Hang on a minute. I need to go where it's quieter. Okay, I'm out on the gallery. Caterine, is that you?"

"Yes, it's me. Don't say anything, just listen. If anyone asks you who the lady was wearing the princess gown, you have to say you don't know.

Understand?"

"What's going on? Where are you?"

"I'm in my car heading home. Elaine, please, it's important. Don't tell anyone who I am."

"Okay, I get it. But why are you going home? Are you all right?"

"Yes, I'm fine. You're not going to believe what I've done."

"What? Wait a minute. Here comes Paul, and there's someone with him. I don't want him to see I'm talking to you."

Caterine had turned into Audubon Place, passing the guard at the gates, and headed for her driveway. When she heard Elaine's next words, she almost hit the mailbox.

"Well, hi, Remi. I'm glad to finally meet you." Elaine continued, "You're looking for whom? I'm sorry. I'm not sure who that could be."

Caterine then heard Paul's voice but couldn't understand what he was saying. Had Paul seen her in the dress? She didn't think so, but she couldn't be sure.

Elaine spoke again. "Cat? Well, yes, the girl you describe sounds like her but, Remi, I'm sorry, Cat wasn't here tonight. She called and told me she couldn't make it. It must have been someone else."

Good girl, Elaine.

Caterine put the car into park and leaned her head on the steering wheel. *This couldn't be happening.*

"If I discover who your mystery lady is, I'll be sure to let Paul know," Elaine concluded.

Seconds passed before Elaine's voice came back on the phone. "Okay, they're gone," she whispered. "Caterine, are you still there?"

"Yes, I'm here. Thanks. You don't know how much I appreciate what you just did."

"You can show your appreciation by telling me what's going on. I swear Remi looks like the guy who tried to help you earlier today."

"He is."

"He is what?"

"The same guy."

"Oh . . . my . . . God, I don't believe this. What's the chance your hero is Paul's friend and partner? This is perfect."

"No, this is not perfect."

"Why, what's wrong? Why do you want to avoid Remi?"

"So that's his real name."

"What do you mean, *that's his real name*? I thought you two had met. Didn't he introduce himself?"

"Sort of."

"Sort of? Cat, what are you talking about?"

"He said he was Jean Lafitte."

"The pirate?"

"That's him."

"Okay, what happened between you and the pirate?"

"We . . . well-l-l."

"Oh, my God, you didn't."

"I'm afraid I did."

"Where?"

"In your arbor."

"What did you say?"

"I said it happened in your arbor. Elaine, I'm home. I'm going to fix myself a cup of tea, then I'm going to try and forget what an ass I've made of myself."

"Wait a minute, you can't nonchalantly tell me you made love to a stranger in my arbor and hang up."

"Honestly, I don't know what happened to me. I went a little crazy. It was like I became another person. God, I was all over him like some Bourbon Street tramp."

Elaine giggled. "Boy, when you said you were tired of the old Caterine, you weren't kidding around."

"I have to say my intentions weren't to go quite that far, but there's more. When I realized who he was, I thought you went back and found him and invited him. Then I sounded like an idiot when I asked him. And you can stop laughing. This isn't at all funny."

"I can't help it. This is too much."

"*Too much* is right." Caterine slammed her car door then quickly glanced up at the second floor window, hoping she hadn't awakened her grandmother. She hurried to her converted carriage house and opened the front door.

"Come on, Caterine, get past all your self-recriminations and get to the good stuff. Was it good?"

Caterine dropped down into an overstuffed leather sofa and sighed. "Okay, if you have to know, it was absolutely the most incredible experience of my entire life, but it's over. I lost my head and let things go too far. For the time being he doesn't know who I am, and we need to keep it that way."

"Oh, for heaven's sake, why?"

"For one thing, I'm extremely embarrassed. Elaine, I just had sex with a total stranger. I've never done anything like that before. I can imagine what he thinks of me."

"Cat, he came looking for you. That tells me he's interested. If he wasn't, he would have just left."

"I don't know. I need time to absorb all this. What if it was nothing more than a one-night stand for him? I don't want to make a fool out of myself."

"Oh, for heaven's sake, the man was trying to find you. Cat, I have to get back to the party. I'll call you tomorrow. I'll see what I can find out about Remi from Paul." With that, Elaine hung up.

Damn. Caterine knew her friend was now on a serious matchmaking quest and nothing was going to stop her. She placed her phone and small handbag on the granite kitchen counter and reached for the kettle. Teacup in hand, she walked through the open living/dining/kitchen area toward her large bedroom in the back. She stopped abruptly in front of a full-length mirror.

"Good God," she cried in horror, almost dropping her tea when she saw her reflection. Her long hair, which had been secured with a clip at the nape of her neck, was now hanging loose down her back and over her shoulders in a mass of tangles. Her lips were red and swollen, and a trace of whisker burn marred her smooth cheeks. Her beautiful gown was crushed and wrinkled. Two of the satin buttons closing her bodice were missing, and one of the little cap sleeves was torn.

She groaned. What could the staff at Elaine's have thought when she ran past? *And what if the police had stopped me on my way home? I look as if I've been on a drunken binge. Well, thankfully I made it home without anyone seeing me and, except for Elaine, no one knows what I was up to this Carnival night.*

She kicked off her shoes, removed what was left of her gown, and dropped the full under-petticoat to the floor. A smile touched her lips as she remembered the feel of her pirate as he entered her. She closed her eyes and whispered, *"Bien fait, monsieur.* Well done."

She picked up her cup and headed for the whirlpool tub, adding a splash of Ma Chérie's Fleur-de-Lis bath oil to the water. As she gathered her hair to pin it on top of her head, she realized her diamond clip was missing. Even though she had copies, this one had belonged to her mother and was a cherished keepsake. She went back to where her clothes lay and quickly searched each garment. Finding nothing, she tamped down her panic. It had to be in Elaine's arbor. She thought of her dash across the lawn. Or somewhere on the grounds. *I'll call her tomorrow and tell her to look for it.*

She sighed with pleasure as she sank gratefully into the steaming bath. Caterine lay back and closed her eyes. Visions of her magical night floated through her mind. With the bubbles surrounding her, she again saw the tender passion in her pirate's eyes as he'd shown her the true meaning of pleasure. At that moment she hadn't cared about her family, her reputation, or Ma Chérie. She could have lain in that arbor with him for the rest of her life. All she had cared about was him and how right she'd felt in his arms.

Then the real world had to rear its ugly head. She reached for her tea. *Reality check, Caterine. You were two strangers, instantly attracted to each other, who let your emotions run wild, and things went way too far. Don't make more out of it than that. Remember Jonathan and take a step back. Don't position yourself for another major fall. Remi's an incredibly sexy man who probably has seduced more women than he can count. Just because he went looking for you doesn't mean anything.*

She wished the level-headed side of her brain would shut up. She wasn't quite ready to let go of her fantasy. She sank lower in the bubbles, reliving how her body had reacted to his every touch. *At least I know I'm not frigid.* Caterine snorted. *What an understatement that is.*

And who do I choose to prove it to but a smooth-talking, sexy pirate who I'll probably never see again? And if she did see him again what would she say? Thanks for showing me I'm capable of feeling passion? She shook her head. Considering her behavior, she doubted if she could look him in the eyes.

She laid her head back and let the gently swirling water surround her. But deep in her heart, she wanted nothing more than to be held in Remi's arms and feel his lips on hers.

Remi cursed as he stepped onto the deserted street outside the LaBeaus' home. *If you want to play games, Princess, I'll be more than happy to oblige.* As he slid onto the leather seat of his black convertible Thunderbird, something sharp stabbed his leg. He removed the offending object from his pocket and switched on the car's interior light.

Well, Princess, it's not a glass slipper, but it's about as grand. Light reflected off the tiny diamonds bordering the fleur-de-lis hair clip. If he had any sense, he'd give the hair clip to Paul and chalk tonight up to an incredible encounter with a beautiful elusive princess.

When he'd approached her, he had never imagined in his wildest fantasy that his princess would turn out to be the woman he couldn't get out of his mind. The lady was certainly full of surprises. One minute her beautiful sky-blue eyes gazed at him with shy unease. The next minute they blazed with desire.

As he sat staring at the hair clip, he could still taste the sweetness of her lips on his. His fingers could feel the silkiness of her skin. "Damn." He leaned back in the seat. Every instinct he possessed told him to walk away.

He turned the key in the ignition. But he knew his attraction for the lady was too strong to ignore. *You're out there somewhere, and like it or not, I'm going to find you. When I do, we'll see if I'm still as love-struck as I am now, or if tonight was nothing more than two strangers caught up with each other and the night.*

When he stopped in front of his apartment in the French Quarter, Remi sat holding the hair clip in his palm. *Princess, if I'm lucky enough that we meet again, I promise to make our next encounter better than a tumble in someone's backyard.*

Chapter Six

Jean Lafitte's hands were slowly making their way down her hot body, his mouth trailing kisses across her sensitive breasts. He teased and caressed his way over her stomach, only stopping when his mouth finally reached her . . .

Caterine sat bolt upright in her bed, breathing hard, blinking in confusion, shaking her head to clear the erotic dream. She reached for the phone that had blessedly awakened her.

"Hello," she croaked.

"My dear, did I awaken you?"

"That's okay, Grandmère." Caterine glanced at the clock. "I didn't plan to sleep this late."

"I thought perhaps you could accompany me to Mass, but I see that's unlikely. Did you enjoy yourself last night?"

"What?"

"Caterine, are you sure you're awake? I'm talking about the party at the LaBeaus'. I assumed since you're still in bed you must have stayed late."

"I'm sorry, Grandmère. I guess I'm not quite awake and, yes, I did enjoy myself last night." *And I pray you never find out how much.* Caterine tossed back the blankets and sat on the edge of the bed. "I can be ready in a few minutes if you wish for me to go with you."

"That's not necessary. I'll have Thomas drive me."

"Okay, then I'll see you later this afternoon."

"Caterine, I need to speak with you in private. I'd like you to join me at Brennan's after Mass. Can you do that?"

"Sure, I'll be happy to meet you. Does this have to do with what occurred at Ma Chérie yesterday?"

"I'll explain when I see you. Please call and make our reservation. Make sure to tell them I wish to have my usual table."

"All right, Grandmère. I'll see you later."

In her kitchen, as she scooped Café Du Monde coffee into a cafetière, the phone rang.

"Hello."

"I found out a little more about your pirate," Elaine said excitedly.

Caterine laughed. "Well, good morning to you, too."

"Cat, I don't have time for pleasantries. Paul is dressing the boys and I don't want him to hear me talking to you. He's already been asking me if I'm sure you weren't at the party."

"What did you tell him?"

"I told him no, you weren't here."

"Did he believe you?"

"I don't know. He looked at me kind of funny. He'll be here any minute to leave for church. Do you want to hear what I found out or not?"

"Of course I want to hear."

"He's thirty-three years old and has never been married. Here's the best part—he doesn't have a current girlfriend. So far so good, right?"

"I suppose."

"What do you mean, *I suppose*? He's absolutely perfect."

Caterine cleared her throat. "He's that, all right."

"According to Paul, he was a damn good cop," Elaine continued. "He said he's never known such an honest, trustworthy person. So when do I get to hear all of the details from last night? I still can't believe you jumped his bones in my arbor."

"I'm having a hard time believing that myself." Caterine sighed. "As far as details, there aren't any."

"Oh, come on. You can begin with how you ended up in my arbor."

"Speaking of which, I need you to look for my diamond clip."

"In the arbor?"

"Yes."

Elaine laughed. "That good, was it? Damn, here comes Paul and the boys. Why don't we meet for lunch and you can fill me in. And don't think you're going to get away with not telling me because I'm going to hound you until you do."

"You can be a real pest, you know that?"

Elaine chuckled. "So where do you want to meet?"

"I can't today. I'm meeting Grandmère at Brennan's after church. How about tomorrow?"

"Tomorrow will work. I'll drop the boys off at my mother's. Where should we go? Pick someplace where we can hide in a corner."

"How about Le Tea Pot? They have that lovely courtyard with a noisy fountain."

"Perfect. I'll see you there at noon."

When once again Remi's face swam through Caterine's mind, she distracted herself by calling Brennan's. After speaking with the maître d', she went to her front door to retrieve the morning paper. She sat at the kitchen counter, nibbling at an apple-filled croissant and drinking black coffee. She tried her best to concentrate on an article dealing with housing reconstruction scams after Hurricane Katrina, but Remi's face kept blurring the print.

"Stop it." She slammed her cup onto the saucer. *You have to stop thinking about him. Stop reliving last night, and definitely stop thinking about seeing him again. When you meet Elaine tomorrow you can't allow her to convince you otherwise. Stop wasting time fantasizing about a man who's probably already forgotten you.*

She placed her plate and cup in the dishwasher and with a determined set to her mouth went to get dressed.

Remi, wearing a black T-shirt and jeans, sat with one booted foot propped up on the wrought iron railing of his small balcony, watching amusedly as Toulouse Street came to life.

Car horns honked, people shouted greetings, a horse and carriage carrying tourists clopped quickly by, and, in the background, always the music.

I love this city. He smiled, watching as an older black man dressed entirely in gold walked past singing.

Remi breathed in the familiar smells of the French Quarter—a combination of spicy food, chicory coffee, spilled beer, and the Mississippi. As he sipped his strong café au lait, his mind drifted back to the night before. He'd awakened that morning hard and ready after a dream in which he was about to enter his princess' sweet little body.

Damn it, Michaud, get a grip. You had a very pleasant encounter with a beautiful woman who for some reason ran away and doesn't want her identity known. She probably ran away because you were all over her like a horny teenager on his first date. He reached into his pocket and pulled out a pack of cigarettes, hesitated, then put them back. Of all the women he'd known, he'd never lost his self-control as he had with his princess.

You've got two choices. Forget about the lady and spend the rest of your life getting a hard-on dreaming about her—and save yourself from being used by another spoiled, self-centered uptown bitch like Desiree—or try your damnedest to find out who she is and give the lady a chance. This time going in with your eyes wide open. If she turns out to be a user, you walk.

As he stood to go into his apartment, a red Mercedes coupe driving slowly by caught his attention. Remi stared in disbelief as, through the open sunroof, he spotted long blond hair held back by a silver fleur-de-lis clip identical to the one now resting on his bedside table.

His heart pounding, unable to believe his luck, he leaned over the rail and called, "Hey, Princess, wait. Damn." He swore as a delivery van pulled up so close to the Mercedes' bumper he couldn't read the plate.

Remi ran through his apartment and down to the street. He reached the sidewalk and cursed fluently in French. The car wasn't anywhere in sight. He turned right on Toulouse toward Royal and headed in the direction she'd been going.

Caterine impatiently tapped her fingers on the car's wooden steering wheel. She was going to be late, and Grandmère wasn't going to be pleased. She glanced at the clock on the dashboard.

First, a fender bender had held her up on St. Charles. Making her way to Conti Street, she'd been rerouted due to a broken water main. Now here she sat in traffic on Toulouse. When the out-of-state car in front of her began to move, she could have sworn she heard a man yelling "Princess."

Glancing in her rearview mirror, she saw a heavyset man smiling at her from the cab of a delivery van.

Making her way to Royal, she stopped in front of Brennan's. Frustrated, she searched for a parking place then spotted her grandmother's driver, Thomas, sitting in a black Lincoln. Caterine rolled down her window. "Hello, Thomas, have you been here long?"

"No, miss, only about fifteen minutes or so. Miss Dauphine is waiting inside."

"I've had one problem after another trying to get here and now I don't know where I'll park."

"I'd be happy to park the car for you if you wish."

"Yes, Thomas, thank you." She jumped from the car and handed him the keys.

As Caterine hurried into the restaurant, Thomas drove away.

Remi, out of breath from running, spotted the car as it turned a corner. With a smile on his face, he ran on, only to be brought up short when he saw a distinguished-looking black man step out. Remi leaned against a wall to catch his breath as he watched the man enter a coffee shop.

Maybe she had turned before he reached the street. He wiped the sweat from his brow as he started back home. He paused beneath Brennan's dark green awning, waiting as a group of tourists went inside.

I know it was her. He scanned the street but didn't see another red Mercedes. As a thought struck him, he smiled. It was nice still knowing people with access to vehicle registration records.

Chapter Seven

"There you are, Caterine." Miss Dauphine glanced at her watch. "You're usually punctual. Did you have a problem?"

"Yes, Grandmère, and I'm sorry I'm late." She kissed her grandmother's cheek before taking a seat across the linen-covered table that overlooked the courtyard. "I encountered one mishap after another getting here. Have you already ordered?"

"Just coffee and onion soup so far. Take your time, my dear, and catch your breath. I don't have another appointment until this afternoon."

Caterine placed her order for coffee, onion soup, and eggs Hussarde, then sat back and took a sip of water. Love and pride filled her heart as she smiled across at her grandmother.

Elegantly attired in her signature Ma Chérie black cashmere suit and lace-edged white silk blouse, Miss Dauphine's petite frame was still erect. Her perfectly quaffed thick silver hair and smooth skin were the envy of women ten years her junior.

"What are you smiling at, my dear?"

"You, Grandmère. You look lovely, as always."

A slight pink tinged Miss Dauphine's cheeks. "Why, thank you. And I must say you're looking especially lovely yourself. It's uncanny, Caterine. The older you get the more you resemble your dear mother." For a second, Miss Dauphine's face took on a pained expression.

"But I digress. What I meant to say is that you have a glow about you, such as a young lady might after a pleasant encounter with a young man. Did you meet someone special at the party last night?"

Visions of Remi's eyes dark with passion flashed through Caterine's mind and she stammered, "W-why, no, Grandmère. I didn't meet anyone." Unable to meet her grandmother's probing gaze, she busied herself refolding her napkin.

"Is there something you wish to tell me, Caterine?"

"No, Grandmère, there's nothing." She let out a sigh of relief when the tuxedo-clad waiters took that moment to bring their food.

As their orders were placed in front of them, Miss Dauphine said, "We'll finish this delicious food before I get to the reason I asked you here. I don't wish to discuss unpleasantness while dining."

Sighing with relief, Caterine gratefully began to eat.

When the empty plates from the flaming Bananas Foster were removed and their coffee cups refilled, Miss Dauphine sat back and sighed. She patted her mouth with her napkin and began.

"Caterine, I've made an extremely difficult decision, but a decision I feel is necessary for the well-being of Ma Chérie. Up until now, my own grandmère's wishes have been honored. Sole ownership was passed down to the first-born daughter, then to me. As I only had sons, my eldest granddaughter should succeed me. Now I find myself having to dishonor my grandmère, and the circumstances forcing me to this decision not only have made me heartsick, but extremely angry as well."

The sudden tears welling in her grandmother's eyes had Caterine reaching for the older woman's hand. "Perhaps there's another way?"

"No, my dear, there isn't." Miss Dauphine dabbed at her eyes with a lace-edged hanky. As she gazed through the window into a courtyard destitute of summer blooms, she visibly composed herself. Then sitting even more erectly than she had before, her mouth set in a determined line, she continued.

"Ma Chérie is what's important. If I can't follow tradition, I'll at least save the business my grandmère worked so hard to create." She took a deep breath. "I intended to leave Ma Chérie to you in my will."

Caterine opened her mouth to protest but her grandmother cut her off.

"Let me finish, Caterine, and don't interrupt. I fear if I were to do this, my sons would feel compelled on behalf of their daughters to contest my will, placing you in a difficult, not to mention unpleasant, position. Therefore I've made an appointment tomorrow with my attorney, Clayton Butler. At my request, he's drawn up the necessary papers for me to turn over total ownership to you while I still live and can deal with my sons myself."

Caterine could only gape. Finally finding her voice, she protested. "Grandmère, you can't do that. Charlotte is next in line, then Paulette."

"Honestly, Caterine, I don't need you to tell me who my granddaughters are. I'm well aware that of all my grandchildren, you're the youngest. You're also dependable, level-headed, and intelligent. But of all your attributes, the one that stands out is that you truly love Ma Chérie. You care about tradition and holding our standards to the highest quality. Your final goal isn't to see how much money you can make, as it is with your aunts and cousins. How my two sons could have married such vulgar, greedy women is beyond me. Other than you, my dear, your mother was the only one who truly cared, but she and my son are gone, so I'm placing the future welfare of Ma Chérie in your hands."

Caterine sat speechless and began to feel sick. She swallowed the lump in her throat. "Grandmère, do you realize how angry this is going to make everyone? Why not tell the family you plan to leave Ma Chérie to me, but you intend on keeping control for now?"

"I thought of that, but after what occurred yesterday I've decided I want this done and over with. I'm weary of listening to their grand ideas. Giving the business to you now should put an end to their plans."

Caterine's voice quavered when she spoke. "Grandmère, you have no idea how much your trust means to me. I'd be honored, but I'm truly afraid that by doing this, we'll have even more problems than we have now."

Miss Dauphine uttered an unladylike snort. "Ma Chérie is mine to do with as I wish. As a matter of fact, so is the house. If they make me any angrier, I might give that to you as well."

"You can't do that."

"I can do anything I want. Your two uncles and their sons have total control of Doucette Shipping. What they do with it is their business. Ma Chérie and the house my grandpapa gave to my grandmère on their wedding day are mine."

Caterine sighed as images of the upcoming confrontation passed before her eyes. If this was what her grandmother wanted, so be it. It wouldn't be the first time she'd clashed with her family, and she was sure it wouldn't be the last.

"This is how I intend to handle the situation," Miss Dauphine continued. "I plan on telling the family my decision tomorrow night after dinner. I want to wait until I've seen my attorney and all the paperwork is signed and finalized. I wanted to explain all of this to you today because you'll need to be present tomorrow. My appointment is at ten o'clock. Tomorrow morning when your Aunt Frances and Aunt Hyacinth arrive for work, tell them you have to leave for a while."

Resigned, Caterine took a deep breath. "All right. If you're sure this is what you feel is necessary, I'll be there."

"Now, I have some news that I hope will put a smile back on your face. I heard from your cousin Robert the other day. He said he will be coming home for the Doucette Mardi Gras party and will stay for at least a week."

"Oh, that's wonderful. I was disappointed he and Becky weren't able to make it home for Christmas."

"So was I. I've never understood why he insisted on going to college up north with all those Yankees."

"Grandmère, the University of Michigan is an excellent college."

"That may very well be, but we have excellent schools right here."

Caterine smiled. "Now, Grandmère, Bobby did go to Loyola. He only went to Michigan for grad school. Besides, if he hadn't gone north, he wouldn't have met and married Becky."

"He could have gone to grad school here as well, but I do love Rebecca, so I'll forgive him." Miss Dauphine sighed. "Caterine, you and your cousin Robert have been thick as thieves since you were children. Heaven forbid anyone might have the nerve to say anything against either one of you in front of the other."

Caterine laughed. "I'm afraid you're right."

"Well, I suppose we should be going. I have a garden club meeting this afternoon." She gathered her gloves and purse. "What are your plans? Will I see you this evening for dinner?"

"Yes, I'll be there. Since I'm already in the Quarter, I'll go on over to Ma Chérie and get some paperwork done."

"That reminds me. With my mind on this other business, I've neglected to call Paul to schedule a time for him to install the new security system. Can you take care of that for me?"

"I'd be happy to."

"Then I'll see you later." Miss Dauphine kissed Caterine's cheek. "Don't work too hard."

"I'll walk out with you. Thomas has my keys, and I don't know where he's parked my car."

Chapter Eight

Caterine stood for several long minutes on Royal Street in front of Ma Chérie, overawed by the responsibility that would soon be entrusted to her. She shook her head. *Grandmère, I hope you know what you're doing.*

In her office, she sat behind the desk and reached for the phone. "Hi, Paul, it's Caterine," she said when Paul LaBeau answered.

"Hey, Cat, how you doing? Too bad you missed the party last night. We had quite a house full."

Caterine said a quick prayer of forgiveness for the lie she was about to tell.

"I'm really sorry I missed all the fun. Something came up here at work that I had to attend to."

"Cat, you need to get a life other than that store. Not only did you miss a fun party, I wanted to introduce you to my partner, Remi. He's a great guy who was with me on the force. I think you two would get along well. I thought the four of us could go to dinner some time."

Great, now how do I get out of this? She couldn't come up with one plausible excuse. Perhaps it wouldn't hurt just to go to dinner. As this thought flickered tantalizingly through her mind, her internal alarm began to scream. *If you have dinner with Remi, where do you think that will lead? Directly to his bed, that's where. Then what?*

Was she ready for a relationship that might mean nothing more to him than sex? She'd only been with him once and already couldn't keep her mind off him. What if the affair were to go on for months? How would she handle the hurt if one day he was gone?

"Cat, are you still there?"

Paul's voice brought her thoughts crashing back. "What? Oh, sorry, Paul. I'm here. What were you saying?"

"I said Elaine's not here. She took the boys to the park. Do you want me to tell her you called? Or you can get her on her cell."

"No, that's okay, I'll try her later. Actually you're the one I wanted to talk to. Grandmère wanted me to ask if you'd have time to install an alarm system here at Ma Chérie."

"Sure, no problem. But don't you already have one?"

"Yes, but it's very old and Grandmère wants to update."

"Well, you're in luck. I had a cancellation and can do the job tomorrow morning. Are you there now?"

"Yes."

"How about if I run over and take a look. That way, I'll know what I need."

"Thanks. That would be great. Ring the bell at the front when you get here."

Caterine disconnected and quickly punched in Elaine's cell number. When she answered, Caterine got right to the point. "We've got trouble."

"What? What's wrong?"

"I was just on the phone with Paul, and he told me he wants to introduce me to his buddy Remi and have the four of us go out to dinner."

"Oh no."

"*Oh no* is right. You have to persuade him that's a really bad idea."

Elaine chuckled. "If he only knew you've already met his buddy Remi— and how well acquainted you two are."

Caterine smiled. "Yeah, well, you need to nip this in the bud."

"Why? Paul says he's a nice guy, and you know he wouldn't introduce you to someone who was a jerk. Besides, I thought you wanted to change your life and start having some fun. Remi sounds like the perfect one to help you do that."

Caterine sighed. "I'm afraid if I pursue this with Remi, I'll be setting myself up for another fall. He could have a string of broken hearts all over

Louisiana. And I'm not ready to take the risk of being the next one."

"How do you know he's going to hurt you? You're making assumptions about him without giving him a chance. Didn't he try and protect you from Jonathan? And didn't he come searching for you last night after you ran away?"

Caterine pinched the bridge of her nose, willing a threatening headache to go away. "I didn't say he wasn't interested in me. I said I don't trust him."

"You trusted him enough to have sex with him. Cat, I know you well enough to know you wouldn't have let that happen unless you felt something for him. So why not take a chance and let him prove you wrong? You can't spend the rest of your life afraid to let people close. Do you want to end up some alone, bitter, sourpuss old lady?"

"Oh, for heaven's sake, aren't you being a little dramatic?"

"No, that's exactly what's going to happen. Cat, if you could survive all the crap your family handed you, I'm sure you can handle whatever happens between you and Remi. You need to give him a chance."

"All right, I'll think about it. But between my aunts, Grandmère and Ma Chérie, I can't deal with Remi right now. So, for the time being, you need to get Paul's mind on something besides matchmaking."

"Okay, but I'm not going to let this go. I'll see what I can do with Paul, but what should I tell him?"

"I don't know. Tell him I'm too busy or something. Elaine, there's the bell. I'll bet it's Paul. I'll see you tomorrow."

Paul walked into Caterine's office and sat in the chair across from her desk. "I've checked out your entry doors, and I have some ideas for a new system."

"Great, what do you suggest?"

"First, you can eliminate changing the locks and worrying about keys by installing a coded key pad."

"What's that?"

"It's a pad that you program with a series of four numbers. It goes right on the door where the lock is now. It's more convenient than messing with keys, and you can change the code whenever you want."

"Could we put one on my office door?"

Paul went to examine the door. "I don't see why not."

"Great."

"As I said, I can have it done tomorrow. If you want, I'll also install cameras so you can see who's at the front and back doors."

"That would be perfect. Paul, I really appreciate you doing this."

He grinned. "Tell me that when you get my bill. I'll see you around nine tomorrow morning. Hey, you know what?" He turned in the doorway, a wide smile spreading across his craggy face. "The guy I was telling you about—Remi—he'll be helping me do the job. You'll get to meet him then."

Not if I can help it, Caterine thought as she followed Paul from the room.

Caterine entered the front parlor of the Doucette Audubon Place mansion as her Uncle Jules was handing around the family's before-dinner cocktails. Just turning sixty, of medium height with silver flecks throughout his chestnut hair, he was still a handsome man.

"There you are, Caterine," Miss Dauphine said, seated in her customary high-backed brocade chair to the right of the Adams fireplace. "I was concerned you wouldn't be joining us."

As Jules handed his mother a glass of sherry, he turned to face Caterine. In a slow cultured drawl he admonished, "Mother said you were at Ma Chérie. On a Sunday." He shook his head. "Caterine, I swear you're working way too hard. You're spending more time there than is good for you. I'm sure your Aunt Frances or Aunt Hyacinth would be willing to take some of your burden. Now, what can I get you to drink?"

"I'll have a glass of Cabernet, thanks," Caterine replied, taking a seat on a deep-rose settee. As she waited for her wine, Caterine inwardly sighed with pleasure at the well-appointed room. Rose and cream moiré drapes were pulled back from floor-to-ceiling French windows that looked out on the wide veranda. A Baccarat chandelier cast a warm glow over the empire-style furnishings arranged upon a thick Aubusson rug of rose, cream, and soft blue.

"Jules is right, Miss Dauphine. As Hyacinth and I have been saying, we'd be happy to take on more responsibility," Frances said, accepting a gin and tonic from her husband. "And since someday Charlotte will be the head of Ma Chérie, it's important that she learns more about the store. Isn't that right, Charlotte?"

Caterine glanced from Frances to her cousin Charlotte, who fidgeted in her seat and looked at her watch. "Yes, Mother, certainly."

"I've always wanted to learn more about the business," Paulette added. "It all sounds so fascinating."

Hyacinth turned her large ice-blue eyes toward Caterine. "I'm sure you'd be happy to teach Paulette anything she needed to know, wouldn't you?"

Not waiting for Caterine to reply, Paulette clapped her chubby little hands. "Oh, that would be wonderful. I can't wait to begin."

Paulette's mood swings always amazed Caterine. One minute she was all sugary sweetness, the next bitter venom. A few months earlier, days before their wedding, Paulette's fiancé, Travis Jenkins, had broken their engagement. Since then, Paulette's venom had surfaced more and more frequently.

Caterine silently shook her head. How Bobby, with his even-tempered pleasant disposition, could be Paulette's younger brother amazed her.

"Miss Dauphine, I hope you've had a chance to think over the ideas we talked about earlier," Frances said. "I understand tradition is important, but it's time for Ma Chérie to leave the nineteenth century and advance forward with fresh new concepts."

"Absolutely," Hyacinth agreed. "Ma Chérie's clothing is too stuffy. We really need to liven up our line and make it more fun and affordable. Like the clothing I make for myself and Paulette."

Caterine peered over the top of her wineglass, waiting for her grandmother's reaction. She knew the only reason they were having this conversation was that her aunts were hoping to gain their husbands' support.

Miss Dauphine's dark eyes went from Hyacinth to Frances. She cleared her throat. "I will say this one last time, then this nonsense will cease. Ma Chérie's clothing has always been, and shall always be, elegant and chic. This is the standard our clientele expects, and this is what our clientele will receive. To do otherwise would be unacceptable not only to me, but to those who have patronized the salon for over a century. There are plenty of other clothing establishments that cater to people with your taste, Hyacinth."

Bravo, Grandmère. Caterine silently applauded. Her attention was drawn to her uncle Markus, whose low nervous chuckle filled the quiet room.

"Now, ladies," he drawled, "you can discuss Ma Chérie business all you wish later, but here's Flora announcing dinner and I'm ready to eat." He rose to his feet. "Mother, may I escort you in?"

As they all stood, Caterine noticed the lines creasing Markus' brow and the dark circles under his eyes. His efforts to keep up with his young nephew Randal seemed to be taking a toll.

"Jules, where are Raymond and Randal?" Frances snapped, clearly furious over Miss Dauphine's rebuke. "I thought you said they'd both be here for dinner."

Jules put his arm around his wife. "They must have gotten delayed. The boys are grown men with lives of their own. You have to stop fussing over them."

Delayed, all right, Caterine thought, trailing the others from the room, *at the casino or in some whorehouse.*

Chapter Nine

The following morning, Caterine sat in her office nervously tapping her fingers, trying to hold back the panic that threatened to overtake her. Her eyes were glued to the digital clock sitting on her polished cherrywood desk, watching anxiously as the time changed from 8:45 to 8:46, and her aunts still weren't there. Paul, with Remi in tow, was due to arrive at nine o'clock to install the new alarms.

Why didn't I give Paul a key so he could let himself in? The digital display now said 8:52, and, for the first time in her life, she was ecstatic to hear the sound of her aunts' voices as they came through the front door. A sigh of relief had no sooner left her lips when Paul's voice had her moving. She grabbed her bag and was halfway out the back door when she heard her Aunt Frances calling her name.

A few hours later, Caterine hurried across Jackson Square and entered Le Tea Pot's hot-pink front door as the St. Louis Cathedral's bells chimed the hour. Directed to the courtyard, Caterine found Elaine ensconced at a corner table, flanked by two tall potted plants.

"Hi. Have you been here long?" Caterine asked, gratefully taking her seat.

"Long enough to order a Bloody Mary. You look as if you could use one yourself."

"You have no idea how much." Caterine caught the waitress' eye and pointed at Elaine's drink.

"Before you tell me all the juicy details of how you ended up with Remi in my arbor, I've been dying to hear how you avoided being seen by him this morning." Elaine cocked her head. "Or did you?"

"Yes, I did, and it was a real nightmare. This is turning into some farcical TV sitcom. I had to tell my aunts I needed them to come in early because I had an appointment, which I did, but not until ten o'clock. They got there seconds before Paul and Remi came through the front door. I literally was running out the back as they came in the front. And you can stop laughing. This situation isn't funny."

"Oh, but it is." Elaine doubled over in laughter.

"Stop that," Caterine demanded, but her own lips were twitching.

"Okay, I'll quit." Elaine wiped her eyes. "But I still don't understand why you're being so stubborn about seeing Remi again. Besides, how are you going to keep from running into him here in the Quarter?"

Caterine shrugged. "I'll have to deal with that if it happens. Now do you want to hear where I've been? And what my grandmère has done?"

"No." Elaine gasped when she'd finished. "You now are the sole owner of Ma Chérie?"

She nodded. "That's right. Grandmère is going to tell the family tonight after dinner."

"I can't believe this. You owning Ma Chérie. How wonderful." Suddenly Elaine's exuberance left her face. "Oh God, Caterine, your family is going to throw a fit when they hear this."

"No kidding. I wish I could let Grandmère tell them on her own, but that would be too cowardly."

Elaine knitted her brows. "I suppose. So how are you going to handle your rampaging relatives?"

Caterine took a long sip of her drink, then her mouth formed a firm line. "Grandmère has entrusted me with a business she holds dear, and I intend to honor that trust. And no matter how loud or how long they scream, there's absolutely nothing they can do about it. Ma Chérie is mine."

The ticking of the parlor mantel clock was the only sound in the suddenly silent room. Caterine held her breath, waiting for the explosion that was sure to come.

"Mother, you can't be serious," Markus said, breaking the silence.

Regally seated in her brocaded chair, Miss Dauphine looked prepared for battle and intent on victory.

"I can assure you, Markus, I am very serious. The papers were signed this morning."

Markus, clearly agitated, rose and headed toward the drinks cabinet. "Can I fix one for anyone else?"

Randal stared at Caterine, scowled and shook his head. "I'll join you, Uncle Markus. The occasion certainly calls for one."

Caterine's eyes went from Randal to Markus and noticed her uncle's hands weren't steady as he poured the drinks.

"Mother, shouldn't you have discussed your decision with us first?" Jules asked.

"No, Jules, why should I have? Ma Chérie is mine to do with as I choose. And I choose to give it to Caterine."

Caterine braced herself as all eyes turned toward her. Her breath caught at the variety of emotions in their faces: confusion, disbelief, envy, distaste, and hatred, all focused on her. She lifted her chin high and stared defiantly back.

Silence again filled the room until Frances, barely able to control her rage, met Caterine's eyes. Emphasizing each word as she spoke, she said, "Well, I hope you're happy. You've just cheated your cousin out of her inheritance."

Caterine opened her mouth to reply when her uncle Jules came to her defense. "Now, Frances, Caterine had nothing to do with this."

"Don't *now, Frances* me, Jules. She's been manipulating your mother since she was a child, and now she's managed to convince her to disinherit your daughter."

Miss Dauphine's eyes flashed with anger. "Frances, I have never been manipulated by anyone, nor do I ever intend to be. As Jules said, Caterine had nothing to do with this. She did not know my intentions until yesterday."

"Mother, do you realize that by doing this you're disregarding your grandmother's wishes?" Markus asked.

Before Miss Dauphine could reply, Frances interrupted. "That's right, Raymond. You're an attorney. Is what she's done legal?"

Caterine and her cousin Raymond's eyes met. To her astonishment, he winked.

As twins, Raymond and Randal had the handsome dark looks of the Doucettes, but that's where similarity ended. Their personalities were as different as salt and pepper. Caterine definitely preferred Raymond.

"Mother, I'm sure Clayton Butler knows what he's doing. He's been taking care of Grandmère's affairs for years."

Miss Dauphine nodded. "Thank you, Raymond. That's correct. And to answer your question, Frances, I've done nothing illegal."

"It's not only Charlotte that's being disinherited. What about my Paulette?" Hyacinth said, glowering at Caterine.

Through narrowed eyes, Paulette looked from Caterine to Miss Dauphine and back to her mother and simpered, "Mother, I don't understand. Why does Grandmère dislike me so?"

Caterine waited for her grandmother's response. Her expression of exasperation warned that they were about to push her beyond the limits of her patience.

"Paulette, my decision has nothing to do with whether I love you or not. I feel Caterine is the right one to take over ownership of Ma Chérie. This is strictly business."

Charlotte jumped to her feet and began to pace. "That's all well and good, Grandmère, but what I want to know is where exactly does this decision of yours leave Paulette and me? Are we SOL or what?"

"Really, Charlotte." Frances gave her a disapproving scowl.

"What, Mother? Don't you think we have a right to know who would inherit Ma Chérie if something were to happen to Caterine?" Charlotte stiffened. "Why are you all staring at me? Anything could happen to her. Why, her own mother was already dead at the age Caterine is now."

A deafening silence filled the room. A chill went up Caterine's spine as she gazed into each face.

Two spots of color stained Miss Dauphine's cheeks as she slowly rose. In a voice taut with anger, she spoke. "Your despicable behavior here tonight has proven to me once and for all that my decision to place the welfare of

Ma Chérie in Caterine's hands was exactly what I needed to do. So there's no confusion, Charlotte, if Caterine were to precede me in death, the business would revert back to me. Currently her will states that after my death Charlotte would be next in line to inherit, but as sole owner Caterine has the authority to leave Ma Chérie to whomever she wishes.

"Now, neither Caterine nor I plan on leaving this world soon, so hear me and hear me well. If any of you try and interfere with my decision, or with Caterine and the running of Ma Chérie . . ." Here she paused. "Trust me, you will live to regret it." Her head held high, Miss Dauphine swept from the room.

With her family's eyes boring into her, Caterine felt like a trapped mouse surrounded by hungry cats. She knew tonight's events had shaken her grandmother more than she let show. She decided to leave her family to stew in their anger and go check on her. She took a deep breath, stood, and confronted the group.

"As Grandmère said, I knew nothing about this until yesterday. I don't really care if you believe me, but believe this—Grandmère has entrusted me with Ma Chérie, and I intend on living up to that trust. As long as I'm alive, Ma Chérie will be run according to Grandmère's wishes."

Caterine hadn't taken but a few steps out into the hall when Frances' voice stopped her. Unable to help herself, she crept silently back and listened outside the door.

"Jules, your mother is eighty-two and becoming senile," Frances was saying. "This situation is outrageous. I want to know what you intend to do about it."

"The papers have been signed. There's nothing I can do."

"I agree with Frances. Miss Dauphine has lost her mind," Hyacinth said. "There has to be some way to stop this."

"Hey, don't y'all look at me," Raymond replied. "I'm a corporate attorney. I told you, Clayton Butler knows what he's doing."

"What about assigning someone to have power of attorney over her affairs?" Frances asked.

"Good luck," Raymond said. "You'd have to get her assent, or prove that she's incompetent to handle her own affairs."

"There's not a damn thing wrong with Mother's competency," Markus said. "She knows exactly what she's doing."

"Mama, I still don't understand why Grandmère gave Ma Chérie to Caterine," Paulette said. "Why does she always get everything she wants?"

"Because she's been pampered and spoiled and raised to believe she's special and better than the rest of you," Hyacinth snapped. "But she's about to learn differently. There are others in this family who have just as many rights."

"I, for one, am sick and tired of the little goody-two-shoes preying on Grandmère's sympathy," Charlotte said.

Her anger rising, Caterine was about to reenter the room when Uncle Jules spoke.

"That's enough. Caterine was devastated when her parents were killed. Who wouldn't have pitied that child? I don't blame Mother and Daddy in the least for sheltering and surrounding her with love and affection. Now, if Mother has decided to give Ma Chérie to Caterine, so be it."

"We'll see about that," Frances said. "I'm not going to sit by and let Caterine walk away with Ma Chérie."

"That's right," Hyacinth added. "Something must be done."

"Y'all can sit here bitching and moaning about the injustice of it all, but you're wasting your time," Randal said. "Caterine has loved Ma Chérie since she was a little girl." He laughed. "So it seems to me the only way to get control of Ma Chérie would be if Grandmère and Caterine were both dead."

Chapter Ten

Caterine stood frozen in disbelief outside the parlor door. After Randal's chilling remark, the room had gone quiet.

Until her uncle Jules broke the silence. "As Randal said, sitting here going on and on about this is pointless. Mother has made a decision. Caterine now owns Ma Chérie. And glowering at me, Frances, isn't going to change that. Like it or not, we have to accept this and go on."

At sounds of her family stirring, Caterine ran into the darkened dining room. She peered through a crack in the door, watching as her uncles and Raymond went into the library, Randal and Charlotte left through the front door, and her aunts and Paulette headed upstairs.

Caterine made sure the entry hall was empty, then hurried into the parlor to retrieve her purse.

"Well, little cousin, you've created quite a family uproar."

Startled, Caterine turned to see Raymond leaning against the parlor doorway.

"For heaven's sake, Ray, you about gave me a heart attack."

He smiled. "Sorry, I was coming out of the library and saw your mad dash from the dining room. So how much did you overhear?"

Caterine shrugged. "Not much." Even though she liked Ray, she wasn't about to let him know she'd heard it all.

"You've managed to really piss off the family this time."

Caterine snorted. "No kidding. It would have been pretty hard to miss that."

"Keep your powder dry, little cousin."

"What's that supposed to mean?"

"It means watch your back."

Caterine's mouth had suddenly gone dry. "Ray, you're scaring me."

"Good." Without another word, he turned and went out the front door.

As she had many times before, Caterine felt alone, an outcast in her own family. She grabbed her purse and, with tears streaming down her cheeks, ran to the solace of her carriage house.

In a bedroom upstairs, Paulette lay propped up against a mound of lace-edged pillows. At the foot of the bed, Hyacinth paced.

"I will not see all my dreams destroyed by that batty old lady nor her brat of a granddaughter."

Paulette scowled. "Yes, well, what can we do about it?" She chose another chocolate from the box by her side. "Once again Caterine has gotten her way. It's really too bad she didn't die with her parents."

Hyacinth snorted. "That certainly would have made things a lot simpler. After the accident, Caterine should have been sent to live with her mother's people in Virginia, but, of course, Miss Dauphine wouldn't allow that. No, she had to stay right here where she could be coddled and pampered. It was enough to make me sick."

"Remember how Charlotte and I used to torment Caterine?" Paulette said with a satisfied smirk. "Like the time I tore the head off her favorite doll and threw it in the pond?" She smiled. "She cried for weeks. And the time Charlotte locked her in the closet and she peed her pants? Grandmère was furious." Anger replaced her humor. "Bobby told Grandmère I was the one who did it. I don't care if he is my brother, I hate him about as much as I do Caterine."

Hyacinth's eyes narrowed in anger. "Bobby is as much mine as you are. I will not have you bad-mouthing him. Caterine has always been a conniving little brat who played on Bobby's sympathetic nature."

"Mother, you always take his side. What about me?"

Hyacinth threw up her hands in exasperation. "Oh, for God's sake, Paulette, why do you think I want you to learn how to run Ma Chérie? Since the day I entered this house, Miss Dauphine has treated me as if I wasn't good enough for her precious son. Well, I'll show her. When you're in charge, they'll all have to respect us. And if she thinks she's outwitted me, she's mistaken."

Paulette frowned. "But what about Charlotte? I can't have Ma Chérie as long as she's around."

Hyacinth gave a dismissive wave. "Charlotte can be easily dealt with. It's Miss Dauphine and Caterine that's our problem."

In a bedroom down the hall, Frances glowered at her husband. "How you can stand by and allow your mother to disinherit your daughter is beyond me. Since your father's death, you're supposed to be the head of this family. For once in your life, stand up to that woman."

Jules rubbed his temples. "Frances, I'll repeat this for the hundredth time. Markus and I haven't any say over Ma Chérie. Besides, I don't know why you're so upset. Charlotte has never shown any interest in the business. I'm sure if you asked her, she'd tell you she couldn't care less."

Frances' back stiffened. "I'll have you know that just last week Charlotte asked me a number of questions regarding the running of Ma Chérie. In the past she hasn't shown an interest because Miss Dauphine has always been healthy, but now she's getting up in years and Charlotte realizes the time is nearing when she's going to have to take over."

Jules shook his head. "Not anymore."

"Are you telling me you won't even consider talking to Miss Dauphine?"

He sighed. "That's exactly what I'm telling you. So will you please let it alone?"

Frances' mouth hardened into a thin line. "No, Jules, I will not leave it alone. Ma Chérie is Charlotte's inheritance, and I intend on making sure she gets it back."

Across town, on the private deck of the casino boat The High Roller,

Randal, Markus, and Charlotte were on their second round of drinks.

"Well, I guess we're all royally fucked," Randal said. "I can kiss this boat goodbye."

Markus gulped his drink. "Yeah, what about my ass when Jules finds out about Doucette Shipping?"

Charlotte held her head in her hands. "I thought for sure this would soon be over."

Randal narrowed his eyes. "Thanks to you, cousin, we're all going down."

Charlotte slammed down her glass. "Don't even try to blame this on me."

Randal lifted one brow. "It sure as hell isn't all my fault."

"Both of you stop it," Markus said. "We all had a part in this, and now we have to figure out a way to get ourselves out."

"If there's anyone to blame, it's Caterine," Charlotte said. "God, I can't stand the sight of her."

Markus sighed. "Caterine isn't to blame any more than Mother is. It's only that Mother's timing couldn't be any worse."

"Yes, well, I never much cared one way or another about Caterine, but right now I'd like to strangle her little neck," Randal added.

Charlotte smiled. "That would take care of one problem, but we still have Grandmère."

Both Randal and Charlotte turned to Markus.

"Don't look at me. There isn't a damn thing I can do now. Perhaps Ray can come up with something."

Randal snorted. "Ray is so pissed he's not about to lift a finger to help us. No, we're on our own, and I, for one, am not about to sit around and watch everything go to hell."

Two days later, after tossing and turning for most of the night, Caterine awoke late for work. Her car, which had never let her down, wouldn't start, so she'd run to catch the streetcar, missing it by seconds. Finally making it to work, she was greeted by her two angry aunts.

"Caterine, you might own Ma Chérie, but as far as I know, your Aunt Hyacinth and I still work here, or am I mistaken?"

Great, this is all I need. Caterine gritted her teeth to keep from screaming.

She took a deep breath and pasted a smile on her face. "Of course both of you still work here. What's wrong?"

"What's wrong is we can't get in," Frances said. "When you decided for some unknown reason to have all of the locks removed and this key pad installed, you conveniently neglected to give us the code, so we've had to stand out here in the damp and cold waiting for you to let us in."

Caterine silently counted to ten. She'd decided to deal with her family's hostility by either ignoring them or killing them with kindness. She wasn't about to give them the satisfaction of knowing they'd hurt her once again.

"I'm sorry. You left before I did yesterday and I forgot to give you the code. Here, let me show you how it works." Sounding as apologetic as she could stomach, she punched in the series of numbers. "See how much easier this is than having to fumble with keys."

Hyacinth sniffed. "I never had a problem with the old locks."

Caterine inwardly sighed. She stood back, letting her two aunts precede her through the door.

By six o'clock, Caterine's head was pounding. She'd spent most of the day trying to trace missing bolts of silk that were supposed to have arrived from France the day before. She'd had to calm an irate client who insisted it was the seamstress' fault, not hers, that the cashmere suit she'd ordered was now too tight. She'd gallantly ignored her aunts' satisfied little smiles as each new problem arose.

Now blessedly alone in her office, she'd decided to work for another hour or so. She rubbed her temples, thinking aspirin and coffee were what she needed. A small kitchen alcove had been equipped with a coffee pot, refrigerator, and microwave. As she made her way down the hall, she noticed through the front windows the thick fog that hadn't been there an hour ago.

Terrific, this is all I need. Thanks to her chaotic morning, she'd forgotten to call AAA and have her car towed to a garage. She'd planned on calling a cab when she was ready to leave. She continued to the alcove and the coffee pot. As she passed the short hall leading to the alley door, she paused.

Out of the corner of her eye, through the frosted glass, backlit by an alley streetlight, she thought she'd seen a dark silhouette. Slowly turning her head, seeing nothing, she sighed. *It's only the fog playing tricks with the light.* With her head pounding harder by the minute, she decided she might as well go home.

Back in her office, she shut down her computer, neatly stacked the next day's orders, and phoned for a cab. Informed they didn't know how long it would take for one to get there, in exasperation she told them never mind and hung up.

I'll just take the streetcar. She gathered her oversized candy apple red bag, matching coat, and umbrella, locked her office door, set the alarm with the remote control, and stepped out onto the sidewalk.

The fog was a lot thicker than she'd thought. Caterine huddled deeper into her coat. *To end this perfect day, the streetcars probably aren't running.* She'd only taken a few steps when someone grabbed her from behind.

"I have a gun," he hissed. "If you make a sound or fight me, I'll kill you."

He began to pull her toward the curb. Her entire body trembling, Caterine could see the outline of a van. Everything seemed to move in slow motion. Franticly she tried to think of a way to draw someone's attention.

"Fuck," the man cursed as distant footsteps could be heard approaching.

Caterine felt her attacker hesitate, the gun still pressed against her back. *This is your only chance,* she told herself. *Do something.* When she realized what she still held in her hand, she pressed the button, praying it would work. As the scream of Ma Chérie's alarm filled the night, Caterine, the remote clenched in her fist, blindly swung it behind her, connecting satisfyingly with her assailant's nose.

"Fucking bitch, I'll still get you." He shoved her hard toward the van. "We're going for a ride."

She cried out in pain as she landed hard on the sidewalk, scraping her hands and knees, the remote skidding into the gutter. Blurry eyed, she spotted her umbrella lying on the ground within reach.

Her attacker grabbed her long hair, jerking her head back. "Get up, bitch."

Tears streaming down her cheeks, fear giving her strength, Caterine grabbed the umbrella and with both hands thrust the point up and back.

As he shouted in pain, his grip on her hair loosened. She rose to her feet and ran, her small figure disappearing into the fog.

Remi, on his way home from a solitary dinner of crawfish étouffée at Oceania, heard the wail of an alarm. Curious, he followed the sound to its source. Stopping in front of the building, he realized it was the same business where he and Paul had installed a new alarm system. As he reached for his phone, two police cruisers pulled up.

"Hey, Remi, is that you?" asked one officer as he got out of the car.

"Hey, Vince. Yeah, it's me."

"What's happened here? Why's the alarm going off?"

"I don't know. I just got here." Remi explained he'd been on his way home and had heard the noise.

"This damn fog is a pain in the ass," said Andre, the second officer. "Can't see a foot in front of you."

"I can at least silence the alarm," Remi said.

"How's that?" Vince asked.

"Because I installed it." Within seconds Remi had the door open and the alarm off.

Vince let out a long whistle as Remi turned the lights on. "Pretty posh place. What kind of business is it?"

"Some kind of fancy ladies' clothing store. The owner is a friend of Paul LaBeau. We installed the system a couple of days ago."

Vince grinned. "Seems you two know what you're doing. It works."

"Hey, what do you expect from two former cops?"

"Yeah, well."

"Everything's secure, Vince," Andre reported.

"We'll still need to get the owner down here to see if anything's missing, but I don't see any sign of a break-in. Do you?" Vince asked.

Remi shook his head.

"Do you know how we can get in touch with the owner?"

"Here's Paul's number." Remi handed Vince a business card. "He'll know."

"So, how you been? You like being off the force?"

Remi smiled. "It's better than getting my ass shot at, *cher*."

Vince laughed. "I hear you."

"I'll leave NOPD's finest to take care of this. Later."

As he was leaving, something on the sidewalk caught Remi's eye. In the semidarkness, he bent to get a closer look and saw it was a red umbrella. His gut clenched as he noticed a familiar object lying only a foot or so away. He reached down and picked up a silver hair clip in the shape of a fleur-de-lis. His gut clenched tighter as his eyes fell upon two fresh streaks of blood on the sidewalk.

"Vince, get out here."

Chapter Eleven

Her breath coming in shallow gasps, Caterine ran blindly through the thick fog. As she rounded a corner, she almost collided with a taxi sitting at the curb. With a sob of relief, she yanked open the back door and flung herself in.

"Drive." When the wide-eyed cabbie only stared, she repeated herself. "Did you hear me? I said *drive*."

"Ah, miss, do you need a doctor?"

"No, I don't need a doctor."

"How about the police? Do you want to go to a police station?"

Caterine hesitated, replaying the attack in her mind. The man didn't try to steal her purse; he was after her. The Doucettes were wealthy, so there was always the threat of kidnapping. One by one the faces of her family and their reactions to her ownership of Ma Chérie swam before her eyes. As suspicion of their betrayal struck her, she began to shake uncontrollably. Was the timing too coincidental? But what could they gain from abducting her? Caterine swallowed back the nausea that churned in her stomach. The only way they'd gain anything from her is if she were dead. *Oh, God, I'm going to be sick.*

"Miss, do you want the police?" the driver asked again.

Caterine gulped the stale air of the cab. If it was her family, did she want the police involved? She had to have time to think it through. She tried to keep her teeth from chattering as she replied, "No, I don't want the police. I just want to leave the Quarter."

"Is there someone I can call to come get you?"

Caterine thought she'd scream in frustration. "Please just drive. I don't care where we go."

"Miss, I can't leave until this fog lifts, and when it does, I have a fare to pick up at the airport."

Caterine gritted her teeth. "Then take me to the airport."

"That will cost you thirty dollars."

She dug her wallet out of her oversized bag that somehow was still hanging on her shoulder, pulled out a fifty-dollar bill, and handed it to him. "Here, keep the change."

The driver looked at her, then at the bill. With a resigned shrug, he took the money and faced front. "The fog is beginning to lift. We can probably leave shortly."

"Thank you."

As police sirens filled the night, the cab slowly made its way through the streets. Another fear entered Caterine's mind—Grandmère. Would they go after her as well? She began franticly searching in her handbag for her cell phone. For the first time in her life, she felt on the verge of hysteria.

The cabbie glanced at her in the rearview mirror. "You okay back there, miss?"

She stifled a sob. "Yes, I'm fine."

"We're almost at the airport. Where do you want me to drop you off?"

"What?"

"At which airline do you wish to be left?"

"It doesn't matter." Caterine had finally dug her phone from the bottom of her bag. With trembling fingers, she tried to scroll down to her grandmother's private number, but she was shaking too badly.

"Here we are, miss."

She glanced up to see they were parked in front of the terminal entrance.

"Are you going to be okay, miss?" the cabby asked as she stumbled from the car.

"What? Yes, I'm fine. Thank you."

Caterine hurried into the terminal and headed for the ladies' room. When she saw her reflection in the mirror, she understood the cab driver's concern. Her hair was a tangled mess. Her clothes were disheveled. Her stockings were torn, and her hands and knees were scraped and bloody.

She splashed cold water on her face, then cleaned herself the best she could with soap and paper towels. Thankfully, she found a brush, another hair clip, and some makeup in her bag. One more glance in the mirror told her she was as presentable as she could be. She left the ladies' room and headed for an area of empty chairs.

Grateful there weren't many people around, she took a seat and again tried to call her grandmother. *Thank God,* she thought with relief when the phone was answered. Hoping she could keep her voice steady, she asked, "Grandmère, are you all right?"

"Yes, I'm fine. Why?"

Caterine hesitated. How could she tell her grandmother she was convinced someone in their family had just tried to have her abducted?

"Caterine, what's going on?"

She took a deep breath. "Grandmère, I'm at the airport and before I say anything else, I want you to know I'm okay."

"What?"

"I don't know any other way to say this, but someone just tried to abduct me at gunpoint."

"What in the world are you talking about, Caterine?"

"I was just leaving Ma Chérie, and I was attacked from behind. I was able to get away and find a cab, and now I'm at the airport and I'm afraid now they'll come after you. So you have to get out of there."

"For heaven's sake, slow down. I can't make sense out of anything you're saying."

Caterine wiped the tears from her cheeks and took a few calming breaths, then repeated the chain of events. "So you see, your life could also be in danger. You have to get out of that house. Thomas can take you somewhere safe."

With a quiver in her voice, Miss Dauphine asked, "What makes you think your attack had to do with Ma Chérie?"

"I can't know for sure, but to me it's a bit coincidental this happens two days after you transfer ownership."

"Oh, sweet Jesus, do you realize what you're saying?"

"Yes, that someone in our family is behind it. Grandmère, I don't want to think that any more than you do, but until we know for sure, we have to be careful."

"I don't understand. What would they achieve by abducting you?"

Caterine hesitated. Her grandmother was upset enough; she didn't need to hear that she thought killing her was their goal. "I don't know Grandmère, but we can't worry about that right now. It's your safety I'm concerned about."

"This is all my fault."

"Don't even say such a thing."

"If you're right, how can I not? I thought I was doing what was best. I never imagined there could be such evil in my own family."

"Grandmère, we'll figure this out later. What you need to do now is leave that house. I'll meet you at a hotel."

"Caterine, I will not be run out of my own home. It's you we have to worry about. Do you have identification and a credit card on you?"

"Yes, I have both. Why?"

"Then get on the next plane and leave New Orleans."

"Grandmère, I can't do that. What about you?"

"I'm of no importance. It's you who's in danger. Until we know what we're up against, I want you out of this city."

"I can go to a hotel. Nobody will think to look for me there."

"For all we know, we're both being watched. We can't take any chances." Miss Dauphine's voice cracked. "Caterine, I couldn't stand it if something happened to you. Please do as I ask and leave."

"All right, I'll go, but I want you to join me. Once we're settled, we'll call Paul and tell him what's happened, and he can advise us on what we should do next."

"I plan on calling Paul as soon as I hang up from you. I want him to send someone to be with you and keep you safe. So as soon as you get where you're going, call me and let me know where you are."

Caterine opened her mouth to protest but, knowing her words would fall on deaf ears, gave up. "Fine, I'll call you. But please ask Paul to send someone to look after you as well."

Caterine dropped the phone back in her bag and looked around for a monitor listing departures. Spotting one, she started to rise, then abruptly sat back down. *No, if Grandmère isn't going to allow them to run her out of her home, then by God I'm not going to let them chase me out of New Orleans.*

An anger she didn't know she possessed burned through her veins. *Damn them to hell. I've had a lifetime of their abuse. No more. I'm going to find out who's behind this, and God help them when I do.*

She rose from her seat and, with a determined stride, headed for the exit.

Remi paced back and forth, smoking a cigarette he knew he shouldn't be smoking, while waiting for Paul to arrive. After he'd found the hair clip and the blood, he'd called Paul only to have the phone answered by a nearly incoherent Elaine. All Remi was able to understand was that her friend Caterine was in trouble and Paul was on his way.

"We got samples of both blood smears, along with the smaller drops we found," Vince said, stopping beside Remi. "And we found this in the gutter." He held out an evidence bag. "It may have traces of blood."

Remi tossed his cigarette into the street and reached for the bag. His eyes narrowed when he realized what he held. "It's the remote alarm for the store."

"Since the damn fog has lifted, we can get some lights out here and see if we find anything else."

Remi nodded and reached for another cigarette.

"Remi, man, you okay?"

"Yeah, I'm fine." He let out a long stream of smoke. "I may know whose blood that is."

"Whose?"

"It belongs to a princess."

"A what?"

Before Remi could explain, a black Mercury Mountaineer stopped at the curb and Paul jumped out.

"Hey, Vince, where y'at?" Paul asked, stopping in front of the two men.

"All right, Paul. I hope you can make more sense than this one." Vince pointed at Remi. "He's telling me the blood on the sidewalk might belong to a princess."

Paul glanced at Remi, then back at Vince. "He's right. It does."

Vince sighed. "Okay, I'm listening."

"Her name is Caterine Doucette, and she's in trouble."

"Doucette, as in Doucette Shipping?" Vince asked.

"That's the one."

Remi lit another cigarette.

"Hey, I thought you quit?" Paul asked.

He received an icy stare in reply.

With a shrug, Paul continued. "Caterine's grandmother just called me. It seems Caterine was attacked earlier when she left work. They aren't sure if it was an attempted kidnapping or family related. She managed to get away and make it to the airport. Her grandmother told her to get on the next plane out of here. I stopped here on my way to talk with Miss Dauphine."

"Did Miss Doucette say whether she got a look at her attacker?" Vince asked.

Paul shook his head. "That's all I know. I'll call you when I learn more."

"I take it this business . . ." Vince indicated Ma Chérie, "belongs to the Doucettes."

Again Paul nodded. "That would be Miss Dauphine Doucette. Vince, I need to get going. Do what you need to do here then lock up. I'll be in touch after I speak with Miss Dauphine."

"Will do."

Paul and Remi headed for the SUV, Remi climbing into the passenger seat.

"Elaine told me what happened between you and Caterine at the party," Paul said after he pulled from the curb.

Remi narrowed his eyes. "Everything?"

"As much as Elaine thought I needed to know. It wasn't hard to figure out the rest."

Remi turned and stared out the side window. "How long have you known her?"

"Caterine, Elaine, and I have been friends since we were kids. Why?"

Remi shrugged. "Just curious. Until tonight I didn't even know her name."

Paul's brows rose. "You two didn't introduce yourselves?"

"Sure. I was Jean Lafitte and she was a princess."

"I can't believe this is Caterine we're talking about. She's always been pretty straight-laced. In fact, I've heard her called a frigid princess. And now you're telling me that you and she, ahhh . . ." Paul hesitated. "Got close and she didn't even ask you your name."

Remi snorted. "We weren't real interested in talkin', *cher*."

"I told her I wanted to introduce her to a friend of mine, and she didn't say a word about already knowing you."

"She didn't know the man she'd met at the party was the friend you were talking about?"

"Actually she did. She found out from Elaine that night who you were."

"Is that right?" Remi scoffed. "I guess when the uptown lady realized who'd she'd just done the dirty with, she didn't want anyone to know."

"Remi, Caterine isn't a snob. She's always been kind and giving. She's never let a person's background or social standing influence her. She cares more about them than about their bank accounts."

"Then why'd she run away from me like the hounds from hell were at her heels?"

Paul sighed. "Buddy, I don't know. Who knows why women do the things they do. But I do know Caterine well enough to tell you it wasn't your background that made her run. And if you're thinking she's another Desiree, forget it."

"Yeah right."

"I'm telling you the truth. Caterine could no more act like Desiree than I could deal drugs to little kids. It's not in her to use people the way Desiree did. In fact, if you remember, I warned you about getting involved with her. So if I thought Caterine would screw you over the way Desiree did, I sure as hell wouldn't have wanted you to meet her."

Remi ran his hands through his hair. "Damn it, Paul. I haven't been able to get her out of my mind since our encounter on the street. And now she's out there somewhere, alone and running scared."

Paul's brows rose. "Wait a minute. What do you mean, since you met her on the street?"

Remi explained what had occurred during the parade and afterward.

"Christ, that must have been Jonathan Day. Caterine's been seeing him for quite a while now."

"Yeah, well, from the little I overheard, he's been seeing someone besides Caterine."

Paul shook his head. "I suppose she gave him an earful?"

Remi grinned. "She seemed to be holding her own when I got there. I still would have loved to knock the asshole on his preppy ass. I just don't understand. She's wealthy, beautiful, and sexy as hell. Why was she with that jerk Jonathan?"

Paul shrugged. "I personally never cared for the guy, but what do I know?"

Remi's eyes narrowed. "I think our midnight encounter was nothing more than a convenient diversion to take her mind off the bastard, and things went further than the lady expected."

"Perhaps Jonathan had something to do with her behavior, but I've been around Caterine long enough to know she wouldn't have had sex with you if she didn't have feelings for you."

"The feelings the lady had for me are called lust."

Paul sighed. "How'd you two get separated anyway?"

Remi recalled the sudden panic in Caterine's eyes and shook his head. "It's as I said, she realized what she'd done and who she'd done it with and ran."

"I still don't believe that." Paul turned into the circular drive of a three-story antebellum mansion. "You know, I wouldn't be at all surprised if it doesn't turn out to be one of the Doucettes behind Caterine's attack. Elaine told me Miss Dauphine just turned over ownership of Ma Chérie to Caterine, and both she and Caterine were afraid of their reactions."

Remi stared in amazement. "Her own family would try and abduct her?"

"Before we go in, I'll fill you in on one of the wealthiest and most dysfunctional families in Louisiana."

"What a fucked up sounding bunch," Remi said when Paul had finished.

Paul laughed. "Except for Miss Dauphine, Caterine, and Bobby, they pretty much are."

"So Caterine was raised by her grandparents? And other than the Doucettes, she has no one?"

"Some relatives on her mother's side in Virginia, but she hardly knows them. Other than Elaine and myself, there's really only a handful of people she's close to." Paul stepped onto the drive. "Now prepare to meet one of the most gracious southern ladies I've ever had the pleasure of knowing."

The double front doors were answered by a middle-aged black woman who told them Miss Dauphine was expecting them.

A curving staircase led up to a wide hall from which they entered a small sitting room.

"It's good to see you, Miss Dauphine." Paul bent to kiss the older woman's cheek. "And you're as beautiful as always."

She smiled. "And you're still a charmer, Paul LaBeau."

"Miss Dauphine, I'd like you to meet my friend and partner, Remi Michaud. Remi, this is Madame Dauphine Doucette."

Remi took her hand. "Ma'am, it's nice to meet you."

"Likewise, young man." Miss Dauphine studied Remi's face before asking, "Mr. Michaud, are you by any chance Annabelle Michaud's grandson?"

"Why, yes, ma'am."

She smiled. "Are you aware your grandmother and I are dear friends?"

"No, ma'am."

"I've known Annabelle since we were young girls at school." She looked from Paul's serious expression to the grim line of Remi's mouth, and the smile left her face. "Paul, would you please close the door?"

"Thank you. Now, if you'll both take a seat." She indicated two chairs. "I'll tell you what Caterine told me and what I need you to do."

Paul shook his head after she'd concluded. "This is unbelievable. And Caterine is sure this person wasn't trying to rob her?"

"No, Caterine was perfectly clear. She said someone held a gun on her and tried to force her into a van. And it's all my fault," she whispered as the tears trickled down her cheeks. "If I hadn't turned Ma Chérie over to Caterine, this would never have occurred."

"Now, Miss Dauphine, you stop blaming yourself. Who could have imagined something like this would happen? Besides, we don't know if your family is involved."

Her breath caught on a sob. "Paul, I'm sure it was someone in this house who tried to have Caterine abducted, and I fear they were planning on killing her."

"You can't really believe that."

She turned her head, visibly trying to compose herself. "Paul, you know as well as I that greed can make people do unspeakable things. My family's reactions when I told them I'd given Ma Chérie to Caterine were despicable. I'm not a stupid woman. Just kidnapping Caterine would gain them nothing." She shook her head. "No, it's too coincidental that Caterine is attacked at this time."

Paul knelt, quietly holding the older woman's hand as tears streaked her face. Remi watched her back straighten as she fought for control. Finally she took her hand from Paul's and removed a lace handkerchief from her sleeve. She dabbed away the tears then daintily blew her nose.

"So which one of you is going to protect my granddaughter and find out who in my family wants her dead? I want her kept safe until we discover the truth and whoever's behind this is exposed."

"I'm the man who's going to protect your granddaughter, ma'am," Remi replied without hesitation.

Miss Dauphine slowly studied his face then nodded. "Young man, I believe you will. Now tell me what you need. Do you know what Caterine looks like? I have a picture of her there on my desk."

Remi turned in the direction she pointed and smiled inwardly as his princess smiled back at him from a silver frame. "Yes, ma'am, we've met."

"Oh, really, where was that?" Then Miss Dauphine's eyes opened wide. "Was it you?"

"Ma'am?"

"Did you meet my granddaughter at Paul and Elaine's costume party?"

Remi's stomach tightened and he could feel sweat breaking out on his forehead. "Why, yes, ma'am, I did."

She nodded. "I had a feeling more happened at that party than Caterine was telling. So, Mr. Michaud, how can I help?"

Realizing she was unaware of what exactly had occurred between him and Caterine, Remi inwardly sighed with relief. "All we can do at this point is wait for Caterine to call. When she does, I'll leave to be with her."

"In the meantime, I'll see what I can find out on my own and whether the police have any leads," Paul said.

Miss Dauphine nodded. "I'll expect both of you to keep me informed of the progress you're making. Also, Mr. Michaud, I expect you to keep Caterine out of New Orleans. I know my granddaughter and she's going to insist on coming back, but you must promise me you won't let that happen."

"Yes, ma'am. I'll keep her away."

"For the time being, I do not want any of my family to know Caterine is gone. When they finally ask, I'll say she had to leave unexpectedly on business. While she is gone, I will take charge of the store. Whoever is behind this will not get their hands on Ma Chérie as long as I'm alive."

"Miss Dauphine, I understand your feelings, but we have to be concerned about your safety as well as Caterine's," Paul said. "I'd feel better if, when Remi leaves to be with Caterine, you go as well."

She shook her head. "As I told Caterine, I will not be run out of Ma Chérie nor this house. I don't believe one of my sons was behind this. Unfortunately, I can't say the same when it comes to either of my daughters-in-law or my grandchildren." Tears again flooded her eyes. "Having money can be a blessing and at the same time nothing but a curse."

Remi was impressed with the strength in this petite but imposing woman.

"Well, Miss Dauphine, at least allow us to have someone accompany you when you leave the house," Paul suggested.

"That won't be necessary. I plan on informing Thomas of what has occurred. He's both a loyal friend and trusted employee. I know I'll be safe in his care."

When Paul's cell phone began to ring, Remi glanced around the well-appointed room. There were a number of family photos in small frames arranged on an ornately carved cherry table. He walked over and picked up one that had to be Caterine around age five or six. Her blond pigtails were tied with pink bows, and she wore a pink party dress. His heart skipped a beat as her happy sky-blue eyes sparkled back at him. *I'm coming, Princess. And if someone hurts you, he's a dead man.*

He replaced the photo and turned as Paul concluded his phone conversation. Giving Remi a look that meant they had trouble, Paul addressed Miss Dauphine. "There's nothing else we can do here. We'll wait to hear from you. Now, Miss Dauphine, it doesn't matter what time Caterine calls you. Call me."

She nodded. "Mr. Michaud, tomorrow morning I intend on going to my bank, where I will open an account in your name that you may draw from as needed. Caterine has her own account, but I want to make sure there're other funds if needed."

Remi hesitated. "That's really not necessary, but if it will make you feel better, that's fine."

"Also, here's my private number." She handed Remi a slip of paper. "I detest cell phones and do not own one. I'll be in touch. Good evening to you both."

When Remi and Paul reached the foot of the staircase, Jules Doucette intercepted them.

"Paul, I heard you were here." Jules patted Paul's back. "How have you been, son? We haven't seen you out this way in quite a while."

"I'm fine, sir. Let me introduce my partner, Remi Michaud."

He shook Remi's hand. "I understand you're here to see Mother. Is something wrong?"

"The alarm at Ma Chérie went off and the police needed to notify Miss Dauphine," Paul replied. "Since LaBeau Security had installed the new system, I felt I should come out in person and speak to Miss Dauphine."

"Is there a problem at Ma Chérie?"

"No. We're thinking it was only a malfunction."

"Has Caterine been notified?"

"Yes, she's aware of the problem."

"Smooth going, *cher*," Remi said as he and Paul walked back to Paul's car. "He didn't suspect a thing."

Paul grinned. "Thanks. I learned one thing being on the force all those years—how to bullshit."

When Paul had pulled out of the drive, Remi asked, "So, who called and what kind of trouble do we have?"

"It was Elaine. She received a call from Caterine, who wants her to bring her some clothes."

"Where is she?"

"Room 221 at the Maison Dupuy."

"What the hell is she doing in the Quarter?"

Paul shrugged. "Elaine said Caterine decided she wasn't going to leave, but she doesn't want her grandmother to know. She plans on hiding out at the hotel until she discovers who hired her attacker."

Remi ran his hands through his hair while cursing colorfully. "Paul, drive me to the hotel."

"What are you going to do?"

"Rescue a princess."

Chapter Twelve

Caterine stood at her hotel room window staring down onto Toulouse. The chain of events that had brought her to this spot kept playing through her mind. Was she wrong and her family wasn't behind the attack? Could it have been an attempted kidnapping and it was just incredible timing? Like a photo album opening, images of the past swam before her eyes. She relived the mean taunts, cruel words, and each petty slight she'd received from her so-called family. Could one of them actually want Ma Chérie badly enough to have her killed? As unthinkable as that was, she knew in her heart the answer must be yes. Mentally and physically exhausted, she let the tears she'd been holding back flow freely.

When her tears turned to sobs, she flung herself onto the bed. She cried and cried and cried until there weren't any tears left.

As she lay there, her emotions spent and her head pounding, a renewed anger built inside her. *Okay, Caterine, you've had your pity party, now get yourself together and figure out how you're going to discover the truth and expose your enemy for the monster they are.* She stumbled into the bathroom and splashed cold water on her face. When she saw her reflection in the glass, she groaned. *Good God, I'll give Elaine a heart attack if she sees me looking like this.*

She stared down at the torn and dirty hem of her dress and shuddered as the fear came rushing back. Knowing she could never wear the dress again without thinking of the attack, she quickly removed it and threw it into the trash. She'd take a quick shower and put on one of the hotel robes. Surely by then Elaine would be there with clean clothes. She'd no sooner dried herself off and wrapped her hair in a towel when a knock sounded on her door. *Finally.* Crossing the suite's seating area, she opened the door and froze.

"Hello, Princess."

Caterine stared in disbelief at the man leaning against the doorframe. Her mouth suddenly gone dry, she whispered, "Remi?"

"At your service."

She opened her mouth and closed it several times before she stammered, "Wha-what are you doing here?"

"Your grandmother sent me."

"Why?"

"Let me in, and I'll tell you."

Without a word, she stepped back to let him pass. He quickly scanned the room. "Nice, isn't it? I've never stayed here, but I've heard it's a great hotel. It suits you. But would you care to tell me why you're here and not on a plane out of New Orleans?"

Caterine's back stiffened. "I don't see what concern that is of yours. I called Elaine and expected either Paul or her to come. So, again, what are you doing here instead of Paul?"

"You're in trouble and need help."

"But you don't even know me."

Remi smiled. "We have met."

Caterine felt her face turning scarlet.

He chuckled. "I take it you remember."

Remember? Oh, how she remembered. She'd relived those moments in his arms over and over again. And here he was standing in front of her wanting to help. It took everything she had not to throw herself at him. "I still don't understand. How did you find out what happened?"

"I was on my way home when I heard Ma Chérie's alarm. I found your hair clip and the blood on the sidewalk. What did that guy do to you?"

She looked away and in a barely audible voice said, "He held a gun to my back and tried to force me into a van."

Remi's jaw tightened. "That *fils de putain* left some blood. If we find him, we have a DNA sample." He reached out and took her hand. "How did you get away from him?"

"First I swung wildly and hit him in the nose with the alarm remote I had in my fist. Then I got him with my umbrella."

"Way to go, Princess."

She gave him a slight smile. "And I'm pretty sure the remote saved my life. I set the alarm off while he held the gun to my back."

"You must have been terrified. I promise we'll get the bastard who did that to you."

She tried to blink back the moisture that suddenly filled her eyes.

"Don't cry." With the tip of his finger, he brushed away the tear that slid down her cheek. "You're safe. I'm here."

As she looked into his deep blue eyes, everything that had happened that day began to fade away. She was taken back to the night she'd seen those eyes turn dark with passion, the night his bold kisses had ignited a flame in her she didn't know she possessed, the hands that had made her cry out in excruciating pleasure, and how right it had felt when he'd entered her.

His voice was low and his eyes turned an even darker blue. He leaned forward until his mouth was inches from hers and said, "I've missed you, Princess."

Her pulse quickening and her breath coming in tiny gasps, she whispered, "I've missed you as well, Pirate."

He took her in his arms and kissed her. All her misgivings over this man vanished as soon as his lips touched hers. She wrapped her arms around his neck and hungrily kissed him back. If she were honest with herself, she'd admit that seeing Remi standing outside her door had been her most fervent wish come true. She had thought of nothing but him since she'd arrived at the hotel. And now here he was. He'd come to protect her and keep her safe.

She gave herself over to the heat of his kisses and the thrill of his hands as they slid over her body.

"Princess, this time I'm making love to you in a bed."

She blinked in confusion. "What?"

"A bed. We need a bed." He carried her into the adjoining room, where they fell upon the large four-poster. From the open balcony doors, the soft chords of a violin could be heard. The glow from the street lamps below was the room's only illumination.

The towel around her head had fallen off, and her wet hair fanned out across the pillow. The belt of her robe had loosened and gaped open.

"God, Princess, you're beautiful."

"I'm not really a princess."

"You're my princess, *cher*."

Caterine swallowed as she felt his finger slowly trace a path down her neck and across her collarbone, stopping where her open robe revealed her breast.

"If you want me to stop, you'd better say so now. Because, trust me, Princess, once we start, there's no turning back."

Her heart was pounding so hard she was surprised he couldn't hear it. His nearness, the smell of his spicy cologne, and the husky sound of his voice had rekindled a flame inside her she knew she was incapable of stopping. "Love me, Remi," she murmured as she wrapped her arms around his neck and opened her mouth to him.

As she surrendered, he groaned deep in his throat. Their tongues intertwined and his kiss became more demanding.

Desire fueled the flames building inside her. Caterine ran her fingers through his hair at the base of his neck and tugged. "Remi?"

"Yes, *cher*, I know." When his teeth gently nipped at her earlobe, she squirmed beneath him. "Remi, I need . . . "

"I know what you need, Princess." He removed her robe trailing hot kisses over her shoulders and breasts. "Your skin is like satin, and I'm going to taste all of you." His hand moved between her legs. "That's it, Princess, get wet for me." He began to gently stroke her. "I want to watch you come."

Breathing in shallow gasps, Caterine stared into his passion-filled eyes as the orgasm slammed through her. As she cried out with her release, Remi's lips covered hers.

"Princess, I'd say we're off to one hell of a start," he murmured.

Unable to form a coherent thought, Caterine just smiled. She ran her hand under his shirt. "Don't you think you should get out of those clothes? I want to feel your skin against mine."

"Excellent idea."

Anticipation coiled in Caterine's stomach as Remi pulled his shirt over his head, and his muscled chest with its expanse of dark soft hair was revealed. Her eyes traveled lower as he removed his belt and unsnapped his jeans, the outline of his erection clearly visible.

"See what you do to me, *cher*?" He quickly removed his boots and slipped out of his jeans. Lying back down next to her, he held her close. "Now, where were we?" He began to softly kiss her neck. Satisfaction filled his eyes when he moved his attention to her full breasts.

"Very nice." He ran the pad of his thumb along her swollen nipple. "Very, very nice."

"Remi," she gasped when he took her nipple between his teeth and tugged.

"You like that?"

"Yes." She moaned when his mouth began suckling one and then the other, giving equal pleasure to both. "Oh, yes." She arched her back to give his mouth better access. The harder he suckled, the higher her climax built until she squirmed beneath him. "Remi . . ."

"Not yet. I can do something that will feel even better."

"I doubt that," she panted.

He chuckled. His hot mouth left her breasts, working its magic over her stomach until he reached the sensitive place nestled beneath her curls.

She screamed his name as his tongue began to stroke her. She dug her fingers into the mattress as the orgasm slammed through her.

"*Mais yeah*. That's it, come for me. Christ, you taste so sweet."

Caterine floated on wave after wave of ecstasy. Abandoning all inhibitions, she spread her legs and allowed his skillful tongue to once again bring her body to the peak, then send her plummeting over the edge.

He rose to his knees, his eyes hot with his need. "You're going to kill me, *cher*."

For the first time in her life, Caterine knew what it was like to hold sexual power. She smiled and raked her nails lightly through his chest hair. "Not before you finish what you started, Pirate."

He made a low sound deep in his throat. He held her hips and sheathed himself deep inside her. Her arms wrapped around his neck and she lost herself to the exquisite sensations he sent through her with each hard thrust.

His mouth close to her ear, he reverted to his Cajun dialect, the sound of which caused the core of her womanhood to ache even more for release.

"Remi," she whimpered as she arched her hips to meet his thrusts.

He raised her slightly and drove harder and deeper. They moved together until she felt her body tighten around his shaft. He covered her mouth and moaned with his own release, collapsing on top of her, both their bodies damp with sweat. Caterine ran her hands down his slick back, sighing with contentment.

"Now I understand what's supposed to be so great about sex," she whispered.

He raised his head and looked into her eyes. "What did you say?"

She smiled. "I said I now understand what's so great about sex. I wish I would have known this a long time ago."

He scowled.

"But I'm glad it was you who showed me, Pirate. Oh," she gasped, as she felt him slowly begin to move inside her. "Again?"

He flashed his white-toothed grin. "Princess, now that I've found you it's going to be again and again. But this time we'll take it nice and slow." His grin faded. "Shit."

"Hmmm."

"Caterine, pay attention."

"Hmmm."

"I didn't use any protection. You do know how babies are made?"

She blinked, trying to focus on his words. "What?"

"Babies, Caterine."

She smiled. "I've been on birth control pills for years. It's okay."

"*Mais yeah.*" He recaptured her lips and sent her soaring once again.

Hours later, Caterine slipped from the bed and quietly made her way to the bathroom. Unable to sleep, she decided to take a shower. As the warm spray washed over her body, she smiled at how happy she felt. *I'm going to remember this night for as long as I live. I'm going to enjoy every minute I have with Remi, and I'm not going to think about what a really, really bad idea it is for him and me to be together in this room doing what we're doing.*

Chapter Thirteen

Remi reached for Caterine. Finding the bed empty, he frowned. They'd spent most of the night making love, and he'd awakened hard and ready for more. He hadn't wanted a woman this much since . . . he put that memory from his mind and, blurry-eyed, tried to read the bedside clock. Eight thirty. He stretched and yawned. The thought of her tight little body had him tossing back the covers.

"Caterine?" he called as he entered the sitting room. He found her asleep, curled up on the sofa. The tenderness he felt for her as he watched her sleep scared the hell out of him. *Watch it, Michaud. Remember who she is and why you're here. Sex is one thing; getting emotionally involved can lead to a place you don't want to go.* But when she opened her eyes and smiled, he was afraid it was already too late. Seeing him standing there naked, she blushed to her roots.

Remi chuckled, strolled into the room, and stopped in front of her. "It's a little late for modesty, isn't it? I'm going to take a shower. Want to join me?"

"I've already showered." Caterine looked everywhere but at him.

Remi reached for her. "It isn't just a shower I have in mind."

She quickly glanced up and batted his hand away. "Go on and I'll order breakfast."

This statement caught his interest. "Food?"

"Yes, they have room service. Tell me what you want, and I'll order. There's another robe and hotel toiletries in the bathroom."

He reappeared a short time later wearing nothing but jeans, his hair damp and tousled. The desire in Caterine's eyes made him smile.

"You keep looking at me like that and breakfast is going to get real cold." He laughed. "You're awfully cute when you blush. You know that?"

"Stop that." She pushed his hands away when he reached for her. "We need food. I thought we'd eat at the table out on the balcony."

He shook his head. "Can't do that. It would be too easy for you to be seen. From now on you don't go anywhere in public."

Caterine's mouth formed a thin line. "Don't be ridiculous. I can't stay hidden away. How else are we going to find out who's behind my attack?"

"Yes, you can. And *we* won't be finding out anything." Remi slipped his shirt on and moved to where the room service tray sat on a round table. "I'm starving." He held out the coffee pot. "Want some?"

Caterine placed her hands on her hips. "Remi, we have to get something straight."

"Yeah, what's that?" He took the lid off his western omelet. "God, that smells good. Did you remember the bacon and grits?"

"They're right there on the tray. Remi, I need you to pay attention."

"I'm listening. Hand me the hot sauce. Don't you want to eat before it gets cold?"

She let out an exasperated breath and joined him at the table. "Remi, I don't appreciate being told what I can and can't do."

He swallowed a bite of toast and shrugged. "Well, I suppose you'd better get used to it. Because as long as I'm in charge of protecting you, you'll do as I say."

She narrowed her eyes. "And who put you in charge of protecting me?"

"I told you, your grandmother hired me. Do you see more jelly?"

"Here." She reached for a packet of jelly and practically threw it at him. "When exactly did she do that?"

"I explained that to you last night."

"What are you talking about? My grandmother doesn't even know where I am."

He glanced up from his plate. "You haven't called her?"

She shook her head. "I don't want her to know I'm still in New Orleans, but I don't know where to tell her I am."

"I don't suppose there's a chance in hell I could persuade you to really leave the city, is there?"

She shook her head again. "I'm staying right here until I discover who attacked me. Did Paul tell you I suspect it was one of my family?"

Remi nodded. "We'll talk about that later. First we have to decide what you should tell your grandmother." He paused. "Do you have your cell phone and charger?"

"Yes."

"Then say you're in . . ." He hesitated. "How about Atlanta? She can keep in touch with you by your cell phone and not know the difference."

Caterine bit her lower lip. "Okay, Atlanta will work. I love to go shopping there, so Grandmère will believe that's where I've gone."

"Good. Remember when you make the call, you haven't seen me. She's going to tell you she's sending me to protect you. And, Princess, do not argue with her. She's scared to death for your safety, so don't make it worse telling her you don't need me."

Caterine stared, the coffee pot still in her hand. "Remi, this isn't going to work."

"What isn't?"

"You and I working together. First, I'm told what I can't do. Now you're telling me what I can and can't say to my grandmother." She sighed. "I know you're trying to help, but perhaps Paul and I would do better together."

Shocked at how much her words stung, Remi snapped, "Is that right? Well, why don't you call him and see what his reaction is when you tell him you plan on doing exactly as you wish and to hell with anyone who tells you otherwise."

He tossed his napkin on the table and headed for the balcony. Leaning on the wrought-iron railing, he lit a cigarette. Was it his curse in life to get involved with spoiled, rich women? Well, Paul could have her. He didn't need this shit.

"Remi."

"Did you talk to Paul?"

"No, would you please turn and face me?"

He did as she asked, and her eyes narrowed in disapproval when she spotted the half-burnt cigarette he held. "Don't even go there, Caterine. Just tell me what you've decided."

"Can we sit down and discuss this?"

He nodded, stubbed out his cigarette, and took a seat next to her on the sofa.

Caterine straightened some magazines on the coffee table before facing him. "You have no idea how hard this is for me. I'm not used to trusting strangers." She held up her hand to stop him when he opened his mouth to speak. "You have to admit that other than sex we don't know each other very well."

He smiled. "I'll give you that."

"And, not only am I not used to trusting strangers, I'm used to taking care of myself. I learned a long time ago, except for a select few, I can't depend on anyone."

He could see the fear and confusion in her eyes and pulled her close. "Princess, you can depend on me." He lifted her chin and lightly kissed her lips. "But you have to decide. Do you want me or Paul?"

She hesitated for only a heartbeat. "You."

He smiled. "Good."

She moved from his embrace. "But we have to have some rules."

His brows rose. "Such as?"

"Such as, we make decisions together."

"Fine, unless it has to do with your safety. Now wait." He stopped her before she could speak. "I happen to have a little more experience in dealing with this type of situation, and I'm not going to budge on this. Either you agree or you can get someone else."

As he watched, a myriad of emotions passed over her face. In the end, she looked grim, but she nodded. He gave her a quick kiss. "Now, call your grandmother. Then we'll discuss what we do next."

While Caterine went into the bedroom to talk to her grandmother, Remi picked up his cell phone and hit the speed dial for Paul. "Hey, it's me."

"I was about to call you," Paul said. "I take it you found Caterine?"

"Yeah, I found her. What I'm going to do with her is another matter."

Paul chuckled. "That bad?"

"She seems to take offence at me telling her what to do."

Paul snorted. "Is that right? So how are you going to handle the situation?"

Make love to her as often as possible. Aloud he said, "I got it covered. We can't stay here, so I'm going to take her to my apartment."

"Buddy, Miss Dauphine isn't going to like that."

"Miss Dauphine will think she's in Atlanta. Caterine is calling her now. I wanted to let you know my plans before Miss Dauphine called you. When she does, you can say you'll get in touch with me and send me to Caterine."

"Got it. Then what's our next move?"

"We need to decide if the Doucettes were truly behind the attack. I'm going to ask Caterine to tell me about her relatives. Perhaps she'll mention something that will give us a lead."

"Good idea. Let me know what you find out. I've spoken with Miss Dauphine's driver, Thomas. He assures me he won't let her out of his sight."

"I'll keep you posted. Later, *cher*." Remi hung up as Caterine came back into the room.

"Well?"

"It's done. Grandmère is calling Paul to send you to me." Caterine sat on the sofa and sighed. "I feel awful lying to her, but I can't leave her here alone. I'm afraid if they can't get to me, they'll go after her." Caterine's face turned white and she jumped to her feet and began to pace. "Remi, Grandmère would never give them Ma Chérie. They'd have to kill her first."

"Will you please relax? We're not even sure your family is behind the attack. But, to be safe, while you were talking with your grandmother, I called Paul. He's already explained the situation to Thomas. He was told not to let anyone else drive Miss Dauphine and not to let her out of his sight."

She nodded. "Thomas is a good man. He'll take care of her." She frowned. "Having Thomas watch out for Grandmère while she's out is all well and good, but my family all live there in the house. It would be easy for something to happen to her there. God, Remi, they could poison her food or tamper with her medication or push her down the stairs or suffocate her in her bed or . . ."

"Caterine, stop." Having gotten her attention, he took her hand and pulled her onto his lap. "First, I don't believe your grandmother is in any immediate danger. If it's someone in your family, they're not going to draw attention to themselves by harming her in her own house."

"But they could make it seem like an accident."

He shook his head. "They're too cowardly and too smart to take a chance of something like that backfiring. They're going to get someone else to do their dirty work. Miss Dauphine is perfectly safe in her own home. Besides, she's sharp enough to grasp the situation. I'm sure she's staying alert to what's happening around her."

Caterine gnawed on her bottom lip. "I suppose you're right. Grandmère isn't young, but she's sharp. Okay, the sooner we figure this out, the sooner I can stop worrying about her. So, what's our next move?"

"As soon as it gets dark we leave the hotel."

"What? Why?"

"You're not safe here."

"Why not?"

"Because you're Caterine Doucette and easily recognized. Whoever is after you is smart enough to have people all over New Orleans keeping an eye out for you. Besides, you don't want to leave a paper trail."

"What kind of paper trail?"

"Who pays your credit card bills?"

"All my expenses go to Tamara Bailey, my accountant. Why?"

"Do you trust her?"

Caterine didn't hesitate. "Yes, absolutely."

"Until this is over, you can't trust anyone associated with your family. It would be easy for your accountant to tell someone just exactly where you are by your credit card transactions."

"You're telling me I can't use my credit cards?"

"It wouldn't be a good idea. It's also too late for you to withdraw money from your bank account. Someone could be watching that kind of transaction as well."

"Then would you like to tell me how I'm supposed to live without credit cards or cash?"

Remi's smiled. "With me, Princess."

Caterine could only stare. "What did you just say?"

"I said you should move in with me. It's the only thing that makes sense. You'd be safe and no one would think of looking for you at my apartment."

"Where's your apartment?"

Remi smiled. "On Toulouse."

Her eyes opened wide. "This hotel is on Toulouse."

"How about that for fate? You chose a hotel two blocks from where I live."

Caterine studied his face then asked, "Remi, do you believe in fate?"

Seconds passed before he replied. Barely audible, his voice was raw with emotion. "Not usually, Princess, but when I saw you for the first time, I knew I had to have you."

"Oh, Remi," she whispered. Wrapping her arms around his neck, she held him close.

"Princess, I don't know what's happening between us, but I know I can't get enough of you."

"I know. I want you, too, Remi."

"This sofa is too small." He got to his feet pulling her up with him. When her robe fell to the floor, he growled. "Princess, we're not going to make it to the bed."

"I don't care. Do something—anything."

Remi backed her against the wall. In one swift move she was lifted off the floor, suspended by the wall and his body.

He cupped her bottom. "Wrap your legs around me and hang on. I hope you're ready. I'm coming in."

"Oh," Caterine cried, for in one hard upward thrust he buried his shaft deep. She wrapped her arms around his neck and entwined her fingers in his hair. When he increased his rhythm, she held him tight and moaned.

"That's it, Princess. Come all over me," he rasped.

As soon as she screamed with one climax, Remi felt her tighten as another built. She pulled hard on his hair and whimpered. "Remi, don't you dare stop. I'm going to again."

"I'm with you this time, Princess. Come with me, baby."

With Remi still inside her and her back pressed against the wall, Caterine gasped for breath. "That was quite incredible."

He chuckled. "You liked that, did you?"

She wiggled her butt. "Very much."

His eyes darkened. "You keep doing that and we might have to do it again."

"That's not possible."

"Is that right?" He began to walk slowly backward, Caterine's legs still wrapped around his waist.

"Remi, What are you doing?"

"I thought we probably entertained whoever is on the other side of that wall long enough, so I'm taking us to the bed. Hang on, Princess."

Caterine laughed. "You're crazy. Put me down."

"I can't. You seemed to be impaled on me."

As he bumped into the side of the bed, he fell backward, Caterine landing on top of him. Pulling her mouth to his, he kissed her long and deep then whispered, "Now it's your turn."

She gave him a quizzical look. "What do I do?"

"You ride me, Princess."

Chapter Fourteen

Hours later Caterine awoke, smiling from a dream in which Remi had been making love to her on a beach. Luxuriating in her contentment, she stretched. She turned and smiled tenderly at the sleeping man who hadn't only awakened the passion in her, he'd unlocked her heart.

When her parents died, she had found out how suddenly love could be torn away. As an adult, afraid of being hurt, she'd avoided any serious relationships. Instead she'd thrown herself into her college studies, then her training in France and now Ma Chérie. If she stayed busy, she didn't think about how lonely she felt.

Perhaps I don't have to be alone any longer. She lightly stroked the hair off his forehead. As she stared into his serene sleeping face, her breath caught at the tenderness encircling her heart. *I could go to sleep with him every night and wake up with him every morning. But what happens once my would-be kidnapper is caught? Do I say, 'thanks for all your help,' then go back to being alone?*

Again she gazed at his sleeping face. "Can you ever love me, Remi? Or will you break my heart?" she softly murmured. The longer she stayed with him, the harder it would be to say goodbye. Could she intentionally open herself to that kind of hurt?

I can't believe this is all happening to me. She closed her eyes, lay back, and inwardly groaned. How could she have gone from being boring

Caterine Doucette to someone running for her life, having mind-blowing sex with a man she hardly knew, possibly falling in love with him, and now contemplating moving in with him?

"What's wrong, Princess? You're frowning." Remi ran his finger across her forehead. "Didn't I please you enough?"

Caterine opened her eyes at his gentle touch. "You please me just fine, Pirate." She ran her palm along his cheek and smiled.

"Then why are you frowning?"

She sighed. "I was thinking about the decision I need to make."

"What decision?"

"Whether to stay with you."

He frowned. "I thought we settled that."

"I didn't say I'd go. There's a lot involved."

"Such as?"

"Such as, what if Grandmère finds out? She'll be furious enough if she discovers I haven't left New Orleans. I can't imagine her reaction if she learns I've been living with you."

"Caterine, we have enough problems without worrying about your grandmother's reaction to us living together. Besides, you're a grown woman. If she does find out, I would think she'd be glad to know you were safe and not be concerned about proprieties."

Caterine laughed. "*Propriety* is Grandmère's middle name."

Remi flung back the sheet and sat on the edge of the bed. "This is a ridiculous conversation." He looked at the clock. "Christ, it's the middle of the night. How in the hell did we sleep so late? Get ready. We're leaving."

"It's the middle of the night because we spent the day making love, and this is not a ridiculous conversation. And I can't get ready because I don't have any clothes."

Remi ran his hands through his hair. "What the hell happened to the clothes you arrived in?"

"My dress was dirty, wet, and torn. Looking at it reminded me of what happened, so I threw it in the trash, and the maid took them away. So all I have is my underwear, raincoat, and heels. Elaine was supposed to bring me other things."

"So wear your raincoat and heels. We only have to go two blocks."

"I can't do that."

"Then wear your robe. This is New Orleans. Nobody will notice or care."

"That may be, but I still didn't agree to go with you."

"For Christ's sake, Caterine, you're coming home with me, and Miss Dauphine will have to deal with it."

"There are other considerations than just Grandmère."

"And they are?"

Such as whether I'm going to open myself to being hurt by you. Aloud she replied, "I'm not sure I can stay with you, for one."

His eyes narrowed. "What the hell is that supposed to mean?"

"It means I don't know if I'd feel comfortable *living* with you."

He laughed sardonically. "You seem to be living here with me just fine. What's the difference if we're in a hotel or my apartment?"

"It's not the same thing."

"Explain to me how it's different."

Caterine stared at her hands. "Somehow living with you in your apartment seems more intimate."

Remi snorted, pulling on his jeans. "Princess, it would be pretty hard to get more intimate than we've already been."

Her cheeks flushed in anger. "I'm not only talking about sex."

He reached for his shirt. "Then what the hell are you talking about?"

"I'm talking about us and what happens to us when this is all over."

As he buttoned his shirt, his hands stilled. Caterine could see the indecision in his eyes.

"Do we have to discuss this now?" He grabbed his cigarettes and headed for the balcony.

"Damn it, Remi. You started this conversation, so you can damn well finish it." She put on her robe and followed.

He stepped out onto the balcony and lit a cigarette. "Go back in, Caterine. It's cold out here."

She pulled her robe tighter around her. "No, I'm not going back in. I want to finish this conversation."

With irritation, he blew out a plume of smoke and turned to face her. "I don't know what the future is going to bring. I just know that right now you're in danger and I'm responsible for keeping you safe. In order for me to do that, you need to stay close to me. Which means staying with me in my apartment." He let out a long sigh before he continued. "So unless you want to get killed, I suggest you stop worrying about the future and concentrate on the here and now."

Her teeth chattering from the cold, she quietly asked, "So you're saying the only reason you want me to stay with you is so I will be safe?"

He let out a long breath. "Caterine, I care about you. No, let me clarify that. I care a great deal about you. I not only want to make sure you're safe, I want you with me." Remi stubbed out his cigarette. "Come on, let's go in. You're freezing." Once inside he took her in his arms and held her close. "Princess, let's get through this family bullshit of yours, then we'll see what comes next."

Caterine wrapped her arms tight around him, pressing her cheek against his chest. "As long as we're in this hotel I can pretend my life is normal and there's no danger. I'm afraid when we walk out that door all the ugliness waiting for us will make everything we've had together disappear."

He held her even tighter. "Whether we're here or in my apartment, Princess, I'll be with you. And I'm going to do my damnedest to give you your life back."

A short time later, Caterine stood wearing nothing but her bra, panties, candy apple red raincoat, and strappy heels, and carrying her large bag. "I don't know if I can do this."

Remi grinned. "Just don't flash anyone and you'll be fine."

She rolled her eyes. "Let's get this over with." As she stepped through the door into the hall, she paused.

"What's wrong?" Remi asked.

"This is the first time I've gone out since the attack." She swallowed hard. "Suddenly I'm afraid."

He put his arm around her shoulder. "You're with me, Princess. I won't let anyone hurt you."

Other than the muffled sound of music coming from distant bars, Toulouse was quiet. Near the corner was a small, all-night cafe. Remi stopped. "They've got great po-boys in here, and I'm hungry. What about you?"

"Sure." As she followed him in, the smells of freshly baked bread and sizzling shrimp made her mouth water.

"What do you want?" Remi asked.

"A shrimp po-boy will be fine." While Remi placed their order, Caterine took in her surroundings. The only other customer in the cafe was a man in a corner booth wearing a dark jacket and a ball cap. He was on his cell phone gesturing excitedly. When he headed for the door, Caterine noticed his cheek had been cut and his nose was swollen. As remembered images flashed before her eyes, her pulse began to race.

"Remi," she gasped, tugging on his arm.

"What?"

It took all of her willpower to control her trembling body. Through stiff lips she whispered, "I don't want to draw his attention, but I think that man leaving is the one who attacked me."

Remi tossed her his wallet and keys. "Pay for the food. My address is on my license. It's on the second floor in the middle of the block. Go there."

She stood frozen as Remi raced for the door, and didn't hear the woman behind the counter until she touched her shoulder. Caterine turned.

"Your po-boys."

"Oh, sorry. How much?" Caterine quickly paid for the food and headed for the door. On the sidewalk she looked for Remi, but the street was empty.

Okay, stay calm. You can do this. She tried to ignore her gathering fear. What if the man was hiding out here, and Remi didn't see him? Should she go back into the store and wait for Remi? No, he said his apartment was in this block. Surely she could make it that far. Her hands shaking, she opened his wallet and withdrew his license. By the light from the sandwich shop, she read the house address.

Frequently looking over her shoulder, she walked as quickly as she could, soon reaching a three-story brick house with light-green shutters. Two lamps glowed beneath the second-floor balcony. She opened the street door, climbed the stairs, and unlocked the door at the top. As she stepped in, she let out a sigh of relief.

Soft light from the street below filtered in through double French doors illuminating her surroundings. As she glanced around, she was pleasantly surprised. There were only three rooms, but narrow floor-to-ceiling windows facing Toulouse would make the apartment light and airy in the daytime. Though not large, everything was neat and clean with comfortable-looking furniture.

Caterine switched on a lamp and placed the sandwiches in the refrigerator. She began to pace in front of a brick fireplace. Where was he? Could she have been overreacting and sent him after the wrong man? She gnawed her lower lip. The sense of danger she'd felt was real enough, but could it only have been her own jumbled nerves? She jumped when she heard a knock at the door.

"Caterine, it's me."

Sending up a prayer of thanks, she flung the door open and hurled herself into his arms. "Are you all right?"

"Hey, it's okay, I'm fine." He turned and locked the door. With her still in his arms, he sat on the sofa.

"I was so afraid he'd hurt you."

"I can take care of myself, *cher*. Now, look at me. Are you sure that was the guy who attacked you?"

She shook her head. "I don't know. There was something about him that gave me the creeps. Then when I saw the cut on his cheek and his swollen nose, well, I panicked "

"When I got out on the street, he was getting into a car that was waiting at the corner. I tried to follow and get the license number, but they headed for Canal and I couldn't keep up. Caterine, this is important. Could you describe him well enough for an artist's drawing?"

She hesitated. "I'm not sure. I mostly saw him from the back. It was when he stood to leave that I got a glimpse of the side of his face."

Remi sighed. "From the little I was able to see, I'd put him Caucasian, below six foot and of medium build."

She nodded. "I also remember his hair was dark."

"Okay, there's nothing else we can do tonight. I'll fill Paul in on all this tomorrow. Now I'm ready for food. How about you?"

Caterine nodded. "My head is pounding. Do you have any aspirin?"

Remi took her by the hand and led her into the bedroom. A queen-sized bed was placed against one wall with a dresser and a tall chest of drawers across from it.

He pointed to the bathroom. "In the medicine cabinet above the sink."

Caterine entered a black-and-white-tiled room with a small pedestal sink but a surprisingly large shower stall. Swallowing two aspirin, she reentered the bedroom.

"It's not the Maison Dupuy, but it works for me," Remi said.

She kissed his cheek. "It's very nice."

"I'll clear out some drawers and make space for your clothes tomorrow."

Caterine laughed. "Considering I don't have any, I won't need much room."

He pulled her into his arms. "Perhaps we should keep it that way. Then I don't have to worry about you going out on your own. Besides, I kind of like you naked. In fact . . ." He began to unbutton her coat. "I can't stop thinking about what you have on under here."

She pushed him away. "I thought you were hungry."

"I am." He again pulled her close. "Food will keep."

"But I won't. I'm starving."

He kissed her long and hard. "Okay, I'll feed you. But then . . ." He nibbled her lip. "We'll have dessert."

After giving her one of his T-shirts to wear, they sat in the dimly lit kitchen eating their sandwiches, Remi drinking a beer and Caterine a glass of wine. As she chewed, Caterine looked thoughtful.

"Why so serious, Princess?"

She swallowed and blotted her mouth with a napkin. "I was just thinking. We really don't know that much about each other. Well, you probably know more about me than I do about you."

Remi took a sip of beer. "Ask me anything."

"Paul said you were an excellent cop. Why did you quit?"

He chewed more of his po-boy before answering. "Let's just say Katrina opened my eyes about a number of things and leave it at that."

"Okay, then where did you grow up?"

"That would be on Bayou Petit Caillou." He smiled. "And before you ask, my papa and uncle were both cops. I have two sisters and a brother, all younger, and my *maman,* who keeps all of them in line, including me." He grinned. "And I have aunts, uncles, and cousins spread from one end of Louisiana to the other."

"It sounds as if you're all very close."

"We are."

"It must be nice having a big family who all like each other."

He laughed. "I didn't say I liked them all."

"Well, I'm sure it's still a nicer family than mine." She tried to hold back the tears that burned the back of her eyes.

Remi stood to refill her wineglass. "Princess, we'll find out if it was one of your relatives behind your attack, and we'll put the bastard in jail."

She stared into her glass of wine. In a soft voice she said, "It's still hard for me to believe someone in my family, someone I grew up with and sit with at the dinner table practically every night, hates me enough to hire someone to do that."

He reached across the table and took her hand. "There're people who care about you, *cher*."

"I suppose."

He stood and pulled her into his arms. Holding her close, he whispered, "I care."

He lowered his head and kissed her with such tenderness that tears once again sprang to her eyes.

"No, don't do that." He held her even closer and deepened the kiss.

Caterine wrapped her arms tightly around his neck. *Whatever this is between us has to be right. He makes me feel happy and safe and . . .*

"Oh," she gasped as he pressed his erection against her.

"It's time for dessert."

Chapter Fifteen

The morning sun shone through the curtains, laying streaks of pale light across the bed. As memories of steamy sex from the night before floated lazily through Remi's mind, he felt Caterine stirring beside him. He turned to find her lying on her stomach. He brushed her long hair off her neck and began to kiss her awake, while his hand caressed her backside.

"Remi?"

"What, *cher*?"

"What time is it?"

"Morning. I had an idea on how we could begin the day." As he slid his hand between her legs, his cell phone rang.

"*Putain de merde.*" He cursed every cuss word in French he knew as he turned from her and reached for his phone.

"What?" he barked.

"Remi, it's Paul. Did I wake you?"

"No, man, you didn't wake me."

Paul paused. "Oh, sorry. Bad timing?"

Remi sighed. "It's all right. What's up?"

"I got a call from Vince that I thought you should know about. They just found a girl critically injured in the Quarter, not far from Ma Chérie."

Now totally alert, Remi swung his legs off the bed. "And?"

"And she was about Caterine's age and resembled her."

"Fuck."

"Fuck is right. She was shot. Now we know shootings in the Quarter aren't unusual, but she wasn't robbed or sexually assaulted."

Remi ran his hand through his hair. "It seems whoever hired the shooter didn't know his target was gone."

"I agree."

"Remi, who are you talking to, and what's going on?" Caterine asked.

"*In a minute*," he mouthed.

"I don't know exactly what Miss Dauphine told her family about Caterine's whereabouts," Paul was saying, "but I intend on finding out. I'm not sure if I should tell her about the shooting. What do you think?"

"I wouldn't. It would only add to her worry. Now let me tell you about our little encounter last night."

"No shit," Paul said when Remi had finished. "So it could have been our guy?"

"Who knows, but he sure as hell was agitated about something. The car that picked him up didn't waste any time getting out of there."

"Perhaps he was a little upset because he'd realized he'd shot the wrong girl."

"Could be. Problem is neither of us can give a clear ID."

"Give me what you've got. I'll run it past Vince."

After Remi gave Paul the information, he ended the call and looked into Caterine's scared face.

"Remi, what's going on?"

He hesitated. "Let's make some coffee first."

"I don't want coffee. I want you to tell me what's happened." Her face paled and her voice quavered. "Is it Grandmère?"

"No, your grandmère is fine." He took a deep breath and explained.

"Oh my God, it's all my fault that poor girl was shot."

"No, Caterine, it isn't your fault. It's the fault of whoever hired the shooter."

"But if it weren't for me, there wouldn't be a shooter."

"Caterine, listen to me. That girl was in the wrong place at the wrong time. You had nothing to do with her being attacked."

"How can you be so unfeeling?"

Because when you're a cop, you have to learn how to stop feeling, he thought. Aloud he said, "Look, I'm sorry she was injured, but getting yourself all upset isn't going to help. We need to focus on finding out who's behind these attacks."

She wiped at her tears. "And how are we supposed to do that?"

"For starters, I need you to tell me everything about your family you can, but first I need coffee." He got to his feet, slipped into his jeans, and headed for the kitchen.

As he spooned French roast into the coffeemaker, Caterine said, "Remi, I have to get some clothes." When he turned to her and grinned, she frowned. "I'm not kidding. I'm calling Elaine and telling her to bring me some of her things."

"How about for now I go get you what you need?"

She rolled her eyes. "Are you telling me you're used to buying women's clothing?"

"No, but it can't be hard. There're hundreds of T-shirt shops around. They're bound to have something." Seeing the disbelief in her face, he sighed. "Caterine, you can call Elaine, but for now humor me. I want to hear about your family, and if Elaine is here we won't get anything done."

"All right," she agreed. "I'll make a list, but I can't imagine what you'll buy."

An hour later, showered and wearing her new jazz festival T-shirt and sweats, Caterine poured herself a fresh cup of coffee and sat next to Remi on the sofa.

"Okay, Princess, tell me about your family."

"Do I have to? Why spoil a perfectly nice day?"

"Come on, Caterine," he coaxed.

She sighed. "What do you want to know?"

"Paul filled me in on some of your background the night I met your grandmother. I need you to go into more detail."

"I suppose I should start with my two uncles, Jules and Markus. They're Grandmère's eldest sons."

"I met Jules the night Paul and I went to tell your grandmother what had happened."

"He's always been kind to me, regardless of his wife's open animosity."

"And she would be?"

Caterine scrunched up her nose. "Aunt Frances, the barracuda."

"She sounds lovely."

"She is if you like greedy, domineering women."

"Oh, yes, please. That's just my type."

Caterine smiled. "If you like the sound of Frances, you must meet her daughter, Charlotte."

"I can't wait. Tell me."

"First you have to understand Charlotte loves Charlotte. She thinks she's perfect in every way. But something must be wrong with her perfection; she's on her second divorce. The good news is that she's chosen men who can keep her in the style she's accustomed to. In other words, Charlotte loves to spend money. She flies back and forth to Europe pretending she's somebody famous. Aunt Frances also thinks Charlotte's perfect, so when she got dumped by two husbands, naturally it was their fault, not Charlotte's."

Caterine paused. "You know, Remi, years ago my cousin Bobby told me he'd heard that Aunt Frances was in love with my father, not Jules, and that's why she always hated me and my mother. But I can't see my father ever being attracted to someone like her."

"How old were you when your parents died?"

"Six."

He put his arm around her and pulled her close. "And how did they die?"

She laid her head on his shoulder. "A hit-and-run driver who was never found. I was in the backseat asleep with my seatbelt on and didn't get a scratch."

He held her tighter. "When did it happen?"

"Late one night during Carnival. We were on our way back from a party, and the rain had turned into an icy mix. I don't remember much except my mother's scream and screeching tires. I was told the police thought someone must have been passing us and cut back in too quickly. They said the left front of the car was smashed and my father must have lost control and hit a tree."

"I'm sorry, Princess." He tilted up her chin and gently kissed her.

Caterine looked into his eyes and smiled, then suddenly frowned. "Remi, your eyes are blue."

He laughed. "You've just noticed that?"

"No, of course not, but I hadn't thought about it until now. So tell me, how does a dark handsome Cajun end up with blue eyes?"

"My eyes are courtesy of my grandmother, Annabelle Michaud. She's a real southern belle with blond hair and blue eyes."

"Annabelle Michaud."

"Yes, that's her name."

"Remi, I know who your grandmother is."

"I know. Miss Dauphine told me."

"Then why didn't you tell me who you were?"

"I had other things on my mind." He bent his head and kissed her.

She smiled. "I suppose you did. So how about your mother? Do I know her as well?"

"I doubt it. My *maman* is about as Cajun as you can get."

She cocked her head. "Do you have a sister, Yvette?"

He nodded.

"This is incredible. Ma Chérie offers scholarships to high achieving young ladies who need a little financial aid. Your sister received one for her grades and her fashion talent. I really enjoyed meeting her."

"No kidding. I knew Yvette was going to France, but I didn't pay any attention to how or why. That's really nice of you."

"I wanted to help those who weren't as lucky as I was. Although I'd have given anything to have grown up in a family like yours. I hope to meet them all someday."

"I'm sure that can be arranged. I'll take you to a Michaud crawfish boil. Now, tell me more about your family."

Caterine sat back against the sofa. "Besides Charlotte, my Aunt Frances and Uncle Jules have twin sons, Raymond and Randal. Ray is an attorney working for Doucette Shipping. Randal is the CFO. He's also part owner of the High Roller, a casino riverboat. Randal has never done anything against me, but I like Ray better."

Her eyes opened wide. "Remi, the night Grandmère told my family about signing Ma Chérie over to me, Ray warned me to watch my back."

He set down his coffee cup. "Tell me exactly what was said that night. It could be important."

After explaining in detail her family's reactions to her grandmother's announcement, she concluded with Ray's warning. "I don't believe Ray had anything to do with my attack. In fact, during a particularly nasty confrontation that night Ray actually winked at me. I took it to mean he was on my side."

"He might not have been behind the attack, but his warning might indicate he knows something. Is he close with the rest of your relatives?"

She shrugged. "I don't know. I've never seen them arguing, but since I've become an adult, I haven't spent a lot of time with them. Other than Grandmère and my cousin Bobby, I'm not close with the rest of my family."

Remi frowned. "That's their loss, *cher*."

"Why did I have to be born into such a mess? People think if you have money, everything is perfect. Well, it isn't. I'd rather be poor and come from a normal loving family than be stuck with the bunch of rich piranhas I've got. The thought of one of them trying to have me killed to get their hands on Ma Chérie makes me mad as hell. Do they actually think that if I'm dead, Grandmère will sign over Ma Chérie to one of them?"

"It seems to me your family doesn't know how tough you and your grandmother can be."

As Caterine began to speak, Remi's cell phone rang.

"Michaud."

"Hey, Remi, it's Paul."

"Yeah, what's up?"

"I'm with Miss Dauphine at her attorney's office. We thought this would be a safe place for us to meet. I wanted to fill you in on what I know before I went in."

"I'm all ears."

"They ID'd the girl they found injured in the Quarter. Her name is Melinda Perkins. According to her driver's license, she's twenty-four and lives on Royal. They ran her through the system and she came back clean. It seems the poor girl's only sin was looking like Caterine—and being in the wrong place."

"I agree. What else you got?"

"Not much. But you'll find this interesting. Miss Dauphine says she didn't tell anyone anything about Caterine leaving until they asked. It seems no one did ask until this morning while they were all at breakfast. I asked her if she thought this was rather strange, since it had been her instead of Caterine opening the shop. She told me they all figured she was still angry over their performances Monday evening and knew better than to question anything she did."

"So none of them realized Caterine was gone?"

"That's right, but they know it now. Miss Dauphine told them Caterine had to go out of town on business for a while and that she will be running the store."

"You got anything else?"

"No, except Miss Dauphine is waiting to speak with Caterine."

"Put her on."

Remi handed Caterine the phone. "It's your grandmère, Princess."

Chapter Sixteen

"Hello, Grandmère."

"Caterine, my dear, how are you?"

"I'm fine, and you?"

"I'm well. I understand Mr. Michaud has arrived."

"Yes, he's here."

"Good. Now, Caterine, I want you to do exactly as Mr. Michaud tells you to do. I only had an opportunity to meet with him briefly, but he seemed both intelligent and competent."

Caterine smiled at Remi, who was watching her closely. "He is both those things, and I'll do as you ask."

"I informed everyone at breakfast this morning that you were out of town on business. I watched each of them closely, but they showed little or no interest. I tell you, Caterine, the thought that someone in our family could perpetrate such a cruel and despicable act, and that they're living under my roof, sickens me." Her voice took on a sterner tone. "I thought about throwing the lot of them out, but I decided I'd rather have them where I can keep an eye on them."

"Grandmère, I'm positive I didn't know the person who attacked me. Remi and Paul feel someone in the family would have had to hire him."

"I understand, and I agree. As for me, I don't want you to worry. I've taken precautions. Clayton Butler has been informed of the situation. For the time being, I've also given him my power of attorney.

"If anything were to happen, his instructions are to insist on a complete investigation. I've informed him that if my death is suspicious, he's to insist on an autopsy, but I really don't feel I'm in any danger. If I thought resuming ownership of Ma Chérie would put a stop to all of this, I would, but one of them may have either tried to have you killed or abducted. As hard as that is for me to accept, I want the person caught and prosecuted. I have total confidence that between Mr. Michaud, Paul, and the police, they will catch whoever is behind this. You need to stay where you're safe."

"I'll be careful, Grandmère. As you said, I have Remi with me."

There was a slight hesitation before Miss Dauphine spoke. "Now, my dear, I mustn't keep you any longer. I love you dearly and will talk to you as soon as possible. But before I hang up, I'd like to speak with Mr. Michaud."

"I love you, too, Grandmère. Here's Remi." Caterine handed over the phone.

"Ma'am?"

"Mr. Michaud, I'd like to begin by thanking you for being with my granddaughter and for keeping her safe."

"My pleasure, ma'am."

"Also, Mr. Michaud, I wish to make myself perfectly clear. Although I have total confidence and trust in you, right now Caterine is scared, feeling alone, and extremely vulnerable. This unimaginable situation has brought the two of you together where emotions may rule over common sense. Therefore I expect you to conduct yourself as a gentleman at all times and not take advantage of my granddaughter's emotional state. Have I made myself clear?"

"Yes, ma'am."

"Then I wish you good luck, and good day to you as well."

"Ma'am." Remi ended the call and looked into Caterine's questioning face.

"Well, what did she say?"

"She told me to keep you safe."

Caterine cocked her head and gazed directly into his eyes. "I have a feeling she said more than that."

Remi shrugged. "Not really. I'm going to go out and have a smoke. We'll continue with your family saga in a minute." Remi stepped out on the balcony and lit his cigarette. He sat in a chair and put one booted foot up on the railing. He thought about Miss Dauphine's words. Was she not only telling him to keep his hands off Caterine, but also subtly telling him not to get any ideas about a future with her granddaughter?

Way to go, Michaud. Once again you've managed to get involved with someone you can't have. What happens when this is over and she no longer needs you? How do you bring yourself to take her back to her world and let her go? For let her go you must. Well, at least this time I know what's coming and won't get sucker punched. He stubbed out his smoke. *So for now, I'm going to enjoy every minute I have with the lady. When it's done, I walk.*

Remi went back in and found Caterine with her head in the refrigerator. "Sorry, there's not much in there. There's a little market around the corner. Make a list of what you want and I'll go get it."

She emerged with a half a loaf of bread and a pack of cheese. "I can make us grilled cheese."

"You can cook?"

"It's not exactly hard to make grilled cheese."

His brows rose. "Sorry. I wouldn't have thought you'd have spent much time near a kitchen."

"Well, you're wrong. Our cook didn't mind when I hung around. In fact, he used to let me help." Caterine banged cupboard doors. "Do you own a frying pan?"

Without a word, Remi opened a drawer and handed her the pan.

She snatched it away and slammed it down on the stove.

Arms folded, he leaned against the doorframe. "Would you like to tell me why you're so mad?"

"Because I know you think I'm nothing but a spoiled rich girl who's had everything handed to her. Let me tell you, I may have been raised with money, but I've worked hard to get where I am at Ma Chérie. My grandmother didn't give the business to me to spite my relatives. She gave it to me because I earned it."

Remi took her in his arms. "Okay, I believe you." He kissed her. "And I'm sorry." He kissed her again. "And the grilled cheese is burning."

A short time later they sat at the kitchen table enjoying their grilled cheese and drinking iced tea. "So, Princess, how about telling me a bit more about your family?"

Caterine made a sour expression. "Okay, let's see, who's next? Uncle Markus, I guess. Uncle Markus is married to Hyacinth. Their children are Paulette and Bobby. Bobby and I are really close. We were pretty much ignored by the others when we were young, so we looked out for each other. He now lives in Michigan with his wife and two daughters. Paulette, on the other hand, seems like an ooey-gooey pastry filled with cream, but when bitten, it tastes sour."

Remi laughed. "What a mental picture you're giving me."

Caterine grinned. "It's true. She's short and kind of plump, and her hair is all these bouncy curls. She has big dimples when she smiles. And she always wears frilly, flouncy clothes."

"How old is she?"

"She's five years older than me, so she's thirty."

"And that's how she dresses?"

"Yes, but I blame that on Aunt Hyacinth. Paulette has never been allowed to grow up or make her own decisions. Hyacinth tells the seamstresses at Ma Chérie how to make her clothes, and Hyacinth has horrible taste. You should have seen Paulette's outfit the year she was Rex's queen for Mardi Gras. I thought Grandmère was going to die of embarrassment."

"I can imagine."

"In spite of her mother, Paulette did manage to get engaged, but he practically left her at the altar."

"What happened?"

She shrugged. "I have no idea. I've run into him quite often since, and he always seems to be a nice, decent guy. In fact, I wondered what attracted him to Paulette in the first place. Perhaps he finally saw her true nature, but I'm probably not being fair to Paulette. Who knows, she might have an endearing side. I've just never seen it. I'm usually on the receiving end of her spiteful retaliations."

"So what are the parents of such a loveable person like?"

Caterine smiled. "Oh, they're both quite something. After college, Uncle Markus went with a friend to Mobile for a few months and came home married to Aunt Hyacinth. From what I understand, Grandmère wasn't pleased. Let me put it this way: Hyacinth is the embodiment of blond hair jokes and isn't exactly what Grandmère had in mind for her son. Frances isn't either, but I don't think Frances was pregnant when she got married."

"Are you saying Paulette came along soon after the wedding?"

"If you do the math."

Remi grinned. "Are your two aunts anything alike?"

"No, not really. Hyacinth isn't quite as bossy as Frances, or as hateful. It's all about image with Hyacinth. She wants so badly to be somebody important. She volunteers for all the right committees. She belongs to the right clubs. She hosts elaborate charity fundraisers, but she doesn't really know what she's doing. She tries too hard and usually ends up looking foolish. I have a feeling Uncle Markus' attraction to her wore off a long time ago. He spends a lot of time with my cousin Randal in the casino and God knows where else."

"Does he cheat on her?"

She shrugged. "If he does, at least he's discreet about it. On the other hand, Randal is usually seen with some bimbo hanging all over him."

"Is Randal married?"

"Not any more. Peggy, his ex, made him pay, and pay well, for his indiscretions." Caterine frowned. "I can't say I really trust Randal. He's the type that would be shaking your hand while he's stabbing you in the back."

"Princess, you've got quite an interesting family."

She pursed her lips. "Now do you understand why I envy you so for having normal relatives?"

Remi laughed and kissed her. "I didn't say they were all normal."

She snorted. "They have to be more normal than mine."

He poured himself more tea. "You need to concentrate on which one of them hates you enough to want you dead."

She laughed without humor. "Oh, that's easy. All of them."

"I'm serious, Caterine. There has to be one who stands out more than the others."

She was silent for a while before she spoke. "It's not exactly pleasant to think of someone in your family wanting you dead. And I'm sure that's what that abduction attempt was all about. Anything else doesn't make sense. They wouldn't be holding me for ransom."

"There's still a chance your family wasn't involved."

She shook her head. "The Doucettes have always been wealthy, and no one has ever threatened us in any way. If my family were nice people, not known to be mean and greedy, I'd say no. Unfortunately they aren't like that. It has to be them. It's just a matter of figuring out who."

"Perhaps I can help." Remi got up and withdrew a tablet from a kitchen drawer. "Think of a reason for each of them to want control of Ma Chérie and I'll write them down. Remember, whoever it was only went after you because you stand between them and their final goal, which we assume is the business."

Caterine knitted her brows. "Okay, well, I'd say for Aunt Frances it would be the total control and power. She acts like it's Charlotte who wants the store, but it's more so her. Although the income would definitely appeal to Charlotte. For Aunt Hyacinth, it would be the prestige and how it would elevate her in society. As for Paulette, I can't think of any reason she'd want Ma Chérie bad enough on her own. She'd be following her mother's lead."

"You're doing well. Go on."

"All that's left is Uncle Markus, Randal, and Ray. I can't see any of them giving a second thought to Ma Chérie. They have their own jobs and incomes."

"What about as a team?"

"What do you mean?"

"Would two or more of them pull together against you?"

She laughed sardonically. "They've been doing that since Bobby and I were kids."

"As adults, how would they pair up?"

Again she knitted her brows. "That's a tough one. I go out of my way not to be around them."

"Think about things they may have in common."

"Charlotte, Randal, and Ray usually go on a skiing trip once a year. Paulette, Charlotte, and the aunts go to New York. As I said, Uncle Markus and Randal hang out together. The two aunts work at Ma Chérie. Oh, and Charlotte and Paulette go off to some health spa once or twice a year. Other than that, I haven't any idea who does what with whom."

"Are any of them addicted to alcohol, drugs, or gambling? Has anyone ever had financial trouble?"

She hesitated before answering. "Randal may have a little problem with each of these. As I said, Charlotte goes through money like water, but I've never heard of her not having enough."

"Paul and I can begin by looking deeper into their backgrounds to see what they might be hiding."

"How are you going to do that?"

"Don't worry. We have our connections."

She frowned. "I hope helping me isn't going to interfere with Paul's business."

"He has others working for him. Besides, your grandmother has hired him, so he's not only helping because he's your friend, it's also a job. And speaking of Paul, we need to get Elaine over here."

Caterine brightened. "Really, that would be great. She can bring me clothes and some essentials."

Remi shook his head. "Actually, we're going to send her on a shopping expedition."

"Why? Her clothes will fit me. We're the same size."

"It's not the size. They're too similar to your own."

"Yes, but why is that a problem?"

"Because the way you dress is too recognizable." Remi thought about how he would miss all that long, sexy, honey-colored hair spread out across his pillow or draped over his chest. "Tell me, Princess, how do you feel about becoming a brunette with short hair?"

She stared, speechless. When she found her voice, she asked, "Are you asking me to cut and color my hair?"

"Not only cut and color your hair, you're going to need a different style of clothing. Your own clothes are too distinctly expensive. I also thought some fake glasses would help."

"You're not serious?"

Remi nodded. "I'm very serious." He smiled. "What's wrong, Princess? Haven't you ever shopped in a normal clothing store?"

She stiffened. "I've never had a reason to, but I'm sure I can manage it just fine."

"You're not going to have to manage it. Elaine will. Until you look nothing like Caterine Doucette, you don't set foot out of this apartment. Although, I don't know how much help Elaine is going to be. She's probably never set foot in a department store either."

"You know, Remi, I don't think it's all that difficult for any woman to buy clothes, no matter where she goes to buy them."

He reached over and tweaked her nose. "You got me there, Princess."

She slapped his hand away. "I still feel this is all unnecessary, but if you think it's for the best, I'll do it." She grinned. "I can't wait to see Elaine's face when we tell her."

Remi glanced at his watch. "It's kind of late to have her come over today. I'll call Paul and see if we can set it up for tomorrow."

She nodded. "That will give me time to make a list."

Chapter Seventeen

Caterine awoke to the peaceful sound of clopping hooves as a horse and carriage went by on the street below. She blinked in surprise as the pleasant clatter of the horse's hooves was replaced by a cacophony of trucks, street cleaners, and honking horns.

"What's wrong?" Remi sleepily asked.

"Does all this noise happen every morning? I don't recall hearing it yesterday."

He shrugged. "It's the Quarter. Some days it's louder than others." He grinned. "You're not uptown anymore, Princess."

She had to raise her voice to be heard over the next onslaught of passing delivery trucks. "Do you ever get used to it?"

Again he shrugged. "Sure. It's how you know it's morning."

She sat up and swung her bare legs over the side of the bed. "With all that noise, I guess we won't be going back to sleep."

"There's something else people like to do here in the Quarter." He put his arm around her waist and pulled her back, easily rolling on top, positioning his morning arousal between her legs.

"Remi, stop that. We have a lot to do today."

"Slow down, *cher*. We'll get there." He nuzzled her neck, whispering, "We do it nice and easy here in the Big Easy, like this."

"Oh," she gasped.

Later that morning, Caterine opened the front door to admit Elaine, who rushed in and threw her arms around her neck.

"I've been so worried about you. I can't believe one of your awful relatives actually tried to hurt you."

Caterine hugged her tight. "I'm so glad to see you."

Elaine stepped back. "Are you sure you're all right?"

"Thanks to Remi and Paul, I'm fine."

Paul was the next to pull her into a big hug. "I didn't do anything, Cat. It was all Remi."

"You're the one who gave me the alarm remote. If I hadn't had it in my hand, I don't think things would have turned out the way they did."

"No kidding. I haven't actually heard how it all happened."

"Have a seat and I'll get us some coffee. While I'm doing that, Remi can tell you about my heroic escape."

"I'll help you with the coffee," Elaine said. "I don't want to hear the details of that night."

When the two women were alone in the kitchen, Elaine lowered her voice. "Okay, Caterine, spill it. Tell me all. And don't you dare leave anything out."

"I thought you said you didn't want to know what happened?"

"I'm not talking about your attack. I'm talking about that gorgeous man in the other room. And what's been going on between you two?"

Caterine busied herself with the coffeemaker.

"Caterine?"

She rolled her eyes. "Okay, what do you want to know?"

"When Paul told me he offered to be the one to protect you, I thought that was one of the most romantic things I've ever heard. What did you do when you saw him?"

"To tell you the truth, I about passed out. Trust me, Remi was the last person I expected to see standing at my door."

Elaine touched Caterine's arm. "Cat, I hope you aren't mad at me. When I got your voice mail, it scared me to death. Then when Paul began to ask me questions, I broke down and told him everything, beginning with Remi and the party, Miss Dauphine and Ma Chérie and your horrible family."

"What did you tell him happened at the party?"

She hesitated. "Well . . ."

"You didn't tell him about the arbor, did you?"

She shook her head. "I said you'd become kind of friendly toward each other. He probably figured out the rest."

"Since I'm living here with Remi, I guess none of that really matters anymore."

Elaine's green eyes twinkled mischievously as she whispered, "So how is it?" She covered her mouth stifling her laughter. "God, Caterine you should see your red face. I take it that means it's great. Lucky you."

She pushed coffee mugs toward Elaine. "Here, do something useful and fill these while I get the milk."

"Does Miss Dauphine know you're living in sin with the man she sent to protect you?"

Caterine put her hands on her hips. "Ha ha ha. I'm glad you think this is all so funny. It's not you who has to face Miss Dauphine."

Elaine's smile widened. "Oh, but this is too good. Who would have ever thought, of all people, you would find yourself in a predicament like this."

Caterine lowered her own voice. "If you would have told me a month ago I'd be having wild sex with a man I hardly knew, I would have said you were crazy." She picked up two of the coffee cups and went out the kitchen door.

Behind her Elaine hissed, "Caterine, get back here. You can't drop a bombshell like that and walk away."

"Checking into their financial records might be the place to start," Remi was saying as Caterine placed the mugs on the coffee table in front of the two men.

"I agree," Paul replied. "What about other motives?"

"There could be some drug or gambling problems we should also check out."

Paul lifted his brows and looked at Caterine. "Really? Who?"

Caterine shrugged. "I've always wondered if Randal might be into things he shouldn't be."

"Not only Randal, what about Charlotte?" Elaine set down the two coffees she carried and took the seat next to Caterine.

"What do you mean?" Caterine asked.

"I saw her at the Hallowells' Carnival party Sunday night. She was looking and acting kind of weird. Paul, don't you remember? I pointed her out to you."

Paul rubbed his chin. "Yeah, now that you mention it, I do."

"Charlotte?" Caterine questioned in amazement. "Elaine, are you sure it was her?"

Elaine nodded. "I'm telling you it was Charlotte, and she was there with Randal, and I swear they'd been arguing. Randal's face was thunderous, and Charlotte looked like she'd been crying. She also didn't seem very steady on her feet. I think Randal was helping to hold her up."

Caterine shook her head. "That doesn't make any sense. Charlotte would never do anything to draw attention or disgrace herself in public. She has to maintain perfection at all times."

"Were Miss Dauphine and the others there?" Remi asked.

Caterine shook her head. "The Hallowell party is for a younger crowd. Grandmère and my aunts and uncles wouldn't have been invited. I usually go, but I was afraid of running into . . ." She hesitated.

Remi frowned. "Who? That guy from the parade? What was his name? Jonathan?"

Caterine nodded.

Remi's frown deepened. "Well, he's someone you don't have to worry about anymore."

"It is a good thing you didn't come," Elaine said. "I didn't think about it until now, but Jonathan was there. I also saw Paulette, and she was with that guy who dumped her. Then later I saw her talking to Jonathan."

Caterine's eyes opened wide. "Paulette was with Travis Jenkins?"

"That's right. And he seemed mad as hell, but she was all sugary smiles."

The incredulity Caterine was feeling must have shown because Remi asked, "What is it?"

"I can't help but find both Charlotte and Paulette's actions unbelievable. As I said, Charlotte is always the picture of perfection. I've never seen her drunk, in public or anywhere else. As for Paulette, the idea that she would speak to Travis, let alone stand there smiling at him, is ludicrous. She was in such a rage when he left her, I heard her screaming that if she ever found out who the woman was that took the son of a bitch from her, she'd kill them both."

"Paulette's temper is that bad?" Elaine questioned in surprise. "I wouldn't have thought she'd say boo to a goose."

Caterine laughed. "Trust me. Not only would Paulette say boo to a goose, she'd be wringing its neck while saying it."

Remi and Paul exchanged glances before Remi spoke. "Caterine, I want you to take your time and think about whether Paulette is capable of hiring someone to kill you."

"Oh, come on, you two. It couldn't have been Paulette," Elaine objected. "She's mean-spirited, but intentionally hiring someone to hurt Caterine, I can't see it. Besides, how would she know how to go about doing such a thing?"

Paul snorted. "This is New Orleans. Trust me. If you have the money, it's not hard to find anything you want."

"Well, Caterine, what do you think?" Remi asked.

Caterine hesitated, then shrugged. "I suppose if Paulette were mad enough, but where's her motive? She's in line behind Charlotte. My death doesn't get her any closer to Ma Chérie."

"Who would get Ma Chérie if both you and Miss Dauphine were to die?" Paul asked.

"Grandmère said that until I make my own will, her original will goes into effect and Charlotte would inherit."

"Who all knows this?" Remi asked.

"As far as I know, my family and Clayton Butler."

"Then all Caterine has to do is make her will and let her family know who she's chosen to inherit," Elaine said. "Then there wouldn't be any reason for them to go after her."

Caterine nodded. "I thought the same thing, but Grandmère told me she wants whoever is behind this caught and prosecuted, no matter who it turns out to be."

"Since Charlotte's next in line, I suppose she's the main suspect?" Elaine asked.

"Not necessarily," Paul replied. "You never assume the obvious. Ma Chérie may not have even been the motive."

Caterine turned to Remi. "Is that true?"

"Sure, an unrelated kidnapping is still a possibility. It's probably unlikely, but we can't rule anything out. That's why doing background checks on everyone is important. You never know what you might find."

The clock on the mantel chimed the hour. "I don't know about y'all, but I'm getting hungry and there's not much here to eat," Remi said. "Paul, do you have to get back to work?"

"No, I've got it covered and my parents have the boys, so we're all yours."

"Oh, good, let's go get lunch." Elaine suggested. "How about the Court of the Two Sisters?"

Remi shook his head. "Sorry, but Caterine can't go out until she changes her appearance."

Elaine looked from Remi to Caterine. "What do you mean?"

"Remi's afraid I'm too recognizable, and we don't want my family to know I'm back in New Orleans," Caterine explained.

"That's where we can use your help, Elaine." Remi said. "We need you to go to a drug store and get a brunette dye, about the color of your own hair, then to a discount department store and buy her some new clothes. She'll need shoes and lightly tinted sunglasses. Caterine has a list."

Caterine couldn't help but laugh at the expression of horror on Elaine's face. She stared at Remi as if he'd asked her to dance naked in Jackson Square.

Paul chuckled. "Come on, Remi. We'll go get some po-boys and beer. We can leave the ladies here to see if they can figure out what one can buy off the rack."

Caterine rolled her eyes at Elaine before smiling at Remi. "Remi, as long as you're going out, would you mind picking up a couple of items for me?"

"Sure. What do you want?"

"I'd like some Perrier, caffeine-free diet soda, freshly squeezed orange juice, and wine. Elaine, you'd like some wine, wouldn't you? We might get really thirsty working on that list." Caterine pursed her lips. "Perhaps a bottle of Arietta Cabernet Sauvignon 2003 would be nice."

Remi bent down and took her chin in his hand. "Princess, there's water in the kitchen tap. There's regular soda in the fridge, along with a carton of orange juice." He kissed her long and hard. "And, Princess, I'm going to introduce you to the delightful bouquet of four-dollar screw-top red."

"Good God, Caterine," Elaine said, fanning herself, after the men had left. "That kiss curled my toes, and he wasn't even kissing me. That is one sexy man. Does he always kiss you like that?"

Caterine grinned. "Sometimes they're even better."

Elaine sighed wistfully. "I remember those days. Since we had the boys, we never seem to have time for romance, or we're too exhausted from chasing them around to do anything if we did find the time. But I love my boys." She grinned. "So Paul and I do what we can, when we can."

Caterine bit her lower lip. "Elaine, can I ask you something personal?"

"Sure. We've been friends long enough we don't have any secrets."

Caterine hesitated, her cheeks turning pink.

"What is it?"

"When you and Paul were first together . . ." Again she hesitated, then blurted, "How often did you have sex?"

Elaine laughed. "Are you kidding? As often as we could. Why?"

Caterine took a sip of her tepid coffee and let out a long breath. "I've never told anyone this, but Jonathan was the first man I had sex with." She laughed derisively. "Well, sort of. When he tried to make love to me, I wanted to respond but the feeling wouldn't come. Then one night it seemed like everything was going well, but it was over in seconds, and he blamed me and I believed him." She leaned forward. "But I had no inhibitions that first night with Remi. In fact, I'm not sure the amount of sex we're having is normal."

Elaine lifted her brows. "Really? Are you saying he, ah, has stamina?"

"Boy does he ever. We can't keep our hands off each other. We even had sex against a wall."

Elaine giggled. "That's nothing. Paul and I once made love with me sitting on top of the washing machine."

"You didn't!" Caterine exclaimed, as they both doubled over in laughter.

"Now I know not to think Remi is strange if he comes up with an idea like that."

"Caterine, making love in my arbor during a party where there's about a hundred guests is pretty crazy and that didn't seem to bother you. How did he get you in there anyway? You never did tell me."

Caterine began to clear the coffee cups. "I'll put these in the dishwasher and get out plates for lunch."

"Hold it. Not so fast." Elaine blocked the kitchen door. "What is it you're not telling me?"

Caterine knew she couldn't hide her guilt. "It wasn't Remi who suggested we use your backyard, it was me. There, now are you satisfied? You know the truth."

Elaine grinned. "Considering how hot he is, I'm surprised you made it to the arbor."

"Tell me about it. I don't know what came over me. I went a little crazy. I guess I wanted to prove I wasn't frigid and do something the *proper* Caterine would never have considered. When Remi smiled at me, I practically melted on the spot. When he held me close while we danced, I began to lose all sanity. When I knew he wanted to make love to me, well, that's when any remaining brain cells I had left turned to mush. For some reason I thought of your arbor, and that's where we went."

"And you told me you didn't want to see him anymore, but you're crazy about each other."

"Don't get excited just yet."

"Why? What's wrong?"

Caterine set a stack of plates and napkins on the counter. "I asked him what was going to happen to us after this is all over and he didn't really answer me."

Elaine frowned. "He didn't say anything about your future?"

"No, only that we needed to get through this stuff with my family then see what happens."

"Paul said you're staying here with him because it's the safest place for you. If you want to come home with me you can. I don't see why you wouldn't be safe with us."

Caterine hugged her friend. "Thanks, I really appreciate your offer but I want to stay here. For the first time in my life, I may be falling in love. I feel toward Remi as I've never felt for any other man. If I'm going to lose him when this is over, I want every minute I can get."

Elaine scowled. "Perhaps he's not such a nice guy after all. Cat, I don't want to see you hurt. You're in the perfect position for him to take advantage."

"I honestly believe he cares for me but for some reason is holding back." Caterine cocked her head. "Elaine, what do you know that I don't? And don't tell me nothing. I can see by the expression on your face that something's wrong."

Elaine glanced at the front door, hesitated, then sighed. "Okay, I'll tell you, but you can't let on to Paul that you know. Promise me, Cat, or I'm not saying a word."

"All right, I promise."

"Let's have a seat." Elaine led Caterine to the kitchen table. "First, I don't know much, only what Paul recently told me. It seems a year or so ago Remi was involved with someone he met while investigating a break-in. They dated and Paul says Remi was crazy about her, so much so he asked her to marry him."

Speechless, Caterine could only stare.

Elaine nodded and took a deep breath. "This is where it gets ugly. I guess Remi had the ring and everything, but when he asked her, she not only said no, she laughed in his face."

"My God, what did he do?"

"Paul said he stayed drunk for about two weeks."

Caterine let out a long breath. "That's awful. How could she do that to him?"

"Remi didn't tell him all the details, but Paul figures she thought it would be fun to have an affair with someone with his background, but that she never intended to marry him."

"What do you mean by that?"

"Cat, she came from money. Remi was a toy to play with, that's all."

Caterine narrowed her eyes. "What a bitch. I wonder who it was?" She leaned closer. "Do you know?"

Elaine nodded. "Desiree Delany."

"What?" Caterine couldn't believe her ears. "Good God, how could he have fallen for that slut?"

"He's a man. Desiree might be a slut, but she's a beautiful slut with a killer body."

"You know, she's one of my cousin Charlotte's jetset cronies. As far as those women are concerned, if a man isn't wealthy, he doesn't exist." She shook her head. "I can just hear her laughing over Remi's proposal. This is great. Thanks to that cruel bitch, Remi now thinks every woman who comes from money is like her."

Elaine put her hand over Caterine's. "You have to prove him wrong."

"That isn't going to be easy." She sighed. "But thanks for telling me. At least now I know what I'm up against."

Elaine nodded. "I suppose we should get started on that list." She grinned. "This is too good. Am I really going to buy Caterine Doucette clothes from the supersaver store?"

"Yes, and I'm sure you won't have any problem. I mean, how different can it be from shopping at a designer boutique?"

"Why did Remi tell me to get hair dye? You're not considering coloring your hair, are you?"

Caterine bit her lower lip. "I don't want to. He also said I should cut it."

"Oh, Caterine, no. You can't do that."

"How do you think I'd look in a wig?"

"Turn around. Let me see how long your hair really is. The wig would have to touch your shoulders in order to stuff your own hair under it."

"Do you know where we could find one?"

"Let me see." Elaine tapped her chin in thought then smiled in triumph. "I know. Let's call Francois."

"Our hairdresser?"

"Yes, who else would know where to get a good wig but the best hair stylist in New Orleans?"

"You're probably right, but you can't tell him it's for me."

"I'll say it's for a friend. You'd be the last person he'd think I was talking about."

Caterine busied herself making more iced tea while Elaine made her call.

"Oh, bless you, Francois," Caterine heard Elaine say. "I'll be over today to pick it up."

"He actually has one there I can use?"

"Yes, do you believe it? Some woman thought she was going to have to have chemo and ordered it."

"That's terrible. Did she die before she had a chance with the chemo?"

"No, that's the best part. It turns out she didn't need to have the treatment, and Francois is now stuck with the wig. He's more than happy to get rid of it. So he said I could have it for my friend. So when Paul takes me to the store, I'll drop by Francois' on our way back."

"Thank you. I really didn't want to have to cut or dye my hair."

"No problem. Now let me see your list."

Caterine handed Elaine the pad she'd been writing on.

"As you can see, I don't even have any lingerie except for what I've been washing out."

Elaine smiled.

Caterine narrowed her eyes. "What are you thinking?"

"How much fun I'm going to have picking out your underwear."

"Don't you dare buy me a thong or anything like that."

Elaine smiled as they heard the front door open.

Chapter Eighteen

"It's absolutely amazing. Your own grandmère wouldn't know it was you," Elaine said a few hours later as they stood in front of the bedroom mirror staring at Caterine's reflection.

The auburn wig was cut in a long pageboy, which fell silkily to her shoulders. Light pink-tinted glasses hid her blue eyes. She wore a low-cut red and white striped tank top that didn't quite cover her breasts or reach the top of her low-slung, form-fitting navy capri pants. Matching navy sandals and a short red jacket completed the outfit.

"I don't know what happened. It didn't look so skimpy or tight on the mannequin."

Caterine rolled her eyes. "Elaine, are all the clothes like this?"

"Not really. The rest are mostly pants, jeans, and T-shirts."

"And the ones that aren't?"

"Oh, just a couple of skirts, a dress, and your underwear. You know I'm getting hungry, and the boys are waiting to take us to dinner."

Caterine glowered. "Elaine, I'd better not have a bag full of naughty underwear."

"*Sexy*, Caterine, not naughty. Come on, let's go." Elaine took Caterine by the arm and led her into the living room where Remi and Paul waited. "Well, here she is."

Remi's eyes open wide, then narrowed. "*Maudit*, Caterine, where in the hell do you think you're going dressed like that?"

Caterine smiled innocently. "I thought we were going to the Gumbo Shop. What's wrong? Don't you like my new clothes?"

"No, I don't like your new clothes. They sure as hell don't leave a lot to the imagination."

Caterine stifled a laugh. "Remi, that's not nice. You'll hurt Elaine's feelings."

"I wouldn't want Elaine wearing something that skimpy either," Paul said.

Caterine put her hands on her hips, which emphasized her breasts and the low-cut capri pants. "The point was for Caterine Doucette not to be recognized." She smiled. "And Elaine achieved that rather well."

"I'd say so," Paul murmured.

"I think it's a cute outfit, and I'm not going to change."

"Damn it, Caterine, you look like you're on your way to work on Bourbon."

"Oh, for heaven's sake, Remi, it's not that bad."

"You know, Caterine, perhaps I should take it back to the store. It really did look different on the rack," Elaine said.

"We can't take it back, we took the tags off. Besides, this is kind of fun. I've never dressed like this before. Come on, let's go hit the Quarter."

Scowling, Remi took her arm and led her out the door.

"Do you realize you're being ogled by every man in here?"

"The only man I'm being ogled by is you, Remi," Caterine said as they sat at a corner table in the courtyard of the Gumbo Shop. "Will you please lighten up and try to have a good time."

"Here's our waitress with our drinks," Elaine said. "Are we ready to order? Is everyone having gumbo? What about you, Paul? Do you feel like gumbo?" Not getting a response, she turned to see what had Paul so enthralled. "Oh no."

"*Oh no* is right. God, what should I do?" Caterine asked, staring in horror at the couple coming toward them.

Remi shifted his attention from Caterine's cleavage. "Who are they?"

"It's Charlotte, and I don't know the man she's with," Caterine whispered anxiously. "Maybe they won't see us. I can't imagine what she's doing here. This isn't her usual kind of restaurant. Remi, what if she sees through my disguise?"

Remi took her hand in his and gave it a reassuring squeeze. "Stay calm, Princess. Just act natural."

Paul turned to Remi and murmured, "Take a good look at the guy."

Remi let out a silent whistle.

"Interesting company for Charlotte to be keeping, isn't it?" Paul said.

Caterine's voice cracked. "Who is he?"

Remi gave his head a quick shake. "Later, here they come."

Charlotte halted a few steps from the table as she recognized Paul and Elaine. A cloud of uncertainty crossed her face as her eyes met Caterine's.

Heart pounding, Caterine willed her hands to be steady as she nonchalantly picked up her menu and began to read. Out of the corner of her eye, she saw Charlotte plaster on a fake smile as she halted next to Paul and Elaine.

"Well, hello. Fancy running into you two."

"Well, hello to you, too," Elaine said, smiling with as much phony warmth. "This is certainly a surprise."

Charlotte gave a nervous-sounding laugh. "I know. Isn't this something? During Carnival, you never know where you might end up." Her eyes flicked around the table, pausing again for a second directly on Caterine.

Paul chuckled. "People do act out of the ordinary during Carnival, don't they?"

Charlotte turned her attention back to Paul. "Isn't that the truth?"

Remi discreetly took this opportunity to study Charlotte's companion who was impatiently checking his watch.

"Well, it was nice seeing both of you," Charlotte said. "Y'all enjoy your dinner. Oh, by the way, Elaine, have you heard from Caterine? I understand she's out of town."

Elaine shook her head. "Actually I've been so busy with the boys I haven't talked to her in a couple of days."

Charlotte's smile brightened. "Oh well, no one ever knows what Caterine is up to. Y'all enjoy your dinner."

"Whew," Elaine said when Charlotte walked away. "I can't believe we pulled that off. When she asked about Caterine, did my answer sound convincing?”

“I think you did fine,” Caterine replied. “Although I thought my heart was going to stop.”

“Tell me about it. I thought I’d pass out when she looked directly at you.”

“I know. I had to dig my nails into my palms to keep my hands from trembling. I guess that proves my disguise works. But I hope I don’t have to go through that again.”

“Did you notice Charlotte’s behavior?”

“No. I tried not to make eye contact,” Caterine said. “Besides, I was more interested in her creepy friend. Was there something wrong?”

“I thought she acted nervous and fidgety. I wonder if she’s on something? You know my cousin Will acted like that, and we found out he had a coke habit.”

“Charlotte putting drugs into her perfect body?” Caterine shook her head. “I can’t imagine that. Remi, what do you think?”

Remi halted Caterine with a wave and spoke to Paul. “Can you watch without being obvious?”

Paul nodded. “Dominic Rivette’s back is to me, and Charlotte is in profile.”

“Think he made us?”

“I doubt it. It was his watchdog we got, not him.”

Remi drained his beer and rose. “I’ll be back.”

As Caterine opened her mouth to ask where he was going, Paul lifted one finger silencing her.

“Here’s the food, and doesn’t that gumbo smell good.” Paul smiled at the waitress. “I’ll have another beer when you get a chance. Ladies, anything for you while she’s here?”

Elaine and Caterine both said no as Remi retook his seat.

“How about you, darlin’, can I get you another beer?” the smiling waitress asked.

“*Oui.*” Remi waited until the waitress had left and turned to Paul, lowering his voice. “Rivette’s muscle is standing at the far end of the bar.”

“Did he see you?”

“Nope. He’s watching their table.”

“Just him?”

“He’s all I saw.”

Caterine's gaze went from one serious male face to the other. "All right, dynamic duo, enough with the cloak and dagger bit. What's going on? Who's Charlotte's date?"

Remi leaned forward reaching for the hot sauce. His voice was barely above a whisper. "Your cousin is in very bad company. That's all I can say. Now relax." Then in a normal voice he said, "How's your gumbo, *cher*? You want some hot sauce?"

Caterine gave him a frustrated scowl and snatched the bottle of Crystal from his outstretched hand.

"Where do we want to go after we're done eating?" Elaine asked. "It's not that often one of our parents offers to keep the boys overnight, so for a change Paul and I don't have to hurry home. We can stay out all night and party if we wish."

Paul frowned. "That's exactly what I thought we'd do—go home to an *empty* house. Besides, I have to work tomorrow."

Disappointment filled Elaine's voice. "We don't have to leave right away, do we?"

"Actually none of us will be leaving until Charlotte and her friend do," Paul replied.

Caterine turned to Remi. "Why not?"

"Because we want to see where they go."

"How are we going to do that? Won't they see us?"

"They won't see Paul and me. You two are to wait right here until we get back."

"When did you decide all this without telling us?"

"We decided to follow them as soon as we saw who Charlotte was with. And I didn't tell you because it doesn't involve you," Remi said. "Caterine, I'm not kidding about this. You and Elaine are to stay put. Do you understand me?"

As their eyes met, Caterine opened her mouth to reply, but before she could speak, Paul spoke.

"They've got company."

"Male or female?" Remi asked.

"Younger male and I don't recognize him."

"You take one and I take the other?"

Paul nodded. "I'll take the young guy since I know what he looks like."

"Change of plans?"

Again Paul nodded.

"Then I'll meet you outside." Remi slipped into his lightweight jacket and leaned toward Caterine. He placed bills on the table and cupped her chin bringing his mouth close to hers. "Caterine, listen to me and do not argue. Do exactly as I tell you. Pay the check. Wait here until Charlotte leaves. Then get a cab back to the apartment and wait there for us. Under no circumstance do you walk home." He slipped her a key, kissed her, and was gone.

Irritated at Remi's terseness and abrupt departure, Caterine turned to Paul and found his chair as empty as Remi's. "So the dynamic duo have left the building," she said. "I assume Paul gave you your instructions?"

"Straight and to the point. I am to go to Remi's and wait."

"What those two handsome bad boys do to you girls? Leave you stuck with the check?" the waitress asked.

Caterine thought quickly and smiled. "No, they were nice enough to leave us the money to pay the check. They saw someone they knew, so they went to see if they could catch up with him."

"Glad to hear that," the waitress replied. "I had a man once say he was goin' to the bathroom, and he never come back. The bum stuck me with an eighty-dollar dinner bill. So you ready for the check, then?"

Caterine turned to Elaine. "Do you want to stay and have a coffee and dessert?"

"Sure, why not? They've got great bread pudding here."

"I understand Remi is trying to keep me safe, but I'm not used to someone ordering me around like he does," Caterine said after the waitress had left. "He's beginning to make me crazy."

"It's the cop in him. He can't help himself."

"I suppose."

Elaine leaned in closer and whispered, "If that man is as bad as Remi and Paul say, I wonder what kind of trouble Charlotte has gotten herself into."

Caterine blew out a breath and lowered her own voice. "I heard she had a new boyfriend. Charlotte always has a man with her, so I didn't think anything about it, but hanging around with scumbags and possibly getting into drugs just isn't like her."

"He seems to be her type, attractive with money. Perhaps by the time she realized what kind of guy he really was, it was too late."

"Can you tell what's happening at their table?" Caterine asked after they'd finished their coffee and dessert. "I'm getting tired of sitting here."

Elaine peered over Caterine's shoulder. "It looks like a pretty heated conversation between the two men. Charlotte doesn't seem to be saying much. In fact, she looks upset."

"I wonder what Remi and Paul are doing."

Again Elaine shrugged. "Hiding outside someplace, I guess. Oh, Charlotte and the men are getting up."

"Are they coming this way?"

"No, they turned in the other direction."

Caterine sighed in relief. "Thank God. Let's pay the check then see if we can get a cab." A few minutes later, looking irritated, Caterine dropped her cell back into her bag.

"What's wrong?" Elaine asked.

"They said it would be at least a half hour to forty-five minutes before they could get here. We could be at Remi's apartment in ten minutes. I'd rather not wait. How about you?"

"No, but the boys will be mad as hell if we walk."

Caterine gnawed on her bottom lip in thought. "The streets are full of people. And if Charlotte didn't recognize me, nobody will."

Elaine nodded. "That's true. And there's two of us. It's not like you'd be out on your own."

"And we have our cells. We could call for help if we needed to."

Again Elaine nodded.

"Then let's go. Remi and Paul will never know the difference."

A black limousine sped down Canal toward the river.

"Were you able to contact him?" Charlotte asked.

The man next to her nodded.

"I know Elaine was lying when she said she hadn't heard from Caterine. Neither of them makes a move without the other one knowing about it. They're thick as thieves." Charlotte covered her mouth and laughed. "Thieves, how appropriate."

Without a word, the man handed her a rolled up hundred-dollar bill and a small mirror framed in gold.

Smiling, Charlotte spread a thin line of white powder on the mirror and inhaled.

When the man spoke, his voice was low with a dangerous edge. "I'll give you all the candy you want, sweet Charlotte." He ran his hand under her dress. "But all pleasure comes with a price. And I expect to be paid in full."

"Oh, listen," Caterine said as they headed up Royal. "I love this song." A three-piece band in front of Rouses Market was playing a lively rendition of "When the Saints Go Marching In." They stopped and clapped along with the crowd. When the music ended, Caterine dropped a five-dollar bill into the open guitar case, and they headed for Toulouse.

Once they'd passed the partiers on Bourbon, the crowd thinned and the streets were quiet. They were on Toulouse and had just crossed Dauphine when Elaine grabbed Caterine's arm and whispered, "There's someone behind us."

When Caterine turned, her blood ran cold. Only a few feet away, moving quickly toward them, was a man all in black. Unable to see his face clearly, Caterine yelled, "Elaine run."

They'd only taken a few steps when something hard slammed into the back of Caterine's head. As she fell, and everything began to go black, she heard Elaine scream.

"Let me go!"

Facedown on the sidewalk, her head reeling and bile burning the back of her throat, Caterine willed herself to stay conscious.

"Where's your friend Caterine?" the man demanded.

"I don't know!" Elaine cried. "Let go of me, you bastard. My husband's a cop."

When she heard the slap and Elaine's gasp of pain, Caterine tried to rise, but blackness again threatened to take her under. She tried to call Elaine's name, but it came out as a croak.

"Well, your hubby isn't here, is he? So I'll ask you one more time, then I'll really make it hurt. Where's Caterine?"

"Go to hell."

No, Elaine, don't, Caterine inwardly cried seconds before she heard his fist strike. Elaine's sob brought Caterine to her knees. Fighting back waves of nausea, she thought she heard the sound of running feet, then her world went black.

"Goddamn son of a bitch," Remi roared as he flung the man from Elaine's crumpled form.

Before Remi could remove his gun from his ankle holster, the attacker was on him. A hard punch to the bridge of Remi's nose and another to his stomach sent him stumbling back.

"You're a fucking dead man," Remi growled as he lunged, tackling the attacker to the sidewalk. They rolled kicking and swinging until the assailant had Remi pinned and was about to bring his fist down on his bloodied face.

Suddenly the man was jerked away, landing hard on the curb. A Smith and Wesson revolver in his hand, Paul shouted, "Now you stay put, motherfucker, or I'll shoot your balls off!"

"Good timing, *cher*," Remi scrambled to his feet and grabbed the attacker by his jacket. Their faces inches apart, Remi yelled, "Who sent you?"

"Go fuck yourself."

"I'll ask one more time, then I'm going to pound your fucking face into pulp," Remi said between clenched teeth. "Who are you working for?"

The man smiled, his split lip dripping blood. "Fuck you."

"I warned you, asshole," Remi said and slammed the man's head down against the pavement.

"The interview might be over," Paul said as he looked down at the unconscious man.

Chapter Nineteen

Remi used his sleeve to wipe blood from his nose. "Glad you showed up, *cher*." He hurried to where Caterine lay.

"What the hell happened?" Paul asked.

"I don't know. When I got here, the guy had Elaine, and Caterine was down." Remi knelt next to Caterine as two police cars pulled up.

"What you boys up to?" Andre asked, jumping from one of the cruisers, followed seconds later by Vince.

Andre nodded toward the man Paul still held at gunpoint. "Who's your friend?"

"This slimeball attacked my wife and her girlfriend," Paul said. "Book him on assault. We'll be in tomorrow to sign the papers."

"Hey, this guy is out cold," Vince said as he tried to pull the assailant to his feet.

"Yeah," Remi said, "I think he tripped and bumped his head."

Paul stepped back and crouched down next to Elaine, taking her into his arms. "It's okay, baby, stop crying. How bad are you hurt?"

"Not too badly." Elaine hiccupped through her tears. "How about Caterine?"

"I'm not sure," Remi replied, his voice tight with fear. "Caterine, can you hear me?"

"Do you need me to call for a medic?" Vince asked, then pointed to the man still on the ground. "I guess I'll have to get one for this asshole anyway."

"Wait, she's stirring. Caterine, it's Remi." When her eyes fluttered open, Remi relaxed for the first time since he'd arrived on the scene.

"Elaine?" Caterine murmured.

"She's all right. Paul has her. Can you sit up?"

"I don't know. I'm kind of dizzy and feel sick." Tears rolled down her cheeks. "Remi, I tried to help Elaine, but I couldn't move."

He sat on the sidewalk and gingerly took her into his arms. "Shhh. It's okay. We got him."

"Is it the same man?"

"I don't know, Princess. You'll have to tell us. Do you think you can do that now?"

Her tears turned to sobs and her entire body shook. "No, Remi, I don't want to look at him."

"It's all right. You don't have to." He rose with her in his arms. "Paul, I'm going to take her home."

With Elaine by his side, Paul nodded. "How about you? You okay? Your face isn't looking too good. How did he manage to get the drop on you anyway?"

"My gun was in my ankle holster. When I pulled the bastard off Elaine, he got me before I could get to it."

"Are you two thinking this is the same guy who attacked Miss Doucette?" Vince asked.

Remi nodded. "Could be."

"I'm going to run him through the system. Chances are he'll have a record. If so, there'll be mug shots. I'll bring them by so Miss Doucette doesn't have to come to the station," Vince said.

"I appreciate that, Vince," Remi said, watching as Andre handcuffed the unconscious attacker and went through his pockets.

"No ID," Andre said.

"I'll call you tomorrow, Remi, and fill you in on what I learned from trailing that guy," Paul said. "I can't go into it now."

"No problem. I didn't get shit off the black limo Charlotte and her friend got into except the plate number. They headed toward the river, and I couldn't keep up with them on foot."

As they stopped in front of Paul's car, Elaine turned. "Tell me the truth, Cat, are you really all right?"

"I'm fine. Truly. Remi, put me down."

Elaine left Paul's embrace and with tears streaming down both their faces, the two girls hugged. "Cat, I was so afraid."

"I tried to get up and help you, but I couldn't," Caterine said, choking back tears as she held Elaine close. "How bad did he hurt you?"

"Not bad, I don't think. How about you?"

"My head hurts, but I'll survive. I love you, Elaine."

"I love you, too, Cat."

Back in his apartment, Remi sat Caterine on the couch. "Let's get that wig off so I can examine your head. If it looks like it needs stitches or I think you need an X-ray, I don't want to hear any arguments. We're going to the hospital." Carefully he removed the wig and parted her hair. "You have a nasty bump, but the skin isn't broken. You know what, Princess? I think that wig may have cushioned the blow. I'm going to get some ice." When he returned, he gingerly pressed a towel to the back of her head.

"Ow." Caterine winced.

"Sorry, but it will help the swelling. Do you remember what happened?"

Caterine took the towel from his hand. "If I tell you, do you promise not to be mad?"

He cursed long and hard. "You didn't take a cab, did you?"

Tears trickled down her cheeks. "No. They said it would be at least forty-five minutes, and we didn't want to wait. Remi, we thought since we were together it would be okay."

Remi tried to hold down his temper. "Caterine, I told you to take a cab for a reason. That guy Charlotte was with is dangerous as hell."

"I don't think the man who attacked us was either of the men Charlotte was with in the restaurant." She began to cry. "Oh, Remi, I could hear him hurting Elaine, and I couldn't help. He kept asking her where I was, and she wouldn't tell him I was right there."

Remi let out a long breath and gathered her into his arms. "Come on, stop crying or you'll make yourself sick."

Caterine buried her face in his chest and sobbed. Stroking her back, he held her until finally, her tears spent, she sat up and wiped her eyes. "Remi, how did that man know who we were?"

"I think Charlotte must have arranged to have Elaine watched. Then when you left the restaurant, he followed."

"But how could Charlotte do something like that?"

"Through her boyfriend, that's how."

Caterine knitted her brows. "But Remi, my family thinks I'm out of town. Why would Charlotte think otherwise?"

Remi shrugged. "There're two possibilities. Either she saw through your disguise, or your family didn't believe Miss Dauphine. Do you usually leave that suddenly?"

"No. I always tell my aunts when I'm leaving and how long I'll be gone."

"And if Charlotte is behind the attacks, she knows you got away and are probably hiding somewhere."

Caterine rubbed her temples. "I'm tired and want to take a shower. Can we deal with this tomorrow?"

"Sure. Come on."

Caterine stood, stared at Remi's face and gasped. "Remi, your face."

"Don't worry about it, I'm fine."

"You're not fine. Your nose is swollen and your eye is turning black. I'm so sorry, I didn't realize how badly you were hurt." She reached for the towel, damp with melted ice, and began to clean his face.

"*Merde*, Caterine, that's cold."

"Hold still and stop being such a baby. I've about got it. There, that's better. You still look awful, but at least the dried blood is gone."

He guided her toward the bedroom, where she removed her jacket and top and looked down at the holes in the knees of her capri pants. "Well, so much for my new outfit."

Remi grinned. "I can't say I'm disappointed, *cher*."

As Caterine slipped out of her pants, she noticed the dried blood where the scabs on her knees had reopened. Without warning, her body began to tremble.

"Hey, Princess, what's wrong?" Remi asked, putting his arm around her shoulder.

"Remi, I'm scared." Her teeth were chattering so badly she could hardly speak. "What if that man finds me?"

Remi wrapped his arms around her and held her close. "As long as I'm with you, Princess, nobody's going to hurt you." He kissed the top of her head. "I promise. Now, let's get you cleaned up, and I'll put you to bed."

"What about you?"

"In case you have a concussion, I'm going to stay up for a while so I can check on you."

After he got Caterine settled, Remi headed for his small drinks cabinet. Opening the door, he pulled out a bottle of Jack Daniel's and a fresh pack of cigarettes, then headed for the balcony.

His body beginning to ache, he sat back in a cushioned chair, took a long swig from the bottle, and lit a cigarette. He couldn't remember the last time he'd been in such an explosive rage. He'd never experienced such gut-wrenching fear as when he had seen Caterine lying on the sidewalk. He thought of what could have happened to the two of them if he hadn't gotten there when he did, then took another swig from the bottle. Here he was doing his damnedest to keep her safe, and what does she do? She ignores him and walks home. Didn't the woman understand the real danger she was in? If the guy her cousin Charlotte was with tonight was involved in this in any way, this could get really ugly before it was over. He tipped the bottle for another long swallow.

"Remi?" Caterine stood in the open door. "What are you doing?"

"I'm just trying to unwind. Why are you up?"

She stepped out onto the balcony. "I can't sleep. I keep thinking about that man." She sat in Remi's lap and wound her arms around his neck. "I need something to take my mind off him." She leaned close and whispered, "Kiss me."

"Caterine, I smell like booze, tobacco, and sweat, and there's nothing nice about me right now. Besides, you're hurt. Are you sure you want this?"

She tightened her arms around his neck. "Yes."

He wasn't going to ask her twice. A few hours of mind-blowing sex was just what he needed to work off his adrenaline rush. Without a word, he lifted her up, carried her to the bedroom and laid her upon the bed. "I have to warn you, Princess, I'm still a little wired."

"Show me what you need, Pirate."

He began to undress. "Don't say I didn't warn you." He gave her a smile that was pure devil. He propped his foot on the chair and, with scraped and cut hands, removed his low boots, unbuckled his ankle holster tossing it on the bedside table, and then hastily removed his shirt. He knew he should tell her just to go to sleep, but he wanted her, and the bad boy in him had a full head of steam. He threw down his shirt and began on his jeans.

Caterine's breath caught as his shirt hit the floor and the bruises from the fight were exposed. "Oh, Remi." She rose to her knees to examine him closer.

"I'm all right. Come here to me." When his mouth covered hers, he poured all his pent-up emotions into a searing kiss. As she wrapped her arms around his neck and hungrily kissed him back, he could feel his self-restraint slipping away.

His mouth left hers, and he looked into her passion-filled eyes. "Caterine, I want you, but I'm afraid with the mood I'm in I'll hurt you."

She ran her hand lightly over his bruised face. "When that man knocked me down, I was so afraid, but I knew in my heart you'd come to rescue me. You could never hurt me, Pirate." She gave him a slow sexy smile. "Love me and make us both forget."

"Gladly, Princess." Red-hot fire seemed to flash through his veins as they fell back onto the mattress and his mouth covered hers. As their tongues intertwined, he slid his hand down her side, over her hip, and squeezed and caressed her bottom.

When his hand slipped between her legs, Caterine groaned, moving against his fingers as he stroked and teased.

"Look at me, Caterine. I want to watch your eyes when you come." He moved two fingers inside her while his thumb rubbed her sensitized nub.

Caterine's breath was coming in shallow little gasps as their eyes met, hers glazed with passion, his dark with lust.

"You've got the sweetest little *cocotte*, Princess. *Mon dieu*, I can't get enough of you. That's it, let it come." He smiled with satisfaction as she shouted his name. "Let's see if I can make you do that again." Slowly he began to lick and kiss his way down her body. When he reached the slick bud between her legs, Caterine gave a low moan as he caressed her with his mouth. As her climax built, she ran her fingers through his hair, whimpering his name over and over until her body shuddered with her release.

"Baby, I love making you scream."

He kissed his way back up her body, lifting her silk nightie as he went.

"I hope you're ready, Princess, because I'm going for what I want." He spread her legs and drove his throbbing shaft deep inside her. "Come on, move with me. We're going for one hell of a ride."

With his hands under her bottom, he lifted her up, driving himself in again and again, harder and deeper. When he felt her nails dig into his back and her muscles tighten around his shaft, he let out a guttural cry and slammed into her one last time before, covered with sweat and breathing hard, he collapsed on top of her.

"Did I hurt you, Princess?"

She ran her hand down his slick back. "No, Pirate, you didn't hurt me."

He lifted his head and kissed her tenderly. "Caterine, I . . ."

"What?" she asked breathlessly.

He opened his mouth to tell her that he thought he was falling in love with her, but he couldn't quite get the words out. So he swallowed them back and instead said, "I think we need a shower. Let's finish this in there."

Chapter Twenty

"Noooo!" Caterine shouted as she swung wildly.

Remi was awakened by a fist landing hard on his chest. "What the hell?" He opened blurry eyes to Caterine's screams. "Hey, baby, wake up." He gathered her into his arms. "It was just a dream. Hush now, you're all right, I'm here."

Caterine clung to him. "Remi, it was that man. I tried to run, but I couldn't move. He kept getting closer and closer, and he had a gun."

"Caterine, look at me." He raised her tear-streaked face. "There's no one here but us. It was only a bad dream. Nobody is going to hurt you." He rubbed her back until her sobs subsided. "That's it, *cher*, you're going to be fine." He kissed the top of her head. "If I recall correctly, I was able to make you smile last night. How about if we see if I can do it again?"

She snuggled closer to him. "You certainly have a way of taking my mind off my problems."

"Anytime, Princess. You know you about caused me to drown in the shower."

She rolled her eyes. "That was all your idea, not mine."

"I don't recall you objecting."

She wrapped her arms round his neck. "I haven't wanted to object to anything you've done."

He bent to kiss her lips. "Does your head hurt?"

"Just a little."

He nuzzled her neck. "Should I stop?"

"I don't ever want you to stop."

As his lips found hers, they were interrupted by the ringing of his cell phone. "*Merde.*"

"Ignore it," she said, rolling onto her back and pulling him on top of her.

"It might be important." He gasped as her hand found his hard erection.

"As important as this?" She slid her hand along his shaft.

"*Cher*, nothing is as important as that." His mouth found hers for a long kiss. Again, his cell phone began to ring.

Cursing colorfully, he rolled off her. "Where is the damn thing?"

"It sounds like it's coming from your clothes," Caterine said, scrambling from the bed.

Remi reached over the side of the bed and rummaged through the discarded clothing, finally finding the phone in the pocket of his jeans. Leaning back against the headboard, he hit the on button. "Michaud."

"It's Paul."

"Yeah, what's up?"

"Well, buddy, I've got bad news and more bad news. Which do you want first?"

"Tell me."

"First, how's Caterine?"

Remi glanced at her shapely butt as she bent over, gathering clothes. He smiled. "She has a pretty good bump on the back of her head, and she woke with a nightmare, but she'll be fine. How about Elaine?"

"She held her own, at least until she got punched in the stomach. Thankfully, that's about the time you showed up. I wish I'd been there with you, man. We haven't kicked ass together in a long time."

Remi chuckled. "We've had some fun, haven't we, *cher*?"

"That we have," Paul agreed. "Now here's my news. I just got off the phone with Andre, and the guy from last night has already been bailed out."

Remi let out a long sigh. "I can't say I'm surprised, especially if he works for Rivette."

"Yep. And in case you can ID him, Rivette will make sure he leaves New Orleans."

Remi ran his fingers through his hair. "Well, *cher*, I'm not sure that guy was the same one who originally attacked Caterine."

"How's that?"

"Before I put my fist into his face, I don't recall seeing any other bruises. Caterine is sure she left some marks on him."

Remi watched Caterine put on a robe and leave the room. "If I had to bet, I'd say that guy from last night was nearby and was sent to see what he could find out. The one we want is still out there."

Paul cleared his throat. "Now for my other bad news. Miss Dauphine knows you're not in Atlanta and that Caterine is staying with you."

"Great. How did that happen?"

"She called here this morning from Thomas' cell phone on her way to Ma Chérie, and Elaine answered the phone. When she asked Elaine if she'd spoken with Caterine, Elaine blurted out that she'd just seen her and she was fine."

Remi murmured a few choice words in French. "How bad is it?"

"Miss Dauphine is planning on paying you a visit sometime today. Once the truth was out, I didn't see any reason not to explain it all to her."

Remi sighed. "Don't worry about it. It had to happen sooner or later. What was her reaction?"

Paul was silent for so long Remi thought they'd lost the connection.

"I get the feeling this isn't going to be at all good," Remi said.

"I'll put it this way and leave it at that: She wasn't pleased."

"Damn." Remi ran his hand through his hair. "How will we know when she's coming?"

"She has your cell number."

"All right, *cher*, tell me about the guy you trailed from the Gumbo Shop."

"He went into a house on Governor Nicholls. I didn't want to get too close and be seen. I had Andre run the address through the system and, lo and behold, guess who the house belongs to?" Paul paused for effect. "Our old buddy Martin Tremaine."

"That low-life scum runs everything from cheap whores to pickpockets. What's one of his boys doing meeting last night with a highflyer like Rivette?"

"Good question. Another is what's Charlotte doing with them?"

Remi frowned. "There's always high-end drugs. You know, he didn't look like the usual sleazebag associated with Tremaine."

"I thought the same thing. But it can't be a coincidence he went into one of his houses."

"You and I haven't had any dealings with Tremaine in quite a while. Could he be recruiting a better class of criminal?"

"I can ask Vince. He'd probably know."

"Give me the address," Remi said. "I want to follow the guy to see where he goes and who he meets."

"When?"

"Tonight."

"Want some help?"

"If you're offering, I can always use someone watching my back."

Paul laughed. "Yeah, since you almost got your sorry ass whipped last night."

"Hey, I didn't do so bad. I got another call coming in. I'll see you, what, around six o'clock? We should get there early in case he leaves."

"I'll be there," Paul said.

Remi groaned when he read the caller ID. "Caterine," he yelled, "get back in here."

When she reappeared in the door, he held out the phone. "The shit's hit the fan, Princess. It's your grandmother. She knows you're here."

Wide-eyed, Caterine took the phone Remi held out and mouthed, "*How?*"

"Elaine spilled it this morning. You'd better answer before voice mail picks up."

Caterine took a deep breath. "Hello."

"Caterine."

"Yes, Grandmère, it's me. How are you?"

"I'm well, Caterine. The question is how are you? I understand you're not in Atlanta, you're here in New Orleans."

"Yes, ma'am."

"I was under the impression you had left for Atlanta and were to remain there until this situation was concluded."

Caterine hesitated. "I couldn't leave you alone, Grandmère. I wanted to be here in case there was some way I could help."

Silence filled the minutes as they slowly ticked by before Miss Dauphine spoke again. "And when exactly were you going to inform me of this change of plans?"

"I wanted to get settled first."

"Is it true, Caterine, that you're staying somewhere with Mr. Michaud?"

"Yes, ma'am. He thought I'd be safer here with him."

"I'm sure he did. Caterine, I wish to speak to both of you in person. I assume this will be possible?"

"Of course, Grandmère. Where are you now?"

"I'm on my way to a meeting, then on to a luncheon appointment. I would like to see you this afternoon."

"That will be fine. Let me give you the address."

"Very well, Caterine. I will see you around two o'clock."

"Yes, ma'am." White-faced, Caterine disconnected and handed the phone to Remi, who was still reclining against the headboard.

"So?"

"She's coming here at two o'clock."

"And?"

"I've only heard that tone in her voice a few times, and each of those times she's been very, very angry."

Remi ran his hands over his face. "What do you think has her more pissed, the fact we've been back and haven't told her, or the fact that you're staying here with me? Or perhaps the fact that I disregarded her wishes and put my hands on you?"

"All of the above," came her soft reply.

"Christ. This is all I need." Remi got out of bed and headed for the bathroom.

Caterine soon had two mugs of chicory coffee and plates of scrambled eggs, bacon, and toast laid out on the small oak kitchen table.

"That smells great." Remi said, taking a seat. "My eggs are usually runny and the bacon burnt, but I keep trying. Now, if you want some good fried catfish, Princess, I can do that."

Caterine smiled. "I've never had fried catfish. You'll have to make us some."

He froze with his fork halfway to his lips. "You grew up in New Orleans and have never had fried catfish?"

She shook her head.

"What about a crawfish boil?"

She shook her head again.

"Well, we'll have to introduce you to all the delicacies you've been missing. The Saturday before Mardi Gras my family all get together and have a big crawfish boil with all the trimmings. Would you like to go with me?"

"Oh yes, Remi, I'd love to."

His heart did a flip at the pure joy that came over her face. "What the hell did you grow up eating?"

This time she shrugged. "Whatever our French chef prepared, although Elaine and I did take a cooking class during college."

He smiled. "And what did you and Elaine learn how to cook?"

She ignored his question and concentrated on her breakfast. Then she stood and began to gather the dishes. "You know, Remi, we should have some kind of pastry to offer Grandmère when she gets here."

He took the plates from her hands and put them in the sink. "Come on, Princess, tell me what you and Elaine learned how to cook."

She placed her hands on her hips. "Sauces. Now are you satisfied?"

His smile spread across his face. "What kind of sauces?"

She sighed in exasperation. "The kind you put over food."

He laughed aloud. "The only sauce I'm used to putting on food, *cher*, is hot sauce."

She rolled her eyes. "If you're done laughing at me, we have a pressing matter to discuss—how to explain our living arrangement to Grandmère."

All humor left his face as he leaned back against the sink. "The only thing we can do is tell her why I feel you're safer with me and hope she understands."

Caterine dampened a cloth and began to wipe off the table. "What if she expects more than that?"

"Such as?"

She busied herself cleaning the top of the stove. "Like about us."

He took a deep breath. "What is it that you want to tell her?"

She stared directly into his eyes, and he knew exactly what she was thinking. *I love you and you love me, and we're going to spend the rest of our lives together.*

He opened his arms. "Come here to me, Princess."

Caterine stepped into his embrace and he held her close. "If your grandmother asks, we'll tell her we don't know, but for now we want to be together." He kissed the top of her head. "But to help us along, I'll run over to Brennan's and get a suicide cake."

Chapter Twenty-One

"Caterine, would you please calm down. You're making me crazy with all that pacing." Remi was sitting on the sofa trying to read the paper. He finally gave up, refolded it and placed it on the coffee table, then stood. "Come on, let's go sit on the balcony and wait."

He watched in exasperation as she snatched the paper from the coffee table, shoved it in a drawer, then hurried to straighten the sofa cushions.

"For Christ's sake, will you chill out? The apartment is fine. You look fine. And I look as good as I can with a black eye and swollen nose."

"God, I hadn't thought of that! How are we going to explain our bruises?"

Remi threw up his hands, mumbling something rude in Cajun. "Let's tell her we got this way by having wild sex on the floor bouncing off the furniture."

"Very funny. I'm serious."

"I don't know what to say. Let's just wing it. She may not even ask."

"How could she not ask?"

Remi was grinding his teeth as he went out onto the balcony. Caterine was right behind him.

"You're not going to smoke while she's here, are you?"

He closed his eyes and counted. "Caterine, if you don't sit down and stop worrying, I'm going to smoke the entire pack."

"Oh no, there she is."

Remi watched as the distinguished black man he'd seen before opened the Lincoln's back door and helped Miss Dauphine step out.

Taking on the thugs from the previous night was definitely more appealing to him than facing Miss Dauphine. He sighed and rose to greet his guest.

When Miss Dauphine entered the apartment, Caterine kissed and hugged her. "Hello, Grandmère. It's good to see you."

Miss Dauphine hugged her back. "I'm pleased to see you as well, Caterine."

"Come in and have a seat." Caterine indicated one of the chairs. "Would you care for a cup of coffee and a slice of cake?"

"No, thank you. I'm fine for now. What I would like is for you to be seated while I ask Mr. Michaud to answer a few questions I have for him."

"I'd be happy to do that, ma'am." Remi took a seat across from Miss Dauphine.

Caterine couldn't believe how calm and confident he sounded. She took her seat, waiting for the explosion that was sure to come.

"Before I begin, would you like to tell me why both of you look as if you've been brawling in the streets?"

"On our way home from dinner last night, we unexpectedly found ourselves in a crowd of rowdy partiers. Unfortunately, Caterine was shoved against the wall and scraped her hands, and I came in contact with some drunk's fist."

Caterine marveled at Remi's ability to lie nonchalantly while appearing perfectly truthful.

Miss Dauphine looked doubtfully from Remi to her before sighing resignedly. Clearing her throat, she turned her attention fully on Remi. "Very well, Mr. Michaud. I'll proceed with my questions."

He nodded. "Yes, ma'am."

"First, would you please explain to me why, knowing full well that Caterine is in danger here in New Orleans, you disregarded this fact and allowed her to stay here instead of leaving for Atlanta?"

Caterine opened her mouth to explain, but Remi quickly silenced her with a glance.

"Miss Dauphine, Caterine is here in New Orleans because she refused to leave, and I couldn't change her mind. To be honest, I don't know that she would have been any safer in Atlanta. It wouldn't be all that difficult for someone with money and connections to kidnap her there."

Caterine glanced anxiously at her grandmother, hoping to gauge her reaction to this answer. She said a silent prayer of thanks when it seemed she'd accepted his explanation.

"I do know my granddaughter can be stubborn when she wants to be. If you believed Caterine would be unsafe in Atlanta, you were right not to go there. That leads me to my next question. Why is it necessary for her to reside here, alone with you, when she could have just as easily obtained her own apartment, or a comfortable hotel room?"

"Caterine is staying with me because I feel that's the safest place for her to be. I can't protect her if she's alone in an apartment or some hotel room."

For long minutes she silently studied Remi. "I have many discreet friends who would have been more than happy to have Caterine stay with them."

"I'm sure you do, but as you say, discretion is of the utmost importance. The fewer people who know Caterine is in New Orleans, the safer she'll be. Besides, I'm sure you wouldn't want to take the chance of putting some innocent person in danger."

Miss Dauphine's dark eyes flashed. "Of course I would not, but there are other options. A guard could be hired to stand outside Caterine's apartment or hotel room."

"Yes, ma'am, they could, but are you willing to take a chance on Caterine's life that a guard couldn't be bribed?"

Caterine watched as her grandmother's back stiffened and her nostrils flared.

Remi sighed. "Miss Dauphine, you hired me to protect Caterine from harm. I'm doing as you asked, the best way I know how. That's by keeping her close to me at all times."

"And safety is the only reason you're keeping my granddaughter with you, is it, Mr. Michaud?"

He met her challenging eyes. "No, ma'am, that's not the only reason."

Again she silently studied Remi before turning to Caterine. "I wish to speak with Mr. Michaud privately. Would you please go and prepare the coffee you offered earlier?"

"Grandmère, Remi and I—"

"Caterine, please do as I ask. I'm sure Mr. Michaud is capable of having a private conversation with me without your assistance."

Caterine stood and gave Remi a "what can I do?" shrug before leaving the room.

Miss Dauphine folded her hands in her lap. "Now then, Mr. Michaud, I believe you're being truthful when you say the safety of my granddaughter is your main priority, but it's not only Caterine's safety that concerns me. For months after her parents were killed, Caterine was inconsolable. My husband and I tried our best not only to comfort her, but to protect her from ever experiencing that kind of anguish again. Now, I'm afraid by doing so we inadvertently left Caterine vulnerable and ill-prepared to deal with life's heartbreaks. Also, I imagine my granddaughter is extremely naïve when it comes to knowing how to protect herself against handsome smooth-talking persuasive men

"I, on the other hand, am neither naïve nor gullible. Obviously, since my granddaughter is residing here with you, and I seriously doubt you're sleeping alone there on that sofa, I can assume you disregarded my wishes and more happened between you and Caterine than just protecting her. Now I'd like to know how you plan on resolving this potentially hurtful, not to mention compromising, situation you've put my granddaughter in."

Chapter Twenty-Two

Caterine reentered the room carrying a tray. "Grandmère, I met Remi at the LaBeaus' ball. And I can assure you he is in no way taking advantage of me."

"Caterine, don't," Remi said. "It's not necessary."

Ignoring both Remi's and her grandmother's annoyed expressions, she placed the tray of coffee and cake on the table. She felt a little sick but was determined to see this through.

"Caterine." Remi's voice had taken on a warning tone.

Still ignoring him, she addressed her grandmother. "I know you don't approve of me being here, and if the circumstances were different I wouldn't be, but I really don't have any other choice. Besides, staying here with Remi is where I want to be."

Caterine narrowed her eyes in puzzlement at her grandmother's triumphant smirk and Remi's pained expression.

"Well, Mr. Michaud, what do you have to say for yourself now?"

"Grandmère, he—"

"Caterine, if you please, let him speak for himself."

"But, Grandmère, Remi isn't to blame."

"I don't blame Mr. Michaud entirely for this *amourette* you find yourself in, Caterine. Have you thought beyond the point in time when the person who hired your assailant is identified and this situation is resolved? Like it or not, our family is well known and very newsworthy. Once the story of your attack and the arrest is made public, everything that has transpired from the beginning to the end will be revealed, including your relationship with Mr. Michaud. You are Caterine Doucette. Do you realize what this living arrangement is going to do to your reputation?"

"Miss Dauphine, my intentions from the beginning have only been for Caterine's well-being. I never intended to hurt or disgrace her in any way."

"And exactly what are your intentions?"

"To do exactly what you hired me to do: to protect Caterine while discovering who in your family wants her dead."

Caterine's eyes traveled from her grandmother's rigid, incensed form to Remi, sitting taut as a bowstring. Miss Dauphine's scolding dark eyes never left Remi's steady blue gaze. Suddenly, taking Caterine quite by surprise, her grandmother nodded once, then sat back in her chair.

"I usually have a good instinct for people," she said. "At our first meeting, I took you to be an honorable man. Even though I'm not at all pleased with this living arrangement, I believe you have Caterine's best interest at heart. So when this is over, I'll expect you to do the right thing and not disappoint me."

Remi nodded. "Yes, ma'am."

"Now, Caterine, I believe I'll have a slice of that delicious looking cake," Miss Dauphine said.

Caterine said a silent prayer of thanks. She wasn't sure how Remi had managed to defuse her grandmother, but whatever he'd done, she thanked God it had worked. "Grandmère, we do have some news." Caterine handed her a plate and coffee mug. "We saw Charlotte last night in the company of two men who Remi said were both bad characters."

"I was under the impression your presence in New Orleans was supposed to remain a secret. What were you doing out in a public place?"

"I have a great disguise. Charlotte stopped at our table and didn't recognize me."

Miss Dauphine turned to Remi. "Who were these men Charlotte was with?"

Remi took the cake and coffee Caterine handed him. "Charlotte came into the restaurant with a man named Rivette. His legal holdings include ownership of the Triple Aces Casino and a very lucrative business importing anything and everything that has to do with Mardi Gras. His not-so-legal activities include drugs, high-class prostitution, and money laundering, none of which has ever been proven in a court of law."

"And you're sure Charlotte was in the company of this person?" Miss Dauphine asked.

"Yes, Grandmère, and they were joined by an unknown younger man who Paul followed to a house on Governor Nicholls. The house is owned by another known criminal. Remi and Paul are planning to follow that man tonight."

"It pains me to think of Charlotte involving herself with people with such dubious reputations. I can't imagine what would have possessed her to do such a thing."

"Drugs *are* a possibility," Caterine suggested.

"Charlotte on drugs? Caterine, that's absurd. Money would be more like it. For some reason, Charlotte never seems to have enough. If this Rivette person is wealthy, unfortunately that's all Charlotte would need to know. I blame Frances and Hyacinth for setting such poor examples for their daughters. I can tell you Frances certainly hasn't shown any remorse for her behavior the evening I informed the family of my decision regarding Ma Chérie. As for Hyacinth, she's become more disgustingly sweet than Paulette."

"Grandmère, Elaine saw Charlotte and Randal at the Hallowell Carnival ball. She said Charlotte seemed upset and was acting drunk or high on something. I guess Randal was with her and didn't look pleased. Oh, you're not going to believe who else Elaine saw. Paulette was there talking with Travis Jenkins." She nodded at her grandmother's evident astonishment. "It's true. Elaine said Paulette was smiling but Travis was very angry."

Miss Dauphine set down her empty plate and massaged her temples. "I don't understand what any of this means or what your cousins have gotten themselves involved in, but I fear no good can come of it. Having been a police officer, Mr. Michaud is used to dealing with this type of person; you certainly are not. Caterine, would you please at least consider going to stay with Robert and Rebecca where I'll know you're safe?"

"Miss Dauphine, as long as Caterine listens to me and does what I tell her, I can assure you she will not come into contact with any of these people."

"Very well, Mr. Michaud, I'll trust you to protect my granddaughter." Moisture suddenly filled her eyes before she blinked it away. "I couldn't bear it if something were to happen to Caterine."

Caterine wrapped her arms around her grandmother. "Oh, Grandmère, nothing is going to happen to me."

"I'll protect her with my life, Miss Dauphine," Remi said, "and that's a promise."

When Remi came back into the apartment after walking Miss Dauphine to her car, he found Caterine kneeling on the floor, rummaging around in his liquor cabinet. "What are you doing?"

She glanced at him over her shoulder. "I'm looking for something to get me drunk."

He laughed. "Now, it wasn't that bad, was it?"

She rolled her eyes. "I love my grandmother dearly, but I hope to never go through anything like that again. Besides her clear belief that I deserved a scarlet letter burned into my forehead, the third-degree she gave you was awful."

He shrugged. "She loves you."

"This will do." Caterine triumphantly held up a bottle of red wine. "Can we open this?"

"You can. Remember, I'm going out. Have you ever been drunk?"

"I don't think so." She rose to her feet. "Although Elaine and I might have been tipsy the night we graduated college."

Laughing, Remi took her into his arms and kissed her soundly. "Don't drink the entire bottle, or I'll find you passed out when I get home."

"When are you leaving?"

Remi glanced at his watch. "I need to get ready. Paul should be here soon."

"But you haven't had any dinner."

He tweaked her nose. "Don't worry about me, Princess. I'm a big boy. If I need food, I'll get it. What about you, though?"

She stood on her toes and tweaked his nose right back. "And I'm a big girl. Besides, who made breakfast?"

Caterine's mouth went dry a short time later when Remi walked out of the bedroom looking much as he had the first night she'd seen him. Dressed entirely in black, he not only exuded danger, he was incredibly sexy.

As he came over to where she sat on the sofa, his cell phone rang. Slipping his leather jacket on over his shoulder holster, he pulled out his phone. "Michaud."

"I'm out front," Paul replied.

"I'm on my way."

Remi bent over until his face was level with Caterine's. "Don't you be giving me that sexy smile when I have to go out." He kissed her hard. "We'll take care of whatever you were thinking about when I get back."

The smile left Caterine's face as she put her arms around his neck. "Remi, please be careful."

"I'll be fine. I've got to go."

"Do you know when you'll be back?"

"When you see me, *cher*. Don't wait up."

Chapter Twenty-Three

"Since it's already dark, let's see if we can find a parking place where we can watch the house," Paul said when Remi slid onto the passenger seat.

Remi nodded.

After the short drive to Governor Nicholls, Paul pulled in behind a parked van. "How's this? The house is across the street about three doors down."

"It's fine with me, but do you have a clear view?"

"Yeah, I should be able to see if he comes out, but it's a good thing we've got a full moon and most of the houses have working porch lights. This street's as dark as hell."

They removed their seatbelts, sat back, and made themselves comfortable.

"So tell me, how did the visit from Miss Dauphine go?"

"How do you think it went?"

"That bad?"

Remi shrugged. "She's concerned that when this situation with her family is resolved and becomes public knowledge, Caterine's reputation will be irrevocably damaged by the revelation that she'd been secretly living in sin with me. Therefore, she'd like to know what my intentions in regards to her granddaughter are."

"Ouch." Paul grimaced.

"Yeah, well, it's what I expected."

"So what did you tell her?"

Again he shrugged. "I told her the only way I could guarantee Caterine's safety was to keep her with me."

"And that satisfied her?"

He nodded. "For the time being."

Paul shook his head. "You must have made one hell of a good impression for her to let you get away with an answer like that."

"Well, *cher*, I'd better do as I said I'd do, because I don't want to have to face her again if I don't."

"Then I guess we'd better get busy." Paul watched a man walking his dog pass the car before he continued. "I asked Vince if he'd heard anything new about our friend Martin Tremaine. According to Vince, Martin lost most of his slum properties to Katrina, which rather put a crimp in his more or less illegal business dealings. This house here," Paul said, nodding down the street, "seems to be the only one left."

"Which means some of his employees may have moved on to greener pastures, so Martin could be scrambling to expand his operations by associating himself with a higher class of scum," Remi suggested.

"It's a possibility. That would explain our boy from last night meeting with Rivette."

"Since Randal Doucette and Rivette both have financial interests in casinos, what are the odds they don't know each other?"

Paul grinned. "Throw in the fact that Charlotte is Randal's cousin and she's keeping company with Rivette. Not likely."

"So tell me all you know about Randal Doucette."

"He and Ray are a few years older than me, so I didn't run with their crowd growing up, although I do know Randal was always the bad boy of the two."

"Bad boy how?"

"He hung around with a rowdier group of guys. Don't get me wrong, they never got into any serious trouble. They just walked a real fine line. Their parents all had money, so if they ever did step over that fine line, daddy would take care of it. My parents said Markus was also pretty wild in his youth. So maybe Randal comes by it naturally."

"Caterine told me Markus spends a lot of time in Randal's company. She also said that when Miss Dauphine dropped the bombshell about giving her

Ma Chérie, Markus was visibly agitated."

"Really? I wonder why," Paul questioned. "As far as I know, Markus and Jules have nothing to do with Ma Chérie. As far as that goes, neither do Ray or Randal. For them it's all about Doucette Shipping."

"Could there be a problem and they need Ma Chérie's income?"

Paul's brows rose. "Interesting point. It might be worthwhile to do some checking into Doucette Shipping's finances." He paused. "Now that I think about it, every time Elaine and I have been at the casino riverboat, Markus has been there. I even saw him and Randal together at the Slick Kitten."

Remi grinned. "What're you doing hanging out at a strip club?"

Paul grinned back. "I was there for Elaine's brother's bachelor party, which Elaine knows nothing about."

"Your secret is safe with me, *cher*."

Paul looked out his window and all humor left his face. "Slide down. It's party time. Our guy is coming this way. No, wait. He's stopping in front of the house, and here comes his ride." Paul could see headlights in his side mirror. A dark green BMW slowly drove past. "Bingo. They just picked him up." Paul waited until the car crossed Treme before pulling away from the curb, then flipped on his headlights and followed.

"Did you get the plate?"

"Yep."

Remi wrote down the Louisiana license plate number as Paul rattled it off.

"We're heading toward the river." Paul hung back as the BMW, now two cars ahead, turned right onto Decatur.

"What you want to bet we're on our way either to the Triple Aces or the casino boat?"

Paul chuckled. "I'd say I'll take that bet."

"And the boat it is," Remi said.

They followed as the car took North Peters to Conti, then hung right onto North Front, leading them to the dock of the brightly lit three-story High Roller.

"Well, well, well, look at who the driver is," Paul said as they watched the two men get out of the car. "It's our old friend Earl, Rivette's watchdog."

Remi swore. "How we going to keep him from making us?"

Paul reached behind the seat and handed Remi a New Orleans Saints cap. "This will have to do for you."

"And you?" Remi watched amused as Paul slipped on dark-tinted glasses, exchanging his windbreaker for a sport coat lying on the backseat.

Remi smiled. "I'm impressed." Turning up the collar on his jacket, Remi tugged the cap low on his forehead. "You got somewhere for this?" He pulled the Glock from beneath his jacket.

"There's a safe under your seat." Paul placed his snub-nosed revolver into his ankle holster. "Is that Glock all you got?"

Remi smiled. "Nope."

Chapter Twenty-Four

A cacophony of ringing bells, beeps, whistles, loud laughter, and thousands of coins dropping into metal trays assaulted Remi and Paul as they entered the glittering glitz of the High Roller's main deck.

"There they go." Paul spotted the two men heading for a burgundy-carpeted staircase.

"Do you know what's up there?" Remi asked, as they followed the two men.

"Randal's office and the high-stakes tables, I believe. I hope to hell we can blend in. Perhaps it would be better if we go up separately."

Remi nodded.

"Go on ahead, then. I'll hold back."

At the top of the stairs, to the right, people sat quietly playing Bourré, blackjack, and baccarat. To Remi's left, the two men headed down a hall that led past restrooms and closed office doors. To his relief, directly ahead of him was a large oval bar packed with people. He took a seat at the bar where he'd have a clear view of the hallway but not be easily seen. Soon Paul took a seat on the opposite side, also having a clear view.

"Oh, excuse me."

Remi silently cursed before turning to the buxom redhead who had purposely pressed her breast against his arm as she took the seat next to him. "No problem." Remi gave her a quick smile before resuming feigned interest in a televised basketball game.

"It's awfully crowded in here, isn't it?" Obviously not deterred by Remi's lack of interest, she leaned forward, giving him a nice view of her cleavage. "I'd love a glass of white wine. Would you mind getting the bartender's attention for me?"

Remi motioned for the bartender. Somehow he had to get rid of the girl. Catching Remi's eye, Paul rose, pointed at his cell phone, and walked toward the stairs.

Seconds later Remi's phone rang. He turned away from the girl and answered. "Yes."

"That girl next to you is a friend of Charlotte's named Laurie Conway. Charlotte, Randal, and our two friends just came out of one of the offices. Charlotte, Randal, and Laurie will recognize me, so you're on your own for now. I'll be down below."

"Right." Remi placed his phone back in his pocket as Charlotte and her party came out of the hall. The three men headed toward the high stakes tables, while to Remi's chagrin Charlotte headed directly toward him, stopping next to the redhead.

"Laurie, what are you doing sitting here? I thought you were playing baccarat."

Remi, seemingly engrossed in the television, strained to hear their conversation. Out of the corner of his eye, he saw the girl shrug.

"After I lost a few thousand, I quit. Besides, I got bored waiting around, so I thought I'd find myself a more interesting distraction."

Remi could feel both women's eyes on him. When the bartender sat down the glass of wine, Remi put on his best smile and turned, hoping like hell Charlotte wouldn't recognize him from the Gumbo Shop. "Here, *cher*, let me get that for you." He laid a twenty on the bar.

The redhead smiled. "Why, thank you, handsome. I'm Laurie." She held out her hand.

Remi gently squeezed it. Something about the woman seemed familiar. "I'm Remi."

Laurie nodded toward Charlotte. "And this is my friend Charlotte."

Remi held his breath as his eyes met Charlotte's. Seeing no recognition, he relaxed. "Hello."

Charlotte smiled. "Well, hello to you, too."

Remi studied Charlotte's dilated pupils and animated face. He'd seen people high on coke often enough to be convinced the guy in the BMW was her candyman.

"Hands off, Charlotte. I saw him first." Laurie placed a proprietary hand on Remi's knee. "Tell me, handsome, are you here all by yourself?"

Remi nodded. Then recognition hit. She was the woman dressed as Cleopatra at the masquerade ball.

Laurie's smile brightened as she ran her hand up his leg. "I'm going to be joining some friends out on the deck. Would you like to come with me?"

Remi grinned. So far his luck had held and she hadn't recognized him. "*Oui.*"

"God, I love to hear a man speaking French."

He got off the bar stool and put his arm around her nearly bare shoulders. Bending close, he whispered in her ear.

"Oh, yeah, handsome, I think you're lookin' good, too." She wrapped her arms around his neck and pressed her breasts into his chest.

"For Christ's sake, Laurie, don't attack the poor man right here."

Laurie swayed slightly as she glanced up at Remi with sultry eyes and slurred, "You don't mind, do you, Remi?"

"No, *cher*, I don't mind, but perhaps we should go out and get some air."

He wasn't sure where the three men had gone, so he hung back as Charlotte led the way past the high stakes tables toward a door marked *Private*. If Earl was waiting on the other side of that door, his ass was busted. As for Rivette, he didn't think he'd paid much attention to them in the Gumbo Shop. He put his hand in his jacket and felt for his cell phone, praying he could hit the speed dial for Paul.

Laurie glanced back. "Remi, what are you doing?"

He smiled, showing her the pack of cigarettes he'd pulled from his pocket. Seconds before they reached the closed door, his phone blessedly rang. It would be Paul calling him back. "I'll be right with you." He stopped as Charlotte opened the door, giving him a quick look out onto a deck where three men sat in shadow around a table.

He took a step back as the door closed. "Yes?"

"It's me. What's up?"

Remi spoke quickly, "I'm with Charlotte and Laurie. We're about to go onto a private deck off the stern. There are three unidentifiable men sitting around a table. Do you happen to know where our two friends are?"

"Earl is about fifteen feet away from me nursing a beer. I don't know about the other one. Do you need me?"

"No, my phone will be on vibrate. Call me if Earl moves." Remi slipped the phone into his pocket and stepped through the door onto the deck, the pungent smell of the river filling his nostrils.

"There you are, Remi." Laurie waved. "Come over here by me and I'll introduce you."

As he stepped closer, he was grateful the only illumination came from the full moon and dock lights, for Rivette was one of the three men at the table.

"This is Randal, Markus, and Dominic." Laurie pointed at each man as she introduced him. "And this is Remi. He was kind enough to buy me a drink, so I invited him to join us."

Remi took a seat next to Laurie, nodding at each of the men.

"Any friend of Laurie's is welcome," Randal said. "Are you from around here?"

"Born and bred on de bayou," Remi replied, thickening his Cajun accent.

Laurie grinned. "I love to listen to you talk." Beneath the table, she ran her hand up his leg.

He stopped her seconds before she reached his crotch.

"Is this your first time on the High Roller?" Markus asked.

"No, I've been a few times. It's a real friendly place, a little more laid back than the Triple Aces."

Laurie giggled, tugging at her hand, which Remi held tightly.

Charlotte chuckled. "Whatever you do, Remi, don't compare the High Roller to the Triple Aces," Charlotte said. "Dominic goes ballistic."

"Don't exaggerate, Charlotte." Dominic's words were low and his smile seemed forced.

Laurie managed to get her hand from Remi's. "Well, there's really no comparison. I mean, Randal, the High Roller is a nice boat, but the Triple Aces is a class act all the way around."

"A nice boat," Randal repeated through gritted teeth. "It's more than just a fucking nice boat."

Before he could continue, Charlotte, with a nervous laugh, quickly cut him off. "How about another round of drinks?"

Randal visibly fought for control, then his eyes softened and a jovial expression again filled his face. "Good idea. Does everyone want the same?"

When they all nodded, Randal put in their order.

"I take it you're Randal Doucette, the owner of the High Roller," Remi asked.

Randal nodded. "At your service. Casino boat owner and Doucette family black sheep. Although, actually, I'm not the only Doucette black sheep sitting at this table. Markus is my uncle, and Charlotte is my cousin."

Charlotte scoffed. "Speak for yourself. My record is clean."

Randal almost choked on his drink. "I'm afraid, dear cousin, you're confusing yourself with Caterine."

Charlotte grimaced. "Not hardly. Who in their right mind would want to be anything like Caterine?"

"Maybe not be like her, but have what she has," Randal needled.

"What in God's name could Caterine have that anyone would want?" Laurie asked as her hand again crept up Remi's leg.

"Not a damn thing," Charlotte snapped.

She's coming off her high, Remi thought, clasping Laurie's hand in his.

Randal snorted. "You'd be surprised, sweet Laurie, how many people do want what Caterine has."

"Well, now, nobody is going to get it, so you two need to let it go," Markus said before taking a long swallow of his drink.

"Get what?" Laurie asked. "What are y'all talking about?"

Randal smiled sardonically. "Why, the jewel of the Doucette crown, what else?"

Laurie's Botox-enhanced mouth frowned. "Randal, I haven't a clue what you're talking about."

Remi, grateful for Laurie's distraction, took the opportunity to remove her hand from his leg.

Charlotte's eyes darted between Randal and Remi. "Don't pay any attention to Randal, Laurie. He's just being an ass."

"I'm sure Remi and Dominic aren't interested in hearing about our family squabbles," Markus said.

Laurie's eyes widened. "Are y'all referrin' to Ma Chérie? What's Caterine have to do with that? I thought Miss Dauphine was in charge."

Randal scoffed. "Not anymore."

"Y'all don't mean Caterine now has Ma Chérie?" Laurie asked. "Charlotte, how can that be? I thought you said you were next in line."

Remi surreptitiously watched Randal, Charlotte, and Markus for their reactions. Markus took another deep swallow of his drink. Randal fidgeted with a cigarette. Charlotte, reaching for her purse, was stopped by Rivette placing his hand on her arm. Remi thought she was probably going for more coke. He knew he'd been under close scrutiny by Rivette since he'd sat down and hoped like hell Rivette had stopped Charlotte because Remi was a stranger and not because he thought he was a cop.

"Well?" asked Laurie. "Isn't someone going to tell me what's going on?"

Markus sighed. "A few days ago Miss Dauphine turned total control of Ma Chérie over to Caterine. That's all."

Laurie's eyes opened even wider. "But Charlotte, I thought you said you needed . . ."

"Can it, Laurie," Randal said tersely.

Looking petulant, Laurie got to her feet, grabbing onto Remi's shoulder for support. "Remi, I'm ready to leave. Would you please take me home?"

Randal sighed. "Sit down, Laurie. I'll take you home."

"You're too drunk to drive and so am I. Besides, I want Remi to take me."

"Maybe Remi doesn't want to take you," Randal retorted.

They're afraid of what she might say if she's alone with me, Remi thought. Aloud he said, "I don't mind. I'll drive her."

He didn't miss the tightening of Randal's mouth or the narrowing of Charlotte's eyes.

Laurie smiled triumphantly, putting her arm through Remi's as he rose. "See y'all later." She gave them a finger wave as she pulled him toward the door.

"Sorry, but I'm going to need to use the gents' before we leave. I'll meet you in the lobby."

"Don't be long, Cajun. I can't wait to get you home." She wound her arms around his neck and kissed him, practically swallowing his tongue.

Once in the men's room, Remi hit redial for Paul, speaking quickly when he answered. "Change of plans. I need you to follow me when I leave. I'll be with Laurie."

"And we're going where?"

"To take the lady home. Give me five minutes once I get her inside, then call me. I'll fill you in on our way back."

"What about Earl? He's still sitting here."

"Leave him."

"I'll be there. This has to be good."

Chapter Twenty-Five

Remi found Laurie leaning against a pillar when he reached the foot of the stairs, then spotted Paul playing a slot machine close to the boat's arched entryway.

"Give me your keys, *cher*." He placed a steadying arm around her.

She smiled drunkenly and dropped the Porsche's key between her breasts. "Come and get it, Cajun."

Remi sighed and could have sworn he heard Paul laugh. Resigned to playing her games, he gave her his sexiest grin then plucked out the key. "Where you parked?"

By the time they'd reached the car, his patience had about reached its limit. Not only did he have to keep her upright, he had to keep her persistent hands off his body.

"Okay, here we are. In you go." Remi poured her into the passenger seat and slammed the door. He scanned the parking lot, relieved to see Paul's Mountaineer coming toward them. He gave him a thumbs-up and slid in behind the wheel of the Porsche.

"Where do you live?" he asked as she flung herself over the console into his arms, crushing her mouth against his as her hand searched for the zipper of his jeans.

"You don't have to wait, Cajun. I can make you feel real good right here," she whispered against his mouth.

Before he could stop her, she had his zipper down and her hand around his semi-hard erection.

"Oh, Cajun, you really are a big boy, aren't you?" She lowered her head.

A car's honking horn filled the silent night. *I owe you one, buddy*, Remi thought, knowing it was Paul.

"As much as I'd like for you to continue what you're doing, *cher*, perhaps we should finish this at your place." He gently sat her back in her seat. He awkwardly zipped up his pants and turned on the ignition. "But I can't get us there unless you tell me where we're going."

Laurie gave him her address and said sullenly, "Can I have one of your smokes? I supposedly quit, so I don't have any."

He handed her the pack and squeezed her knee, hoping to mollify her. "Don't worry, I intend on finishing this." He slid his hand farther up her leg under her skirt, stopping when he reached the juncture between her legs.

She blew him a kiss and relaxed back against the seat.

He gave her a reassuring smile before pulling out of the parking lot. *I hope you're worth all of this.* Her eyelids began to droop. *Just don't pass out on me quite yet.*

"So tell me, what was that all about back there on the boat?"

"What do you mean?" She yawned.

"Everyone getting bent out of shape over someone named Colane owning a place called, what, Ma Pirie or something like that."

Laurie laughed. "That would be Caterine Doucette and Ma Chérie."

Remi nodded. "That's it. So what's the big deal?"

Laurie blew out a stream of smoke. "Ma Chérie is a high-class boutique in the Quarter owned by Charlotte's grandmother, Miss Dauphine Doucette. I don't know why Randal had to get so pissy with me. Everyone knows Charlotte expected to inherit. Maybe what everyone isn't supposed to know is that the last time Charlotte went to New York, she lined up a buyer for Ma Chérie. As soon as it belongs to her, she's going to sell, and she told me this would be happening real soon." Laurie yawned hugely. "I don't blame her in the least for wanting her inheritance now. I mean, why wait when you can have all that lovely money right away? Besides, who'd want all the work of running a store when you have someone ready to take it off your hands?"

"I thought you said this place was owned by Charlotte's grandmother.

How can she sell if it doesn't belong to her?"

Laurie yawned again and stubbed out her cigarette. "Miss Dauphine is old. Maybe she's sick and Charlotte was going to get her to sign the business over to her. But I guess none of that matters now that the scheming little bitch, Caterine, managed to get her hands on it first."

Remi had to bite back a scathing reply. He'd had about enough of these people trashing Caterine. When he looked over, Laurie was out cold. "*Putain de merde*," he cursed under his breath. Now how was he supposed to get her into the apartment? He stopped in front of her building and got out. He scanned the street for Paul, spotted him at the corner, and waved.

With Laurie's arms around his neck, Remi managed to lift the half-conscious woman out of the car and carry her inside. He stood her on her feet and sighed in exasperation when she rallied enough to begin unbuttoning his shirt.

"Where's your bedroom?"

She began to kiss his neck. "It's down the hall but, Cajun, we could start right here. I definitely want more of what I had a taste of." She again went for his zipper.

He lifted her into his arms and carried her to a large bedroom dominated by a king-sized bed. He laid her on the bed and kissed her long and hard. "I'll be right back, *cher*."

As he went into the adjoining bathroom, he prayed she'd soon pass out. He'd give her a few minutes. Then, if she wasn't out, hopefully Paul would call and he'd make some excuse and leave. He quietly reentered the bedroom and said a prayer of thanks. Laurie was curled up on her side sleeping soundly.

Remi slid onto the passenger seat next to Paul and sighed. "What the hell are you smiling about?"

"Had your hands full, did you?"

"Just drive the damn car."

Paul chuckled. "So how did you manage to get away from lusty Laurie? From the way she was all over you, I see she hasn't changed. I hope I did the right thing by interrupting back there in the parking lot."

Remi grinned. "If I didn't have Caterine waiting for me, I might have let her have her fun. The lady certainly knows what she's doing, but thanks for helping out. I take it you know her."

"Oh yeah. I couldn't believe our bad luck when she sat next to you. So tell me you got more out of tonight than a good workout fending off the lady's advances."

"For starters, I'm pretty sure our boy from tonight isn't anything more than Charlotte's candyman."

"No shit, she's really got herself hooked on coke?"

"I'd say so."

"Randal, too?"

Remi shook his head. "He and Markus were both a little drunk, but that's all."

"So do we have Vince pick up our guy with the coke?"

Remi nodded. "Who knows, if he's working for Rivette, there's a chance he might talk."

"You said there were three men on the deck. Who was the third?"

Remi smiled. "Rivette."

Paul's brows rose. "Did he recognize you from the Gumbo Shop?"

"Not that I could tell, though he kept his eyes on me the entire time."

"Do you think he smelled cop?"

"Could have. Or, due to the line of work he's in, he's naturally suspicious."

Paul frowned. "Learn anything else?"

"Oh, yeah. According to Laurie, Charlotte's plan was to sell Ma Chérie as soon as she had it in her greedy little hands, and since Charlotte already had a buyer, she was planning on this happening real soon."

Paul let out a long whistle. "I wonder who all knew this?"

"I'd say only Laurie, Randal, and perhaps Markus. Considering Frances' plans for improving Ma Chérie, I seriously doubt she knew what Charlotte had in mind."

"So could Charlotte have been pissed enough to actually hire someone to kill Caterine?"

Remi ran his hands over his face. "I don't know. She's the most obvious suspect. And she definitely has a coke habit."

Paul arched his brows. "And coke can be an expensive toy."

"Caterine told me Charlotte spends quite a lot of money. And Laurie was very clear that Charlotte expected to inherit."

"And what does that suggest?"

"That Miss Dauphine was the original target, not Caterine."

"Could be," Paul said. "Then she messed up Charlotte's plans by handing the business over to Caterine. God, this is getting sicker by the minute."

"Sick is right." Remi scowled. "Which makes me think if Charlotte and Randal are as close as Caterine says, then Randal is in it up to his neck."

"So what's next? Do we check into Doucette Shipping and see what we find?"

Remi shrugged. "I'd say so. If Charlotte's motive is money to support her habit, then we need to know what Randal's might be."

Paul nodded. "Okay, come by the office tomorrow. We'll sic Vince on Charlotte's candyman then see how far we can get digging into Doucette Shipping."

When Remi let himself into the apartment, he found Caterine curled up in a blanket, fast asleep on the sofa. He removed his jacket, boots, and shoulder and ankle holsters and walked over to where she slept. As he stood there, his feelings for her hit him like a physical blow. He shut his eyes and tried to envision his life without her. The stark image his mind produced snapped his eyes back open. *Christ, what a mess. I might be falling in love with someone who would probably no more consider marrying me than some tramp off the street.* He now knew the way he'd felt toward Desiree had been nothing but lustful infatuation.

His feelings for Caterine went to his very soul. He looked around his apartment. *This is a far cry from where you came from, Princess.* He made a good living working with Paul, but he could never give her what she was used to. *If I weren't such a selfish bastard, I'd break this off before it went another day, take her to her cousin in Michigan, and tell him to make her stay there no matter what.* But he knew he couldn't let her go, not yet.

Remi ran his fingers through his hair. It had taken everything he'd had tonight to sit there and let her family put her down without telling them they were nothing but scum compared to her. His experience tonight had only heightened his determination to find which of them was evil enough to have her attacked, then put the *putain de merde* behind bars.

He knew he wasn't going to do what he should, so instead he would do what he wanted to. Remi swept Caterine, blanket and all, into his arms.

Chapter Twenty-Six

Caterine automatically put her arms around his neck and snuggled closer. "Remi?"

"I hope it's me." He laid her on the bed and followed her down. As the blanket slipped away, his breath caught at the sight of the lacy black teddy she wore.

She gave him a sleepy smile. "Do you like it?"

"You're driving me crazy. You do know that, don't you?"

She smiled smugly. "I'll take that to mean yes."

"Oh, I like it all right, Princess." He slowly ran his hand across her breast, over her hip, stopping at the junction between her legs. "And what do we have here?"

She chuckled. "Snaps."

"You trying to keep me out, *cher*?" As he spoke, he ran his finger in a circle over the silk nestled between her legs.

She gasped. "Just making you have to work a little bit."

A grin spread across his face. "I love a challenge." He bent his head, placing tender kisses on the sensitive spot below her ear.

With a thrill of delight, she inhaled, then froze. Expecting to smell his spicy aftershave, instead her nose filled with the unmistakable scent of perfume. Confused, she stiffened beneath him.

"What's wrong? Did I hurt you?"

She opened her mouth to speak, then spotted a trace of red lipstick on his neck. Unable to form the words, she pushed against his chest.

"For God's sake, Caterine, what's wrong?"

She fought for breath. In a voice she didn't recognize, she asked, "Where were you tonight?"

"You know I went with Paul. What's this all about?"

"Get off of me!"

"What? Why?"

"Remi, get off me right now."

"No, Caterine. I'm not moving until you tell me what the hell is wrong."

"You reek of perfume, and you have lipstick on your neck. That's what's wrong!" she yelled, bucking her hips while pushing at his shoulders.

"If you would only listen, I can explain. *Merde*, Caterine, stop trying to hit me."

"Let go of my hands and let me up!"

"You're going to have the police here if you don't stop yelling. I didn't do anything. Will you please just listen to me?"

Remi pressed her body deeper into the mattress, grabbing her flailing hands in one of his and pulled them over her head. "Will you please be still and let me explain?"

She swallowed hard and tried to hold back her tears. With an icy glare, she nodded.

"Paul and I followed that guy tonight to the High Roller. I'll go into more details tomorrow, but I ended up with Charlotte."

"What?"

"Wait a minute. Let me continue before you let loose on me again. Charlotte, Randal, Markus, and that guy Rivette that Charlotte was with were all there."

"If you're about to tell me that lipstick is Charlotte's, you can save your breath. Charlotte wouldn't be caught dead wearing that trampy color or that perfume."

"I did what I had to do in order to get information, that's all."

"What?"

"Fuck, I didn't mean it that way. Oh, the hell with it. Caterine, there was this friend of Charlotte's named Laurie and she—"

"You were with that whore Laurie Conway? Ahhh!"

"Christ. What's the matter with you? Damn it, stop screaming."

"Not you, too."

"What are you talking about?"

"You and that bitch. You're no better than Jonathan!"

"What?"

"It doesn't matter, just get away from me." Her dreams of a future with Remi were crumbling around her. How could he have done this to her? He was tearing her heart into pieces.

Remi visibly fought for patience. "Caterine, I wasn't with Laurie. Well, not in the way you think."

"Then in just what way were you *with* that slut in order for her perfume and lipstick to be all over you?"

He gave her an exasperated scowl and rolled off her to sit on the side of the bed. "For the hundredth time, I didn't do anything wrong. It's late, and I'm tired. Do we really have to do this now?"

"You're damn right we're going to discuss this now. But I'm not going to listen to anything you have to say until you go shower off every trace of that bitch," she shouted as she got out of the other side of the bed and wrapped herself back in the blanket.

Remi cursed nonstop as he took off his clothes, tossed them on the floor, stomped his way into the bathroom, and slammed the door.

Caterine willed herself not to cry as she threw down the blanket and hurriedly tried to dress. She'd never been so hurt or so angry. Her hands were shaking so badly she could hardly button her blouse. *Take some deep breaths and get yourself under control*, she silently demanded. The thought of Remi touching another woman the way he touched her made her physically ill. *Stop it. Remi wouldn't hurt you like that. He's going to have a reasonable explanation for why he was with that slut.* First Jonathan and now Remi. This couldn't be happening.

She froze as she recalled Elaine telling her about Remi and Desiree Delany. Now he was with Laurie. *Oh, God, I'm going to be sick.* She quickly sat back down on the bed, willing her roiling stomach to settle. What could it be about that kind of woman that attracted men? Then her eyes opened wide as the realization hit her. *Sex.* It had to be sex. She put her head in her hands. Remi knew ways to make love she'd never heard of, but she'd bet Desiree and Laurie knew them and probably more.

What a fool she was. What would Remi want with a novice like her when he could have sex with women like Laurie? She swallowed back another wave of nausea. *I knew better than to fall in love with him, and this is what I get.* She stiffened her resolve. *Well, there's only one thing for me to do. I'll listen to what he has to say. Then, if I feel he's lying, tomorrow I'll go to Elaine's.*

When Remi entered the living room a short time later, he found Caterine dressed, sitting on the sofa and drinking a rather large glass of wine. He ran his hands through his damp hair and took the glass of Jack she silently handed him, then seated himself in the chair across from her. As he sipped the whiskey, he studied her rigid face, sighed, then began to explain everything that had occurred from the time he and Paul had followed their man to the riverboat, ending with him leaving Laurie passed out on her bed. He decided to put off telling her about Charlotte's plan to sell Ma Chérie until she had a chance to calm down. "And that's all that happened."

As he retold the night's events, her lack of trust in him not only hurt, it began to piss him off. Didn't she realize how much he cared about her? Did she really think so little of him that she thought he'd screw around on her the first opportunity he got?

"I would have thought you knew me well enough by now to know I wouldn't be out messing around on you. For Christ's sake, Caterine, why would I? It's not as if I'm not getting all the great poontang I want right here."

Caterine jumped to her feet. Hands on her hips, eyes blazing, she spat out, "Don't be crude, Remi. And don't you dare sit there acting all indignant because I got upset that the man I happen to love came home smelling like he'd been rolling around with a French Quarter whore."

Color suffused her face. She looked as if she wished the floor would open and swallow her whole. Her words, *the man I happen to love,* seemed to reverberate throughout the silent room.

"Oh, Princess, come here to me." Remi clasped her in his arms, holding her tight. He brought his mouth down on hers, pouring every ounce of love he felt for her into that one kiss. "You're so beautiful, Caterine." He nibbled his way along her neck, nipping her ear. "Do you have any idea how much I love the taste of you?" He placed hot kisses across her cheek. "Do you know how much I love touching you?" His hand slid down her back and caressed her bottom. "I love watching the pleasure on your face when I make love to you."

He took her in his arms and carried her back to the bed, where he gently laid her on the mattress. With hands that weren't too steady, he slowly unbuttoned her blouse then slid her jeans down her legs.

"Caterine, you are the sexiest, most desirable woman I've ever known, and I don't want anyone else." He quickly removed his own clothes and lay next to her.

Remi pulled her close as a warm river breeze blew softly through the open window, caressing their bodies, and the low sultry blues notes of a sax filled the room.

Caterine wrapped her arms around his neck and whispered, "I'm so sorry I doubted you. When I smelled the perfume and saw the lipstick, I lost all reason. I'm sorry I don't know more about lovemaking, but I want to learn all you want to teach me."

His brows rose in surprise. "And I'd love to teach you, Princess, but what made you say that?"

"I know you weren't expecting someone my age to be so naïve, and I'm really not sure how to please you, but . . ."

Clarity dawned in his eyes and he gently turned her face so she had to look at him. "You please me just fine, Princess. I love the fact I'm the only man who's ever given you pleasure in return. And I have no interest in, or desire for, Laurie Conway or anyone like her."

"Remi, I love—"

"Hush, Princess." He stopped her with a long kiss. "Lie there and let me please you. I want to enjoy every inch of you while I remove this lacy thing you're wearing."

She smiled tentatively. "I want to touch you, too, but this time I'm going first."

His chuckle quickly turned into a groan as he felt her hand gently surround his hard erection and squeeze.

She smiled coquettishly into his eyes as she ran her hand slowly along his shaft. "Am I doing this right?"

He gritted his teeth. "*Mais yeah*, Princess, you're doing just fine."

A thrill of anticipation shot through him when she boldly pushed him onto his back, sliding down until she lay between his legs. He soon lost all sanity when he felt her mouth close over him. "Christ, Princess, you're going to kill me."

She ran her tongue over the length of his shaft. "Do you like this?"

"Oh, yeah."

She took him deep into her mouth.

As he watched her, Remi balled his hands into fists and gritted his teeth. "Princess, you have to stop," he panted through a haze of pleasure. "I can't take much more."

She swirled her tongue over the swollen head, and he groaned aloud.

"Caterine, did you hear me? Do you understand what I mean? I can't hold back much longer."

"Then don't."

"Christ," he shouted hoarsely with his release.

When he could breathe again and his vision cleared, he pulled Caterine up next to him. He grinned and rolled on top of her. "You're looking extremely pleased with yourself. Now let's see what I can do."

With his teeth he tugged on the ribbon, loosening the tie between her breasts. As the lacy fabric fell away, he ran his tongue between her firm mounds. Her pink-tipped nipples invited him to taste his fill. "I believe I'll start here."

"Remi." She squirmed as he circled each nipple with his tongue.

"Tell me what you want, Princess."

"Remi."

"Come on, tell me."

She moaned deep in her throat. "Suckle me."

"I'll be happy to."

She ran her fingers through his hair as he licked and sucked one breast, then the other, until she squirmed beneath him.

"Remi?" She pushed on his shoulders.

He gazed into her eyes and grinned. "What do you want me to do now?"

She rubbed herself against him. "You know."

"You'll have to tell me." He positioned himself between her legs, running his finger along the damp silk nestled there. "You're so wet, *cher*, you've dampened all the way through."

She dug her fingers into his shoulders. "Put your mouth on me now."

His chuckle was low. "I thought you'd never ask."

She whimpered her pleasure as he slowly undid each snap between her legs. "Come for me, Princess."

She screamed, raking her nails over his shoulders as his tongue found and teased her swollen bud.

"Yell like that again, *cher*, and they'll be selling tickets down on the street." He covered her mouth with his as he slid his shaft deep into her heat.

The next morning, Remi was awakened by the unmistakable aromas of fresh coffee, cinnamon, and frying sausage. Curious, he followed the enticing smells to the kitchen where he found Caterine busily frying French toast and sausage patties.

He stopped behind her, put his arms around her, and nuzzled her neck. "Work up an appetite, did you?"

She grinned. "No, but I thought you probably did."

He swatted her backside. "That I did." He poured himself a cup of coffee, then opened the refrigerator for milk and frowned. "Caterine, where did all this stuff come from?"

"That nice little market around the corner."

He took a deep breath, hoping for patience. "And how did it get here?"

"I wanted to surprise you, so I went and got it this morning. I hope you don't mind. I didn't have enough money, so I had to take some out of your wallet."

He closed his eyes and counted. "What if someone had recognized you?"

She turned to him and sadness filled her eyes. "I wore my disguise, but to be honest I ran the entire way there and back." She swallowed back tears. "Remi, never in my life have I been afraid to walk the streets of the Quarter. I hate that man and my family for doing this to me."

He reached around her and shut off the stove. "Come here, *cher*." He held her close as she cried.

"Remi I hate being like this. I want my life back."

"I know, baby, I know."

She stepped from his arms and wiped her tears away. "I'm not a violent person, but I'm telling you when I find out who in my family is behind this, God help them."

She turned back to the stove and in a few minutes slid two slices of golden French toast onto his plate along with three plump sausage patties, then poured him a tall glass of fresh orange juice.

"I appreciate you wanting to surprise me with food, but please don't go out alone again."

She placed her own plate on the table and said, "When we were kids, Bobby used to tell me that it was easier to ask forgiveness than permission, so I followed that rule this morning."

He scowled. "Just don't push it too far."

"Oh, for heaven's sake, eat your breakfast and tell me what we need to do next. I still can't believe Charlotte actually has gotten herself hooked on cocaine. Is there some way you can have that man who sold her the stuff arrested?"

"I hope so. I'm meeting Paul at the office today, and we're going to explain all of this to a buddy of ours on the force." He smiled and took another bite of toast. "Mmm, this is almost as tasty as you, Princess."

She rolled her eyes and cleared her throat. "You didn't say last night if you thought Randal was on dope as well?"

He shook his head. "But I feel he's somehow involved in all of this." Remi knew he'd delayed long enough. He had to tell her about Charlotte's plan to sell Ma Chérie. He laid down his fork and began. "Caterine, there's something else you need to know."

Her first reaction to the news was to sit staring at him in stunned silence. Then her face turned red with fury. "That scheming little bitch. Here I was feeling sorry for her for getting hooked on drugs, and all along her only plan was to get the money from the sale of Ma Chérie!" With each word her voice increased in volume. "Well, that will happen over my dead body." She seemed to realize what she'd said and the high color drained from her face. "Oh my God, Remi, so it was Charlotte who tried to have me kidnapped?"

He reached across the table and took her hand. "I don't know. Cocaine is an expensive habit, but that doesn't mean Charlotte is hooked bad enough to kill over it."

"And Laurie is the one who told you?"

He nodded.

She narrowed her eyes. "You never did tell me what Laurie was doing to get her perfume and lipstick all over you."

"I told you she was so drunk she could hardly stand. I had to practically carry her to her car."

She made a disgusted face. "Laurie has been a tramp from the time she was a teenager, and it sounds as if things haven't changed. I can't believe Ray actually wanted to marry her."

Remi's brows rose. "Ray, not Randal?"

She shrugged. "I imagine she's been with Randal by now, but Ray did love her at one time. In fact, it was Bobby and I who caused their breakup."

"What happened?"

"We were all out at the house on Lake Pontchartrain for a big Fourth of July party when Bobby and I saw Laurie go into the summer cottage with Curtis Dobbs."

"State representative Curtis Dobbs?"

"That's the one."

"He's quite a bit older than she is, isn't he?"

She nodded.

"What happened?"

"Bobby and I went and got Ray. We probably shouldn't have, but I couldn't stand Laurie even back then. As I said before, I always got along well with Ray."

"What the hell did Ray do?"

"Needless to say, there was quite a scene. He called Laurie all kinds of nasty names and punched Curtis in the nose."

Remi smiled. "Good for Ray, although I probably would have done more than punch the son of a bitch in the nose."

"Yeah, but what about Laurie? I'm sure Curtis didn't drag her into the cottage."

"Trust me, Princess, you never want to know what I'd do if I caught the woman I loved in that kind of situation."

"Yes, well, that's not something we have to worry about."

His eyes softened. "I wouldn't think so. So tell me, what was Ray's reaction to you and Bobby being the ones to show him what Laurie was really like?"

"Actually, after he calmed down, he thanked us for stopping him from almost making the biggest mistake of his life, though he soon married someone who was only interested in his money. That marriage didn't work out. I'm sure he married her on the rebound."

"Could it have been his way of repaying you, warning you that night to watch your back?"

She frowned. "I don't know. He didn't say it in a menacing way. In fact, when I told him he was scaring me, he said good, as if he wanted me to be on alert."

"Damn, I wish there was a way we could talk to Ray alone." Remi stood and began to pace the small kitchen.

"Perhaps Paul could arrange a meeting."

He stopped and turned. "Caterine, this is important. If Ray were told about the attempt on your life, could he be trusted not to tell your family?"

"Ray is an attorney. Even though he mainly does corporate work for Doucette Shipping, if we met with him and paid him for his time, wouldn't attorney-client privilege apply?"

Remi looked thoughtful. "If he's honest and ethical, he'd be obligated to keep whatever we told him to himself."

"Then I say let's do it." Caterine began to clear the table. "Call Paul and see if he'll set up an appointment at his office this afternoon."

Remi rubbed the back of his neck. "I'm still not sure about this. We'll be taking one hell of a risk. What if you're wrong and Ray goes directly to your family and tells them everything?"

"Even if he does, which I don't think he will, what can he tell them but that I know that one of them tried to either kidnap me, kill me, or both?"

"That's our problem. If that person is forewarned, we may never find out who they are and you'll spend the rest of your life looking over your shoulder, not knowing if they'll try again."

"Remi, I want this all over with and my normal life back, and if that means taking a chance on Ray, I'm willing to take that risk."

He studied the determined set to her jaw and acquiesced. "All right, but when we're talking to Ray, do not tell him where you're living, or that your grandmother hired me, or about our relationship. We don't want to give him any more information than necessary."

Caterine smiled, wrapped her arms around his neck, and gave him a quick kiss. "It will be okay. Really. I'm sure we can trust Ray."

He held her tight before watching her hurry off to change. *For both our sakes, Princess, I hope you're right.*

Chapter Twenty-Seven

"Remi, you're making me nervous. Will you please stop pacing and sit down," Caterine said as they waited in Paul's second-floor office for Ray to arrive.

"Caterine's right. You're making me crazy as well." Paul took a seat behind his desk. "Instead of wearing out the carpet, let's decide how much we're going to tell Ray."

"I'm too geared up to sit." Remi leaned against a table stacked with papers. "What did you say to Ray in order to get him here?"

"I said I needed to speak with him about something of great importance to him and his family. That's all."

"And his reaction was?" Caterine asked.

"He started to ask questions, and I told him I'd explain when he got here. I also said this was to be confidential."

"Shouldn't I tell him exactly what happened to me?" Caterine asked. "Including the fact that Grandmère has been told?"

"You probably shouldn't say anything about Miss Dauphine's knowledge until after we see how he reacts," Paul said. "If he reacts badly, it may be in her best interest to keep her name out of this."

"I agree. Caterine, just explain what happened to you after you left Ma Chérie and nothing more."

"So I shouldn't mention the silhouette I thought I saw outside the back door?" She frowned. "What's wrong? Why are you two staring at me?"

Remi took a calming breath. "Caterine, what are you talking about?"

"Didn't I tell you?"

Remi's jaw clenched. "No, you didn't."

Caterine shrugged. "It was the evening of the attack. I was planning on working late and decided I wanted some coffee. I was on my way to the alcove where we keep the coffeemaker, and out of the corner of my eye I thought I saw a man's silhouette through the frosted glass of the alley door."

Remi desperately tried to hold on to his temper. "Then what did you do?"

"I thought it must have been the fog playing tricks with the light. It had been a trying day, and by then I had a headache. I knew I wouldn't get any more work done, so I called for a cab. They said due to the fog they didn't know when they'd get there, so I decided to take the streetcar back home."

Remi ground his teeth, unable to believe what he was hearing. Before he could speak, Paul asked, "Why didn't you have your car?"

"When I went to go to work that morning, it wouldn't start." She knitted her brows. "You know, that was really unusual. That car never gives me any trouble. I couldn't even get the door open with the remote. I had to use my key."

Remi slowly walked over to where she sat. Bracing his hands on either side of the chair, he leaned toward her until his face was inches from hers. His voice was harsh with suppressed anger. "Let me get this straight. You're telling us that after Ray's warning, and after your car mysteriously wouldn't start, and after you thought you saw someone outside the door, you decided to go out into the fog and walk all those blocks alone to catch the streetcar. What the hell is the matter with you? For Christ's sake, Caterine, you acted like those stupid women in movies who are alone and hear some sound in the basement and go down to investigate."

Caterine winced as Remi's voice rose.

"Cool down, Remi," Paul said. "I'm sure she didn't realize she was in that kind of danger."

"Thank you, Paul. As for you, Remi, I didn't actually think someone in my family would try and hurt me. Make my life miserable, yes, but cause me harm, no. And I don't appreciate being called stupid. Perhaps I showed bad judgment, and if I had known then what I know now, I wouldn't have left on my own."

Remi glowered while renewing his pacing. "If there was any doubt that someone in your family was behind the attack, what you've just told us clinches it. Your car had to have been tampered with sometime during the night. I wish we could get our hands on the car. Not only am I curious as to how it was disabled, there's a chance they left prints."

"Why not have the car towed here or to my house?" Paul suggested.

Remi smiled. "I have an even better idea. It so happens my cousin Antoine owns a garage and towing service that isn't far from the Quarter."

Paul glanced at the clock. "You've got about ten minutes until Ray arrives." He handed Remi the cordless phone from his desk. "Call the man."

"He'll need these?" Caterine held out her car keys.

Still on the phone, Remi took the keys from her hand and put them in his pocket. After giving Antoine the Audubon Place address and warning him not to get his fingerprints all over the car, Remi hung up. "He said he'd go get it today, so we should be able to go over there and dust it for prints after we're done talking to Ray."

Caterine frowned. "I don't understand. If none of my family has a police record, how will you know if any of their prints are on the car? Besides, anyone could have walked past and put their hand on the hood or door handle."

"I seriously doubt it was someone in your family who tampered with your car," Remi said. "We're hoping whoever was hired to do it does have a record and left his prints."

"So do I tell Ray everything that happened that night or not?" Caterine asked.

Remi turned to Paul. "What do you think?"

"I don't see where it can hurt. Just not anything from the time you got into the cab."

At that moment, Paul's secretary buzzed his office phone to announce Ray's arrival.

Tall and lean, in his late thirties, with dark brown hair and intelligent brown eyes, Ray Doucette exuded power and confidence as he strolled into the room. His eyes flicked past Paul and Remi to settle on Caterine. "Hello, Cat. So, what's this all about? I thought you were out of town? When did you get back?"

"Have a seat, Ray, and we'll explain." Caterine motioned to the chair next to her. "You know Paul, and this is his partner, Remi Michaud."

Ray shook both men's hands then took the seat indicated. "Okay, I'm listening."

Caterine swallowed hard before she began. "Ray, I have to ask you something first. Will you swear to me that everything you hear today will be kept in total confidence no matter what is said?"

Ray looked from face to face before settling on Caterine. "What's going on? What kind of trouble are you in?"

"Ray, please, I need to know if you can be trusted to keep quiet about what you hear."

He stared at Caterine and sighed. "Unless you're about to tell me you murdered someone, or robbed a bank, you have my word anything said in this room won't go any further. Now tell me what the hell is going on."

Caterine smiled and kissed his cheek. "Thanks, Ray. I knew I could count on you. It seems a member of our family hired someone to kidnap me to get their hands on Ma Chérie."

The color drained from Ray's face as she described the events leading to her attack.

Paul rose from his chair behind the desk and opened a cabinet built into a nearby bookcase. He took out a crystal glass, poured two fingers of Knob Creek Bourbon, and handed it to Ray, who downed it in one swallow before handing the glass back.

"What proof do you have that it was someone in our family?" Ray asked when Caterine had finished.

"Because it wasn't a random robbery. The man who attacked me wasn't interested in anything but getting me into that van, and you yourself warned me to watch my back."

"Ray, Caterine's car was sabotaged two days after your family was told about her ownership of Ma Chérie." Paul said. "Now, if these were random acts, whoever did this to her car could not have known that it would create the perfect setup for abducting Caterine that very night. Don't you agree it's all a little too coincidental?"

Ray rubbed his forehead. "Okay. Still, I ask, where's your proof? What motive would any of them have to want Ma Chérie badly enough to abduct

Caterine?"

As Caterine watched, Paul and Remi silently seemed to communicate. Then Paul nodded. Leaning forward in his chair, he rested his arms on his desk. "Ray, why would you tell Caterine to watch her back if you weren't afraid she was in some kind of danger?"

Ray smiled, showing even white teeth. "Don't you and your partner over there try to pull any bullshit cop interrogation tricks with me, Paul."

Paul spread his hands. "No bullshit, Ray. You must have had a reason. I'm asking what it was."

"And I'm asking you what motive you think someone in my family has to want Caterine hurt?"

"How about being hooked on expensive drugs and needing to inherit Ma Chérie in order to be able to sell it?" Caterine asked.

Ray's eyes searched hers. "And who might that be?"

Her patience was about at an end. "That would be Charlotte. Not only is she hooked on cocaine, she's hanging around with a well-known criminal. Not to mention that she already has a buyer for Ma Chérie. So you can just stop with your attorney crap. You damn well know something, and unless you want to help me, you might as well leave."

"Hold on, Caterine. I didn't say I wouldn't help. Accusing someone of attempting to kidnap and hurt you is pretty damn serious. I want to know what evidence you have to make such an accusation."

"You were sitting there the night Grandmère told the family she'd given me Ma Chérie, and you saw their reaction. I didn't want to believe someone in that room could hate me this much but, Ray, it has to be one of them. Nothing else makes any sense. And you know that as well as I do, or you wouldn't have warned me."

Ray closed his eyes and sighed. "You didn't tell me how you got away from the attacker."

"I hit him in the nose with the alarm remote and tried to run. You can still see the scrapes on my hands from him knocking me down." She held out her palms. "Ray, he grabbed my hair and tried to pull me into a van at gunpoint."

The color, restored to Ray's face by the bourbon, drained away again. "Grandmère told everyone you went out of town on business. That wasn't true, was it? You've been hiding out somewhere, haven't you?"

She hesitated before answering. "No, I didn't go out of town, and yes, I've been hiding out."

He smiled. "And you're not going to tell me where you're staying, are you?"

She shook her head. "Can I still count on your help if I don't?"

"If you're asking if I know who's behind this, I can honestly tell you I don't."

"Okay, you say you don't know who hired the attacker, but you do know something. Ray, there's someone living under Grandmère's roof who is evil. Maybe if you tell us what you do know, it will help stop whoever it is before they make another try, and perhaps succeed, at having me killed."

"For Christ's sake, Caterine, of course I don't want you killed. In fact, I'm on your side. For that matter, I've always been on your side. I had no problem with Grandmère's decision to give Ma Chérie to you."

"Then help me get on with my life by telling us what you know."

Ray stood and stared out the window onto Magazine Street. Minutes passed in silence before he turned. He looked resigned and a little pissed. He spoke directly to Caterine. "You've put me in a position I'm not at all happy about, but I can't take a chance with your life to save another's pride. So, Paul, if you'll refill that glass, I'll tell you what I know."

Chapter Twenty-Eight

Ray took a sip of the bourbon, cleared his throat, and began. "I found out about Charlotte's addiction and her relationship with Dominic Rivette this past New Year's when we all went skiing in Tahoe. I thought it was a little strange we were going there instead of Aspen like we normally do, but the skiing is great in Tahoe as well, so I didn't think any more about it. It wasn't until Randal, Charlotte, Markus, and I arrived at the condo that I was told it belonged to Rivette and that he'd be joining us. I'd never met him, but I sure as hell knew who he was.

"Needless to say, I wasn't pleased to find out Charlotte had been dating someone of such dubious reputation. Not to mention, by accepting his hospitality, I'd be putting my own reputation on the line. I actually checked into getting my own accommodations, but everything for miles around was booked. I let Randal and Markus convince me that even though Rivette had been accused of illegal activities, nothing had ever been proven, so what would it hurt to be seen in his company? I wanted to ski and the condo was in a perfect location, so I thought what the hell and ignored my unease."

Ray placed his empty glass on Paul's desk and began to pace as he continued. "The second night we were there, I came home unexpectedly and caught Charlotte snorting coke. I can tell you there was quite a scene. I may have my own vices, but I detest drugs of any kind. After Charlotte calmed down, she told me she started playing around with the drug last summer while sailing the Mediterranean on Rivette's yacht. Now not only was she hooked, she was under his control, being in debt to him for a great deal of money. When she told me how much, I wanted to shake the shit out of her for being so stupid and getting herself in such a mess."

Ray stopped his pacing and turned to Caterine. "Cat, you're probably going to want a drink before I continue, because at this point this story really begins to go south."

Caterine looked from Ray to Paul to Remi, then back to Ray's grim face. "Okay, I'll have a glass of wine if you have it."

"As I said," Ray continued, "Charlotte had managed to get herself deeply in debt, but I knew Doucette Shipping could cover it. Once Charlotte was out from under Rivette's control, we'd send her away to some clinic where she could get some help. That's when I learned that sometime last fall, Randal's big buddy and partner in the High Roller, Dickie Boone, had disappeared with most of the casino's cash. So, while a private investigator hired by Randal tried to locate Dickie, the casino expenses began to pile up. Then Randal and Markus came up with the brilliant idea of covering them with money from Doucette Shipping, putting us in a real bind."

Caterine gasped. "Oh my God, Ray, how bad is it?"

Ray gave her a thin smile. "We won't starve, little cousin, but Doucette Shipping's finances aren't the only problem. It seems Rivette found out about the High Roller's financial difficulties and talked, or threatened, Randal into letting him lend him money, then gave him a deadline to repay it or he wants the riverboat."

"Son of a bitch," Paul swore. "Randal really has his nuts in a vise this time."

Ray scoffed. "And for once it isn't totally his fault. Skimming money from Doucette Shipping is, but not being ripped off by Dickie or getting muscled by Rivette."

"You're saying the money they took from Doucette Shipping wasn't enough to cover all of Randal's debt so he let Rivette bail him out?" Caterine asked.

Ray nodded. "They'd been extracting the money in small amounts so they wouldn't draw attention to themselves, then one of our accountants found a discrepancy in the books and came to me."

"When's Rivette's cut-off date?" Remi asked.

"Midnight of Mardi Gras," Ray replied.

Paul shook his head. "That sure as hell doesn't give him much time."

"Nope." Ray shrugged.

"Ray, I don't understand how Randal thought he'd get his hands on Ma Chérie. Before Grandmère turned the business over to me, Charlotte wouldn't have inherited until Grandmère died, and she's pretty healthy for her age."

"I know, Cat, but Markus was sure he could convince Grandmère to retire and turn ownership over to Charlotte. Then once Charlotte had control, she could sell the business and pay off their debts to Rivette."

"But Miss Dauphine gave Ma Chérie to Caterine instead, ruining all their plans," Paul surmised.

Ray nodded, retaking his seat.

"I can't believe Randal and Uncle Markus actually thought they'd be able to talk Grandmère into retiring. Ray, that seems idiotic."

"By this time they were desperate, and that was their only hope because when I found out they'd been taking money from Doucette Shipping, I put a stop to it."

"So there's no way the shipping company can bail Randal out?" Paul asked.

Ray shook his head. "Not now. Randal is my brother, and God knows I've gotten his ass out of a number of tight spots, but this time my hands are tied. He's going to lose the boat to Rivette, and there's not a damn thing I can do about it."

"Who else is aware of this?" Caterine asked.

"No one, as far as I know."

"Not even Uncle Jules?"

"Not yet, but he'll be finding out soon."

Caterine knitted her brows. "Charlotte and Paulette are pretty close. I can't imagine Paulette isn't aware of Charlotte's little problem."

Ray hesitated. "Charlotte told me no one in the family knew except Randal and Markus. Paulette can't keep anything to herself, so I can't see Charlotte taking a chance of telling her. Besides, if crossed, Paulette can be a vindictive little bitch. If she were to get pissed off at Charlotte, she'd tell all just to get back at her."

"You're probably right. So, Ray, who do you think was behind my attack,

Randal or Charlotte?"

Ray rubbed his temples. "For Christ's sake, Caterine, you're accusing my brother or my sister. I can't believe either of them could be capable of doing something that evil."

Caterine sighed. "I don't want to believe it either, but someone sure as hell did."

Remi turned to Paul. "What about Rivette?"

"That's a possibility. He would have had to know about Miss Dauphine handing over Ma Chérie to Caterine that very night in order to have tampered with her car and set up a hit two days later. Although, if it had been one of Rivette's boys doing the hit, I would have thought the job would have been done right."

"Ray, could Rivette have been told of Grandmère's decision that night?" Caterine asked.

"I have no idea. I rather doubt Randal would have hurried off to inform him. Why would he? It would be tipping his hand. As far as Charlotte, if she were high enough, God only knows what she'd say."

"Charlotte and Randal did leave together that night," Caterine said. "But you're right, it wouldn't have been in Randal's best interest to have told Rivette ahead of time of his plans to use Ma Chérie to pay him off."

"Charlotte did tell me that Rivette wanted the High Roller and wanted it bad," Ray said. "So one could assume if he did know, he'd do all in his power to prevent Randal from getting his hands on Ma Chérie."

"If Rivette did his homework on the Doucettes, he may have thought it would be easier for Randal to get control of Ma Chérie from Miss Dauphine than from Caterine. With Caterine out of the way, ownership would revert back to Miss Dauphine," Remi said.

Paul rubbed his chin. "That's true."

"So, Ray, who were you warning Caterine to look out for?" Remi asked.

"I honestly don't know. I knew trouble was coming. To whom, from whom, I wasn't sure. I knew things were bound to get ugly, and Caterine had unknowingly landed right square in the middle of it all."

Caterine took a sip of wine and frowned. "As I see it, Ray, no matter how difficult it is for you to suspect Randal or Charlotte, it sounds as if they're both pretty desperate for the money from Ma Chérie. Not that either of them has a chance of getting their hands on it, but I guess they think if I'm out of the way, they'll be able to wear Grandmère down until she turns the business over to Charlotte."

Ray scoffed. "Not if she thought one of them was responsible for your death. She'd probably kill both of them herself. What I should do is tell Randal and Charlotte you know everything and that if something were to happen to you, I'd go directly to the cops and tell them everything."

"No!" Paul and Remi shouted simultaneously.

"Okay, why not? Wouldn't that be one way to keep Caterine safe?"

"For the time being perhaps," Paul said. "But someone wanted her out of the picture, and we need to discover who that person is. If they're forewarned, they'll step back and we might never know the truth."

"Ray, we know it has to be Rivette or someone in our family. I can't go through the rest of my life wondering who it is, or if they'll strike again."

"So what are we supposed to do?" Ray asked. "Put you out there like a sitting duck and wait to see who shoots first?"

"You know . . ."

"Don't even think about it, Caterine," Remi said sharply before she could continue. "We're not using you as bait, and that's final. I mean it. Get any ideas of that sort right out of your head."

Ray studied Caterine's stubborn expression and Remi's determined glower and turned to scowl at Caterine. "When I arrived, I was so surprised to see you I neglected to inquire what Paul's and Remi's roles were in all of this, but I'm beginning to somewhat catch on. Paul being an old friend of yours and an ex-cop, it's understandable you'd go to him for help after the attack. But why does Michaud sound as if he has the right to speak to you in a way that suggests he knows you more intimately than he should?"

"Oh for heaven sakes, Ray, what business is that of yours? I'm an adult, and what I do or don't do is nobody's business but my own."

Ray rose and pointed his finger in her face. "You have to answer to me, Caterine, because somehow you've managed to be the only Doucette grandchild living in New Orleans who hasn't yet brought scandal or disgrace upon our family. So for Grandmère's sake, as long as she's alive, I plan on doing everything in my power to keep it that way."

Caterine batted his hand away from her face and stood. "Are you crazy?" For God's sake, Ray, when this all comes to light, it's going to be the biggest scandal to ever come down on our heads, and you're worried about my reputation."

Ray's voice was harsh with emotion. "At this point, Caterine, you're the victim, not the scandal. My idiot brother losing his business to a known criminal is a scandal. Uncle Markus skimming money from Doucette Shipping is a scandal. Charlotte being hooked on cocaine is a scandal. One member of our family perhaps being implicated in your attack is a scandal, but you are innocent in all of this. So I don't want any reporters to have any fuel to drag your name through the mud with the rest of us. Since you've been in hiding, and I don't think you've been staying with Paul, that leaves me to wonder what's going on between you and Michaud."

"Hold on, Ray," Remi said.

"I can handle this, Remi," Caterine said. She placed her hand on Ray's arm. "I appreciate your concern, and I have to say you've taken me totally by surprise. I didn't think that other than Bobby and Grandmère anyone else in the family cared enough to worry about me. Ray, Remi, and I have been discreet. In fact, other than you and Grandmère, no one else in the family need know I'm back or where I'm staying. Besides, your list of Doucette scandals should be enough to keep the press in a feeding frenzy for weeks. I truly believe my living arrangements will be of little interest to anyone."

It was Ray's turn to look speechless.

Paul cleared his throat. "Perhaps we should get back to the matter at hand."

"In a minute, Paul," Ray said. "I want to finish this with Caterine. God knows, Cat, you've got every reason to believe no one in the family gives a shit about you, but it isn't true. I care, my father cares, Uncle Markus cares, and we sure as hell know Bobby cares." He gave her a grin. "You deserve Ma Chérie and everyone knows it, including Charlotte, Paulette, my mother, and Aunt Hyacinth, even though they'd never admit it. Cat, I not only want you to stay safe, I want you to stay away from any backlash that's going to come from this."

Caterine blinked back tears while giving Ray a hug. "I'll be okay. Really, don't worry about me." She stepped back and gazed into his troubled face. "I know it had to be awfully difficult for you to tell us about Randal and Uncle Markus. I'm sorry I had to put you in that position, but I truly thank you for helping me."

Ray cupped her under the chin. "I said I cared about you. I didn't say you weren't a pain in the ass. And whether you like it or not, I'm still planning on having a long talk with your boyfriend over there."

Caterine rolled her eyes and smiled. "Go right ahead. I'm sure he's up to it."

Chapter Twenty-Nine

Shit. Remi cursed under his breath. Dealing with Miss Dauphine was one thing. Being challenged by an irate and overprotective Doucette male was a different matter altogether. "Ray, I can assure you my number one priority is keeping Caterine safe."

"And?"

"And what?"

"And what about Caterine after this is done?"

"For now, keeping her safe is all I can offer."

Ray narrowed his eyes. "What if that's not enough?"

Remi shrugged. "It will have to be. Instead of worrying about my relationship with Caterine, you should be more concerned about persuading her not to use herself as bait to draw out her attacker. Trust me, I've been around Caterine long enough to know that idea is still floating around in that pretty little head of hers."

Ray turned back to Caterine. "Is he right? If so, you can just forget it."

Caterine's mouth opened in astonishment. "What's going on? A minute ago you two seemed ready to attack each other. Now you're taking sides against me?"

Remi smiled with satisfaction. "If that's what it's going to take for you to see reason, Princess. Perhaps you'll actually listen if there're two of us, and then do as you're told."

Caterine's face flamed with anger. "Do what I'm told? I've been doing as I've been told and where has that gotten us? Remi, how can we ever flush this person out if they don't get the chance to try again?"

The smug *I told you so* smile Remi gave Ray made Caterine even more furious. She folded her arms across her chest. "And just what brilliant idea do you all-knowing superior males have for catching this person?"

"You know, I've been sitting here going over what we've been discussing, and I'm beginning to wonder if we were right that Rivette is somehow involved in this," Paul said. All eyes turned his way. "We've already concluded that the person who set up the hit on Caterine would need to have moved quickly to have her attacked that soon after Miss Dauphine's announcement. If they are involved, the only way I can see Randal or Charlotte being able to make this happen is through Rivette. Honestly, what are the chances of either of them knowing how to go about lining up a hit man that quickly?"

There were a few moments of silence while they all digested Paul's theory. Then Remi asked, "Is there any way we could have been looking at this all wrong and the attack had nothing to do with Ma Chérie?"

"What do you mean?" Caterine asked.

"Could you have an enemy that hasn't any interest in whether or not you own Ma Chérie?"

Ray laughed. "You don't know Caterine as well as you think you do, Remi, to have even considered that possibility. Outside of my family's ill-founded envy of Caterine, everyone else who knows her loves her."

Caterine dismissed Ray's statement with a wave of her hand. "You're exaggerating, Ray. There're plenty of people who think I'm a spoiled, prudish snob and would like nothing better than to see me take a fall. But I don't think any of them dislike me enough to try and have me kidnapped or killed."

Ray smirked. "Perhaps there're some women who feel that way about you. But if you had let any of the males who showed an interest in you over the years get close to you, you'd have had them falling at your feet. I'd be willing to bet your lack of response has broken more than one male heart."

Caterine rolled her eyes. "Yeah, well, the theory that I may have some love-struck rejected suitor is too farfetched."

Remi frowned. "Caterine, you didn't steal the affection of one of these men away from another woman did you?"

Caterine threw up her arms in exasperation. "Oh, for heaven's sake, this conversation is becoming ridiculous. Instead of trying to conjure up some mysterious jilted suitor of mine, or a phantom jealous girlfriend, we should be putting our energy into figuring out how to expose the real person behind my attack. Today is Thursday, and Mardi Gras is next Tuesday. Perhaps if we can flush this person out, and it turns out to actually be Rivette, we may be able to save the casino boat for Randal."

"How do you see that?" Remi asked.

"If Rivette is arrested for attempted murder, wouldn't he go to jail? Then he'd lose his hold over Randal."

Remi smiled. "Reasonable assumption, but this is Rivette we're dealing with. He's the epitome of the 'Teflon man'. Nothing ever sticks. Plus, it wouldn't have been Rivette who tried to kill you. He would have contracted that out so his hands would be clean."

"How likely is it that if the hired attacker were caught, he'd implicate Rivette?" Ray asked.

Remi shrugged. "It all depends on whether he's offered a deal. If he's deep in Rivette's organization, he may go down before giving up his boss. On the other hand, if he's someone from out of town that Rivette brought in, he might spill his guts to save his own ass."

Caterine knitted her brows. "Then wouldn't it make sense to have me visible to lure this person out?"

"Damn it, Caterine. No," Remi exclaimed.

"What if she were in an environment where we could guarantee her safety?" Ray asked.

Before Remi could reply, Paul spoke up. "Such as?"

"First, I no more want Caterine hurt than you do," Ray began, "But I think she may have a point. How can we catch this person if they don't come into the open? Every Mardi Gras the Doucettes throw a ball at the Audubon Place mansion. What if it's known that Caterine is back in town and will be attending the party? It's somewhere she knows well, and you could have your own people placed throughout the house. As she moves around, we could make sure someone has her in sight at all times."

Caterine smiled. "Oh, Ray, that's a great idea. Remi, what do you think?"

Paul held up his hand to forestall Remi's objection. "That might be something worth considering. Let's think it through."

Remi shook his head. "You know as well as I, we could have fifty men stationed around the house and still not guarantee Caterine's safety. No, it's too risky."

"There could be one other potential problem," Ray added. "The party is a costumed affair, so our man wouldn't know which was Caterine."

"But if I were to wear the same princess gown I wore to Paul and Elaine's party, everyone in my family would know it was me. The gown is a Ma Chérie. None of them could miss that."

"The problem is that not only will you be in costume, so will our assassin. How would we know it's the right person if he approaches you?" Paul asked.

Caterine tapped her lower lip in thought. "How about if we have some kind of signal for me to give if someone approaches me that I don't recognize?"

"And you could just as easily mistake some innocent party guest you're not familiar with for a would-be assassin." Remi shook his head. "This plan has the potential for major disaster."

"On the other hand, being a costume party, it would be easy to place you and me and Vince and Andre, and whoever else we could find to help, close to Caterine, and no one would be the wiser," Paul said.

Remi ran his fingers through his hair. "Christ, Paul, we already know the attacker carries a gun. He could easily shoot Caterine before anyone knows what happened."

"Hundreds of people attend the Doucette Mardi Gras party. I can't see the assassin taking a chance on not getting a clear shot. If it were me, I'd try and get her away from the ballroom and alone."

"Okay, with that many people, he could easily stab her, then lose himself in the crowd," Remi countered.

Paul rubbed his chin. "I'll give you that one."

"Excuse me," Caterine interrupted. "I'd hardly stand there and not make a sound if someone came at me with a knife."

"They could take you from behind," Remi said. "You'd be down before you knew what happened."

"Not if I kept my back to the wall. Or if you made sure someone was behind me at all times."

"We'd need to know what costumes the Doucettes were wearing," Paul said. "And someone would have to call Audubon Place security with a list of the names of those who will be helping us."

"I could take care of both of those," Ray replied. "And you could count on me to help keep an eye on Caterine."

Remi began to pace, clenching and unclenching his fists. "I still don't like it. Too many things could go wrong. I promised Miss Dauphine I'd keep Caterine safe. What do I tell her if this plan goes all to hell?"

"We'll explain everything to her ahead of time," Caterine said. "I'll make sure she knows I want to do this and you're not responsible if something goes wrong."

Remi snorted. "Oh, that really makes me feel better."

Caterine gave Remi an annoyed scowl. "Being sarcastic isn't going to help. This is my life we're talking about, and if I want to take this chance, it's my decision to make, not yours."

Remi stopped pacing in front of her chair and leaned down so his face was inches from hers. "Since it will be my job to save your sweet little ass, Princess, I sure as hell have a say in whether or not you put yourself in that kind of danger."

"Fine," she said through gritted teeth. "Then I suggest instead of wasting time telling me everything that could go wrong, you come up with a plan that will work, because with you or without you, I'm going to be at that party Tuesday night."

"No, you won't, Caterine," Ray said. "And you can get that stubborn look off your face. If Paul or Remi think there's a chance this plan will place you too much at risk, it's not happening."

"Good. Then that takes care of that because I say no."

Furious, Caterine rose to her feet and pointed her finger in Remi's chest. "Hear me and hear me well, Remi Michaud." She emphasized each word with a jab of her finger. "Just because you and I are in a relationship doesn't give you the right to control my life. I will do as I wish, when I wish, and you and your domineering arrogance had better damn well get used to it."

Remi narrowed his eyes, his voice low. "Stop poking me with your finger, Caterine."

Ray sighed. "Sit down, Caterine, and don't take your anger out on Remi.

I'm the one who suggested the party idea."

"Yes, and what I said to Remi goes for you as well. Neither of you is going to dictate my life."

"Cat, perhaps Remi and Ray are right and exposing you at the party really is a bad idea," Paul said.

Caterine's eyes filled with angry tears. "Paul, I thought at least you were on my side in this. You know what? The three of you can just go to hell." She turned on her heel and ran out of the office.

Chapter Thirty

"Damn it to hell, Caterine, get back here!" Remi yelled.

Caterine heard footsteps behind her, increased her pace, and ran down the stairs. As she reached the front door, a strong male arm went around her waist, lifting her off her feet, pressing her back against a very hard chest.

"Damn it, Caterine, where the hell do you think you're going?"

Caterine fought to break his hold. "Remi, let me go. I've had enough of your male arrogance."

"And you know what, Princess? I'm tired of your temper tantrums."

Angrier than she'd ever been, Caterine pounded his arms with her fists. "Remi, let me go . . ."

"All right, you asked for this." Remi flipped her facedown over his shoulder and smacked her butt. "Now stop it."

Caterine screamed, pounding his back. "How dare you, Remi. If you don't put me down this second I'll—"

"Caterine Doucette, what is the meaning of this?" Miss Dauphine demanded, poised in the open doorway.

Caterine froze, her hands raised for another onslaught against Remi's back. *Oh God, tell me this isn't happening.* She heard Remi curse under his breath as he placed her back on her feet. Attempting to look calm and composed, Caterine brushed her hair from her face and turned to confront her outraged grandmother. Sending up a silent prayer for help, she plastered a smile on her face. "Grandmère, how nice to see you. We weren't expecting you."

Miss Dauphine glared. "Obviously not." Her eyes moved from Caterine to Remi, then up the stairs to where Paul and Ray stood, and back to Caterine.

"I haven't heard from you, Caterine, so I tried Mr. Michaud's cell phone and got his recorded message. So I decided to stop by and see if Paul had any news he might wish to share with me."

"Well, actually Grandmère, we've been discussing a plan that may lead to apprehending my assailant."

"I'm glad to hear there's been at least something productive occurring here. Before you enlighten me on this progress, perhaps you might retire to the ladies' powder room and attend to your disheveled appearance. But first, pray do tell me, what it is exactly that you're wearing?"

Caterine grimaced as she looked down at her fashionably torn faded jeans and tie-dyed dancing crawfish T-shirt. "It's part of my disguise, Grandmère."

"I see." Miss Dauphine sniffed. "Well, it's certainly an effective disguise. I thought perhaps you were in costume for Mardi Gras." Miss Dauphine turned and addressed Thomas. "I shouldn't be long. Perhaps you could get yourself a cup of coffee while you're waiting."

Thomas nodded. "Fine, m'am. There's a café up the street. If I'm not back when you're ready to leave, Paul or one of these young men can come get me."

Miss Dauphine turned back to Caterine. "I'll go up now and find out why Raymond is also here. I expect to see you shortly."

"I'll stay here and wait for Caterine," Remi said.

Miss Dauphine's lips formed a thin line. "I have no idea what that unfortunate imbroglio I just witnessed was about, Mr. Michaud, but I do not wish to ever see my granddaughter put in such an undignified position again. Am I clear?"

"Yes, ma'am."

Arms folded, Remi leaned against the mahogany newel post at the foot of the stairs, waiting for Caterine to come out of the bathroom.

She stopped in front of him. "Of all people to walk in at that moment, it had to be Grandmère."

"You're lucky Paul owns the building and it was only Miss Dauphine who got to witness your performance."

Caterine bristled. "My performance? It wasn't me, Remi, doing a 'me caveman, you woman' routine."

He smiled. "The next time, Princess, I'll make sure your bottom is bare when I do that."

She narrowed her eyes. "There had better not be a next time. I don't appreciate being manhandled, and I won't put up with it."

"Yeah, well, it seemed the only way to stop your tantrum."

She stomped her foot. "I was not having a tantrum."

"No, *cher*? What would you call it?"

"I call it utter exasperation caused by dealing with three overbearing men."

"Three men who only want to keep you safe and alive. And if that's being overbearing, then so be it."

Tired of arguing with him, Caterine hoped he'd listen to reason. "If there's a chance to flush out my attacker at the Mardi Gras party, I'm willing to take a risk. I realize there's some danger and I understand your concern, but please try and see my side in this. I want this to be over and my life back to normal. I want to be able to go back to work at Ma Chérie. I want to be able to go out in public dressed as Caterine Doucette. I want to be able to see my friends and attend parties and functions. But most of all, I want you and me to be able to begin a relationship without this hanging over our heads, controlling our lives."

He pulled her into his arms and held her tight. "Princess, I hear what you're saying, and I want to be the one who makes this evil all go away and gives you your life back, but I want to accomplish that without putting you in danger. Caterine, if something were to go wrong at the Mardi Gras party and you were killed, they might as well kill me, too."

She wrapped her arms around his neck. "If we plan this right and don't take any unnecessary chances, I know it will work. Please." She kissed him. "*Please?*" She kissed him a little harder. "At least let's try and figure out a way where no one will get hurt, and we can put an end to this." She kissed him long and passionately. "What do you say?" she asked when they came up for air.

He grinned. "I say you've made a good start, but it's going to take more than a few hot kisses to convince me."

She grinned back. "Such as?"

Remi's teasing grin turned pure devil. "Such as . . ." He bent to whisper in her ear.

Her pulse quickened as he explicitly described his request.

"So will you do that for me, Princess?" He nibbled her earlobe.

"Ah, excuse me you two, but Miss Dauphine is wondering what's taking so long?" Paul called down the stairs.

"Damn," Remi swore, pulling away. "You'd better go up first. We don't want Miss Dauphine to see the condition I'm in."

She laughed at the distinct outline of his erection visible through his jeans. "I should guess not. I'll tell her you're on the phone."

"There you are," Miss Dauphine said as Caterine entered Paul's office. "Please be seated." She indicated the chair Ray had vacated next to her. "Raymond has just concluded informing me of the latest scandal Randal, Charlotte, and Markus have managed to bring upon this family. Now I wish to hear how all this idiocy involves you."

"Well, Grandmère, it all boils down to the ownership and subsequent sale of Ma Chérie. Randal needs the money to pay Rivette off and maintain control of the High Roller, and to pay back the money he and Uncle Markus took out of Doucette Shipping. Charlotte needs to pay off her cocaine and any other debts she owes Rivette."

"I don't understand. How did they intend to obtain Ma Chérie before I handed it over to you?"

Caterine shrugged. "Supposedly Uncle Markus was convinced he could persuade you to retire and let Charlotte take charge. You threw a wrench in their plans when you gave it to me instead."

"Have they all lost what intelligence they had?"

"They're desperate, Grandmère," Ray said. "And desperate people do stupid things."

"I'll put a stop to this nonsense this very evening. I'll inform them I know of this plan and that hurting Caterine will not get them Ma Chérie. As far as I can tell, all that needs to be done is for Caterine to stay out of sight until after Mardi Gras when this Rivette person takes control of Randal's boat. Then the sale of Ma Chérie will be a moot point. At that time, Charlotte will be sent to a private clinic in Europe to overcome her addiction. And that will put an end to all of this."

"That may take care of the immediate problem," Caterine said, "but we still won't know if there's someone living under your roof who tried to have me killed. And even though Randal can be an incredible ass, if he wasn't involved in my attack, he doesn't deserve to lose the riverboat to a criminal."

Remi entered the room and leaned against the table, his arms crossed over his chest. "Miss Dauphine, Caterine wants to use herself as bait during the Doucette Mardi Gras party to draw this person out."

Caterine jerked her head around. "Remi, don't," she commanded through gritted teeth.

"If we decide to try this harebrained idea of yours, your grandmother has to be told exactly how we're going to pull it off."

Miss Dauphine held up her hand forestalling Caterine's reply. "I'd like to hear this plan. Please explain it to me, Mr. Michaud."

Remi smiled. "Well, that's our first problem. We don't actually have a coherent plan. Caterine thinks if it is known she's back in town and will be attending the party, the assassin will show up, then proceed to waltz up to her and attempt to murder her. But before this ghastly deed can be completed, either myself or one of our undercover operatives stationed around the ballroom will rush in just in the nick of time to vanquish the villain and rescue the Princess."

Miss Dauphine gave Remi a slight smile. "I get the impression you're not greatly enamored of this plan of Caterine's."

"As far as I'm concerned, this idea is a recipe for disaster."

When Caterine opened her mouth to speak, Remi cut her off.

"But if Caterine is determined to go through with it, I'll do my damnedest to make it work."

"Raymond, Paul, what do you think of this scheme?" Miss Dauphine asked. "Is Mr. Michaud correct that this has potential for disaster? I must say I have my own concerns about placing Caterine in such a situation."

"Grandmère, I know there's some risk involved in this, but as I told Remi, in spite of his dire predictions I'm willing to take a chance. I want this over and my normal life back."

"Miss Dauphine, I'm not going to lie to you. There's a certain amount of risk involved if we expose Caterine this way," Paul said. "But if we plan it properly and Caterine does exactly as she's asked, it just might work."

Remi snorted. "Now there's a perfect example of how this could go wrong, expecting Caterine to do as she's told."

Caterine gave Remi a strained smile. "If I feel what I've been asked to do seems both sensible and logical, I'm more than happy to comply."

Again Remi snorted. "Is that so, Princess? You'd damn well better this time, because your life is going to depend on it."

Miss Dauphine cleared her throat. "Raymond, I haven't heard your opinion."

Ray stood staring down at Magazine Street. "Grandmère, I empathize with Caterine wanting to see an end to this. On the other hand, I understand Remi's concern for her safety. I suppose if Caterine is willing to put herself in danger, the least we can do is help her catch this person, no matter who it turns out to be."

Caterine stood and went over to Ray and placed her hand on his arm. "I know what you're thinking and what you fear. What if this person we're after turns out to be your twin brother? I know it wasn't Randal who held that gun to my back that night, and if it turns out that he hired that man, then we'll try to make sure he receives the help he needs."

Ray turned, sorrow filling his eyes. "And if it's Charlotte? Then what?"

"Then we'll try to get her help as well."

Miss Dauphine got to her feet. "Caterine, if you're sure you wish to go through with this idea, and Paul and Mr. Michaud come up with a plan which will minimize the danger, I agree that we need to put an end to this. I expect to be kept informed of the final decision. Raymond, I wish to speak with you privately. I'll send Thomas home with my car and you can escort me home in yours."

"Grandmère, I'll be back at Ma Chérie tomorrow morning," Caterine said. "So you need not come in."

Remi gritted his teeth. "What are you talking about now, Caterine?"

"If we're going to let it be known I'm back in New Orleans, what better way than for me to show up at Ma Chérie? And before you list all your objections, hear me out. You can take me to work and pick me up. I promise I will not leave the store for any reason. There isn't a better way to let my family know I'm back and planning to attend the ball than by way of Aunt Frances and Aunt Hyacinth. Besides, wouldn't you think it will take a couple of days for my attacker to be notified and their own plans made?"

Remi scowled. "What if you're left alone in the store?"

"Mr. Michaud, if it will make you more at ease with Caterine coming into Ma Chérie tomorrow, I can assure you I will be there as well and will not leave her side," Miss Dauphine said.

"That certainly eases my mind," Remi mumbled under his breath as Caterine walked Ray and her grandmother to the door. "Then if they get their shit together quickly enough, they can kill both of you at the same time."

Chapter Thirty-One

"It seems we have four days to decide on how we're going to catch a killer while keeping Caterine safe," Paul said once he and Remi were alone in his office.

"Make that three days," Remi corrected. "I promised Caterine I'd take her to my family's crawfish boil on Saturday."

Paul smiled. "And you don't want to disappoint the lady."

"She told me she's never eaten fried catfish or been to a crawfish boil."

Paul shrugged. "That doesn't surprise me. She wouldn't have ever been exposed to that type of food."

"She lit up like a Mardi Gras parade when I told her I'd take her. And I wouldn't want to disappoint her. So we'd better get to work. I'll call my cousin and see if he has Caterine's car. If so, I'll go over there and dust it for prints."

"Okay, while you're doing that I'll call Vince and see how many additional men we can line up. Since this is going down on Mardi Gras night, it's going to be damn near impossible to get a lot of help."

"I hear you. That's why I'm not only going to my family crawfish boil to make Caterine happy, I'm going to recruit as many of my relatives as I can."

"Then the bastard isn't going to know what hit him."

Remi laughed. "That's the plan. While you've got Vince on the phone, give him the information we have on Charlotte's candyman."

While Paul made his call, Remi placed his own to his cousin and had just ended his conversation when Caterine walked back into the office.

"Who was that?" Caterine asked as she dropped down into a chair and sighed. "What a day."

"That was my cousin, Antoine. He's got your car, and I told him I'd be right over."

Caterine frowned.

"What's wrong?"

"I'd forgotten about the car. I was hoping we could pick up something to eat and go home. I'm afraid between Ray's revelations and the unexpected arrival of Grandmère, I'm feeling mentally exhausted."

"You don't have to go with me. We can get something to eat and I'll drop you off at home."

"That's okay, I'll go. Someone is going to have to drive my car back to your place."

Remi shook his head. "Your car is too easily recognized. It's one thing if your family knows you're back. I don't want them knowing where you're living. I'm sure Antoine won't mind if we leave your car parked there for the time being."

Caterine yawned. "All right, let's eat. Then you can drop me off. I need to see what clothing I have to wear to work tomorrow." She smiled. "Grandmère wouldn't appreciate me arriving in one of my 'Caterine-in-disguise' outfits."

Remi grinned. "I like you in T-shirts and jeans, Princess."

Caterine knitted her brows. "That reminds me, Remi, what should I wear to your family party on Saturday?"

"Trust me, this is not a fancy affair. You look fine the way you are right now."

Caterine shook her head. "I can't meet your family dressed this way." She paused. "I could get Elaine to bring me some things."

Remi shrugged. "Whatever, Princess." He turned his attention to Paul, who had just hung up the phone.

"Vince says he and Andre could help us out Mardi Gras night. And he'll see who else he can get. I told him you'd be stopping by to pick up the things you'll need to fingerprint Caterine's car. I also filled him in on what we learned from Ray."

"What's his opinion of using Caterine to try and draw them out?"

Paul shrugged. "About the same as yours and mine. It's chancy, but it might work."

"Chancy is right. Crazy is what it is. All right, Caterine and I are going to take off. I'll call you if I get anything from the car. What time do you want to meet tomorrow?"

"I have a security installation job scheduled in the morning. I'll go over there long enough to make sure my guys know what I want done, then I'll be back. Let's meet around ten o'clock."

Remi nodded. "I'll be here."

"Where're your wig and glasses, Caterine?" Remi asked as they got into his car.

"In my bag. I thought since Caterine Doucette is going to resurface tomorrow, I wouldn't need them anymore."

"I suppose." Remi pulled away from the curb. "Where do you want to eat?"

"Let's go to the Chartres House. It's close to the apartment, it's casual, and the food is good."

"Sounds perfect. I could really use a beer."

"Tell me about it. I know my family has always been about as wacky as you can get, but this latest stuff from Charlotte and Randal is too much. I suppose Randal isn't totally to blame for the mess he's in, but Charlotte getting hooked on cocaine?" She shook her head. "I mean, she can have pretty much anything she wants, so why mess around with drugs?"

"Boredom, I suppose. Has she ever had a job?"

"Charlotte work? You've got to be kidding." A bakery sign caught her eye as they drove past. "Remi, you haven't said what we're supposed to take to the party on Saturday."

"What?"

"Your family's party, what should we bring? I've never been to that type of gathering, but I would assume everyone is expected to take some type of dish to contribute. Or am I wrong?"

Remi shrugged. "I've never paid any attention." He smiled. "The food appears and I eat it."

"Well, it doesn't appear out of nowhere. People must help out. I can't imagine your mother cooks it all herself."

"I'm sure she wouldn't expect you to bring anything."

"Does she know I'm coming with you?"

"I haven't mentioned it."

"You can't just take me without informing your mother."

"Why not? It will be fine. Don't worry about it. I told you this is an informal party. People come and go all day long."

"That may be, but I'm not going unless you tell her I'm coming and we bring something."

"Oh, for Christ's sake." They'd stopped to let a tour group cross the street, and Remi reached for his cell phone. "Hello, Maman. *Comment ça va?*" He paused. "Yeah, I'm coming on Saturday, and I'm bringing someone with me." He paused again. "A girl." Another pause. "Her name is Caterine." A longer pause followed. "I've got to go, Maman. I'll see you on Saturday."

"What did she say?" Caterine asked.

"She said she was looking forward to meeting you."

"She said more than that."

Remi gritted his teeth. "Caterine, you're making me crazy. I'm telling you that's all she said. And if it will make you feel better, bake a cake or something."

"Fine, I'll bake a cake." Digging around in her bag, she came up with her cell phone.

Remi watched as she scrolled down her phone list until she came to the number she wanted. She waited as the phone on the other end rang.

"Who are you calling?" Remi asked.

"Gambino's Bakery." Then she spoke into the phone. "Hello, Anice. This is Caterine. How are you? I'm fine, thanks. I was wondering if I can get a large chocolate and lemon Doberge cake by this Saturday morning?" She turned to Remi. "What time are we leaving on Saturday?"

They were parked in front of the restaurant, and Remi couldn't keep the irritation from his voice. "Around nine or so, I guess."

"Thanks a lot, Anice. I'll be there at nine thirty. Also, if you need to get in touch with me, please call my cell number." Caterine ended the call and dropped the phone back into her bag. She turned to Remi and frowned at the angry look he gave her. "What's wrong?"

"Who were you talking to?"

"The bakery my family uses for parties. Why?"

"Do they exclusively bake for your family?"

"Of course not."

"It's Mardi Gras, Caterine. Did you ever consider they might be busy with other orders?"

Speechless, she stared. "What is this all about?"

"It's about Caterine Doucette deciding she wants a cake, so Caterine Doucette makes a call and gets her cake. No matter if it's going to inconvenience the person who has to bake the damn cake. You want it, and your family are good customers, so some poor bastard will work his ass off to get you what you want."

When her face filled with hurt and confusion, Remi sighed in exasperation. "Oh, for Christ's sake, forget it." He opened the car door. "Come on, let's go in. I'm thirsty and hungry."

Caterine sat, her eyes filling with tears and her hands balled into fists.

"Are you coming?" He got out and slammed the car door. He watched through the window as she pulled her phone from her bag. Remi flung open the door. "What are you doing?"

"I'm canceling the cake order."

"Give me that." He reached inside the car and grabbed the phone out of her hands. "Caterine, just leave it alone. If you want to order a cake, then order a cake. It's not a big deal."

"Evidently it *is* a big deal to set you off like that and for you to tell me what an inconsiderate, unfeeling, spoiled brat I am."

He let out a long breath. "Caterine, I'm sorry. I'm just cranked over everything that's happened today, and I'm not used to being able to ask for anything I want and have it magically appear. That's all."

"Then I'll call Anice back and ask her if my order will cause her to become backed up on other orders, and if she says yes, I'll cancel the order and make the cake myself."

He smiled. "Have you ever baked a cake, Princess?"

She narrowed her eyes. "Go to hell."

His smile widened. "That's the second time today you've told me to go to hell."

"Then why are you still here?"

"Oh, I'm sure I'll get there soon enough, *cher*. No reason to rush it. Now let's go eat. I smell crawfish étouffée."

Caterine got out of the car. "Remi, give me my phone back."

He ignored her and put the phone in his pocket. "Not until after you've simmered down. I don't trust you not to go into the bathroom and cancel the order."

She stood on the sidewalk, hands on her hips. "You know what? I don't know how you have the gall to stand there and criticize me for asking for what I want when you have to be the most demanding person I've ever met. If you don't get exactly what you want, you either hound a person until they give in or you pout like a little boy until you get your way."

Remi scowled. "I don't pout, Caterine. And I'm not going to stand out here on the street arguing with you. I'm going into the restaurant. If you're coming with me, then let this go and come on. Otherwise, wait in the damn car." He hadn't taken two steps when he heard a male voice behind him.

"Why, hello, Caterine. It's great to see you, but I almost didn't recognize you in that outfit. N-not that there's anything wrong with y-your outfit," the voice stammered. "You always look great in whatever you wear."

Remi turned to see a tall blond man around his own age standing close to Caterine, grinning at her.

"Hello, Travis. It's nice to see you as well. How have you been?"

"Fine, Caterine. I'm staying busy. And you?"

"I've been pretty busy as well. Travis, let me introduce you to my friend, Remi Michaud. Remi, this is Travis Jenkins."

As Remi shook hands, he studied the man's face. The blush that spread across his cheeks told Remi the man's only threat was having the hots for Caterine. "How ya doin'?" Remi asked.

"Fine, it's nice to meet you," Travis replied.

"Travis, I've noticed a number of the blue tarps are beginning to disappear from the roofs. Are you still with your father's construction company?" Caterine asked.

"Ah, yes. I'm still working with my dad and, ah, some others. The reconstruction work is moving right along."

"That's great to hear. I was beginning to wonder if anyone cared whether

New Orleans ever got rebuilt. I know Doucette Shipping was bringing in large quantities of building supplies. Perhaps they're also doing business with your father's firm?"

"Um, well, I'm not sure about that. I'd have to ask my dad."

She scares the poor guy shitless, Remi thought, watching Travis look everywhere but at Caterine.

"Well, Travis, it was nice seeing you again. Remi's hungry, so we'd better go in."

"Oh, yes, sure thing, sorry. I didn't mean to keep you. Take care of yourself, Caterine."

"Travis, before you go, I heard something that I'm curious about."

"Oh, really, what is that?"

"I heard you were with Paulette at the Hallowell party. Is that true?"

Travis' demeanor went from flustered to thunderous in a matter of seconds.

"Where did you hear that?"

Caterine hesitated. "I'm not sure. Travis, I'm sorry. I didn't mean to upset you."

He took a deep breath. "No, Caterine, it's me who should apologize. I did run into Paulette at the party, but by no means was I *with* her. Take care of yourself. It was good seeing you."

Caterine stood open-mouthed watching as, without a backward glance, Travis strode away.

"What on earth?" Caterine turned to Remi. "I knew there was some kind of problem between him and Paulette, but did you see his face? If I didn't know him better, I'd say he looked downright murderous."

Chapter Thirty-Two

"I still can't get over the change in Travis when I mentioned Paulette," Caterine said as her fried shrimp was placed in front of her. "I'd love to know what happened between those two."

"Whatever it was, he's definitely not over it," Remi said before digging into his crawfish étouffée. "I do know you make the poor guy a nervous wreck."

She frowned. "What are you talking about?"

"Didn't you notice he could hardly look you in the eyes, and he kept stumbling over his words?"

"But that's Travis. Every time I've been around him that's the way he acts."

"Did he act that way around Paulette?"

She knitted her brows. "Now that you mention it, I don't think he did."

"Face it, Princess. The guy has the serious hots for you."

"Oh, for heaven's sake, I hardly think so. He's just shy around me for some reason. Perhaps it's because he doesn't know me that well."

Remi snorted. "Yeah, well, whatever you say. Eat up. It's getting late and I want to get over to Antoine's and check out your car."

"Hey, Remi, where y'at?" Antoine asked when Remi walked into the garage office.

"Awright, Toine, how about you? You keepin' outta trouble?"

Antoine chuckled. "I'm trying, *cher*. I'm trying."

Remi snorted. "That's not what I'm hearing. I heard a pissed off Suzette caught your ass where it shouldn't have been."

"Yeah, well, the woman acts more like a wife than a girlfriend." He gave Remi a conspiratorial grin. "But I used my considerable Michaud charm and *sweet* Suzette has forgiven me. Since we're talking about girlfriends, how'd you manage to get a girl rich enough to live in Audubon Place to give your sorry ass a second glance?"

Remi smiled. "You ain't the only Michaud who's got the killer charm. Now, how about showing me where you've parked the lady's car."

"You said you wanted it out of sight, so I closed it up in the first bay." He came out from around the counter. "So what's the story with the lady and her car?"

As they walked, Remi filled him in on Caterine's situation.

"No shit, someone in her family is after her over ownership of some dress shop?"

"It's a little more than just a dress shop, but that's what it seems her family is attempting to do. And now Paul and I have the job of not only keeping Caterine safe, but also finding out who hired her attacker." Remi explained the plan to bring Caterine's assassin out in the open at the Doucette Mardi Gras ball. "So I'm going to be needing some help."

"You can count me in. I'd love the chance to catch the *salaud*. Besides, if she's your girl, she's now part of the family, and the Michauds take care of their own. Will you be at the boil on Saturday?"

He nodded. "I'm bringing Caterine."

"Well then, I'm sure you'll be able to recruit others to help."

Remi smiled. "That's what I'm counting on."

Antoine cocked his head. "The lady must be something special for you to be going to all this trouble. I can't wait to meet her."

"Yeah, well, you can meet the lady and that better be all. Don't make me have to kick the shit out of you for coming on to my girl."

Antoine snorted. "I'm not worried about you kicking my ass. It's a pissed off Suzette who scares the shit out of me."

"That's what you need, Toine, a woman who keeps your ass in line."

"Yeah, well, look who's talking. Does the lady who drives this Mercedes keep your ass in line?"

"She tries, *cher*, she tries." Remi began to examine the car. "So tell me, in your professional opinion, what's the quickest and easiest way to put a car out of commission?"

Antoine rubbed his chin. "On newer models like this, that isn't as easily done as it used to be."

"Really? Why?"

"Because the engine isn't as easily accessible."

"Well, someone got to it somehow."

"Wait a minute. Let me finish. I said it was difficult, not impossible. But the engine isn't what was tampered with. My guess is the car was tased."

"What the hell is that supposed to mean?"

"You were a cop. What do you think it means?"

Remi shook his head. "You telling me this car was hit with a Taser?"

Antoine nodded. "That's exactly what I'm saying. I'll have to take a closer look, but I'll bet you a twelve-pack I'm right."

"I'm not crazy enough to take that bet. You're the car expert, not me. So, saying you're right, how exactly does that work?"

"Easy, hit any metal part of the car and it will short circuit all of the electrical components."

Remi let out a long whistle. "No shit. How common do you think this knowledge is?"

He shrugged. "Since I'm in the business of repairing cars, not destroying them, I have no idea. But I'll bet one of your buddies on the NOPD could tell you."

"How long before you'll know for sure that's what happened?"

Antoine smiled. "If you hadn't threatened me with bodily harm for getting my prints on the car, I'd have already known."

"It's all yours. Let me see if I get some prints from around the door and hood and I'll let you get to it."

"I'll let you know what I find out tomorrow."

"Thanks, Toine. I owe you one."

Antoine grinned. "Just make sure to remind Suzette what a great catch I am."

Remi chuckled. "Yeah, right."

When Remi arrived back at his apartment, he found Caterine sorting through a mound of clothes piled on the bed.

"You and Elaine didn't waste any time. What'd she do, empty out her closet?"

Caterine jumped at the sound of his voice. "For goodness sakes, Remi, you startled me. I didn't hear you come in."

"Sorry." He came farther into the room. "Where are we going to put all this?"

"I'm not keeping them all. I'm just going to pick out something to wear on Saturday. I haven't the slightest idea what one wears to a crawfish boil, so Elaine brought me a selection."

"Princess, I told you most people will be in jeans and T-shirts. Will you please stop worrying? Now if you clear off the bed so we can get into it, I'll tell you what I found out about your car."

She smiled and stepped from his arms. "I think you had better tell me first. I'm afraid if you wait until we're in the bed, I'm not going to learn anything that has to do with my car."

He grinned. "How right you are. Okay, you clear and I'll talk."

"A Taser?" Caterine exclaimed in disbelief after Remi had explained what Antoine had told him. "Someone hit my car with a Taser?"

He nodded. "That's what Antoine believes. We'll know for sure tomorrow."

"What kind of damage are we talking about?"

"A lot. If this is true, your car is toast. No pun intended."

Her eyes filled with tears. "Damn them all to hell. First they come after me, and now my car."

"Hey, Princess, I'm sorry. I didn't know the car meant that much to you. Come here." He took her into his arms. "Don't cry. I don't know that much about cars, but Antoine does. Perhaps I was wrong and it can be fixed."

"I . . . want . . . that . . . bastard . . . caught, Remi. Do you hear me?" She gasped out each word. "I don't care what you have to do. Find him."

He lifted her tear-streaked face from his dampened shirt. "Okay, stop crying. I promise I'll do as you ask." He bent his head and kissed her until her tears stopped flowing.

Chapter Thirty-Three

"I'm still not comfortable with this," Remi said as he parked in front of Ma Chérie early Friday morning.

"It will be fine. We're here well before anyone else, so they won't see you drop me off. I promise I won't leave until you come back to pick me up. I want to be in my office when my aunts arrive so I can gauge their reaction to seeing me. Besides, I had to come in early to find something to wear."

"And you couldn't use anything from all that stuff Elaine brought over?"

"Elaine didn't send over anything designed by Ma Chérie. I can't work with clients and not be wearing one of our own creations."

He scowled. "Well, excuse the hell out of me for being so ignorant."

"You really aren't a morning person, are you? Why don't you go get some coffee and a couple of beignets? That should improve your mood." She opened the car door and stepped out onto the sidewalk. An unexpected wave of fear washed over her as she stood once again on the spot where the attack had taken place.

When she grabbed for the open car door, Remi got out and came around to where she stood.

"Caterine, what's wrong? You're white as a sheet. Here let me help you." He guided her away from the car.

"I'm okay. For a minute, I relived the night of the attack. I didn't realize coming here would affect me this way."

"It's understandable that you'd be rattled. What happened to you that night isn't something you'll forget quickly. Come on, I'm going in with you."

She shook her head. "You don't have to do that. I'm fine now." She knew by the stubborn set of his jaw that he wasn't going to leave until he had her safe inside. Resigned, she led him to the front door. "Wouldn't it be just my luck if my aunts changed the code on me?" Laughing lightly, she punched in the sequence of numbers and sighed as the lock clicked.

"Where is your office?" He followed her in, closing the door and resetting the alarm.

She pointed toward the back of the shop. "I'll show you."

"Wait a minute." He placed a restraining hand on her arm. "Let me check around out here first." Satisfied all seemed as it should, he motioned for her to follow behind him as he made his way to the rear of the store.

When it was clear no one else was there, he turned. "When do your aunts normally get here?"

"Not until nine o'clock. I have plenty of time to go through the auction clothes to find something to wear."

"Auction clothes? What are those?"

"Clothes clients order and, for one reason or another, decide they no longer want. Each year Aunt Hyacinth gathers them and holds an exclusive fashion show and auction. All the proceeds go to charity."

Remi lifted his brows. "That sounds like a very generous thing to do, not to mention a lot of hard work."

She snorted. "Trust me, Hyacinth doesn't do it because it's a kind and generous thing to do. She does it because of the notoriety it brings her." Caterine glanced at the clock on her desk. "And you'd better get going so I can get changed. Before the others get here, I want to go through the orders Grandmère received in my absence. I'll call you when everyone has left and you can come back and get me."

Remi moved to where she stood behind her desk. "You look awfully professional and sexy standing here in your office, Princess."

"Remi, what are you doing?"

A wicked grin spread across his face as he lifted her onto the desk, positioning himself between her parted legs. "We're about to do something

I'm sure proper businesswoman  Caterine Doucette never imagined would happen on her fancy antique desk."

At nine o'clock sharp, Caterine heard her aunts' unmistakable voices as they entered Ma Chérie's front door. Nervously she paused in front of a cheval mirror and straightened the cranberry silk pinstriped jacket and smoothed out the matching skirt. *Okay, here you go. Remember, as far as they're concerned, you've just returned from a business trip. Pay close attention to their reactions when they see you.* She hadn't taken two steps out into the short hall when Aunt Hyacinth's words stopped her in her tracks.

"I'm telling you, Frances, it was Caterine that Paulette saw standing in front of the Chartres House looking like a dirty street person in the company of some rough-looking guy. We only have Miss Dauphine's word that Caterine's been away on business. What if that's not true? What if the prospect of owning Ma Chérie and all that entails sent her over the edge? Perhaps she's had some kind of breakdown and she's run away and doesn't know who she is, and Miss Dauphine is trying to cover the whole thing up. Frances, do you realize what this could mean if it's true? Caterine can't run Ma Chérie if she's crazy. Miss Dauphine won't have any choice but to turn control over to Charlotte."

"For heaven's sake, Hyacinth, take a breath," Frances said. "If it was Caterine, and I doubt it was, I can guarantee you that taking over Ma Chérie wouldn't cause her to have a breakdown. Miss Dauphine has been training her since she was old enough to walk through the store's front door. I'm sure she's been away on business, as Miss Dauphine said."

"But what if you're wrong and it was Caterine," Hyacinth insisted. "What's she doing dressed like a bum, in the company of some nasty looking biker? Or perhaps Caterine has a double life," she continued excitedly. "And when she's not being proper Caterine, she runs around with a bunch of trashy people."

"Really, Hyacinth. Can you actually imagine Caterine not only filthy but dressed like a bum? She may have her faults, but not dressing stylishly isn't one of them. As far as I can tell, Caterine doesn't have much of a single life, let alone a double one. No, Hyacinth, whoever Paulette saw, it couldn't have been Caterine."

"Aunt Frances is right, Aunt Hyacinth. It wasn't me," Caterine said, coming out of the hallway.

Hyacinth threw her arms in the air and let out a piercing scream.

"For God's sake, Caterine, what's the meaning of this? You've about given us both heart attacks," Frances scolded. "Have you now taken to eavesdropping? And why are you wearing that suit?"

Hyacinth pointed an accusing finger. "It's one of mine for the auction. She's stealing it!"

"It's rather difficult to steal from oneself." She came farther into the room. "Now, what's all this about Paulette seeing me with a . . . what did you call him, Aunt Hyacinth, *a nasty looking biker*?"

Frances gave a dismissive wave. "Obviously Paulette was mistaken. When did you get back?"

"I arrived late last night."

Frances knitted her brows. "That's odd. I didn't see your lights on in the carriage house either last night or this morning."

"As I said, it was late when I got in, and I wanted to get caught up on my paperwork, so I came to work early."

Hyacinth narrowed her eyes. "How did you get here? Charlotte told us a towing company took your car away yesterday."

"Someone vandalized my car to the point it may not be repairable so I had to call a cab." Caterine watched their faces, but neither showed anything but surprise.

"That's disgraceful. You can't even park your car on Royal Street anymore without someone vandalizing it," Frances said with disgust.

"It wasn't parked on Royal when it happened. It was parked at home, outside the carriage house."

"What?" Hyacinth gasped. "When did this happen?"

"Right before I left town."

"That's impossible, Caterine," Frances said. "No one could have gotten back to where your car is parked, tampered with it, and not been seen. Audubon Place has a security gate, and the grounds of the house are surrounded by tall shrubbery."

"Impossible or not, it happened," Caterine replied.

"What's not impossible?" Miss Dauphine asked.

The three women turned as one as Miss Dauphine strolled into the room.

"My car being tampered with while it was parked in front of the carriage house." Caterine kissed her grandmother's cheek. "It's good to see you, Grandmère. It was late when I got in last night and I didn't want to wake you."

"It's good to see you as well, my dear. How did your trip go?"

"It was very successful. I'll fill you in later."

"That will be fine. Now back to the subject you were discussing when I came in. What is this about your car?" She listened while Caterine explained, then nodded decisively. "Lately, I have been concerned about the security of the house and grounds, so I've called Paul LaBeau and requested he go over the house, inside and out, and let me know what he recommends. In fact, he and his partner were arriving as I was leaving."

Hyacinth frowned. "But Miss Dauphine, the security system we have now seems to work fine. Why replace it?"

"Because it's probably out of date. A criminal might find the house an easy target."

Hyacinth's voice rose. "But the party is on Tuesday. We can't have the mess of a new system being installed right now."

Miss Dauphine's mouth thinned into a straight line. "Really, Hyacinth, is it necessary to speak in that most unpleasant manner? I promise you, Paul and his men won't interfere with your party arrangements. Now, Caterine, I wish to hear about your trip." Without a backward glance she swept from the room.

Hyacinth's lips formed the word *bitch* before her eyes met Caterine's. With a defiant glare, she turned her back on Caterine and headed toward the coffee alcove with Frances right on her heels.

"Come in and close the door, Caterine." Miss Dauphine took the seat behind the desk.

Caterine couldn't stop the blush that stained her cheeks at the thought of what had happened on that desk earlier.

"Are you all right, my dear?"

"Ah, yes, ma'am, I'm fine. Hyacinth just makes me so angry sometimes."

"The woman has the brains of a goose. Now have a seat and I'll tell you the latest news. As you heard, Paul and Mr. Michaud are at the house planning where the security should be placed the night of the party."

"That was clever having Paul pretend to install a new system."

"It's no pretense. He's been instructed to do just that. After leaving Paul's office yesterday, I got to thinking about their plan and wondered how I could be of the most assistance. So late last night I called Paul, and we spoke for quite a while. Paul is the one who suggested upgrading the house's security, and I agreed."

"And he can have it done in time for the party?"

"I'm not sure he'll have everything installed, but he promised me the important items will be."

"Such as?"

"Hidden surveillance cameras, for one."

"But, Grandmère, if anyone in the family sees him installing hidden cameras, it will tip our hand."

"That's why they're working this morning. The house should be empty for most of the day. Now, what is this about your car?"

Caterine explained Antoine's theory then related the conversation she'd overheard between Frances and Hyacinth. "I can't wait to tell Remi he was described as a nasty biker."

Miss Dauphine smiled. "I imagine Mr. Michaud will find that rather amusing. But what happened to your car is most distressing."

"I know. I loved that car."

"I'm not talking about the loss of your car being distressing, Caterine. It was only a car, which can be replaced. What disturbs me is the thought of some criminal skulking around outside the house. I always thought the shrubbery surrounding the grounds was not only useful for privacy, but a form of security as well. Obviously I was mistaken. I intend on notifying Audubon Place security of the vandalism to your car. Now for our next problem. I'm wondering if we should be concerned over Paulette seeing you yesterday, although I suppose since you've made your presence known now, it doesn't really matter."

"Probably not. I'm surprised Paulette didn't also mention seeing me talking with Travis Jenkins. She must have driven by seconds before he showed up."

"Caterine, what on earth are you talking about?"

"I'm sorry. I haven't told you about the peculiar encounter I had with Travis Jenkins."

Miss Dauphine sighed when Caterine was done. "I don't know what happened between those two. But if I had to guess, I'd say Travis figured out what a spiteful, spoiled brat Paulette is and called the wedding off while he still could."

"If you're right, it's really too bad for Paulette. Travis seems to be a really nice guy who would have been good for her."

"I suppose we'll never know the truth. Now, is there anything else I need to know about?"

Caterine hesitated. "Only that Remi's taking me to his family's crawfish boil tomorrow and I'm a nervous wreck."

"For heaven's sake, why are you nervous?"

"I've never been to a large family gathering like that, especially with people whose lifestyle is so foreign to me. What if I do or say something inappropriate?"

Caterine was surprised at the annoyance that flashed in her grandmother's eyes. "Caterine, whether one is attending a gala ball or a crawfish boil, proper decorum, etiquette, and graciousness are always appropriate behavior. I've never known you to be lacking in any of these. Conduct yourself in the manner in which you've been taught and you'll do fine."

"Yes, ma'am."

"Well, what do you think?" Paul asked as he and Remi concluded their tour of the Doucette mansion, ending with the spacious third-floor ballroom.

"I think we've got us a lot of work to do in a short amount of time. And I sure as hell shouldn't be taking tomorrow off to go to a crawfish boil."

Paul rubbed his chin in thought. "You're right about the work, but wrong about taking tomorrow off. You need to go and recruit help. I say we begin working on securing the ballroom first. We'll get the surveillance cameras installed in here and outside on the gallery."

Remi nodded. "Sounds good. Let's get at it. How long did Miss Dauphine tell you she thought we had until people started coming home?"

"Most of the day. It's Charlotte, Randal, and Markus I'm concerned about."

"I wonder if Ray could help us out by keeping them away?"

Paul smiled. "Good idea. I'll call him right now."

While Paul talked to Ray, Remi walked the ballroom's perimeter. *Just this one room is bigger than the house I grew up in,* he thought, reality again hitting him in the heart like a fist. *What made me think I could take Caterine from this world and expect her to get used to living in mine? Well, tomorrow she'll see for herself where I come from and the kind of lifestyle I'm used to and comfortable in. So, Remi old boy, you may not have to worry about how you're going to let the lady go. She'll probably run away from you on her own.*

Paul interrupted his thoughts. "It's all taken care of. Ray is going to call a special Doucette family board meeting."

Remi grinned. "That should keep them busy for most of the night."

Paul grinned back. "And punish them for bad behavior as well."

"Right on, *cher.*"

"Okay, let's get busy."

"When Caterine calls, I'll have to leave and go take her home, but I'll come right back."

"I could ask Elaine if she could go get her."

Remi snorted. "Don't you remember what happened the last time we left them on their own?"

"But Elaine will have the boys. They can't get into too much trouble with a three-year-old and a five-year-old along."

"It won't be too dangerous for Elaine and the boys?"

Paul shook his head. "Until this morning, no one knew Caterine was back in town. Besides, they're not going to try and hit Caterine in broad daylight with witnesses."

Remi hesitated. "You're probably right, and it would save time if I didn't have to leave."

"I'll call Elaine and make sure she doesn't have plans. If not, I'll tell her to let Caterine know she'll be picking her up."

"All right, but tell her to call us when she and Caterine are safely in the apartment. I won't relax until we hear from them."

Chapter Thirty-Four

"Here we are safe and sound." Elaine ushered the boys into Remi's apartment behind Caterine.

"Yes, believe it or not, we managed to get ourselves all the way from Royal to Toulouse without mishap." Caterine sat down and kicked off her shoes. "Elaine, you'd better call Paul before Remi has the NOPD over here checking on us."

"Aunt Caterine, do you have juice boxes?" five-year-old Spencer asked.

"And animal crackers?" three-year-old Mark added.

"Why no, boys, I'm sorry. I don't," Caterine said. "I have some orange juice. Would that be okay?"

"I have juice boxes and crackers here in my bag," Elaine said. "Would you boys like to go sit on the balcony and drink your juice and have a snack?"

"Yes," was their unanimous reply.

As Caterine watched Elaine get the boys settled, a powerful yearning to have her own children overwhelmed her, surprising her with its intensity. Shaking her head clear of the mental picture of herself holding Remi's baby, Caterine went into the kitchen to see what there was to eat.

"Okay, they're enjoying watching some guy painted copper doing baseball poses," Elaine said, coming into the kitchen.

"Have you called Paul yet?"

"No, why?"

"Find out if they're going to be late. If so, why don't you and the boys stay and we'll order pizza."

Elaine smiled. "That sounds great. The boys would love that."

"Too bad the Pizza Kitchen doesn't deliver. Their pizza is the best."

"I could go pick it up."

Caterine frowned. "I'd love to say the heck with it and we all go over there and eat, but Remi would have a fit. I don't want him mad at me when we're going to his family's tomorrow."

"Before we make any decisions, let me call them."

"Mom, come see. Now he's juggling baseballs." Excited voices came from the balcony.

"I'll go," Caterine said. "You call Paul."

"What's so funny?" Elaine asked as she came out onto the balcony.

"Aunt Caterine gave us quarters, and the copper man is catching them," Mark shouted as Spencer tossed another coin.

Elaine peered over the railing. "You two thank the copper man for putting on such a nice show for you. Then he can be on his way, and we can order pizza. How does that sound?"

"I take it Paul said they'd be late?" Caterine asked.

"Yes, they want to keep working as long as they can. So I told him we'd have pizza then I'd take the boys home."

"Great, you call in the order while I go change. After we eat, you can help me narrow down my choices of what to wear tomorrow."

With the boys happily watching Nickelodeon, Caterine took Elaine into the bedroom where clothes were spread across the bed.

"Caterine, I don't understand why you're making such a project out of this. It's just going to be like a picnic."

"I know, but I'm going to be meeting all of his family. I'm not sure they know who I am, but if they do, I don't want to come across looking like some snooty rich girl."

Elaine laughed. "You are a rich girl, and you couldn't look snooty if you tried. Just be yourself and you'll do fine."

Caterine moved clothes out of the way to sit on the edge of the bed and sighed. "I know I'm overreacting to this, but believe it or not this is the first time a guy has taken me home to meet his family."

"What are you talking about? Over the years you've met lots of guys' parents."

"Not any I didn't already know from school or social events. You and I have been brought up in a select circle where our families have known each other for decades. We're raised to know what to expect at social events and how we're expected to act. I'm afraid I'm going to do or say something foolish. What if I just don't fit in?"

As a tear trickled down Caterine's cheek, Elaine sat next to her and took her hand. "I'm sorry, Cat. I didn't realize how much this meant to you. Listen to me. You couldn't possibly do anything to embarrass Remi. As I said, be yourself. These people aren't from another planet. They just may party differently than we're used to. But I'll bet Remi's family will be a lot more fun than some of those parties our parents dragged us to." She squeezed Caterine's hand. "Now I know there's more to this than you're telling me. So what else is bothering you?"

Unable to reply, Caterine brushed at her tears.

"Oh God, Cat, you've really fallen in love with him, haven't you? That's why this means so much, isn't it?"

Caterine bent her head and nodded.

Elaine let out a long breath. "Have you told him you love him?"

She nodded. "Once."

"And?"

"And nothing. He held me and kissed me, but never told me that he loved me. Every time I try to tell him how I feel, he stops me."

Elaine frowned. "Stops you how?"

Caterine cleared her throat. "Well, he . . ."

"Oh, don't you see? That's his way of telling you he loves you. Some men have a hard time saying the words, so they show you instead."

Caterine brightened. "Do you really think so?"

Elaine nodded vigorously. "He went to you the minute he heard you were in trouble. He has you living here with him. He's willing to take on your family to find a killer in order to make you safe. How can you even question whether he's in love with you?"

"Well, when you put it that way, maybe you're right."

"I know I'm right. Give him some time. You have to admit your relationship right now isn't exactly normal."

Caterine laughed and gave Elaine a hug. "Oh, thank you. I knew you would make me feel better."

"Now, stop worrying about tomorrow. Go and have a good time, and call me as soon as you can. I'll be dying to hear all about it."

"Mom, Spencer is changing the channel."

Elaine sighed. "I'm sorry. They're getting tired and cranky. I'll have to take them home."

"That's fine." Caterine stood and gave Elaine another hug. "Thanks again for bringing the clothes and listening to my paranoia. Now I'd better get these off the bed before Remi gets home. He also gets cranky when he needs to go to bed."

"What do you think about this one?" Caterine asked the next morning, coming out on the balcony where Remi sat smoking impatiently.

"That looks as good as the other five or ten outfits you've had on. But if we don't leave soon, it won't matter what you wear because the party will be over."

"I don't want to look out of place."

Stubbing out his cigarette, his eyes traveled from her white, scooped-neck peasant blouse to her black and white plaid, knee-length skirt, and down to her black sandals. He smiled. "Princess, you'll be the prettiest girl there. Now, can we leave?"

"I can't believe how nervous I am. What if they don't like me?"

Remi gritted his teeth. "Caterine, trust me. They'll like you." Putting his arm around her shoulder, he guided her toward the door.

With the Doberge cake stowed safely in the trunk and Waylon Thibodeaux playing on the CD, Remi had the T-bird's top down so they could enjoy the mild February morning air. As they drove along Highway 90 toward Bayou Petit Caillou, Caterine felt happier than she had in a long time. Glancing at Remi, she smiled. *Who would have ever thought a man in a black T-shirt and snug faded jeans could be so sexy.*

"You keep staring at me like that, *cher*, and I'll have to pull off the road." He ran his hand up her leg under her skirt. "What do you have on under there, Princess?"

"That's none of your business." She playfully batted his hand away. "Just pay attention to your driving."

"I'd rather pay attention to you."

"You should probably pay attention to your speed and that police car behind you before you get a ticket."

Remi looked into the rearview mirror and grinned, increasing his speed.

"What are you doing?" Caterine shouted as the wind whipped her hair. "Remi, slow this car down!" She gasped as the police car sped past, the driver flipping Remi off as he flew by.

"I take it you know that officer?"

Remi slowed to a safer speed. "My Uncle Sosa. He must be on his way to the boil."

"Exactly how many of your relatives will be there today?"

He shrugged. "It's hard to say. If they're not working, they'll be there."

"Are the majority of them police officers?"

"No. We have everything from cops to fishermen to mechanics to bar owners to general store owners to swamp boat guides."

Caterine's eyes grew wide. "What, no firemen?"

"Oh yeah, there's a couple of those as well, including my brother, John."

"What about the women?"

"Homemakers, a nurse, an accountant, waitresses, a librarian, a singer, and one dental hygienist."

She grinned. "That's quite a combination."

"That it is." He glided onto exit 182 toward Houmas.

"I wish I had an interesting family, instead of the dysfunctional group I'm stuck with."

He reached over and squeezed her hand. "As long as you're with me, you can call the Michauds, Thibodeauxs, and Robicheauxs your family."

Caterine laughed. "I'd love to. Do you have many relatives on your grandmother Annabelle's side?"

He shook his head. "Those that are left moved up north. We sometimes see them at Christmas."

A motorcycle going in the opposite direction reminded Caterine she hadn't told Remi about the description of them Paulette had given Hyacinth. Chuckling to herself, she turned toward him. "Remi, there's something I forgot to tell you."

She repeated the conversation she had overheard from the hallway.

"She said what?"

"She said I looked like a bum and you were a rough, nasty biker type." She couldn't see the expression in his eyes behind his Ray-Bans, but his lips were twitching.

"Is that right? Well, *cher*, after this is all over, we'll have to borrow my brother's Harley and fulfill Paulette's fantasy." He slowed, pulling into the gravel lot of Thibodeaux's General Store.

"Why are we stopping here?"

"Getting beer. What do you want to drink?"

"I don't know. Wine, I guess."

Remi grinned. "Cecil isn't going to have anything that doesn't have a screw top."

"Then get me some soda or something."

"I'll be back."

As she waited in the car, she took in her surroundings. A stenciled wooden sign above the store reading *Gas-Ice-Bait-Beer* was flanked by two round, red Coca-Cola signs. The store itself, with its corrugated metal roof, weathered wood, and front porch with railings, fit in perfectly with the rural surroundings. The bayou channel bordered the lots along the east side of the highway. Flat marshland spread off to the other horizon. A hand-painted sign advertised Thibodeaux's swamp boat tours.

They're probably all members of Remi's family, Caterine thought, batting a mosquito away. She watched as Remi and a middle-aged woman came out on the store's front porch and headed toward the car.

"Caterine, I'd like you to meet my cousin, Diane Thibodeaux. Diane, this is Caterine Doucette." Remi placed a paper bag and a couple of six-packs of Turbodog in the backseat.

Diane smiled and held out her hand. "Hello. Welcome to Terrebonne Parrish."

The warm, friendly smile Diane gave Caterine helped calm her unease. "Thank you. It's nice to meet you."

"So Remi's going to introduce you to a Michaud family gathering? You've got guts to meet them all at once. Just don't let them overwhelm you. They're loud and have a tendency to all talk at the same time, but they're a lot of fun."

Caterine laughed. "Thanks, I'll remember that. Are you coming?"

"Later on. My husband and I are taking turns going over until we close the store. Then we'll both be there."

Remi slid into the driver's seat. "We'll try and save you some mudbugs."

Diane stepped away from the car. "You'd better, or no more family discount for you."

A few minutes after leaving the store, Caterine asked, "I take it we're almost there?"

"Just around the bend."

"Ah, Remi, what exactly is a mudbug?"

"You don't know what a mudbug is?"

She shook her head.

"They're the same as a crawfish or crawdad. Down here some of us call them mudbugs. I suppose you don't know the proper way to eat one either?"

Again she shook her head.

Remi grinned mischievously. "It's easy, *cher*. You twist the tail and suck the head 'til the eyes go clear."

Chapter Thirty-Five

Still laughing at her horrified expression, Remi parked the car behind a line of pickup trucks, cars, and motorcycles.

As they approached the house, Caterine stared in amazement. She'd attended parties, gala openings, and fund-raisers where there had been hundreds of people, but all those events had seemed well-ordered compared to the sight she now beheld. A sea of constantly moving bodies spread out in noisy waves of mass confusion: adults, young and old; running, playing children of all ages; and friendly barking dogs. They flowed across the lawn, up the steps to the house, and down to the dock and the stand of mature black willows that screened the bayou.

Like islands in this seething mass of humanity, there were large pots of boiling water set on charcoal fires. Long trestle tables spread with white paper and coolers of soda and beer rested in the shade of water oaks. Horseshoes were being pitched, and a croquet game was in progress. A hand-built stage held musicians tuning their instruments.

They received greetings of "Hey, Remi where y'at?", "Whoo-ee, Remi, how'd you manage to get a pretty girl like that?", "Remi, where you been keeping yourself?", "Remi, who's the pretty lady?", and "Remi, when we going fishing, *cher*?" as they tried to make their way through the crowd to the stairs and the wide, screened porch.

After stopping to acknowledge each greeting and for Remi to introduce

Caterine, they finally reached the screened door to the porch. Caterine's mouth dropped open at the tables laden with food spread out before her.

"Remi, there you are, *cher*. I was beginning to wonder if you'd changed your mind about coming."

Caterine watched as a smiling plump woman in a snowy white apron, her dark hair pulled back in a bun, rushed out of the house onto the porch and hugged Remi.

"Hey, Maman, how you doin'? I told you I'd be here." Remi bent to kiss her cheek. "Besides, we're not that late. Maman, I'd like you to meet—"

"Miss Doucette!" screamed a female voice, breaking into Remi's introduction.

Caterine blushed to the roots of her hair as everyone standing within hearing distance stopped what they were doing and stared.

Remi's mother turned horrified eyes toward her daughter. "Mary, Mother of God, Yvette, what's wrong with you, screaming at a guest like that? You apologize this minute."

Caterine wasn't sure whose face was redder, hers or Yvette's.

Yvette swallowed hard and stammered, "I-I apologize for my r-rudeness, Miss Doucette." Then, without hesitation, her words rushed out. "I was so excited to see you standing there. I couldn't believe my eyes! You are actually here. I didn't know you knew Remi."

Yvette's words halted as quickly as they'd begun. Once again, all eyes turned to Caterine, but before she could form a reply, Remi calmly spoke. "Yvette, she didn't tell you she knew me because she didn't."

Caterine couldn't help but smile. "Hello, Yvette. It's nice to see you again. Your brother's right. When you and I spoke, he and I hadn't met."

Yvette bit her lower lip, then said, "Miss Doucette, I have an entire book of designs. Would you like to see them?"

"That's enough, Yvette. Caterine is here as our guest. She's not to be bothered with your drawings," her mother scolded.

Caterine's heart went out to Yvette at the dejected look that came over her face. "Please, Mrs. Michaud, it's okay. Yvette, I'd love to see your drawings. And please call me Caterine."

Yvette lit up like a Fourth of July sparkler. "I'll go get them."

"Yvette, no, you won't. If Caterine is kind enough to look at your drawings, she can do so after she's had a chance to meet everyone and has had something to eat. Now, leave our guest alone and make yourself useful by taking this beautiful cake she's brought and set it out on the dessert table. Again, my apologies for this rude welcome. As you've guessed, I'm Remi's maman, Annette. Welcome to our home."

"Thank you, ma'am. Please don't apologize. Yvette's welcome was extremely flattering."

"Hello, Caterine. I'm Remi's normal sister, Chloe." Chloe was as petite as Yvette was tall, and as fair as Yvette was dark.

Caterine smiled. "Hello, it's nice to meet you."

"And I'm Remi's handsome brother, John, who would be more than happy to take you away from Remi if you'd only let me."

Caterine laughed. "Thanks, but for now I'll stay with Remi."

John sighed. "I figured as much, but I had to try."

"You know what, little brother? You can go get the beer and wine coolers out of my car and get them iced down." Remi pushed John toward the porch door. "And you can forget you've ever met Caterine."

"Hello there, young lady. I'm Remi's daddy, Samuel, but everyone calls me Sammy. Come with me and I'll take you away from all this craziness. There's someone here who's been waiting to see you."

Caterine smiled up into dancing brown eyes in a round, friendly face topped by sparse gray hair. She allowed Sammy to take her by the elbow and guide her off the porch and across the lawn to where a strikingly pretty older woman in a huge straw hat sat in the shade of a large live oak draped with Spanish moss.

"Mother, may I present Miss Caterine Doucette? Caterine, this is my mother, Miss Annabelle Michaud."

Caterine smiled and took the older woman's hand. "I'm pleased to see you again, ma'am."

"I'm pleased to see you as well, Caterine. Why, you were only a girl the last time I saw you. Please sit and visit with me for a while. Sammy, I believe Caterine and I could each use a glass of lemonade."

"I'd be happy to get that for you two lovely ladies. I'll be right back."

Caterine sighed with relief as she sat in the chair next to Annabelle.

Annabelle's deep blue eyes twinkled with amusement. "They can all be rather overwhelming, can't they?"

Caterine smiled. "Yes, ma'am. Remi tried to warn me, but I must say his description didn't come close."

Annabelle's laugh was light and girlish. "I don't suppose anything can prepare one for meeting this family for the first time. Now tell me, how is Miss Dauphine? It's been quite a while since I've seen her. We were inseparable at school and college, but once we both married and began having families, well, we became busy with our lives. She was living there in New Orleans and I was down this way at Willows, my family's plantation. You can't imagine my delight when she called to tell me you'd be coming with Remi."

Caterine couldn't hide her surprise at learning that her grandmother had spoken with Annabelle. "Why, Grandmère is doing well, thank you. She didn't tell me she'd called you."

Annabelle studied Caterine's face before speaking. "Child, even though your grandmère and I haven't spoken lately doesn't mean there still isn't a close friendship between us. She not only called to tell me you were coming, she explained to me what's been happening with you, Remi, your family, and Ma Chérie."

"She told you *everything*?"

"Yes, my dear, and I offered to have you come stay with me at Willows." She pursed her lips. "I have to say, Caterine, I agree with Miss Dauphine regarding your current living arrangements. I love Remi dearly, but he is a man. I know she and I sound like two old fuddy-duddies but as the saying goes, 'why buy the cow when you can get the milk for free?' "

The shock on Caterine's face had Annabelle laughing out loud.

"You two sound as if you're getting along just fine," Sammy said, handing them each a glass of cold lemonade. "I've just been challenged by John to a game of horseshoes. For some reason he's convinced he can beat me. I have to go and set the boy straight."

Caterine looked toward the horseshoe pits and smiled at John, who was waving at her.

"I didn't mean to shock or embarrass you, my dear," Annabelle continued after Sammy had left. "Your grandmother and I just have your best interest at heart."

Caterine hesitated, not wanting to sound ungrateful. "I appreciate both your and Grandmère's concern, ma'am, but due to the unusual circumstances of our relationship, Remi and I feel the safest place for me is with him. And I wouldn't want to put you in any danger by staying with you, but thank you for the offer."

"Offer of what?" Remi asked, kissing his grandmother's cheek before popping the top on a beer and sitting on the grass next to Caterine's chair. "So what have you two been talking about?"

"I've been telling Caterine about my conversation with Miss Dauphine," Annabelle replied, "and my offer to have Caterine come stay with me at Willows. Caterine was saying that she feels safer living in New Orleans with you."

"You've spoken with Miss Dauphine?" Remi asked in surprise.

"Yes, we had a nice long chat. In fact, I'm considering attending the Doucette Mardi Gras ball. I haven't been to one in years, and it would be lovely to see Dauphine again."

"I'm sure she'd enjoy that, Pet."

Annabelle smiled. "I believe I'll speak to your father about driving me up tomorrow. I'll get a room at the Royal Orleans. Then I can visit Ma Chérie and Miss Dauphine on Monday. Now, I believe I'll go get some of that wonderful-smelling food. Caterine, it was lovely visiting with you. I'm sure I'll see you again before you leave."

Remi watched with narrowed eyes as his grandmother hurried off. "Damn it to hell. All I need is both our grandmothers interfering with our plans."

"They're both concerned about our living arrangement," Caterine explained.

Remi snorted. "Is that right? Well, I like our 'living arrangement' just fine."

"What was that you called Annabelle?"

"What? Oh, *Pet*. It's what we've all called her since we were kids. She refused to be called grandma, and she thought grandmother was too stuffy."

"She really is sweet, Remi."

"Yeah, well, she needs to stay out of our business." Standing, he crushed his beer can. "So are you ready to try some mudbugs?"

"Oh, Remi, I don't know."

He took her hand. "Come on, Princess. I'll show you the right way to eat them. If you don't like it, there're plenty of other things to eat."

Reluctantly she allowed him to take her to one of the tables where mounds of steamed crawfish lay in trays.

"He finally going to feed you, *cher*?" asked a handsome man sitting at the table with a pretty redhead.

"Caterine, this funny guy is my cousin, Antoine, and his girlfriend, Suzette."

"Antoine, are you the mechanic who looked at my car?" Caterine asked.

"That I am."

"Do you know if it can be fixed?"

Antoine hesitated before answering. "I don't think so. It was fried pretty bad, but you could have your own mechanic check it out."

She tried not to let her disappointment show. "Well, thank you for trying."

Antoine cocked his head. "How do you feel about classic cars?"

"I've never really thought about it. Why?"

"Because if I'm right, your insurance company will total that car, and I happen to have a two-seater Mercedes convertible for sale at the shop. I normally don't handle cars like that, but it belonged to a doctor friend of Chloe's, and she asked me to sell it for her. It's a sweet little car, with hardly any mileage and in great condition."

"Really? I'd love to see it."

Suzette scowled. "You didn't tell *me* about the car, Antoine."

He kissed her. "I wouldn't want you out driving around in a fancy car. Some rich guy might take you away from me."

Suzette seemed to be somewhat mollified, but Caterine was taken aback by the hard look she gave her. Tamping down her enthusiasm over the car, Caterine said, "Perhaps sometime next week Remi can bring me in to see it."

Antoine smiled. "Sure, any time."

Remi took a seat next to Caterine, handed her a wine cooler, and opened another beer for himself. Pulling a tray of mudbugs toward them, he said, "Okay, Princess, here's how it's done." He twisted the tail, yanking it away from the head, then pinched the base of the tail, squeezing out the tender meat. "See how easy it is?" Remi grinned at the dubious way she stared at the remaining heads. "Don't worry. You don't have to eat those."

Hesitantly she did as Remi instructed, then smiled in surprise. "This is very good."

"I told you. Here, have some more."

Suzette snorted. "I can't believe you've never had mudbugs, Caterine. Where are you from anyway?"

"Not everyone eats the same things, Suzette," Antoine said with exasperation. "Let's go see what kind of desserts Aunt Annette has hidden on the porch. Remi, bring Caterine in to look at that car."

Remi nodded.

"For some reason, I rub Suzette the wrong way. Did I say something I shouldn't have?" Caterine asked.

"No, and don't worry about it. Antoine's been caught more than once where he shouldn't have been, and Suzette's leery of any pretty new face. Have you had your fill of mudbugs? If not, there's all kinds of other food up on the porch. If you stop eating, Maman will think you don't like her cookin'."

"Actually, the red beans and rice looked awfully good, and so did the potato salad, and those creamed beans, and I'd like another one of these." She waggled the wine cooler.

Remi laughed. "Where you gonna put all that food?"

Caterine shrugged. "All of a sudden, I'm starving."

"Okay, you go get your food and I'll get your wine cooler."

As Caterine made her way across the grass, watching all the activity around her, she didn't notice the little girl until she came crashing into her legs. Startled, Caterine looked down to see a smiling face streaked with strawberry ice cream looking up at her. Caterine bent down and smiled back. "Well, hello. What's your name?"

The girl, whom Caterine guessed to be around two, just giggled.

"Bridget, where are you?" Caterine heard a voice call.

"I have a feeling that's you." Caterine stood to see where the voice was coming from. She spotted Remi's sister with an identical little girl in her arms and called, "She's over here, Chloe."

"Thanks, Caterine. She got away from me while I was cleaning up Britney," Chloe said.

"They're adorable. How old are they?"

"Almost two, and they're a handful."

"Can I help?"

Chloe smiled. "If you wouldn't mind holding Britney while I clean Bridget's face, I'd appreciate it."

Caterine took the little girl, who immediately grabbed for the silver hoops in her ears.

"Is your husband here?"

"No. I'm divorced."

"Oh, I'm sorry, I . . ."

"It's okay. You had no way of knowing."

"It must be tough raising the girls on your own."

"Yes, but I'd rather do that than deal with a husband who's a lying, cheating asshole."

Okay, time to change the subject, Caterine thought.

"Do you and the girls live close by?"

"Not too far. I'm an RN. I work at the hospital in Houmas. There, now they're both presentable again." Chloe released Bridget and took Britney from Caterine. "So are you enjoying yourself?"

"Yes, very much, thank you. I was on my way to the porch and more food."

Chloe smiled. "Maman will love to hear that. She's not happy unless everyone is so stuffed they can't move."

"I've never seen so much food. Did your mother do all of the cooking?"

Chloe rolled her eyes. "She used to but, thank God, she lets others help out now. You have no idea what it was like having to help prepare all those dishes. That's probably why Yvette hates to cook."

"I'm the opposite. I was never allowed to cook, so I want to learn."

Chloe laughed. "Don't let my mother hear you say that. Trust me, you'll regret it. So tell me, have you and Remi known each other long?"

Caterine shook her head. "Only a few weeks. I met him at a friend's costume ball."

"Oh, so you live in New Orleans?"

Caterine hesitated. Not wanting to go into details, she nodded.

Remi walked up and handed Caterine a wine cooler. "Hey there, squirt." Grabbing one of the twins, Remi tossed her in the air.

Amid her sister's squeals of delight, the other twin yelled, "Me, too, Emi."

Chloe grinned at her brother. "He's great with kids. He'll make a great father someday."

Caterine's heart filled as she watched Remi tossing first one then the other little girl. "I'm sure he will."

Curiosity showed clearly in Chloe's eyes as she looked from Caterine to Remi.

She's wondering how serious our relationship is. Well, Chloe, so am I. Aloud Caterine said, "I love children. There aren't any in my family, so I enjoy my friend's two boys."

"So you'd like to have kids of your own?" Chloe asked.

Caterine smiled. "Oh yes."

After eating more food than she could ever remember eating in her life, Caterine sat contentedly with Remi, listening as a new group of musicians tuned their instruments.

"Are they all members of your family as well?"

"Most of them. Some are family friends."

"Hey, Remi, come on. You do the first number with us," called an older man from the makeshift stage.

Caterine was surprised when Remi stood. "You can sing?"

Giving her a smug smile, he walked toward the stage.

"He thinks he can," John said, sitting in the spot Remi had vacated.

"You're just jealous, John, because Remi can and you can't," Yvette said, sitting on Caterine's other side.

Caterine smiled with delight when Remi strapped on a guitar and began to sing and play.

"Do you know what he's saying?" John asked.

Caterine smiled. "Only about half of it, but he sounds great."

John winked. "He's singing you a love song."

"No kidding? I'll have to have him translate it to me later."

"I've never heard him sing this to anyone before." Yvette gave Caterine a wide smile. "It's called 'Madame Sosthene.' "

Caterine could feel her cheeks turn pink as all eyes seemed to be on her and Remi.

"Can you dance to this?" John asked as the band switched to a lively two-step.

Caterine eagerly nodded.

"Then let's go."

They stomped and clapped along with the crowd as they twirled their way around the grassy dance floor. She was out of breath and laughing by the time Remi took her from his brother's arms.

"You've had enough, little bro. She's mine now."

Caterine, feeling happier than she ever had, smiled up into Remi's eyes. Wrapping her arms around his neck, she kissed him. "You are a sexy singer. Did you know that? Your sister told me you were singing a love song to me, and I having a wonderful time."

Laughing, he kissed the top of her head and held her tight as they swayed to the music. "I'm glad you're enjoying yourself, Princess."

"Oh yes, Remi. Thank you so much for bringing me. Your family is terrific."

"I'm sure they think you're pretty terrific yourself, especially Yvette, who's sitting over there with a rather large book on her lap looking like she's sitting on a mound of fire ants. I'm going to leave you with her while I take care of some business. All right?"

Caterine nodded.

"You ever been on a swamp boat?"

"No. Why?"

A mischievous glint came into Remi's eyes as he smiled. "After I've finished with my business, I'll take you for a ride."

Chapter Thirty-Six

Remi sat Caterine next to Yvette, then gathered a select few of his male relatives and ushered them onto the dock. There he privately explained Caterine's situation and asked for their assistance at the Doucette Mardi Gras ball. Waiting for their responses, he leaned against a post and lit a cigarette.

"You'd better not let Maman see you smoking that," John said. "She'll kick your ass."

Remi snorted. "Yeah, well, it's a good thing my maman doesn't see half the things I do."

"How exactly can we help?" Remi's cousin Cecil asked.

"I'll need someone to keep an eye on Caterine at all times and to look out for anyone acting out of the ordinary."

His Uncle Sosa grinned. "It's Mardi Gras. Everyone is acting out of the ordinary."

Remi smiled. "Acting suspiciously, then."

"Are you telling us we get to go to a fancy-ass ball, eat fancy food, and all we have to do is keep an eye on a pretty girl?" Antoine asked.

"That's it. Along with catching the *fils de putain* who's trying to kill her."

"Will she be wearing a wire?" Sosa asked.

"*Mais yeah,*" Remi replied. "I'll be the one listening on the other end."

"Will concealed weapons be required?" his Uncle Bernard asked.

Remi nodded. All humor left their faces.

"We're with you, *cher*. Tell us where to be and when," his cousin Philippe said.

Remi smiled. "Thanks. I knew I could count on all of you."

Antoine snorted. "You haven't heard our price yet, *cher*."

"Do you really mean it, Caterine?" Yvette exclaimed.

"Yes, I really mean it. You're very talented, and I'm sure we'll have a place for you at Ma Chérie. We need to appeal to young professionals, and your designs are exactly what I'm looking for."

"Oh, thank you, thank you!" Yvette threw her arms around Caterine's neck.

"For God's sake, Yvette, don't choke her," Remi said, stopping in front of the two women.

"Oh, Remi, I'm going to work at Ma Chérie!" Yvette squealed again, jumping up and throwing her arms around her brother. "I've got to tell Maman." Grabbing her design book, she gave Caterine one more hug before running off.

Remi watched her go, then turned to Caterine. "That was nice of you, but you didn't have to do that."

"I didn't do it to be nice. I did it because your sister is very talented and I could use her at Ma Chérie."

Remi smiled. "Okay. Now, Princess, are you ready for your swamp boat ride?"

Caterine stared at the unusual looking boat tethered to the dock. "I suppose, but are you sure you know how to drive that thing? I mean, aren't there snakes and alligators out there?"

"Princess, I've been driving that boat since I was big enough to reach the wheel. And yes, there're snakes and alligators out there, but we're not going swimming, just for a ride." Remi cocked his head at seeing her pensive expression. "Can you swim?"

"Yes, but I don't want to end up in that bayou."

"Unless you jump off, you're not going to end up in the bayou. Wait for me on the dock. I'll be right back."

Caterine stood at the end of the dock and studied the airboat with apprehension.

"Nice, isn't it?"

She turned to see Remi's Uncle Sosa standing behind her. "I've never seen one close up before. They're rather unusual, aren't they?"

Sosa shrugged. "I suppose they'd look strange to someone who wasn't used to being around them, but they're a part of life down here."

The flat-bottomed boat lay low in the water. Approximately fifteen feet long, it had a tilted bow. Behind a raised seat, an encaged motor with a large propeller was mounted at the stern.

"How fast can it go?"

Sosa smiled. "Remi taking you for a ride?"

Caterine nodded.

His smile widened. "Make sure you hang on, *cher*."

"Ignore him, Caterine." Remi stepped around Sosa to set a small cooler in the boat. "Here, give me your hand. I'll help you in."

Caterine hesitated, looking from Remi's outstretched hand to Sosa's grinning face and back to the boat.

Remi sighed. "It will be fine. Trust me."

She took a deep breath and held on to his hand, taking a seat in the middle of a padded bench.

Remi sat in front of the engine and motioned for Sosa to push them away from the dock. "Hang on, Princess," Remi called as the powerful engine propelled them out into the bayou.

Once Caterine realized she was perfectly safe and Remi wasn't going to dump them into the water, she relaxed and took in her surroundings. The open waterway narrowed as he slowly steered the boat into a channel. Tall cypress trees with their spiky knees stood along the banks of waving marsh grass. Turtles of every size sunned themselves on fallen logs. "Oh, Remi, look." Caterine pointed delightedly at a family of wood ducks as they bobbed in the gently moving water.

Her delight soon turned to unease as the snout of an alligator suddenly appeared alongside the boat. Happy to leave the reptile behind, her eyes opened wide as, rounding a bend, Remi steered the boat into a secluded cove.

He cut the engine and sat down next to her, opening the cooler he'd brought along. He handed her a wine cooler and popped the top on his beer.

"It's pretty here, isn't it?"

Caterine took in her surroundings and wondered how she was supposed to answer him. Pretty wasn't the word she'd use—spooky would be more like it. Thick, reedy marsh grass covered the banks. Tall cypress, oaks, and willows shaded the murky water of the cove.

"Ah, it's . . ."

Remi laughed. "I take it you're not that impressed."

"I wouldn't say that. The landscape is certainly impressive. It's calling it pretty I have a problem with."

"You should see it in the spring when the water lilies are in bloom. See all those leaves floating in the water?" He pointed to hundreds of large green leaves. "The blossoms are all white, and their fragrance is incredible. We'll have to come back." He tossed his empty beer can in the cooler and took her still full wine cooler from her hand. "In the meantime, I want to do something I've been wanting to do all day." He took her in his arms and laid her back on the seat.

"What are you doing?"

"I'm going to see what you have on under this skirt."

"Remi, we can't. What if someone sees us?"

He laughed. "There's no one to see us except the gators, and I doubt they're interested."

"This bench isn't big enough for the two of us," she declared as he removed her sandals, then his sneakers.

"Watch and see. When this boat was built, my uncles made sure the seat would serve another purpose than just sitting." He lay on his side next to her.

She chuckled. "The Michaud men think of everything, don't they?"

"That we do, *ma jolie fille*, my pretty girl," he murmured as he rolled on top of her, covering her mouth with his.

As the leaf-filtered sun warmed their bodies, Caterine wrapped her arms around his neck and hungrily kissed him back.

Breathing hard, his eyes dark with need, Remi broke their kiss. "Honest to God, Caterine, I can't get enough of you. I haven't acted like this since I was eighteen years old. I brought you out here intending on taking my time making love to you, but you've got me ready to rip your clothes off."

Caterine smiled. "So who's stopping you? I've never made love outdoors.

It's kind of exciting."

"Oh, Princess, it hasn't begun to get exciting." He rolled off her and quickly removed his clothing.

"Now, let's see what you have on under here." As he raised her skirt, he slowly ran his hands up her legs, kissing her calf, her knees, and her inner thigh. He nearly lost his self-control when the hot pink thong she wore was revealed. "*Mon dieu,* Caterine, you're killing me." He licked the pale skin above the triangle of curls covering her sex. "And you taste sweeter than any honey." His mouth covered the slip of fabric nestled between her legs. His tongue found her sensitive nub beneath the silk. She cried his name as the sharp pleasure of her orgasm slammed through her.

He rose above her and eased off her thong, then her top. When her puckered nipples were revealed through the sheer silk of her strapless bra, he let out a groan of pure pleasure.

Unable to resist, he sucked and licked the hard buds through the silk.

"Remi, stop. I need you now," she whimpered, digging her fingers into his bare back as she writhed beneath him.

"Come for me again, Caterine." His mouth sucked harder, his fingers stroking the slick wetness between her thighs. Feeling her body tighten with the beginning of her release, he slid his hard shaft into her heat as the full intensity of her orgasm overtook her. "*Mais yeah, vien, ma jolie fille, vien,*" he murmured as she matched him stroke for stroke until, with his mouth on hers, he cried out with his own release.

As the boat rocked gently beneath them, they lay in satiated bliss until Caterine shattered the silence with a piercing scream.

"*Merde!*" he exclaimed, rolling off her, almost falling from the seat in his haste. "What the hell are you screaming about?"

Unable to speak, she pointed at the large black snake hanging in the tree above them.

"Damn it to hell, you about gave me a heart attack." He stood and reached for his jeans.

Caterine scrambled to her feet, also grabbing for her clothes. "Get me out of here, Remi. I hate snakes. What if it falls on us?"

"Hey, Princess, it's okay." He put his arms around her pulling her close. "Look, it's going away." He turned her so she could see the snake slithering down the tree on the other side. "Your scream must have scared the shit out of him as much as it did me."

Caterine exhaled and sat back on the bench. "I'm sorry, but I absolutely hate snakes of all kinds."

Remi smiled. "I got that." Pulling his shirt over his head, he sat down next to her to put his shoes back on. "Next time I make love to you outdoors, I'll make sure there aren't any trees."

Caterine snorted. "Who says there'll be a next time? And trees are okay. It's the snakes that live in them that I can do without."

Remi pulled her on his lap and kissed her soundly. "Trust me, Princess, there'll definitely be a next time. Now I'd better get us back before Maman sends out a search party."

"There you two are," Annette said as Remi and Caterine came through the door onto the screened porch. "What on earth have you done to this poor girl, Remi?"

"I took Caterine for a boat ride, Maman. She nearly jumped overboard when a little snake tried to join us."

Annette narrowed her eyes.

Caterine had a hard time following the rapid-fire exchange that ensued between mother and son, but from Annette's tone and the few words she did understand, Caterine decided Remi was getting chewed out over something.

Caterine excused herself to use the bathroom and made her way through the house in the direction Annette had indicated. She locked the door and turned, coming face-to-face with her reflection in the mirror. She closed her eyes and groaned. From her disheveled hair to her kiss-swollen mouth and her wrinkled skirt, there wasn't any doubt what she and Remi had been up to on that boat. *Caterine, you have no shame when it comes to that man.*

She tried her best to straighten her appearance. All she needed was to have Annabelle tell her grandmother about this. She glanced in the mirror one last time and left the security of the bathroom. On her way back through the living room, she spotted a group of family photos sitting on a table. She paused and smiled at the many pictures of Remi as a small boy.

"He was as ornery as a child as he is as a man," Annabelle said from behind her.

Cringing inside, Caterine turned. "He's still just as cute as well."

Annabelle's twinkling eyes gazed into Caterine's. "He's a good boy who has a wild streak, like his grandpapa." Annabelle pointed to a wedding picture sitting on the mantle.

Caterine stepped closer and gasped.

"The resemblance is quite something, isn't it?"

Caterine nodded. "It's amazing. Except for the clothing, he could be mistaken for Remi."

A tender smile crossed Annabelle's face. "When I told my parents I was going to marry Rex Michaud, my papa got madder than I'd ever seen him. He threatened to send me up north to boarding school. In order to keep the peace, I agreed not to marry until after college. I know my parents thought by then my attraction for Rex would have waned and I'd have met someone they considered more appropriate. I loved Rex Michaud from the time I was sixteen years old until the day I lost him sixty-five years later. Remi just needs someone to love him that much and he'll settle down, just like his grandfather did."

"I love him that much, Miss Annabelle," Caterine blurted. Shocked at her outburst, she clamped her hand over her mouth.

Annabelle smiled and patted her arm. "I know, child, and I believe he loves you as well. You two need to get through this mess with your family and everything else will fall into place."

Caterine sighed deeply. "I'm afraid Grandmère doesn't favor Remi and me having a future." Horrified at how that sounded, she hurried to clarify. "Not that she isn't fond of Remi—she is. I just don't think she feels he's the right one for me."

Annabelle gave an unladylike snort. "Your grandmère wouldn't have let anyone or anything come between her and Pierre Doucette, and don't let her tell you otherwise."

Caterine smiled. "Really?"

Annabelle took Caterine by the arm, and they headed toward the porch. "Yes, really. Her papa wasn't in favor of that match either, but don't tell her I told you so."

Night was beginning to fall as they stepped onto the screened porch. Caterine could tell by the increased volume on the lawn that the party had taken on a rowdier tone.

"Remi's down there singing again," said Chloe, a sleeping twin in each arm.

"Caterine, he's not in any condition to be driving home," Annette said with annoyance. "You're more than welcome to stay the night."

"Thank you, ma'am, but I can drive if he'll let me."

Annette frowned. "I should have put that boy over my knee more often, then maybe he'd have better manners."

Chloe looked at Caterine and rolled her eyes.

"You didn't put *any* of us over your knee, Maman," Yvette reminded her.

"And that's what's wrong with all of you."

Caterine smiled. "I'm going to go see about Remi. I'll bring him up to say good night."

Remi was back on the makeshift stage, singing and playing his guitar. Caterine's eyes blazed and her hands closed into fists as she got closer. Dancing directly in front of Remi was a scantily clothed buxom girl making sure Remi saw every suggestive move she made, and Remi seemed to be enjoying every minute of it.

Caterine folded her arms, also making sure she stood in his line of vision. When his eyes finally left the girl's bouncing breasts and met her eyes, she motioned for him to come to her.

Remi nodded. As soon as the song was over, he handed his guitar to another man and jumped from the stage, only to be brought up short by the brunette.

Caterine watched in mounting rage as the girl threw her arms around Remi's neck and kissed him soundly.

"She's a real slut, isn't she? She's been after Remi for years."

Caterine turned to face Antoine's girlfriend, Suzette.

Not waiting for her to respond, Suzette continued, "I'll warn you now, Caterine, you can't trust any Michaud men. I've learned that the hard way. If I were you, I'd go over there and slap the shit out of both Remi and the slut."

Caterine thought she wouldn't mind doing exactly as Suzette suggested, but she knew her upbringing would never allow her to disgrace herself in public. Instead she smiled at Suzette, and waited to see what Remi would do next. To her relief, Remi gently but firmly pushed the girl away, said something to her that made her smile, and walked toward where she and

Suzette stood.

"What's up, *cher*? You ready to go?" he asked, as he put his arm around her. "Hey, Suzette, where's Antoine?"

"If he's anything like you, he's up to no good. Remember, Caterine, I warned you." Suzette gave Remi a disgusted look and walked off.

"What the hell was that about?"

"I believe it's time to leave, and I'm driving," Caterine said. "We need to go thank your parents and tell them goodbye."

Remi narrowed his eyes. "Caterine, what's got into you? Are you pissed off over Kathleen kissing me? If so, she's harmless. She's just had a little too much to drink."

She put her hands on her hips. "Remi, she's not the only one who's had too much to drink. So have you. I'm not getting in a car with you driving. So you have two choices. Either I drive or we spend the night here. It's your decision."

"You've been talking to my mother, haven't you?"

Not answering him, she held out her hand. "Give me the keys, Remi."

He gave her a defiant glare and opened his mouth to speak, then hesitated. He swore in Cajun, reached in his pocket, and handed her the keys. "You'd better be a damn good driver, Princess, because I don't want my car messed up."

Chapter Thirty-Seven

Caterine was awakened early Sunday morning by the ringing of her cell phone. Sleepily she answered, "Hello."

"Cat, it's Ray. Grandmère has fallen and is on her way to the emergency room in an ambulance."

All sleepiness gone, Caterine sat bolt upright in bed. "Ray, what happened? How did she fall?"

"She was leaving the house to go to Mass and tripped over the newspaper, which was tucked under the front door mat."

"What was the paper doing there?"

"Cat, I don't know. Perhaps the delivery kid put it there because it's raining and didn't want it to get wet."

Caterine turned toward the rain-streaked windows. "How badly is she hurt?"

"I'm not sure. She's got a nasty bump on her head, and it looks as if she may have broken her ankle."

"Who found her?"

"Thomas. He'd just pulled the car up when she came out of the house and fell."

"I'm on my way." She threw the blanket off and got out of bed. "Is the entire family going to the hospital?"

"I imagine. As you know, Hyacinth won't leave the house until she's looking perfect, and Charlotte isn't known for moving quickly in the morning. But I expect sooner or later they'll all show up."

"I'll be there as soon as I can."

"I'll meet you in the emergency room lobby," Ray said and hung up.

"What's going on?" Remi asked, now sitting on the side of the bed.

Caterine explained as she headed for the bathroom. "Will you drive me? If you'd rather not, I can take a cab."

"I'm driving you. I'll wait in the car until you find out how bad Miss Dauphine's hurt."

As they sat waiting at a light on South Claiborne, Caterine peered impatiently through the windshield. "Damn this rain, and why is there so much traffic out here on a Sunday morning?"

"Relax, we're almost to the hospital," Remi said. "I've been thinking about Miss Dauphine's fall, and I don't like it."

Caterine turned to face him. "What do you mean? She just tripped over the paper."

"Has the paper ever been put under the mat before?"

Caterine shrugged. "I don't know. I'm not the one who gets it off the porch. We'll have to ask Grandmère or Uncle Jules."

"Does Miss Dauphine always go to early Mass?"

"Usually."

"Does she normally go alone?"

"Yes. Everyone else goes later, if they go at all. Are you thinking someone intentionally put the paper there so Grandmère would trip?"

He shrugged. "I don't know. I feel we need to question anything out of the ordinary that happens to either you or Miss Dauphine."

"Well, that takes care of that. We're getting Grandmère out of that house. As soon as she's released from the hospital, I'm taking her to the Royal Orleans. She can stay there with Miss Annabelle."

"Wait a minute," Remi said. "I understand your concern, but logistically that doesn't make any sense. And before you argue with me, let me finish. First, Miss Dauphine will be more comfortable in her own home where people can take care of her."

"Such as the person who might have intentionally made her fall?"

"There're others in that house as well. What about the staff? Are they loyal to your grandmother?"

She nodded. "Yes, they've been with us for years."

"And what if I ask Pet to go stay with her? She wanted to come up anyway. This way she could keep Miss Dauphine company and, since she knows the situation, keep an eye on her as well."

"That's a great idea. Would she do it?"

He snorted. "Are you kidding? I'm sure she'd jump at the chance to not only help out Miss Dauphine but to get involved in all this as well, the prospect of which doesn't really thrill me."

"Oh, for heaven's sake, they're two old ladies. How much mischief can they get into?"

Remi laughed derisively. "Princess, I'd hate to imagine."

"Yes, well, it's still a good idea."

"I'll call while you're in the hospital. She can have either my father or John drive her up as soon as she's ready. Until we know more about Miss Dauphine's injuries, Pet can stay at the hotel. One other thing, Paul and a couple of his men were planning on working at the mansion today on the pretense of trying to finish before the party. I wasn't going to help him because I don't want to be seen by Charlotte, Randal, or Markus. If everyone will be at the hospital, I can go over and help. Can you get Ray to drive you back to the apartment?"

Caterine hesitated. "I'm sure he would, but I need to get some of my things from the carriage house, and it would be easier if I had my own car. We're going to be going by Paul's house. What if I drop you off there and I take the car? Paul can give you a ride home."

Remi scowled. "I let you drive my car last night because it was easier than arguing with you and my mother. I'm sure Ray wouldn't mind taking you by the carriage house."

"Oh, for heaven's sake, Remi, I drove your precious car just fine last night, but if you're so concerned just drop me off at the hospital, and I'll call for a rental car to be delivered to me there."

Remi scowled. "I need my car in case I have to leave your grandmother's house."

"Fine, I'll call the rental company."

"Caterine, I'll get you a damn car. What do you have to get at the carriage house that's so important?"

"I need to take my princess gown to Ma Chérie tomorrow so it can be repaired in time for the ball."

"What happened to your gown?"

She smiled. "A pirate tore it trying to get it off of me."

Caterine not only found Ray waiting in the emergency room lobby, Uncle Jules, Uncle Markus, and Aunt Frances were sitting there as well.

"Hello, Caterine." Her Uncle Jules rose and kissed her cheek. "I heard you were back in town."

"Yes, I got back Thursday night. Have you spoken to a doctor yet?"

"No. Mother is still in the examination room."

"Ray said she tripped over the paper. Is it normally put under the mat?"

Jules shook his head. "No, it most certainly is not. I'm usually out there in my bathrobe searching for the damn thing in the bushes. Now, come over and sit down here with us. Would you like me to get you a cup of coffee?"

"Thank you, but I can go get it."

Ray stood. "I'll come with you. I could use another cup myself."

Caterine waited until they'd reached the coffee machine before saying. "Ray, Remi and I are afraid Grandmère's fall wasn't an accident. We're going to ask someone to come and stay with her."

Ray looked into his empty coffee cup then back up at Caterine. The pain in his eyes had her blinking back sudden tears. "Ray, I'm so sorry. I know the thought of Randal or Charlotte intentionally hurting Grandmère has to be devastating to you. But there're others who live in that house who could have just as easily placed the paper under the mat."

"Like who, Caterine? One of my parents? Or how about Uncle Markus? Christ." He angrily tossed his cup into the trash. "I kept telling myself whoever was behind your attack had to be someone outside our family, but this certainly blows that idea all to shit, doesn't it?"

Caterine placed a hand on his arm. "Ray, we need to make sure Grandmère stays safe. Her old friend Annabelle Michaud happens to be Remi's grandmother. I met her again at a family function Remi took me to. She said she would be happy to come stay with Grandmère and help keep an eye on things in the house."

"How much did you tell her?"

"I didn't have to tell her anything; Grandmère had already taken care of that.”

His brows lifted. “You’re kidding, right? I can’t imagine Grandmère sharing our dirty family secrets with anyone.”

Caterine shrugged. “Well, she did. She probably felt Miss Annabelle was the one person she could trust. In fact, Annabelle said she’d been considering coming to the ball anyway.”

“How are we going to explain her suddenly appearing and staying at the house?”

“We’ll say she was going to visit Grandmère, heard about her accident, and thought she could be of help. I doubt anyone will be interested enough to question it.”

Ray nodded. “You’re probably right.”

“There’s one more thing. Remi is going over to help Paul at the house, and I still don’t have a car, so I may need you to take me to a car rental company.”

“Sure, no problem. Speaking of our family, I found out that for the ball my parents will be dressed as Robert E. Lee and his wife, Uncle Markus as Mark Twain, and Randal as a riverboat gambler.”

Caterine snorted. “How appropriate for him. He won’t need a costume.”

Ray smiled. “That’s what I told him. I’ll let you know as soon as I find out about Charlotte, Paulette, and Aunt Hyacinth.”

“Is Charlotte bringing that Rivette person?” Caterine asked as they headed back toward the hospital lobby.

Ray scowled. “She had better not. I told her I wouldn’t have that scum in the house. It’s incredible what a mess she’s managed to get herself into. I’m on her ass so bad over the coke that I’m not my sister's favorite person right now. I’ve already lined up a clinic in Switzerland for her to go to. She doesn’t know it yet, but she leaves next week. And if I have to handcuff her to me and take her there myself, that’s what I’m going to do.”

“Good for you, Ray. Hopefully someday Charlotte will realize you were only trying to help her. Look, the doctor is talking to Uncle Jules.” She hurried over. They arrived in time to hear the doctor say that Miss Dauphine had a slight concussion and they were taking her to have her hip and foot X-rayed.

As they stood with the doctor, Caterine’s cell phone rang. “Hello.”

“Randal, Charlotte, and some people I assume to be Paulette and her mother are heading toward the entrance," Remi said.

Caterine turned as the four came through the door. "Yes, that's right," she replied, moving away from the others.

"I'm going to go ahead and go to the house. I spoke to Paul, and he's already on his way over. Also, you'll have a car within the hour."

"Oh really? How's that?"

"Antoine's bringing you one."

Caterine sighed. "He didn't have to do that."

"It's all right. He doesn't live that far away, and he owes me for all the times I've gotten his ass out of trouble. He's going to call your cell when he gets here, and you can come out and get the keys."

"Okay, thank you. I'll call you when we learn anything more about Grandmère."

"I've also spoken with Pet. As I guessed, she's happy to come stay with Miss Dauphine. She's having John bring her, and she's going to check into the Royal Orleans until Miss Dauphine is released."

"Then I'll talk to you later."

"If for some reason I see you at the mansion, remember you don't know me, but I'm hoping to be out of there before anyone gets back."

Caterine ended the call and went to join the others in the waiting room. Taking a seat, she realized this was the first time she'd been with all of them since the attack.

Charlotte lifted one perfectly arched brow. "Well, if it isn't Caterine back from her mysterious trip."

"There wasn't anything mysterious about it, Charlotte. I was away on Ma Chérie business."

Charlotte smirked. "Oh, well, pardon the hell out of me."

Paulette gave Caterine a smug smile. "Since you haven't been staying in the carriage house, and your car was taken away, what I do find mysterious, Caterine, is where you've been living and who's been driving you around. Could it be your new biker boyfriend I saw you with?"

Determined not to let her anger show, Caterine stared without speaking until the smugness left Paulette's face. Then, in a voice sounding like Miss Dauphine at her haughtiest, she said, "I haven't the slightest idea what you're talking about, Paulette. Besides, where I'm staying and who I'm staying with isn't your or anyone else's business. And, speaking of my car, you wouldn't happen to know who damaged it beyond repair, would you?"

"Don't be absurd, Caterine," Charlotte said. "Why on earth would any of us know what happened to your car?"

"Because it had to have been tampered with while it was outside the carriage house. I find it hard to believe that out of all the cars parked at the house, someone would only target mine."

Paulette's face was flushed with anger. "I don't know anything about your damn car, but I do know you're a filthy little liar. I did see you dressed like a tramp, standing with some dirty Cajun."

"For heaven's sake, Paulette, lower your voice. We're in a public place," Hyacinth hissed, scanning the area for eavesdroppers.

Charlotte snorted. "Really, Paulette, Caterine wouldn't be so daring as to be seen with someone inappropriate. What if Grandmère were to see her? She might take Ma Chérie away from her."

"That's enough," Jules said. "I'm in no mood to listen to your bickering." He turned to Caterine. "What's this about your car?"

After Caterine had explained, Jules shook his head. "That's incredible. What can I do to help?"

Caterine smiled. "Thanks, but I have a friend bringing me a car."

"Really? Are we going to get a chance to meet your new boyfriend?" Paulette asked.

"No. I'm meeting the *mechanic* in the parking lot."

Charlotte's brows rose. "Is he so bad that you won't let us meet him?"

What a difference between the friendly family I was with yesterday and this school of piranhas I'm stuck with now, Caterine thought. Aloud she said, "Speaking of new boyfriends, Charlotte, I heard you've been seeing someone. Why haven't you brought him around? Or isn't he suitable? I understand he has quite a dubious reputation."

Charlotte gave Caterine an icy glare and mouthed, *Bitch.* "I'm going to the ladies'."

Hyacinth and Frances rose as well. "We'll join you."

As the women walked away, Caterine turned to see Randal closely studying her before he stood abruptly. "I'm going outside for a smoke."

Caterine's eyes met Ray's. Shrugging slightly, he followed Randal.

"Are those blue jeans you're wearing, Caterine?" Paulette asked.

She looked at her jean-clad legs, then opened her eyes wide. "Yes,

Paulette, I'd say they're blue jeans."

Paulette scrunched up her face in distaste. "Imagine that, Caterine Doucette in blue jeans, and cheap ones at that. Tell me, Caterine, are they part of your new persona? Does your boyfriend like it when you look cheap and tacky?"

Caterine cursed inwardly. She'd been in such a hurry to leave for the hospital she had just grabbed a pair of the jeans Elaine had bought for her. She made a mental note to collect more of her own clothes when she stopped by the carriage house. "I didn't realize you paid that much attention to what I wear, Paulette. How flattering."

When her cell phone rang, Caterine sighed with relief. Rising quickly, she headed for the door as she answered. "Yes, this is Caterine."

"Hey, *cher*, this is Antoine. I have a car for you."

"That's what I understand, but you didn't have to do this."

"No problem."

"Where are you?"

"Remi told me to stay out of sight, so I'm in the back of the visitors' lot."

"I'm on my way." Expecting to see Ray and Randal in the outdoor smoking section, Caterine was surprised to find the area empty. The rain had stopped, but the day was still gloomy. A misty fog now covered the parking lot. As she tried to spot Antoine, she could vaguely make out a figure waving in the distance. She waved back and quickened her steps. Halfway to where Antoine stood, she thought she heard a car engine accelerate.

"Caterine, watch out!" she heard Antoine yell, as she realized the car was behind her.

To Caterine, everything that followed took on a dreamlike quality—Antoine coming toward her through the mist; the car's roaring engine; the jolt of their bodies as Antoine slammed into her, hurling them to the ground between two parked cars; the sound of screeching tires as the car drove away; and Suzette's piercing screams.

"Motherfuck!" Antoine exclaimed. "Caterine, are you all right?"

She lay face down on the dirty, wet parking lot, gasping for breath with Antoine on top of her. "I don't know."

Antoine rolled off and helped her to her feet. He swore a string of Cajun as he stared in the direction the car had disappeared.

"Oh my God, are you two all right?" Suzette threw her arms around them both. "What the hell was wrong with that person? Didn't they see Caterine?"

"Suzette, could you tell what kind of car it was?" Antoine asked.

She shook her head. "I was so scared I closed my eyes."

"Remi is going to have my ass for this."

"What are you talking about, Antoine?" Caterine's teeth were chattering so badly she could hardly speak. "You saved my life."

"I should have been paying closer attention. I couldn't make out a damn thing about the car," Antoine said. He ran his eyes over Caterine. "Are you okay?"

"I think so, just a little scuffed up."

"No, Antoine, she isn't all right. Her arms and cheek are scraped, and she's shaking from head to toe. She needs to sit down," Suzette said. "Should we take her into the hospital?"

"No!" Caterine cried. "My family's in there. I don't want them to see me like this."

"Wait a minute, your family are all in there?" Antoine asked.

She nodded.

"Then we need to go see if anyone is missing because if they are, they just tried to run you down."

Caterine's voice broke on a sob. "Maybe it wasn't any of them. Maybe the driver just didn't see me."

Antoine laughed without humor. "Yeah, and come Christmas, I'm Papa Noel. Besides, if that were true, why didn't they stop?"

"I don't know." Caterine hugged herself, trying to control her shaking. "I can't believe they had the nerve to try and kill me right here in a public place."

Suzette looked from Caterine's stricken face to Antoine's angry glower and frowned. "I don't know what's going on, Caterine, but if you need me to go into the hospital with you, I will."

"There you go. Take Suzette and go find out if your family are where you left them."

Caterine took a deep breath and wiped the tears from her eyes. "Antoine's right, Suzette. I need to go in. And I would appreciate it if you'd go with me. Antoine, will you wait outside the door for us? I don't want my family to see you, but I'd like to know you're close."

"If that's what you want, I'll be there."

As she went back into the lobby, Caterine noted that only Uncle Jules, Uncle Markus, and Aunt Frances were still sitting in the waiting area. She walked over and stopped in front of them.

Frances gasped. "My God, Caterine, what's happened to you?"

She ignored her aunt and demanded, "Where's everyone else?"

"I don't know," Jules said. "They said something about getting coffee and perhaps something to eat." Concern filled his face as he stood and put his arm around her shoulders. "Darlin', what's happened to you?"

"I almost got hit by a car in the parking lot. This is my friend, Suzette. It was her boyfriend who saved me."

"Have Ray and Randal come back in?"

"We're right here, Cat. What's going on?" Ray stopped behind Caterine.

Without answering, she studied each man. "Where have you two been? You weren't out in the smoking area."

"I needed cigarettes, so we went to get some. Why?" Randal asked.

"Because a few minutes ago, I almost got run over in the parking lot, and I wondered if you'd seen anything."

Caterine watched as Ray's face paled and Randal looked surprised.

"No, we just got back. Do we need to call the police?" Ray asked.

She shook her head. "I'm not hurt, and the car is gone. I don't know for sure if the driver even saw me." The sound of heels clicking on the tile floor made her turn to see Charlotte, Paulette, and Hyacinth coming their way.

Charlotte was the first to speak. "Good grief, Caterine, what's happened to you? You look as if you've been rolling around in the dirt."

Caterine watched as Paulette studied Suzette from her curly red hair and tight blues festival T-shirt to her low-riding jeans. The disdain that filled Paulette's face had Caterine's temper rising. "Where have you three been?"

"In the cafeteria, if it's any of your business," Paulette replied. "Is this one of your new friends, Caterine?"

Caterine's back stiffened and her anger soared. "Yes, Paulette, Suzette is my friend. Do you have a problem with that?"

Paulette's eyes opened wide. "Temper, temper, Caterine. Why are you being so defensive? Is it because your little friend knows what you've become and what kind of trash you've been hanging around with?"

"Caterine, is this person related to you?" Suzette asked, giving Paulette a scornful look in return. "If so, I'm sorry, but she has to be one of the rudest people I've ever met."

Paulette's eyes flashed with anger. "Why you little—"

"That's enough, Paulette," Ray said. "Can't you see Caterine's hurt and upset?"

"Will you all be quiet," Hyacinth hissed. "You're bringing attention to yourselves."

"Aunt Hyacinth, someone almost ran me down in the parking lot. I'm really not concerned about people overhearing."

Charlotte rolled her eyes. "Oh really, Caterine. Always the drama queen."

Suzette opened her mouth to speak and Caterine shook her head. "It's not worth it."

"Thank God, here comes the doctor," Hyacinth said. "Perhaps now we can all get out of here."

"Miss Dauphine is a lucky lady," the doctor said. "There aren't any broken bones, just some bruising and a sprained ankle, but she does have a slight concussion. I'm going to keep her overnight for observation. They're taking her to a room, and as soon as they have her settled you can go see her."

"If Miss Dauphine isn't hurt badly, I don't see any reason we all have to go up. There are things I should be doing at home to get ready for the ball," Hyacinth said.

"I agree," Charlotte added. "I have things to do as well. Randal, will you drive us home?"

Randal shrugged. "If that's what y'all want to do."

"Well, Frances and I are staying until Mother gets settled," Jules said, his tone expressing displeasure at his family's mass exodus.

"I'm staying as well," Markus said. "How about you, Caterine?"

"I don't want Grandmère to see me in this condition. It might upset her, and she's already had enough for one day. Uncle Jules, please tell her I'll be back later this evening. Come on, Suzette, let's go." Caterine could feel her family's eyes boring into her back as she walked away.

"What a nasty bunch," Suzette said when they reached the pavement.

Caterine smiled without humor. "They're a far cry from Remi's nice normal family."

"Antoine can be a pain in my butt, but like the rest of the Michauds, he's good people."

"Speaking of Antoine, do you see him?"

"Over there." Suzette pointed to a cherry-red Mercedes parked not far away. "That's the car he brought you."

Caterine blinked back tears as she saw Antoine's grinning face. "Suzette, I don't want my family seeing me in that car. I'll call a cab. You two meet me at Remi's apartment."

"I had to follow Antoine, so you can drive his car. Here're the keys. The car is back there." Suzette pointed to the rear of the lot. "It's the black Mustang."

"Thanks." Caterine gave her a quick hug, then walking toward the car, called Remi's cell. "Remi, it's me. Get out of there. Some of them are on their way home."

"What's wrong? You sound funny. How's Miss Dauphine?"

"Grandmère isn't hurt badly, and I can't go into anything else right now. I'm taking Antoine and Suzette back to the apartment. Get there as soon as you can."

Caterine smiled for the first time that day as she sat behind the wheel of the two-seater Mercedes parked outside Remi's apartment. The rain had stopped and the sky had cleared, so with delight she had put the top down. "Oh, Antoine, I love it. Thank you for bringing it to me. I'll write you a check as soon as we go in."

"Wait a minute. You don't have to do that. I just brought it for you to use."

Caterine's face fell. "Isn't it still for sale?"

"Yes, but I don't want you to feel you have to buy it."

"Antoine, I *want* this car."

He smiled. "It's yours."

"Don't you even have to ask how much?" Suzette asked.

Caterine hesitated as she felt her cheeks turn pink. "I probably should, but you know how it is when you really want something."

"I hear you, but I usually can't afford to do that."

Caterine was surprised not to hear sarcasm in Suzette's voice, only admiration.

"Shit, here comes Remi," Antoine said, as the T-bird pulled in behind the Mercedes.

Caterine rolled her eyes. "Antoine, I can't believe you're afraid of Remi."

"You haven't seen that boy when he's really pissed. Trust me, it isn't pretty."

"You're looking awfully proud of yourself sitting there, Princess," Remi said, coming up next to the car.

"Isn't it great? I just bought it."

Remi and Antoine exchanged glances before Remi asked, "How you going to do that, *cher?*"

"I'm going to write Antoine a check. Give them the keys to the apartment and get in. I want to go for a ride."

"Wait a minute. What the hell happened to you?" Remi bent lower, examining her scraped face and dirt-streaked shirt.

"There was a slight accident at the hospital. Get in and I'll explain."

Remi turned to Antoine. "What's going on?"

Antoine shrugged. "I'll let Caterine tell you."

"I'm not going to like this, am I?"

"Nope."

"Shit." He handed Antoine the apartment keys and slid into the passenger seat.

"Hang on. I want to see what this car will do." Caterine accelerated up the ramp onto I-10.

"Christ, slow down." Remi grabbed onto the dashboard. "Don't think I can get you out of a speeding ticket."

"I'm alive," she said with a grin as the wind blew through her hair. "And I'm going to enjoy it."

"You won't be alive for long, and neither will I, if you don't slow this car down."

"Killjoy." She eased her foot from the accelerator and took an off-ramp, turned around, and headed back toward home. Once they were cruising at a normal speed, she explained. To her relief most of what Remi hollered was in Cajun.

"It had to be someone in your family," he yelled. "I can't believe they'd actually try and run you down where anyone could have seen them. Someone is very desperate or just crazy." He ran his fingers through his hair. "I'm telling you, this latest attempt has me even more convinced that exposing you at that ball is a really stupid idea. This person has proven they'll do anything to get to you."

Chapter Thirty-Eight

"For the last time, Remi, we're going through with it," Caterine said back in his apartment after Antoine and Suzette had gone.

"I'm telling you this is idiotic. All we're going to accomplish is getting you killed."

Caterine prayed for patience. "You told me you're going to have two NOPD officers, along with members of your family, stationed around the house. You and Paul have all the surveillance equipment in place, and I'm going to be wearing a wire, which means you'll be listening to everything that goes on around me. I can't be much safer than that."

Remi paced back and forth across the living room. "That doesn't guarantee that somehow, some way they won't manage to get to you. My gut keeps telling me this is all wrong, and trust me, my gut instincts have saved my ass more than once."

Caterine sighed with frustration. "Remi, please, I promise I'll do exactly as you tell me. I don't want to get myself hurt either. I want this over with and to get on with my life. After what happened today, I'm more determined than ever. Now, I need to get cleaned up to go see Grandmère. Why don't you call John and see if he and Miss Annabelle have left yet? If so, perhaps when she gets here, she'd like to go with us to the hospital." She took two steps then stopped. "Damn."

"What?"

"I just remembered. I didn't go by the house to pick up my princess gown. I have to take it with me to work tomorrow so there's time to have it repaired." Her mouth thinned into a stubborn line. "I'm going to drive my new car over to the carriage house and get what I need. And if any of my family gets in my way, they'll regret it."

"Hold on, Princess. You can't drive your new car until you get the title and registration put in your name."

"Damn." She stomped her foot. "I've about had enough of all these restrictions, Remi."

Remi's brows rose. "Well, for now, that's the way it is."

Caterine narrowed her eyes. With each word her volume increased. "That's easy for you to say. You can come and go as you please. You can wear your own clothes. You can go to work without having to have a bodyguard. And you can drive your own car."

"Calm down and stop hollering at me. Remember, I'm the one who's trying to help you. Now go get ready and I'll take you to get your things. Then we'll see if Pet has arrived before we go to the hospital."

Caterine wrapped her arms around his waist, leaned her cheek against his chest, and sighed. "I'm sorry. All that's happened today has taken its toll and my patience has worn thin."

He kissed the top of her head. "It's okay, *cher*. God knows you deserve to let loose once in a while. We'll wait and go after dark. Chances are I won't be seen then."

When Caterine stepped into the carriage house, tears welled up in her eyes at the peaceful normality she'd once known. It was hard to believe it had only been a few days since her life had been turned into turmoil. Grateful for the automatic timers she had plugged a few lights into, she moved through the dimly lit rooms. She pulled a suitcase from a closet and quickly packed. Reaching for the gown, she hesitated, replaying in her mind the night the glittering princess had met her dark, handsome pirate. She smiled at the memory before folding the gown over her arm. On impulse, she dashed into her bathroom to collect Fleur-de-Lis bath oil, body cream, and perfume. She took one last look around, then closed and locked her front door.

Remi popped the trunk for her to put her things inside. As she slid onto the passenger seat he smiled, turning the car and heading out of the driveway. "I'm impressed. You did that in less than ten minutes."

Caterine snorted. "I would have been quicker, but I got all sentimental when I picked up my gown."

Remi reached over and squeezed her knee. "Were you remembering the first time I made you scream? We did have us a good time in that arbor, didn't we?"

Caterine chuckled. "We certainly did. I can still hear Elaine's shocked voice when I told her what I'd done."

"You know, I've never asked you why you ran from me that night."

Caterine stared out the side window then turned back to him. "Because, for the first time in her life, Caterine Doucette had done something reckless and potentially scandalous. So, not knowing what else to do, I ran."

"Answer me this . . . if all that has occurred since that night hadn't happened, would I ever have seen you again?"

She hesitated. "I don't know."

"That's what I thought," he scoffed. "The princess had her fun, but she's not taking the pirate home."

"That's not fair, Remi. I wanted to see you again. In fact, I had a very risqué dream about you that night."

"I didn't say you wouldn't come looking for sex. I said you wouldn't have taken me home to the big house."

"Damn it, Remi, neither of us knows what we would have done. I can't believe you can sit there and say something like that to me. After all we've been through, you don't know me any better than that? Do you honestly think where you come from and who you are would have made a difference to me?"

Remi knew his words had stung, but deep inside he still wondered, if forced to choose, whether she would leave her privileged life to be with him.

"Besides," Caterine said, breaking into his thoughts, "what we *would* have done really doesn't matter, does it? I once asked you if you believed in fate, and you said yes. Well, so do I. I believe we were meant to be together, and here we are. I only wish the circumstances that brought us together had been different."

"So do I, Princess."

As they waited at a light, Remi's cell phone rang. "Michaud."

"Hey, Remi, we're here at the hotel," John said. "And Pet is anxious to go see Miss Dauphine."

"We're on our way. Tell her we'll be there in about five minutes. Are you staying in New Orleans tonight?"

"Yeah, as soon as you pick up Pet, I'm meeting up with a buddy of mine."

"Okay, stay out of trouble. I don't want to have to haul your ass out of jail."

John laughed. "It's Carnival time in New Orleans. What kind of trouble can I get into?"

"I hate to imagine, *cher*."

"Hello, Grandmère." Caterine kissed Miss Dauphine's cheek. "You're looking well."

"I do not look well, Caterine. I have a lump on my head, and my foot is throbbing. Where have you been? I've been anxious to discuss my accident with you and Mr. Michaud."

"I'm sorry, Grandmère, we were unavoidably delayed. We have a surprise for you." Caterine stepped back so her grandmother could see Miss Annabelle standing in the doorway.

Caterine smiled at the utter joy that filled the older women's faces. "Would you like us to give you two a few minutes alone so you can do some catching up?" Caterine asked.

"No, we'll have plenty of time for that later." Annabelle brushed tears from her cheeks. "I believe Dauphine is anxious to tell us about her fall."

Miss Dauphine nodded. "Annabelle is right. You need to hear what I intend to do. I'm convinced that newspaper was purposely placed under the doormat so I'd trip over it. The absolute gall of someone thinking they could get away with that amazes me. Since I can't be sure which of them is the perpetrator, I'm considering throwing them all out on their ears."

"Now, wait a minute," Remi said. "I understand you're upset and you have a right to be, but let's step back and look at the situation before you do something rash. We need to see if there's a way to talk with the kid who delivered your paper. Then we'd know for sure. And we can't do that until tomorrow morning."

Again Miss Dauphine nodded. "That's a reasonable point. Can you take care of that for me?"

"I'll see what I can do."

"Then what should I do if we find that the paperboy did not place the newspaper under the mat?"

"For now, nothing. Please let me finish," Remi said, as anger filled Miss Dauphine's eyes. "If we're hoping to flush this person out, they need to be in the house and at the ball Tuesday night."

Miss Dauphine sighed. "Again you're right."

"I don't believe either Jules or Markus is behind this, Dauphine," Annabelle said. "Both your boys love you too much. They couldn't intentionally want you hurt. On the other hand, those daughters-in-law of yours are a different story."

Miss Dauphine scowled. "You're so lucky, Annabelle. Your boys married kind, decent women. And in my heart I can't believe either of my sons would want to harm me." She turned to Remi. "All right, I won't banish any of my ungrateful offspring. But rest assured I'll be more aware of my surroundings."

"And you won't be on your own, Grandmère. Miss Annabelle is going to stay with you," Caterine said.

"Now, Caterine, Dauphine hasn't yet said she wants me to stay at the house with her. I can easily remain at the hotel."

"Nonsense, Annabelle," Miss Dauphine said. "Of course you'll come to the house. We have a lot to talk about. Let whoever it was try something underhanded with the two of us on alert. Why, we might catch them ourselves."

Caterine had to hide her smile when Remi turned to her and mouthed, *great.*

Clearing her throat, Caterine asked, "So, Grandmère, when did the doctor say you'd be released?"

"Tomorrow morning. Jules is going to pick me up. We can then go by the hotel and get Annabelle. Unfortunately with my ankle as it is, I'll not be able to assist you at Ma Chérie."

Remi frowned. "I don't like the idea of Caterine being there alone with

Frances and Hyacinth."

"Remi, I won't be alone with my aunts. Clients will be coming and going, and there's a full staff of seamstresses. And before you start arguing with me, I promise I won't leave the shop."

"I can go and be with her for a while," Annabelle said. "I wanted to stop by there anyway."

Miss Dauphine nodded. "That will be fine. Plan on Jules and me picking you up. Mr. Michaud, will you be able to drive your grandmother from the hotel to Ma Chérie?"

"*Oui*, I can do that."

"Now that we have everything settled, Caterine, would you like to tell me how you got that nasty scrape on your face?" Miss Dauphine asked.

"I tripped in the parking lot earlier."

"Caterine, I always know when you are lying to me, and you're lying to me right now. I'll ask again. How did you get that scrape on your face?"

"Grandmère, it was foggy this morning. I was in the parking lot and a car didn't see me. I had to jump out of the way and I fell. That's all."

For what seemed hours to Caterine, her grandmother studied her face closely before finally sighing. "Very well. Now, I believe the medication they have me on for pain is beginning to take effect. I'm becoming rather tired." She stifled a yawn. "I'll bid all of you good night."

"I really wish we could convince our grandmothers to stay away from the ball." Remi sat propped up in bed, watching Caterine hang up her princess gown. "I have enough to worry about without wondering what a couple of Miss Marple wannabes might get up to."

"I'm sure they'll be fine." Caterine was closely examining her torn gown. "Grandmère can hardly walk, and Annabelle isn't going to go off and leave her. I'm sure they'll seat themselves in the ballroom, making sure they're in the best spot to see and be seen."

"What are you doing over there?"

"I'm checking the extent of the damage to my gown. I must say, Remi, you weren't a bit careful."

He grinned. "There was something under that gown I wanted. Say, Princess, that reminds me." He opened the drawer of the bedside table and extracted a silver fleur-de-lis hair clip studded with tiny diamonds. "Look what I have." He held up the clip.

Caterine could only gape. "Remi! I thought I lost that, and you've had it all this time." She hurried over and happily took the clip from his outstretched hand. "I have many copies, but this was my mother's. I was so upset I had Elaine scouring her garden for it. I didn't have the heart to tell Grandmère." She did a little dance back to where her dress hung. "Now I can wear it with my gown to the party. I'll bet it will bring me good luck."

Remi grinned. "I've got an idea. Why don't you put the clip and gown on now and come back over here?"

She glanced over her shoulder at him lying naked against the pillows as a familiar thrill tingled through her body. "Why? So you can tear my gown even more?"

His grin widened. "No, I don't need to tear it to get to where I want to go. *Viens ici, Princess. Viens, ma jolie fille. J'aime te faire l'amour avec toi,*" he whispered as she slipped the gown over her naked body.

Chapter Thirty-Nine

"Here you go, *cher*." Remi stopped the car in front of Ma Chérie early Monday morning. "I'll be back after awhile with Annabelle. Now, Caterine, I can trust that under no circumstances you will leave the store, correct?"

Caterine rolled her eyes as she got out of the car. "Yes, Remi. I won't leave the store."

"You know, that habit of rolling your eyes like that is really annoying."

Leaning over, she smiled as she closed the car door. "And you know what, Remi? Constantly being reminded what I can and can't do is also annoying." Blowing him a kiss, she didn't wait for his reply.

Caterine turned on the lights as she made her way through the store heading for the staircase in the back that led to the sewing area upstairs. She placed her gown on one of the long tables and looked around in satisfaction. Everything was neat and tidy. Bolts of cloth were folded on tall shelves. Works in progress were laid out on tables or draped across dress forms. State-of-the-art sewing machines lined the far wall, where large windows offered the best light and a view of the street below. *And it all belongs to me.*

As she stared onto Royal Street, she felt the weight of responsibility pressing down on her. *What if I destroy something that took decades to establish?* She stood there for a long while before she sighed and turned from the window. *All I can do is promise you, Grandmère, that I'll do my very best with what you've entrusted to me and hope it's enough.*

Back in her office, Caterine busied herself with paperwork until she heard her aunts arrive. Expecting only Frances and Hyacinth, she glanced up when she heard Paulette's and Charlotte's voices as well. As she reached the main salon, she was in time to see all but Frances disappear up the stairs.

"Aunt Frances, what are Paulette and Charlotte doing here?"

Frances' back stiffened. "Since Ma Chérie is closed tomorrow, they've come to get their costumes for the ball. Is that a problem?"

She softened her tone. "Of course not. I forgot about them needing their costumes. So what are they dressing as?"

"I believe Charlotte is going as Aphrodite, Paulette as Little Bo Peep, and Hyacinth as Scarlet O'Hara."

Caterine watched as her aunt and cousins made their way back down the stairs. *They should be going as the three witches in Macbeth.*

"Isn't that the princess gown you wore to the LaBeaus' party lying up there, Caterine?" Paulette asked.

Caterine nodded.

Paulette's brows lifted. "Judging by the condition of your gown, it must have been quite a wild party. The gown looks as if it were torn off you. Tell us, Caterine, is that where you met your Cajun boyfriend? I hear those Cajuns can get pretty rough with their ladies. Or perhaps you like it rough?"

"You really shouldn't speak of things you know nothing about," came a sweet southern voice. "My husband was Cajun, and he was nothing but kind and gentle with me."

Caterine had to bite her lip as she turned to see Annabelle Michaud, outraged as only a southern belle could be.

"I beg your pardon?" Paulette stiffened at the woman's rebuke. "And just who do you think you are?"

"Paulette, let me introduce Miss Annabelle Michaud, a dear friend of Grandmère. Miss Annabelle, these are my cousins Charlotte and Paulette, my Aunt Hyacinth and Aunt Frances."

For seconds silence filled the room, then Frances plastered on a bright smile and hurried over to take Annabelle's hands.

"Miss Annabelle, how good it is to see you again. When did you arrive in

New Orleans? Miss Dauphine is going to be so surprised to see you. Where are you staying?"

Annabelle, at her haughtiest, smiled. "Why, Frances, Dauphine already knows I'm in town. In fact, she and Jules will be stopping here after she's released from the hospital. I'll be accompanying them back to the house, where I'll be staying with Dauphine. I came in to see your new designs and to congratulate Caterine on her ownership of Ma Chérie."

Behind her Caterine gleefully heard Charlotte snort and Paulette hiss. With difficulty, Caterine controlled her impulse to run over to Annabelle and throw her arms around her neck. As Caterine bent to kiss her cheek, she whispered, "Thanks."

In a louder tone, she said, "It's good to see you again, Miss Annabelle. Come to my office and I'll show you our design books." Caterine looked back over her shoulder and smiled. "Aunt Frances, I believe Annabelle and I would enjoy some coffee. Would either you or Hyacinth see to it? Oh, some of those pastries would be nice as well."

Once safely behind Caterine's closed office door, both women collapsed into chairs and tried to stifle their laughter.

"Oh, my dear, I'm afraid I may have made things more difficult for you." Annabelle wiped at her tears. "But I couldn't stop myself. Those women are worse than I remembered."

Caterine smiled. "Trust me, the looks on their faces were worth any retribution that may come my way."

"Before they arrive with the coffee, Remi wanted me to tell you he'll be spending the day with Paul going over last minute details for tomorrow and for you to call him when you're ready to leave."

Caterine sighed. "Remi worries too much about me. I can't wait for tomorrow to be over. Hopefully there will be an end to all of this."

"Of course he's worried. He loves you, my dear. He's going to do everything in his power to make sure you're safe."

"I guess we're as ready as we're going to be," Remi said. He was sitting in Paul's office as they reviewed the plan. "We'll have men stationed inside and out. The surveillance cameras will be monitored, and Caterine will be wearing a wire. So how come with all this I'm still afraid somehow we'll fuck up?"

"Because no matter how well orchestrated this is, there's still a chance something can go wrong. But we're good at what we do, and we'll make sure not to screw this up. Remi, you're too close to the situation to be objective or feel secure. If this were a different bust, you'd have a lot more confidence."

Remi ran his fingers through his hair. "I know you're right. I just can't let her get hurt."

Paul played with a pen sitting on his desk. "Buddy, can I ask you something personal?"

"*Oui.*"

"Are you in love with Caterine?"

Remi stood and walked over to the window. After a long minute he turned back to Paul. "*Oui.*"

"Are you going to ask her to marry you?"

His smile was without humor. "You think she'd have me?"

Paul nodded. "In a minute."

Chapter Forty

Remy lay awake, his arms folded behind his head, watching as the shadows danced across the bedroom ceiling. Unable to sleep, he'd played and replayed in his mind all that could possibly go wrong that evening at the ball. With a sigh, he looked over at Caterine's beautiful sleeping face. Once again he marveled at being the one she'd chosen to give her closely guarded love to. His heart clenched in fear every time he thought about the chance they were taking with her life. If something were to go wrong and he lost her, he honestly didn't know how he'd go on alone.

He knew that despite the difference in their backgrounds he couldn't allow his pride to let the woman he loved walk out of his life without a fight. He would ask her to marry him. Then it would be up to her to choose either the life he could give her or to go back to the life she'd known. *Great timing, Michaud. You finally decide to stop being a stubborn ass and marry the girl. Now if you make one mistake tonight, she could be taken from you forever.*

He threw back the covers and reached for his shirt and jeans. He stomped into the living room and grabbed the bottle of Jack Daniel's and his cigarettes and headed for the balcony.

"Remi, what's wrong?" Caterine asked, coming out a short time later.

"Nothing, Princess. Go back to bed."

She walked closer and brushed the hair from his eyes. "It's two in the morning. Tell me what's wrong."

"I can't sleep. That's all. I've got a lot on my mind."

She took the bottle of Jack from his hand and extinguished his cigarette, then sat across his lap, wrapping her arms around his neck. "I know a way to get your mind off your troubles." She gently kissed him.

Remi tightened his hold on her and returned the kiss. All his fears and anxiety came crashing over him. The thought that his luck might run out and this would be the last time he'd have her in his arms had him tightening his hold and deepening the kiss.

Caterine ran her fingers through the thick hair at the base of his neck, moaning into his mouth.

Remi slid his hand under her oversized nightshirt and began to squeeze and tease her breasts.

"Remi, we're outside. Someone will see you."

He chuckled. "It's the Quarter. Trust me, nobody cares. Besides . . ." His hand drifted lower to caress the slick bud between her thighs. "As you said, it's two in the morning."

Her breath was coming in tiny little gasps. "Remi, we should go in."

"You want me to stop, *cher*?"

"No, but Remi—"

He covered her mouth to swallow her cry of pleasure as her body convulsed around his hand.

"Move your leg so you can straddle my lap."

"What? What are you doing?"

He unzipped his jeans, smiling devilishly. "I'll show you, Princess." Lifting her hips he guided her onto his hard shaft.

"Remi, we can't do this out here!"

His chuckle was low. "It seems we already are. Now move your sweet little ass."

With his hands on her bottom she rode him until, unable to hold back any longer, he pulled her mouth down to his and swallowed both their screams.

Caterine's eyes flew open as they heard a burst of applause. "Remi!"

He was laughing as he carried her inside to the bed.

Caterine was awakened from a deep sleep by what sounded like an entire marching band passing beneath their window. She put the pillow over her head and groaned. After Remi had carried her back to bed, they'd made love for what was left of the night. Now all she wanted to do was sleep.

"Happy Mardi Gras, Princess." Remi pulled the pillow off her head. "Let's go get breakfast."

Caterine snatched her pillow back. "You go get breakfast, Remi. I want to sleep."

"Ah, come on, *cher*. It's ten o'clock, and it's Mardi Gras. Let's go have some fun while we still can."

Caterine lifted the pillow high enough to look at him with one eye. "Why aren't you exhausted?"

"You charged my batteries, Princess. Now get up." He patted her backside. "That's unless you want more?"

"No. For God's sake, enough." She batted his hand away. "Go take a shower."

Chuckling, he stood and stretched. "Today is going to be just for us. So let's go have some fun." Remi plucked the pillow off her head and flung back the covers. He lifted her into his arms and headed for the bathroom.

"Remi! Put me down."

"Sure thing." He stood her naked body in the shower and turned the cold water on full blast. Laughing at her shocked expression, he joined her under the spray.

"You've got powdered sugar in the corner of your mouth, Princess." They were seated at a wrought iron table in the sun outside the Café Du Monde drinking café au lait, eating beignets, and watching costumed Mardi Gras revelers filling the streets. "Here, let me get it off for you." Remi leaned closer and ran his tongue along her lower lip, licking the sweet sugar. "Mmm." He slid his tongue into her mouth, caressing her sugary tongue with his. "You know where I'd like to put some of this powdered sugar, then lick it off?" he murmured into her mouth.

Caterine felt her face flame and her toes curl. "Stop that. We're sitting in a public place. What's gotten into you today?"

He sat back and chuckled at her embarrassment. "It's Mardi Gras. You're supposed to act naughty."

She rolled her eyes. "I can't remember the last time I was actually on the streets of the Quarter on Mardi Gras. I'd forgotten how crazy it really is. Oh, look, there's the copper man." She pointed at a young guy, probably in his twenties, painted copper from cap to shoes, doing baseball stances.

Remi turned in the direction she pointed. "You know him?"

She nodded. "Well, no, I don't know him personally. The day Elaine brought me home from work he entertained the boys while they were out on the balcony. He's really quite talented."

Remi glanced at the copper man then back to Caterine and smiled. "Whatever you say, *cher*. If you're done with your coffee, let's go among the masses and see what parades we can find." He leaned forward until their lips were a hair's breadth apart. "But don't you go flashing for beads, Princess."

Chapter Forty-One

Talk about déjà vu, Caterine thought as she stood in the glittering Doucette third-floor ballroom dressed in her ice princess gown.

She watched as a handsome, black-clad masked pirate walked toward her. *He can make my pulse race as much tonight as he did the first time I laid eyes on him.*

"I believe this dance is ours, Princess." Remi gave her a devilish grin she now knew so well.

She opened her eyes wide. "Oh, I don't know. I hear pirates can be dangerous."

He moved in closer, caressing her body with his eyes. "I'll bet we'll discover that you enjoy what dangerous pirates can do, Princess."

She chuckled. "Since I'm wearing a microphone, I hope nobody but you is listening."

"Where did you put the mike?" Remi took a step back.

Caterine gestured between her breasts. "It seemed like the safest place."

He stepped close and looked down. "I don't see it."

She pushed him away. "You're not supposed to. Trust me, it's there. The ballroom is beginning to fill up. Are all your men in place?"

Remi nodded. "They're all dressed as pirates, and the code word is *vien.* If anyone you don't know, or who makes you feel uncomfortable, approaches you, say *vien* and I'll hear you."

"*Come*. That's original."

He smiled. "It works. Well, I hope it does. If this room gets really noisy, I may have difficulty hearing you. If you need to, scream my name."

"Oh, there's Elaine." Caterine waved to Marie Antoinette. "But where's Paul? I don't see him with her."

"Right here, Cat."

Caterine jumped at the voice behind her and looked up into Bluebeard's grinning face. "For heaven's sake, Paul, you about gave me a heart attack."

"Sorry, I couldn't resist." Paul turned to Remi. "I just spoke with Ray. He's helping get Miss Dauphine and Annabelle settled into chairs." He pointed to the ballroom entrance. "Ray said the family is all here except Randal."

"What's Ray dressed as?" Caterine asked.

Paul's grin widened. "A bandit. I think he's Jesse James."

"This is like déjà vu," Elaine said, joining the small group.

Caterine smiled. "I know. I had the same thought."

"Yes, but this time I'm a nervous wreck and I'm not leaving your side."

"No, Elaine, you can't do that," Paul said. "Caterine has to be alone in order for the perp to approach her."

Elaine scrunched up her nose. "The what?"

"The person who's after her," Remi clarified. "Now, Paul and I need to disappear into the crowd. We don't want to draw too much attention to ourselves. Remember, Caterine, someone will have you in sight at all times. Do not stand with your back to the doors leading out onto the gallery. Do not leave the ballroom without making sure someone knows where you're going. Understand?"

"Yes, Remi, I understand. I won't do anything stupid. But I can't just stand here in this same spot. I have to mingle a little."

"That's fine. Just pay attention to your surroundings. Don't get yourself in the middle of a tight crowd of people where my men can't see your back. Try and keep yourself out on the fringes."

"I can stay with Caterine for a while, can't I?" Elaine asked.

"Sure." Paul nodded as he and Remi walked away.

"There goes our dynamic duo," Caterine said. "You know, Elaine, sometimes I wonder if Remi regrets leaving the police force."

"I know. I wonder the same about Paul. But I'm a lot happier now that I don't have to worry every time he leaves the house." Elaine reached out and squeezed Caterine's hand. "Are you okay, Cat? You have to be a little scared."

She squeezed Elaine's hand back. "I'm okay, but I'm more than a *little* scared. I'm anxious as well. I just hope whatever's going to happen happens quickly."

"I can't believe Remi and Paul actually expect someone to come after you in the middle of all these people."

Caterine nodded. "They think they'll either try an attack here in the ballroom where they can just vanish back into the crowd, or try and lure me outside. Either way I'll be ready. Actually I'm more angry than anything else. Whoever is behind this has—without provocation—tried to have me killed, attempted to hurt Grandmère, and has totally disrupted my life. When I find out who it is, Remi may have to be more concerned about what I do to them than what they might do to me."

Elaine smiled. "Let me know if you need help, because if it turns out to be Charlotte or Paulette, I'll happily get in a couple of slaps. Oh, I see my parents are speaking with Miss Dauphine; I should go join them. Who's the lady sitting with her?"

"She's Remi's grandmother, Miss Annabelle Michaud. She and Grandmère have known each other since they were girls at school. I didn't know about the connection with Remi."

"Wow, isn't that something? That reinforces my conviction you and Remi were meant to be together. By the way, best friend of mine, you didn't call me and let me know how it went at Remi's family party. Was I right and you had yourself all worked up for no reason?"

Caterine grinned. "Okay, yes, you were right. They were all very nice to me, and I didn't say or do anything to embarrass Remi." Visions of them making love in the swamp flashed through her mind and she smiled to herself. "And you'll have to wait to hear all about it tomorrow, because if I'm not mistaken here comes Remi's cousin, Antoine."

"Good God, dressed like that he could pass for Remi. How can you tell them apart?"

"Oh, trust me. I'll know if it's Remi."

"Hey, *cher*, I had to come over and tell you how beautiful you are. If this is the way you looked the first time Remi saw you, no wonder the poor bastard lost his heart. It's a good thing he got to you first, because otherwise you'd be mine."

Caterine raised her brows. "And what about Suzette? She might have something to say about that."

Antoine smiled. "Suzette would definitely be a problem. And who's this lovely lady?" He turned his attention to Elaine.

Caterine did the introductions. "Elaine was on her way to go visit with my grandmère. Antoine, would you take Elaine over and introduce her to your grandmother?"

"I'd be happy to." Giving Elaine a gallant bow, he held out his arm. "May I escort you, Your Majesty?"

"You certainly may," said a smiling Marie Antoinette as she took the offered arm.

Momentarily on her own, Caterine took the opportunity to study the people around her and the elaborately decorated room. Aunt Hyacinth certainly hadn't spared any expense. She must have emptied every greenhouse for miles. There were fragrant flowers placed in vases of every size throughout the room. Elaborate bows of intertwining green, purple, and yellow fabrics were tied around the vases and brass wall sconces, and more bows held back the filmy white curtains around the open French doors. White-jacketed waiters and waitresses moved efficiently through the crowd, carrying silver trays of crystal flutes filled with champagne and an assortment of tasty canapés. Against the far wall, a stage had been erected where the Crescent City Kings, a popular local jazz band, began to play.

Caterine gazed in amusement as flouncy, frilly Little Bo Peep went dancing past in the arms of Mark Twain. *For God's sake, Paulette even has a crook tied with a big white bow,* she thought in amazement.

The smile left Caterine's face as her eyes met Scarlet O'Hara's glower. *She's caught me laughing at her little girl, and Mama isn't pleased.* Caterine took a sip of her champagne and turned her attention to Aphrodite, who seemed to be getting a rather stern lecture from Jesse James. Miss Dauphine and Annabelle were holding court at the ballroom's entrance, and Robert E. Lee and his wife were happily greeting guests.

It all seemed perfectly normal. *How could there be a killer lurking among them?* Caterine smiled as she recognized an old friend from school approaching her. She then spent a couple of uneventful hours speaking with friends, dancing with boys she'd grown up with, and catching up on New Orleans gossip. When Remi appeared in front of her and asked her to dance, she had almost forgotten why they were really there.

"You look as if you've been having fun, Princess." Remi led her onto the dance floor for a slow blues number.

She wrapped her arms around his neck. "I'm having a good time. I feel like the old Caterine again."

Remi scowled. "It's still early. Don't let your guard down."

"Excuse me, mind if I butt in?"

"Bobby!" Caterine cried, leaving Remi's arms to wrap hers around the neck of a tall, handsome man with light brown hair, blue eyes, and a friendly smile.

"Hey, Cat, how's my favorite girl?" Robert Doucette picked Caterine up and twirled her around.

She laughed delightedly. "Bobby, put me down before I get sick. I want you to meet someone. Bobby, this is Remi Michaud. Remi, this is my cousin, Bobby."

Remi shook Bobby's hand. "I've heard a lot about you."

"And I've just been hearing a lot about you from Ray," Bobby said, returning Remi's handshake. "What the hell's going on here, Cat? Ray has somewhat filled me in, but I'm not sure I'm following it all."

"I can explain," Remi said. "But let's move from the middle of the dance floor."

"Okay. First I'll take my things upstairs and say hello to Grandmère. Then I'll be back down."

"Bobby, weren't you supposed to get here earlier?" Caterine asked.

Bobby snorted. "Yeah, Cat, about four hours ago. Thanks to the snow, my flight kept getting delayed. I'm lucky I made it out at all. Becky and the girls are staying with her parents, so at least I don't have to worry about them. You two do know there's a blizzard hitting the Midwest, don't you?"

Simultaneously Remi and Caterine looked toward the open French doors where the curtains billowed in a gentle breeze.

Bobby laughed. "Okay, obviously a snow storm a thousand miles away isn't of major interest here." He bent and kissed Caterine's cheek. "I'll be back as soon as I can get away from Grandmère."

"She's right over there." Caterine pointed to where the two women had been sitting. She frowned. "Well, they were sitting over there a minute ago."

"Ray told me Grandmère's foot was beginning to hurt, so they decided to go to her sitting room to be more comfortable. I'll go see her and be right back."

Remi guided Caterine off the dance floor. "I need to speak with you, Caterine. Let's go over here where it's more private." As they reached a secluded alcove, Vince and Andre, with troubled expressions on their faces, joined them.

"What's happened?" Remi asked before either man spoke.

"Remi, we've got to leave. We just got a call some fucking nut in a devil costume shot up the Triple Aces casino and is on the loose."

At Caterine's horrified gasp, all three men turned.

"What?" Remi asked, his hard eyes boring into hers.

Caterine stared into their rigid faces. Even if Randal was an incredible ass, he was still her family. She found herself blinking back tears before saying, "I haven't seen Randal all night."

"Are you talking about Randal Doucette?" Vince asked.

"Yes, but he's not supposed to be dressed as a devil. He's supposed to be a riverboat gambler."

Vince turned to Remi. "Considering what you told us about Randal and his dealings with Rivette, is there a chance Doucette's gone off the deep end?"

Remi shrugged. "I don't really know him. You need to talk to his brother, Ray. That's him over there." He pointed to where Ray stood speaking to a beautiful girl dressed as a flapper.

"We'll talk to Ray, then we're out of here. Remi, I'm sorry we've got to leave you short-handed," Vince said. "Good luck."

Remi put a restraining hand on Vince's arm. "Wait. Did they say whether anyone was killed?"

Vince and Andre exchanged glances before Vince replied, "We shouldn't be telling you this, so keep it to yourself. There're five people down, and they think one of them might be Rivette."

Remi swore. "Good luck trying to find one costumed devil among hundreds on Mardi Gras."

Vince scoffed. "No shit."

Tears trickled down Caterine's cheeks. "Oh, Remi, it can't be Randal. He couldn't do something like that."

Remi put his arm around her and held her close for a second before releasing her. "Ray's leaving with Vince and Andre." He pointed behind her. "But what the hell's wrong with Bobby?"

Cold fear gripped Caterine's heart at the stricken expression on her cousin's face as he hurried toward them, Paul right on his heels. In a voice barely above a whisper, Caterine asked, "Bobby, what's happened?"

"Grandmère's missing, and Annabelle's been knocked unconscious. Remi, you've got to come."

Chapter Forty-Two

"Oh . . . my . . . God," Caterine cried. "Remi, I'm going with you."

"No, you're not!" Remi had to shout to be heard over the band's lively music. "Listen to me. You have to stay right here where you're safe. Do you understand? Now calm down, and let me find out what's happened."

"I'll stay with her, Remi," Paul said. "Just go."

Without another word to Caterine, Remi turned to Bobby. "I have to find my cousin, Antoine. Then you'll have to show me where Annabelle is."

Dread constricted Caterine's heart as she watched Remi and Bobby disappear into the crowd.

Paul put a comforting arm around her shoulders and bent close. "It will be all right, Cat. Whoever's got Miss Dauphine can't get far. I need to alert my men outside not to allow any cars to leave. It's too loud in here for them to hear me on my two-way radio. I'm going to take you over and leave you with Elaine."

As Paul stepped away, Caterine heard him grunt, then saw him crumple to the floor. She looked up into Travis Jenkins' angry face. As she opened her mouth to speak, he held a black gun against her ribs.

"Don't say anything, Caterine. If you want to see your grandmother alive, turn into my arms and dance your way out the closest French door. We have two minutes to get outside. If we're stopped, you'd better act natural or Miss Dauphine dies."

Caterine looked at Paul's still form and began to shake. "Travis, what have you done?"

"Damn it, Caterine, he's not dead. I just tased him." Travis jabbed her in the side again. "Now, move."

Caterine felt as though her body had a mind of its own. She slowly placed one trembling hand on Travis' shoulder, holding his hand with her other. Everything took on a dreamlike quality as she allowed him to twirl her around and around until, unchallenged, they slipped through the door onto the third-floor gallery.

When they reached the cooling night air, Caterine's mind began to clear. She stepped quickly out of his embrace. In a shaky voice she demanded, "Travis, why are you doing this? What have you done with Grandmère?"

He shoved her toward the steps and snarled. "Don't blame me for any of this. I wanted no part of it. That bitch and her fucking partner are forcing me."

"What? Who are you talking about?"

"Paulette. Who else would I be talking about?"

Caterine stopped halfway down the stairs. "Are you telling me Paulette is threatening to kill Grandmère?"

"Yes, now keep moving." Stabbing the gun into her ribs, he jerked her arm.

Caterine cried out in pain and quickened her steps.

"Damn it, I don't want to hurt you, Caterine. Don't you understand? I love you. You're the reason I had to break my engagement to Paulette."

Caterine stumbled on the stairs in her stiletto heels. "Travis, what are you talking about? I hardly know you."

"Oh, my sweet Caterine, I fell in love with you the first time I laid eyes on you. I thought you looked just like an angel. I knew then we were meant to be together and you had to be mine. I couldn't marry Paulette when I knew it was you I loved. But when I told her, the bitch told me she'd never let me go. I made the mistake of telling her I found out about my father's crooked reconstruction deals after Katrina, and she told Jonathan. Now they're forcing me to help them."

"You're telling me Jonathan Day has something to do with this?"

Travis snorted. "Yeah, well, you must have really pissed him off. Besides, he's not the only one."

Her mind in a whirl, Caterine tried to process all Travis was saying. When she realized he was steering her in the direction of a waiting van, she began to panic. Once he got her inside, she knew she wouldn't have a chance of escape. "Is Grandmère in that big white panel van?" she asked as loudly as she dared.

"Keep your voice down," he ordered. "Yes, she's in there, along with the crazy bitch and her mother."

Caterine's head snapped up. "Aunt Hyacinth is part of this?"

He laughed derisively. "Hyacinth part of it? Whose idea do you think it was to kidnap you and Miss Dauphine? Can you honestly imagine it was Paulette's? The only thing that bitch knows how to do is how to trap a man with kinky sex."

As they approached the van, Caterine saw a figure standing beside it.

"It's about time," Jonathan said. "We were beginning to worry you fucked things up." He turned to Caterine and smiled. "Well, if it isn't the ice princess herself. Perfect costume for the most frigid woman in New Orleans. Now, get in the van. We're going for a little ride."

Caterine desperately prayed the hidden mike was working and Remi could hear her. Not caring how loudly she spoke, she said, "Jonathan, you and Travis will never get away with kidnapping Grandmère and me. And where are you taking us?"

Jonathan grabbed her and jerked her head back, clamping his hand over her mouth. "Shut up. I've wanted to knock you on your ass since you humiliated me in front of that low-life Cajun. Now I get to watch the mighty Caterine go down."

"Wait a minute," Travis said. "You told me Caterine wouldn't be harmed. The plan was just to kidnap her."

Jonathan laughed. "You really are stupid, aren't you? We needed you to get her out here. Now get in the van and drive."

Jonathan shoved Caterine hard through the van's open side door.

Kicking and screaming, she landed half in and half out of the van, her long gown tangling around her legs. She fought Jonathan's attempt to push her the rest of the way in. Every minute she could delay, the better chance Remi had of finding her.

"Travis, you idiot, zap her with the Taser," Caterine heard Hyacinth cry from the front passenger seat. "We have to get out of here before that coon-ass boyfriend of hers finds us."

Caterine knew that for her and her grandmother's sakes she needed to stay alert. She stared directly into Travis' eyes and silently pleaded with him not to use the stun gun. When Travis hesitated, she mouthed, *please don't.*

"Give me the damn thing," Jonathan said. "I'll knock the bitch out."

"I'm not as dumb as you all think," Travis said as he pressed the stun gun against Jonathan, smiling as his body fell slowly to the ground. "Caterine will not be hurt."

Limp with relief, Caterine lay on the van's steel floor, watching Travis slam the door shut and the brightly lit windows of the mansion—and their chance of rescue—disappear before her eyes. *The gate*, she thought. To leave they had to go past the security gate. It would be her chance to get help. As she was about to rise and throw herself into the front seat, Paulette spoke.

"Well, Miss Perfect, you're not so superior now, are you?" Paulette gave Caterine a vicious kick in her side. "Stay down, you little whore."

Caterine grunted in pain. She knew they had to be close to the guardhouse and the gate. When she tried to get to her knees, Paulette grabbed a handful of her hair, jerked her head back, and slapped her hard across the face.

"I've been wanting to do that for years." She sneered. "You know what else, whore?" Paulette bent down inches from Caterine, a menacing smile spread across her face. "I'm going to love watching every minute as your unconscious body sinks slowly into the swamp. Imagine that, precious Caterine Doucette is going to be alligator bait."

Caterine fought back tears of fear and pain as she felt the van turn onto St. Charles. Her chance to alert the guard was gone. Where were Remi's men? The cameras should have picked up Travis leading her down the outside stairs. She had to think clearly. It might be up to her to get Grandmère out of this because, by God, she wasn't going down without a fight.

Caterine realized she hadn't heard a sound from her grandmother, and her gut clenched in horror. Had they already killed her? Searing anger temporarily replacing her fear, she shot off the floor and backhanded Paulette with such force it knocked her backward off her precarious seat on an empty paint bucket, slamming her head hard against the metal wall of the van. "I'm going to kill you if you've hurt Grandmère."

Her flaming rage fueling her, Caterine grabbed for Paulette. They kicked, scratched, and punched as they rolled around in the confined space.

"Travis, give me the goddamned Taser!" Hyacinth screamed.

Caterine had just landed a hard blow to Paulette's nose when she heard a weak voice call her name.

"Caterine, please stop. I'm here. I'm alive. They've got me back here."

Breathing hard, Caterine untangled herself from Paulette and brushed her hair from her eyes with scratched and bleeding hands. She scrambled through the dark interior toward her grandmother's voice and found Miss Dauphine wrapped in a blanket, lying on the dirty van floor. She ran her hands along her grandmother's body. "Grandmère, are you all right? Have they hurt you?"

"Except for my throbbing ankle, I'm fine." Miss Dauphine's voice shook slightly but sounded strong. "I foolishly believed Hyacinth and Paulette when they told me they had you and they'd kill you if I didn't come with them. Tell me, did they harm Annabelle?"

"I don't know. Remi left me with Paul and went to check on her. That's when Travis got ahold of me."

Caterine heard her grandmother sigh. "What part that young man, or Jonathan Day, have in all of this is beyond me. Now, please get me out of this blanket so I may sit up and address this situation."

Before Caterine could explain Travis' forced compliance, Hyacinth's shrill voice cut through the darkness.

"What are you two whispering about back there? Don't think you have a chance of escaping." Hyacinth left the passenger seat and knelt next to a sobbing Paulette. When she spoke, each word dripped scorn. "You're going to pay for hurting my little girl, Caterine . . . you and your bitch of a grandmother who's treated me like the dirt beneath her shoes from the day I married her *precious* son.

"But you know what, *Miss Dauphine*? I get the last laugh because once you and your perfect granddaughter are dead and Charlotte is sent away for her nasty drug addiction, the pride of the Doucettes will belong to my daughter. How do you like that? Ma Chérie belonging to my daughter—not your dear dead son's little girl, but *mine*. Do you understand what I'm telling you, you old crone?"

"I understand perfectly well what you're saying, Hyacinth," Miss Dauphine replied, her cultured voice dripping with contempt. "You're telling me you're nothing more than the gold-digging little tramp I always knew you to be. As far as Paulette's paternity, you're mistaken if you believe your confession is a surprise to me. Markus has always been gullible and naïve when it came to scheming women with pretty faces.

"This idea of yours that killing both Caterine and myself will somehow bestow ownership of Ma Chérie upon your daughter again displays what little intelligence you possess. Do you honestly imagine I would allow someone not of my blood to own it? If Caterine hasn't changed the will, it states quite clearly that upon my and Caterine's deaths, ownership goes directly to my legitimate grandson, Robert Doucette. At least you did manage to produce one honorable child, although as my son is his father, perhaps that accounts for Robert's ethics. Breeding does tell in a person. Now, I can't imagine Robert would wish to inherit Ma Chérie by the means of our murders, so I would suggest you stop this nonsense and tell Mr. Jenkins to turn this vehicle around and take us home. Killing us will gain you nothing."

As her grandmother verbally lashed Hyacinth, Caterine was aware that Travis had left the highway and was slowing the van down to a crawl. Fear again clutched at her chest. She could see nothing but impenetrable darkness through the windshield. When Travis brought the van to a complete stop, Caterine began to shake. Was this it? To her surprise, Travis jumped from the van. The only sounds inside now were Paulette's soft whimpers. What was Travis doing? Before Caterine could think of a way to escape, he was back.

"I opened the gates," Travis said as he climbed back into the van. "Should I close them behind us?" Getting no answer, he drove on.

Suddenly, with a scream straight out of a horror film, Hyacinth lunged for Miss Dauphine. "I won't let you win, you crazy old bitch!"

Instinctively, Caterine rose, throwing herself toward Hyacinth, blocking her from her grandmother. As their bodies connected, Caterine felt something sharp rake across her side.

"I'll kill you first, you little whore. Then your precious grandmother can watch as piece by piece I feed you to the gators." Hyacinth's deranged laugh echoed between the metal walls as she plunged the knife toward

Caterine's chest.

"No, not my lovely Caterine. You can't hurt her." Travis, sobbing, slammed on the brakes and dove between the two front seats toward the struggling women. In his haste to save Caterine, Travis tripped over Paulette's outstretched foot, hurling him into Hyacinth and knocking her off balance.

Caterine grabbed her grandmother, just managing to pull her out of the way of the two falling bodies. She heard Travis let out a brief cry, then for a heartbeat the interior of the van went silent.

My God, she's killed him, Caterine thought, seeing Travis' limp form inches from where she sat. Then her grandmother let out a low moan.

"Dear God, Caterine, you're bleeding."

In the dashboard's faint illumination, Caterine followed her grandmother's eyes to the red stain seeping through the tear in the side of her gown.

"How badly are you injured?" Miss Dauphine asked.

Now that she was aware of the stinging cut, she had to swallow back sudden nausea. "It's not that bad. Don't worry, Grandmère, I'll be fine."

"This situation has become intolerable," Miss Dauphine said. "Hyacinth, I demand you take Caterine and myself home immediately."

A triumphant smile spread across Hyacinth's face. "Oh, you do, do you? Well, Miss Bitch, for once you're not going to get your wish. For Christ's sake, Paulette, stop that sniffling. Find the damned Taser and get us some lights back here. Then come over here and help me get these two out of this van."

"Mama, I want to be the one to zap that whore for luring my Travis away from me," Paulette said peevishly as she got to her feet. "Then *I* want to throw her into the swamp."

"Whatever you wish, Paulette. Just find where that buffoon Travis dropped the Taser."

By the dim glow of the weak interior light, Paulette saw Travis lying at her mother's feet. As blood dripped from her nose, she let out a deafening scream. "Mama! You didn't kill Travis, did you? Once Caterine's dead, he'll marry me."

"Paulette, stop it. I don't know if he's dead or not, but we can't worry about that now. Go find that goddamned Taser."

The insane determination in Hyacinth's face told Caterine her aunt was way beyond reasoning with. If she wanted to save her and her grandmother's lives, she'd better do something and do it quickly.

While Hyacinth was distracted by Paulette, Caterine leaned close. "I'm going to try and get us out of here, Grandmère. Do you feel anything you can use as a weapon?"

"Save yourself, Caterine. I'm an old woman and it doesn't matter if I die."

Caterine opened her mouth to protest, but Miss Dauphine cut her off.

"Don't argue with me, Caterine. There's no time. Do as I say and save yourself."

"Here's the Taser, Mama." Paulette came up next to Hyacinth. "Can I use it on Caterine now?"

Hyacinth smiled. "Yes, that will make it easier to drag her out." A pained expression briefly crossed Hyacinth's face. "If that idiot you hired to kidnap her had done his job, we wouldn't be in this damned situation. All we'd have to worry about is Miss Dauphine."

"It's not my fault, Mama," Paulette said. "Charlotte's boyfriend said that man could handle it. Remember it was *you* who put that newspaper under the mat to hurt Miss Dauphine and then tried to run Caterine down. It's just Caterine's incredible luck that she always escapes."

"Well, she's all out of luck. Neither she nor Miss Dauphine is getting away this time." Hyacinth's smile was back in place. "I'll take care of old granny here after you deal with Caterine."

"Hyacinth, you and your despicable daughter are both mentally deranged and are not fit to be among decent civilized people," Miss Dauphine said. "I can guarantee that if you harm Caterine, you both will be locked away for the rest of your lives."

"I hate you, Miss Dauphine!" Paulette shouted. "I hate you. I hate you. I hate you."

As Paulette shoved the Taser at Miss Dauphine, Caterine lunged, screaming Remi's name.

Chapter Forty-Three

"It looks as if someone hit Miss Annabelle from behind," Bobby said as he, Remi, and Antoine hurried from the ballroom and through the upper hall toward Miss Dauphine's sitting room. "I found our housekeeper, Flora, and asked her to sit with her until we got back."

"Remi, what the hell happened?" Antoine asked.

"I've been an idiot. I should have realized they'd use Miss Dauphine to get to Caterine."

"Who's the 'they' you keep talking about?" Bobby asked. "All Ray told me tonight is that you were hoping to set a trap for whoever was behind Caterine's attack."

Remi scoffed derisively. "Yeah, well, it seems they set the trap for us instead. *Merde*," he swore as they entered the sitting room and he saw Annabelle's slight form crumpled in a chair.

"Oh, Mr. Doucette, I'm so glad you're back," Flora cried. "I think she's coming around."

Remi fell to his knees in front of Annabelle, taking her limp hand in his. "Pet, can you hear me? Pet, please open your eyes. Bobby, call for an ambulance," Remi demanded. Then to his relief Annabelle's eyelids began to flutter. Blue eyes, so like his own, opened slowly, regarding him quizzically.

"Remi, what happened? My head hurts abominably." Annabelle's voice was a hoarse whisper.

"Someone hit you, Pet. We called an ambulance."

Annabelle slowly sat up and hesitantly placed her hand to the back of her head, wincing in pain as she felt the tender bump. Fear quickly replaced the pain in her eyes as she frantically looked around the room. "Remi, where's Dauphine?"

Remi hesitated, carefully considering his words. "Pet, listen to me. Before the paramedics get here, I'm going to need your help. I want you to be strong and stay calm for me. Can you do that?"

She slowly nodded.

Hoping to reassure her, Remi squeezed her hand. "I need you to tell me the last thing you remember."

Her eyes filled with tears, and her voice quavered. "Remi, please tell me. Is Dauphine dead?"

"I don't know, Pet. We're not sure where she is. What do you remember?"

Annabelle took a deep breath. "We were sitting in the ballroom when Dauphine's ankle began to hurt. We decided she'd be more comfortable in here, and we'd finally have an opportunity for a nice long chat. Markus and Jules helped to get Dauphine settled. We were entertaining ourselves by gossiping about some of our acquaintances when Paulette and Hyacinth walked in unannounced. Dauphine immediately became angry and asked them to leave." Annabelle's face crumpled, and once again her eyes filled with tears. "I'm sorry, Remi, that's all I can remember."

"It's okay, Pet." Remi squeezed her hand again. "Do you recall what Paulette or Hyacinth said when they came in?"

She started to say no, then hesitated. "I don't recall either of them saying anything, but I do remember I didn't like the looks on their faces."

"What do you mean?"

"I thought they looked smug and, well, rather cruel. Remi, I'm so sorry. I was supposed to be here to help you, and I failed."

Remi scowled and got to his feet. "You didn't fail me, Pet. I failed you." He turned to Bobby and Antoine, then silently cursed at the pale anger on Bobby's face.

In a low voice filled with emotion, Bobby asked, "What the goddamned hell's been going on around here? And what do my mother and sister have to do with Grandmère's disappearance?"

As Remi opened his mouth to reply, his blood went cold. Caterine's voice, clear but faint, came through from her hidden microphone to his earpiece.

"Travis, why are you doing this to us?"

Remi stood motionless, then heard Travis say, "Shut up and walk, Caterine."

Antoine gave Remi's arm a shake. "What's wrong?"

"It's Caterine."

Their portable radios screeched. "Yes," Remi yelled into his radio.

"Remi, it's Sosa. Can you hear me?"

"Yes. Where's Caterine?"

"I don't know. I just found Paul LaBeau down. He's been tased."

Remi swore long and hard in Cajun.

"Remi, it's Philippe." Antoine held up his radio. "He says the gallery camera showed Caterine going down the back stairs with some guy."

This time Remi cursed in English as he headed for the sitting room door, calling over his shoulder as he ran, "Antoine, stay with Pet and go with her to the hospital."

"Wait for me." Bobby was right on Remi's heels. "If my mother and sister are involved, I'm coming with you."

"What's the quickest way to the back?" Remi asked as they ran.

"This way." Bobby led them along the hall, around a corner, then down a flight of stairs that took them into the large kitchen. As they made their way through the house, patches of Caterine's conversation with Travis came through Remi's earpiece.

"This leads to a courtyard and the parking area by the old stables." Bobby pushed open a heavy wooden door, and they charged into the night.

As they rounded the courtyard wall, Remi saw a white panel van halfway down the drive on the far side of the parking area. Then in his ear he heard a woman scream, "Zap her with the Taser, you idiot. We have to get out of here before that coon-ass boyfriend of hers finds us."

Remi was breathing hard when he spotted a figure lying on the ground near where the van had been parked. Fearing it was Caterine, he quickened his pace. Relief washed over him when he realized it wasn't her.

Next to him, Bobby panted. "My God, is that Jonathan Day?"

Bending to get a closer look, Remi realized the man on the ground was the one he'd stopped from bothering Caterine.

"Is he dead?"

"No, I'd say he's been tased."

"What the hell does he have to do with this?" Bobby asked.

"I don't know. He'd been dating Caterine, and she broke it off with him. How he's involved is anyone's guess."

"Now what do we do?"

In a voice as hard as steel and as cold as ice, Remi replied, "We go get Caterine."

Something sparkling on the ground caught his eye. Reaching to pick it up, his heart lurched. In his palm rested a silver and diamond fleur-de-lis hair clip. He heard Bobby's sudden intake of breath.

"My God, that's Caterine's. Remi, do you think Caterine and Grandmère are both in that van?"

Remi nodded. Closing his hand around the clip, he said a prayer before placing it in his pocket. "Come on, we've got to follow them." He ran toward his car.

"What about Jonathan?" Bobby asked as he followed.

"Leave him."

Bobby jerked open the T-bird's passenger door and slid into the seat. "How are we supposed to find them?"

Remi smiled. "With this." He flicked a switch, and a blinking white dot appeared on a screen mounted to the dashboard.

"A tracking device?"

Remi nodded as he turned onto St. Charles. "It's part of Caterine's hidden mike. Another precaution we took."

"Does she know she's being tracked?"

"No. I figured the less she knew the better." Watching the white dot, Remi narrowed his eyes. "Where the hell are they going?"

Bobby studied the screen. "What's wrong?"

Remi scowled. "They're crossing the river on 90 toward the west bank."

"It looks like they're turning onto 45," Bobby said. "The Jean Lafitte preserve is in that direction."

"Fuckin' A." Remi increased his speed.

Bobby narrowed his eyes. "It's time for you to tell me what the hell's going on, and how my sister and mother are involved."

Remi glanced over at Bobby's confused, scared face and sighed. "All right, but this involves more of your family than just your mother and sister. And I imagine you're going to have a hard time believing most of it."

Bobby stared straight ahead, his hands clenched into fists, listening as Remi began.

After he'd concluded, minutes passed in silence. Then in a voice full of rage and contempt, Bobby said, "I always knew I came from a messed up family, but this is too fucking much. You're telling me that right now, in that van, my mother, my sister, and Travis Jenkins have kidnapped Caterine and Grandmère and are planning to kill them to get their hands on Ma Chérie? You realize that sounds crazy, right?"

Remi sighed. "I said you wouldn't believe me."

Bobby laughed without humor. "I didn't say I don't believe you. I just said it's crazy. Unfortunately, I believe every word." He turned his attention to their surroundings as Remi slowed the car. "Where are we?"

"They're following a damn service road." The taillights of the van came into sight and Remi killed his headlights, driving by the light of a sliver of a crescent moon.

He knew he had to remain calm and focused, but he could feel his self-control slipping as, through the earpiece, he heard Miss Dauphine ask Caterine how bad she was cut and someone he assumed to be Hyacinth telling Caterine she was going to feed her to the gators.

"Bobby, I've been able to listen off and on to what's happening in the van. Caterine and Miss Dauphine are still alive, but it sounds as if Caterine is hurt." He hesitated before continuing. "And I'm sorry, but your mother is threatening to kill Caterine."

An ominous thump came from under the car as it jerked to a stop.

"Fuck."

"Christ, what did you hit?"

"Hell if I know." Remi put the car in reverse, trying to back off whatever had them hung up. Grinding sounds came from under the car. "*Merde. Fils de putain. Putain de merde,*" he cursed, slamming his fist against the dash. "Come on, Bobby, we're going the rest of the way on foot."

Remi grabbed a flashlight from under his seat and jumped from the car.

He hadn't taken two steps when he clearly heard Caterine in his earpiece screaming his name.

"Grandmère," Caterine sobbed as Paulette's thrust from the Taser left Miss Dauphine lying limp on the van floor. All the hurt and cruelty these two women had subjected her to throughout her life manifested itself into a strength Caterine didn't know she possessed. Ignoring the blood streaming down her side from the knife wound, and with a guttural sound that was pure animal, Caterine came off the floor kicking and swinging. Paulette was the first to feel her fury. Raking her nails across her cousin's face, Caterine let out a string of cuss words that would have made Remi proud. Before Paulette could react, Caterine slapped her with as much force as she could muster. As she reared back for another onslaught, Caterine winced in pain as her hair was practically ripped from her scalp and a hard object was shoved into her back.

"I'm going to love watching you die, you haughty little slut," Hyacinth hissed into Caterine's ear. "You were born into privilege, but you've shown your true nature by spreading your legs for that scum. Once you're dead, my little girl is going to take your place in society as head of Ma Chérie. We'll finally be shown the respect we deserve."

Caterine could feel her strength waning and knew it was a matter of seconds before Hyacinth pulled the trigger on the Taser, rendering her incapable of movement. She had one more chance to escape. She drove her stiletto heel down hard onto Hyacinth's foot. As Hyacinth cried out, Caterine jerked away. She shoved Paulette toward Hyacinth and scrambled to the front of the van. She made it to the passenger seat, fumbling with the door handle. Finally able to get the door open, she half crawled and half fell out onto the hard dirt road.

The heady smell of a bayou filled her nostrils. Wispy tentacles of Spanish moss dangled eerily from the branches of live oaks. In the dark, something slid into the water with a faint splash. Shaking uncontrollably, feeling slightly dizzy, she stumbled into the moonlit night. She hadn't taken more than a few steps when she heard the back of the van open and Hyacinth's taunting laughter.

"Remi-Re-Remi, pl-please, Remi, help us," Caterine sobbed as she tried to put distance between her and her pursuer. As she heard Hyacinth's footsteps gaining on her, she increased her speed only to be brought up short as she stepped in an unseen hole. She felt her ankle twist and fell to her knees. She tried desperately to stand, but Hyacinth was upon her. This time, instead of the Taser pressed to her back, Caterine felt the tip of a knife against her throat.

"Thank you for making this so easy for me," Hyacinth said, laughing gleefully. "Now get up, whore."

She grabbed Caterine's arm and jerked her to her feet. Determined not to give Hyacinth the satisfaction of hearing her cry out in pain, Caterine bit down on her lip until she tasted blood.

"I love you, Remi," she whimpered as she felt the knife slice into her neck.

Chapter Forty-Four

"I love you, too, Princess," came a reassuringly familiar voice from the darkness.

Not sure it wasn't her imagination, Caterine tentatively spoke, "Remi?"

"I'm here, Princess. Don't move. It's all over, Hyacinth," Remi said, his voice low and menacing. "Drop the knife and step away from Caterine. Her Cajun loverboy is standing right behind you with a gun pointed at the back of your head. I suggest you don't give me a reason to use it."

"Mama, please, what's wrong with you? Let Caterine go," Bobby pleaded.

Caterine felt the knife blade on her neck begin to tremble as Hyacinth slowly turned them both around to face Remi and Bobby. Hyacinth's shrill, startled voice quavered.

"Bobby, what are you doing here?"

He cautiously approached. "Mama, please, I want you to let Caterine go and give me the knife."

"Bobby, no, go away," Hyacinth wailed. "You shouldn't be here! You're ruining everything I've worked for."

Tears filled Caterine's eyes at the torment on her cousin's face. "Bobby, I'm so sorry," she murmured.

"Mama, stop." Bobby's voice broke on a sob. "Please, Mama, this isn't right. You have to let Caterine go."

"No. Don't come any closer."

Bobby was steps away from Caterine when Remi fired.

Caterine felt the weight of something strike her back, then Hyacinth's piercing scream. The knife swung away from her throat, and Caterine dropped to her knees. Whimpering, she turned, expecting to see Hyacinth's dead body. Instead, by the light of Remi's flashlight, she saw the thick black snake curled next to her. Stifling her own scream, Caterine tried to get to her feet and felt herself lifted into Remi's comforting embrace. She wrapped her arms tightly around him, buried her face in his neck, and sobbed.

He held her close as her tears dampened his skin. "It's okay, Princess. It's over. I've got you. You're safe."

"Is she dead?" Caterine gasped.

Remi looked over to where Hyacinth stood silently crying, clasped in Bobby's arms. "No, Bobby has her." He took a deep breath. "Princess, are you all right?"

Caterine sniffed. "I thought you'd never get here. But how did you shoot that snake right out of the tree—in the dark?"

Remi smiled. "I was just lucky. I didn't even know it was there. I shot up in the air over Hyacinth's head to scare her, and the snake fell right on top of her."

Caterine shuddered. "I thought it was Hyacinth's dead body hitting me." She lifted her tear-streaked face, her nose inches from his. "Remi, you sure pick a hell of a time, a hell of a place, and a hell of a way to finally tell me you love me."

A shaft of moonlight illuminated their faces. With his mouth now a breath away from hers, he spoke so only she could hear. "Trust me, Princess, this isn't the way I planned on telling you or showing you that I love you more than life itself. But rest assured that when I get you home I plan on telling you and showing you over and over again under more pleasant circumstances. For the meantime—"

"Excuse me, Mr. Michaud, if you could possibly refrain from displaying your affection toward my granddaughter, I would appreciate some assistance out of this vehicle."

"Grandmère. Oh, God, she's all right." Caterine squirmed in Remi's arms. "Put me down. I have to go to her."

"I'll go. Just wait here." Remi placed her gingerly back on her feet. "You won't get far on that ankle."

As he stepped away, he noticed streaks of red on his hands. "Christ, Caterine, you're bleeding. Where are you hurt?"

Caterine touched her neck where Hyacinth had pressed the knife and felt a shallow cut with sticky drying blood. "The cut isn't that deep, and it seems to have stopped bleeding."

He shone the flashlight along her body. "For Christ's sake, Caterine, your face, hands, and arms are smeared with blood." He peered closer. "And it's streaming from your side."

"Whoa." She swayed slightly. "I'd forgotten about my side. I thought it had stopped bleeding. I guess moving around started it up again."

"Damn it, Caterine, hold on to me before you fall." He shone the flashlight around the area until he spotted a fallen log. He picked her up, carried her over, and sat her down. "What are you wearing under that dress?"

"Petticoats. Why?"

"Let me see how badly you're cut." He held the flashlight close to her side. Cursing, he reached under her gown and tore off a long strip of petticoat. He made a thick pad out of the cloth and pressed it to her side. "Hold this tight while I go help your grandmother."

Caterine smiled. "I don't think there's any saving my gown this time. You know, Remi, every time I wear this something inconceivable happens to me."

He grinned wickedly. "Nothing as inconceivable as the first time, Princess."

As he stood, all humor left her face and she put her hand on his arm. "Remi, wait. Travis is in the van, and I'm afraid he might be dead." Her breath caught. "He was stabbed by Hyacinth while trying to save me."

Hyacinth moaned loudly, rocking back and forth in Bobby's arms.

"Hush, Mama, hush." Tears rolling down his face, Bobby brushed his mother's hair back. "We'll take you someplace where you can get some help."

Caterine's heart broke at the anguish in Bobby's voice. Ignoring Remi's instructions to stay put, she rose and tentatively reached out her hand, lightly placing it on his arm. "Bobby, I'm so sorry. I had no idea things were this bad."

He looked at her with bleak, tear-filled eyes. "I know, Cat. Neither did I. I can't help but wonder had I been here would this have still happened?"

"Don't do that to yourself. We have no way of knowing how ill she is and how long this has been coming on."

"Robert, we'll see to it your mother gets the best possible care," Miss Dauphine said as Remi helped her walk to where they stood. "Mr. Michaud isn't certain how seriously injured Mr. Jenkins is, but one can only hope he'll live. If Mr. Jenkins survives, whether he will press assault charges is another matter. Unfortunately, we have another problem. Robert, I'm afraid Paulette has lost all sanity as well."

"What?" Bobby turned to Remi.

Remi sighed. "She's in the van curled up on the floor around Travis and won't leave. She keeps saying he's going to marry her. I've called the police." Remi held up his cell phone. "Someone should be here soon."

Caterine put her arms around her grandmother and held her tight. "Oh, Grandmère, I thought when Paulette got you with the stun gun she'd killed you."

Miss Dauphine's mouth tightened into a thin line. "Whatever that contraption was supposed to do to me, it must not have worked properly. I felt strange for a minute then it passed."

"The Taser probably wasn't fully charged," Remi said. "You're lucky, Miss Dauphine. I don't know what would happen if someone your age were to be hit with a full charge."

"Well, Mr. Michaud, I never intend on finding out. Pray tell me, how did you and my grandson find us?"

"I'm wearing a hidden microphone, Grandmère," Caterine answered. "Remi was able to hear everything that was going on." She frowned and turned to Remi. "I didn't know where Travis was taking us, so I wasn't able to tell you where we were. How did you find us?"

"Your mike also has a tracking device." Remi scowled. "What I'd like to know is how in the hell Travis was able to get you out of the house without any of my men stopping him."

"Travis tased Paul, then told me they had Grandmère. After that, things moved rather quickly."

"It doesn't matter how quickly things moved, Caterine, someone should have stopped Travis."

"Everyone stay nice and quiet," a voice spoke from the darkness. "Remi, we've got you covered."

"You boys are a little late, aren't you?" Remi said with irritation. "Come on out. I've got everything under control."

Caterine watched as four large shapes carrying guns materialized out of the darkness.

"We saw you leave. We weren't that far behind," Remi's Uncle Sosa explained.

"Yeah, well." Remi glared as his eyes moved from Uncle Sosa to Uncle Bernard to his cousins, Philippe and Cecil. "Would one of you like to tell me how Travis was able to get Caterine out of the house and out here to the middle of the goddamned swamp without anyone getting in his way?"

Before Sosa could answer, another voice came out of the darkness. "It wasn't their fault, Remi, it was mine." Paul stepped into the clearing. "I was stupid enough to let Travis hit me from behind. Then, while the boys were checking on me, Jules and Markus insisted on knowing what was happening, so we wasted more time filling them in. I told them to stay put there at the house and we'd call as soon as we found you. As we were leaving, we found Jonathan Day coming to on the driveway. I assume that means he also had a part in this?"

The men listened in amazement as Remi relayed the sequence of events as heard through Caterine's microphone.

"At least we were smart enough to put tracking devices in all of our cars," Bernard said. "Otherwise, we wouldn't have found you."

"I still can't believe Travis and Jonathan were part of this." Paul shook his head in wonder. "Who would have thought? Paulette and Hyacinth don't surprise me in the least, but those two?"

Wailing sirens pierced the quiet night, and three sets of lights could be seen flashing through the trees.

"You boys had better put your guns away," Remi suggested. "We don't want to confuse New Orleans' finest as to who the bad guys are."

Paul saw to the loading of Travis into the ambulance while a medic cleaned and bandaged Caterine's wound. When she promised to have the cut seen to as soon as possible, the medic reluctantly agreed not to take her along in the ambulance.

After Remi, Caterine, and Miss Dauphine gave statements to the police, Bobby helped his mother and sister into the backseat of one of the cruisers. "I'm going along with Mother and Paulette to the police station." Bobby turned to Caterine and his grandmother. "I called home and spoke with my dad. I didn't tell him exactly what's happened. I just told him to meet me at the station. He didn't know where Ray had gone, so I'm going to try and get in touch with him as well. Hopefully, he can meet us there."

Caterine recalled why Ray had left the party and sighed. "Bobby, Ray might be hard to get in touch with. He left the party with two police officers."

Frowning, Bobby looked quizzically at Caterine. "Why would he do that?"

Caterine bit her lower lip. She wasn't sure how many more family disasters her cousin would be able to take. She took a deep breath. "It's all too complicated to go into right now. Just go to the police station, and I'll try to find Ray for you."

For a second, Bobby stared into Caterine's face, shook his head, then bent and kissed Miss Dauphine's cheek. He hugged Caterine, and got into the front seat of the cruiser. Paulette and Hyacinth sat silent and unmoving in the backseat.

"God knows what will become of those two," Miss Dauphine said as she and Caterine watched the police car's taillights disappear into the night. "My heart goes out to Robert for what he's going to have to face. Now, Caterine, tell me what you didn't want to tell Robert regarding Ray and the police."

Caterine hesitated. "Grandmère, you've been through enough for one night. It can wait until I know more details myself."

"Caterine, considering all that's happened tonight, I can't imagine anything you told me could be much worse."

As she debated how to tell her grandmother that Randal might have shot five people, Remi and his uncles and his cousins joined them.

"Bernard and Cecil have offered to take you to the hospital to see if you need stitches, then see that you and Miss Dauphine get home safely," Remi said.

"What will you be doing?" Caterine asked.

"I have to see if we can get my car off whatever it's stuck on. If it's not drivable, I'll have to get Antoine to tow it to his garage. Hopefully that won't be necessary. I'll see you at home as soon as I can."

Miss Dauphine cleared her throat. "Mr. Michaud, there aren't words to express my gratitude for all you've done to save both our lives."

Remi smiled. "My pleasure, ma'am."

"Well, Mr. Michaud, since this unpleasantness has now reached a conclusion, I no longer feel it's necessary for Caterine to reside with you. Therefore, I will be expecting her to come home where she belongs."

Remi's expression went cold as his eyes met Caterine's. "What will it be, Princess? Are you going back to your old home in Audubon Place or your new home with me on Rue Toulouse?" His jaw tight and his gut clenched, Remi watched the indecision in Caterine's eyes as they traveled from him to her grandmother and back to him.

He silently cursed at his utter stupidity in imagining she'd ever leave her world of wealth and privilege for a simple life with him. The intervening silence grew until, unable to stand there another minute, he spoke quietly to his four male relatives, then walked away into the darkness.

Chapter Forty-Five

"Remi, wait!" Caterine called. The anger, hurt, and betrayal she'd seen in his eyes was like a blast of icy water hitting her in the face. The moment he'd walked away, she knew she'd just made the biggest mistake of her life. Even though she loved her grandmother dearly and understood her responsibility to Ma Chérie, Remi and her love for him had to come first in her life. "Remi, no, please wait. Listen to me." Caterine started after him.

"Hold on there, *cher*." Uncle Sosa put a restraining hand on her arm. "That's one hurt, angry man. I suggest you let him cool down first before you try and talk to him. Trust me, I've seen him like this before, and it can be real ugly."

"Caterine, my dear, it's best if you let him go." Miss Dauphine said.

For the first time in her life, Caterine felt true irritation toward her grandmother. She forced a smile and turned to Remi's uncles and cousins, who looked uneasy and uncertain as to what they should be doing. "Sosa, would you and the others please give my grandmother and me some privacy for just a few minutes? Then I'd appreciate it if one of you would please take my grandmother home and another take me to Remi's." At Sosa's nod, Caterine took a deep breath and addressed her grandmother.

"Grandmère, I love you dearly and I appreciate all you've done for me throughout my life, but I also love Remi Michaud. I love him with every ounce of my being, with every breath I take, with every beat of my heart.

And if he'll have me, I want to spend the rest of my life married to him. Now, I hope you can accept that, but if you can't, I'm sorry. Neither you, nor anyone, nor anything is going to stand in my way of having the man I love." In the silence that followed her declaration, she stood holding her breath, waiting for her grandmother's reaction.

Minutes passed while Miss Dauphine stared into her eyes, then she sighed. "I would have preferred to have this conversation with you in a more private and comfortable setting, but if you wish to discuss this now, so be it. Let me make myself perfectly clear. I do not dislike Mr. Michaud. I find him an honest, hardworking, honorable man who would make you a fine husband. What I am opposed to is you and him rushing into a marriage based on a relationship that had its beginnings in what could only be described as stressful and emotional circumstances. I'm afraid once you begin living normal lives, you'll discover what you thought of as passionate love is nothing more than the result of two people being caught up in the excitement of the moment. I blame myself for sheltering you and not letting you experience more of life. I can't change the past, but I can try and prevent you from making a huge mistake with your future."

Caterine opened her mouth, but Miss Dauphine continued without giving her a chance to speak.

"Now, I can certainly see how Mr. Michaud could sweep a young girl off her feet and make her think she's hopelessly in love with him, but a lasting relationship isn't built on sexual gratification alone. All I'm asking is for you and Mr. Michaud to give your relationship time and not hurry into something you'll both regret. I'm also asking you to spend this time living back in your own home. Now I've had my say. You do what you feel is right."

"But Grandmère, I—"

"As for me, I'm tired, cold, and weary of all this. I wish to go home and check on Annabelle, then go to bed. I expect Frances and Jules dealt with our house full of guests. That's one good thing I can say about Frances— when hit with a crisis she can handle a situation promptly. I have to say this will be a Mardi Gras I won't soon forget. Now, if one of these young men would oblige me, I'd appreciate a ride home."

Caterine swallowed hard then threw her arms around her grandmother. "I love you, and I promise I'll think about what you said, but first I have to find Remi and make things right between us."

Miss Dauphine patted her shoulder. "You go find your young man. I'll speak with you tomorrow, which will be soon enough to deal with this ugly situation."

Remi sat on a barstool at Erin Rose, downed his third shot of Jack Daniel's, and lit another cigarette. Strengthened by his seething anger after leaving Caterine, he'd managed to drag out the rotten log that had been wedged under his car. Then he'd driven home, dropped off his car, and begun to walk, ending up here. He knew, considering the mood he was in, that sitting there getting drunk wasn't a smart thing to do, but he couldn't bring himself to go home to his apartment alone.

In all his years on the police force, he'd never felt such gut-wrenching terror as when he'd seen Hyacinth holding that knife against Caterine's throat. In that moment he'd known that if he managed to get her safely away, he'd fight anyone at any odds to make Caterine his for the rest of their lives. *Well, it seems the lady has other plans that don't include you.*

He finally told her he loved her, and what did she do but throw it back in his face? Christ, it was only last night he'd made love to her for most of the night, and now she was gone. *You stupid shit, you knew this day would come. Now here you sit, acting as if you hadn't expected her to choose a life of wealth over staying with you.*

He signaled for another shot. *She'll find some guy of her own class and forget you ever existed.* The thought of another man touching Caterine sickened him and fueled his growing anger. *I'm the only man who can please you, Princess. We'll see how long it is before you come back, wanting what I can give you.* Images of Caterine's pleasure as she writhed beneath him had him downing that shot and ordering another. *A few more of these, and maybe I can drink her out of my mind.*

But the more he drank, the more the images of Caterine tormented his alcohol-fogged brain. His melancholy thoughts were interrupted by a group of rowdy Mardi Gras celebrants crowding around the bar. Jostled, he turned, ready to punch whoever was standing behind him. As he stared into the scared eyes of a skinny college kid with glasses, Remi realized he was way too drunk and just looking for a fight. He needed to get the hell out of there, so he tossed down more bills than necessary and made his way through the mass of people. Out on the street, he took deep breaths trying to sober up. Deciding it was hopeless, he headed home.

Caterine paced from Remi's balcony into the living room and back out again, checking up and down Toulouse each time she stopped. *It's three in the morning. Where is he?* She knew he had to be someplace close because his car was parked out front. She'd been surprised to find the apartment empty when she'd arrived. She needed to tell him she loved him and that she wanted to stay here with him. She also wanted to tell him she'd spoken with Ray. Randal had been tracked down in the company of that tramp, Laurie Conway. Thankfully, he had not been dressed as a devil or shooting people at the Triple Aces. Whoever that had been had managed to kill Rivette, though, ending any threat to Randal and the High Roller and canceling Charlotte's debt.

Hyacinth and Paulette were on their way to the state hospital in Baton Rouge for psychiatric evaluation. Annabelle had been treated and released, and she was back at the house with Grandmère.

As she once again leaned over the balcony railing, Caterine heard footsteps approaching from the direction of Bourbon Street. She said a quick prayer of thanks when she saw it was Remi and that he was safe. She waited for him to see her, but he seemed to be having difficulty getting his key out of his pocket and walked right beneath her without looking up. She smiled and went to wait for him inside.

As she heard him fumbling with his key, she hurried to open the door. She took a step back at the sight that greeted her. He looked disheveled, drunk, and a little dangerous.

She moistened her lips before she spoke. "I've been waiting for you. Are you all right?"

Remi leaned against the doorjamb and tried to focus. Was he so drunk he was seeing things? He closed his eyes and opened them. No, she was really standing there. "What the hell are you doing here, Caterine?"

Confusion filled her face as she took a step back. "I live here. I've been waiting for you. I have things to tell you."

He came into the room and slammed the door behind him. "Is that right? What is it, Princess, you've come to tell me? Could it be the fact that you're done with me? Have I served my usefulness and now you're going back where you belong? Or could it be you've come back for one last fuck before you go back uptown?"

Her eyes opened wide then narrowed. "Remi, you're being vulgar and crude. Obviously, you're still angry and this isn't a good time for us to talk. You should just go to bed."

"Talk about what? About how you got what you needed out of me and now I'm not good enough for you anymore? I was sure good enough to spread your legs for. I was sure good enough to put my mouth on your little *cocotte* and my dick inside you. I was sure good enough to save your sweet ass from being killed, but when it comes down to it, I'm not good enough for uptown Caterine Doucette to marry. Well, Princess, if you came wanting sex, I'll be happy to oblige."

As he talked, he'd been backing Caterine toward the sofa. Now as he reached for her, she adeptly scooted around to the back, putting the sofa between them.

His smile was pure satisfaction. "You want to play games, Princess. Then let's play."

"Remi, you're very drunk and acting extremely mean and nasty. I don't want you to come near me until you sober up and calm down."

"Is that right? Then you shouldn't have come here, because you're right—I am drunk and looking for a fight."

"Well, I don't want to fight with you." Her own anger visibly rose. "I came here to talk to you about us."

His laugh was humorless. "What *us*? You dumped me. Remember?"

Caterine put her hands on her hips. "I did *not* dump you. And I'm not going to try and explain anything to you while you're in this condition. You know what, Remi? You're right. I need to leave. I'll call you tomorrow and we'll talk."

She edged her way toward the end of the sofa closest to the door and began to run. Remi caught her, tumbling them both onto the thick rug in front of the fireplace, with him landing on top.

As he looked down into her startled face, all the fight in him slowly drained away, replaced by his love for her. He swallowed hard. "I can't lose you, Princess." He brought his mouth down on hers for a crushing kiss. Expecting resistance, he moaned deep in his throat as her mouth softened under his.

When he broke the kiss, she gently brushed the hair from his forehead. "I love you, you idiot. I don't want to leave you. That's what I've been trying to tell you."

He gazed into eyes full of love and tenderness. When he spoke, his words were raw with emotion. "God, Princess, don't leave me. I can't live without you. I'll love you until the day I die."

Caterine's eyes flooded with tears. "I love you with every breath I take, and I'll never leave you, Pirate."

He blinked back the moisture that filled his own eyes. "How did I not only get lucky enough to find you but lucky enough to have you love me as well?"

She smiled. "I'm the lucky one. You showed me I don't have to be afraid to give my heart and love to someone."

His lopsided grin was pure devil. "I'd carry you to the bed, Princess, but I think I'm too drunk to make love to you. And besides, I'm afraid we wouldn't make it that far."

She began to unbutton his shirt. "I kind of like it right here. I believe the floor is one place we haven't made love."

As she watched, his eyelids slowly began to close. "Oomph." A whoosh of air escaped her lips as his full weight fell upon her. "Remi?" She shook him. "Remi, wake up you're squishing me."

She tried to shove him off, but his body was dead weight. He began to snore. "Great. Now what?" She wriggled and pushed until she was finally able to get herself out from under him.

Chapter Forty-Six

I'm going to kill whoever is ringing that fucking bell, Remi thought as his eyes slowly opened. Blinking, he tried to clear his pounding head. As his eyes focused, he stared uncomprehendingly at the cream and green pattern beneath him. Where the hell was he, and why did his head feel like an entire zydeco band was playing inside it?

Untangling himself from a blanket, he rolled onto his back on the hearth rug and groaned. In the background, he could hear a quiet female voice. Memories of the night before began to trickle back into his whiskey-soaked brain. He put his hands over his face to block out the morning light and attempted to listen to Caterine's phone conversation, but the accordion playing in his head was way too loud. He sensed her standing above him and eased his hands off his face, tentatively opening his eyes.

"Shut the drapes, Caterine. It's too damned bright in here. And why in the hell am I still in my clothes and sleeping on the floor?"

Caterine glared down at him. "Remi, you're usually not a pleasant person in the morning, but with a hangover, you sound like a roaring alligator. You're fully clothed and sleeping on the floor because after you passed out on top of me, I couldn't move you." She cocked her head. "How much of last night do you actually remember?"

He placed his hands back over his eyes and pressed hard. "I need hot coffee, a cold shower, and food. Don't even think about having a conversation with me until I've had all of them."

She smiled. "You're in luck. The coffee is already made, and you can take a shower, but there isn't anything to eat. So while you're getting cleaned up, I'll run to the little market around the corner." She clapped her hands and twirled around. "Isn't it wonderful, Remi? I can finally go outside on my own. I can go to work. I can drive my new car. I can go anywhere I please and no one wants to kill me."

Remi gritted his teeth as he rose from the floor. "Caterine, if you don't quiet down, I'll be the one who kills you."

She threw her arms around his neck and kissed him soundly. "No, you won't, because you love me and want to spend the rest of your life with me."

He gazed into her happy smiling face. "Is that right, Princess? Says who?"

"Says you. Or don't you remember?"

He ran is hands through his hair. "I seem to remember saying something like that. I also recall saying some really ugly things to you."

"Yes, you did, and I'd better never see you like that again. You were kind of scary."

The humor left his face, and he pulled her into his arms. "I'm sorry, Princess. You have to know I'd never harm you. I was hurt, angry, and very, very drunk. I know that's not an excuse, and I normally don't get in that condition. Actually, I'm usually a pretty friendly drunk. In fact, I usually find myself getting rather horny."

She rolled her eyes. "If I had my choice, I'd take the horny drunk. Seriously, Remi, I'm sorry to be the one who caused you to get yourself into that condition. Years of doing what I thought was expected of me, and always wanting to please my grandmother, is why I hesitated when you asked me to choose."

He sighed. "I should have never placed you in a position like that. I never wanted you to have to choose between me and your grandmother."

She reached up and stroked his cheek. "I'm not going to choose. I love you both, and Grandmère is trying to accept that. She told me you'd make a good husband, but she's afraid our relationship is built on nothing more than being brought together by intense circumstances and great sex."

He rubbed her backside and grinned. "What's wrong with a relationship built on great sex?"

She laughed and gently pushed him away. "Go take your shower, and I'll go get us something to eat. Then while we're eating, I'll fill you in on what I've found out."

After a handful of aspirin and a cold shower, Remi sat on the balcony drinking his second cup of coffee and began to feel somewhat human again. Watching impatiently for Caterine to return with food, he was surprised when she finally appeared hurrying down the street, not a grocery bag in sight. "What's your rush, *cher*?" he called. "Where're the groceries?"

"Oh, Remi, it's for sale. Come quick. I told the man we'd be right back," she said with excitement.

He frowned and leaned over the railing. "Caterine, what are you talking about? I'm starving. Where's the food?"

"Remi, hurry up. I haven't been to the grocery yet. I saw the For Sale sign and I had to go in."

"What For Sale sign?"

"The For Sale sign on the house. Oh, Remi, it's perfect and I absolutely love it. Please come down. We have to go quickly; there're other people looking at it."

"You want to show me a house? What about breakfast?"

She bounced up and down on her toes. "Oh, for heaven's sake, forget about breakfast. You can eat later. We have to go now. Remi, please come on."

Sighing, he did as she asked.

"Wait until you see it. It's perfect," Caterine said excitedly as they made their way along Toulouse. "It's a fully renovated two-story Creole with a porte cochere leading back to a lovely courtyard. It has wrought iron balconies, three bedrooms, three baths, a wonderful modern kitchen, two fireplaces, and a cozy library. The master bedroom is huge with a private bath and French doors leading out onto a gallery overlooking the courtyard."

As Caterine chattered on, dollar signs danced before Remi's eyes. He knew damn well what houses cost in the Quarter and was sure he wouldn't be able to afford the one she was describing. Not wanting to burst her enthusiastic bubble, he walked solemnly along beside her.

"Look, there it is." She pointed.

He could understand why she was so excited. The tall, creamy yellow house with dark green shutters also appealed to him.

"Caterine." He hesitated. "I'm sorry, but I don't see how I could ever afford this house."

Caterine, momentarily speechless, looked into his apologetic eyes and swallowed. In a soft voice she replied, "I can."

He shook his head. "I won't have you and your Doucette money supporting us. If I can't afford it, we don't get it. And that's final."

He knew it was his pride talking, but he couldn't help it. If she married him, she'd damn well have to get used to living on his income.

Her mouth opened and closed, then she took a deep breath. "I thought when two people were married they shared each other's incomes. It won't be Doucette money I bring into our marriage, it will be money I've earned by working at my own business. Doucette money has nothing to do with Ma Chérie."

Reluctantly, he knew she was right, but still he couldn't bring himself to let her purchase the home they'd be living in. He looked into her eyes and she turned away, but not before he saw the tears she was trying to hide.

She took a deep breath and turned back to him. "Okay, let's go get you something to eat." Without another word, she began to walk away.

He put a restraining hand on her arm. "Are you really willing to give up this house, Princess?"

"If you say we can't afford it, then yes."

He put his hand under her chin and tipped up her face. His heart melted, seeing the tears she'd been trying to hold back brimming in her eyes. "You'd do that for me? You'd give up something you want this bad, just because I say so?"

She nodded. "I love you and I want our marriage to work. If my money makes you uncomfortable, we'll live on what you make. I'll put the money I earn into a trust fund for our children."

Remi took a deep breath and sighed. "I suppose I should do this first." He gathered her into his arms and kissed her. "Princess, will you marry me?"

This time, the tears that filled her eyes were full of happiness. "Oh, yes, Pirate, I'll marry you."

His devilish grin was back in place. "In that case, Princess, you can buy me a wedding gift. Let's go see our new house."

Epilogue

Toulouse, France.
Four months later.
A warm June sun shone down upon the little white rowboat as Caterine and Remi floated lazily through the city on the quiet waters of the Garonne River.

"Are you hungry?" Caterine asked. "Madame Laroche packed us enough food for five people."

Remi yawned. "I'm always hungry. Especially when you keep me up most of the night making love."

She rolled her eyes. "Oh, right. Just who was keeping whom awake?" Sighing happily, she lay back and enjoyed the beautiful landscape passing by. "I'm so glad we came here for our honeymoon. The Laroches seem to be nice people, and I love their inn."

"Uh-huh," Remi murmured. "Why don't you open that basket, and let's see what we've got." He chuckled as she brought out bread, cheese, *saucisson*, fruit, wine, and juice. "With that much food, we could stay out here all day."

"That's fine with me. Isn't it wonderful we can be here and not have any worries?" As his brows rose, she shrugged. "Well, not too many worries anyway."

Remi couldn't help but smile. "If you say so, Princess." To himself he thought, *just a few little worries.* Such as Travis surviving the knife wound and suing the Doucettes, Markus divorcing Hyacinth while she and Paulette were locked away in a clinic, and Charlotte doing rehab in Switzerland. Not to mention the citizens of New Orleans, who were glued to the front page of the *Times-Picayune*, relishing all the scandalous details.

Remi chuckled. "No, Princess, there's nothing to worry about."

She gave him an annoyed glance. "You have to admit our lives are a lot calmer now. We had a lovely little wedding on the bayou, we're in our new home, and Grandmère is happily spending the summer with Annabelle at Willows. Yvette will be coming to work for me and, wonder of wonders, Aunt Frances has done an about-face and is actually helping at Ma Chérie instead of obstructing me.

"With Ray turning Doucette Shipping over to Bobby and helping Randal run the High Roller, I'll have my favorite cousin nearby and the family finances will be put back in order. So I'd say, all-in-all, things are going rather well. Even Antoine is going to settle down and marry Suzette."

Remi grinned and leaned over, popping a chunk of bread with a slice of buttery cheese into her open mouth. "You're absolutely right, Princess. Our lives are much calmer now."

She swallowed the bread and leaned close. "You didn't let me finish. I was about to say, 'and there's the baby.' "

Remi froze, his wineglass halfway to his lips. "What did you just say?"

She smiled triumphantly. "I said, *and there's the baby.*"

"Whose baby?"

Her smile widened. "Our baby."

"How did that happen?"

Caterine laughed. "How do you think it happened? I'm afraid during all the confusion, I ran out of birth control pills. I figured I'd been on them long enough that it wouldn't hurt to go without them for a few days."

Remi could only stare in shock and disbelief.

The smile left her face, replaced by fear and doubt. "What's wrong? Aren't you happy with the news?"

"What?" He shook his head, trying to clear it of the mental images of the woman he loved holding his baby. He saw her eyes fill with tears, and he reached out and pulled her close. "*Viens ici,* Princess. Of course I'm happy. *Je t'aime*—I love you, Caterine." He kissed her long and tenderly. Exactly when will I be a papa?"

"Around Christmas. Oh, Remi, are you really pleased?"

He pushed the remaining food out of their way and pulled her next to him. "*Mais yeah, cher*, I'm happy." He brushed her lips with his. "I love you, Princess."

Caterine smiled. "I love you, Pirate."

Acknowledgments

I'd like to thank the ladies of my editing team: Andrea McKay, Allison Hoover, and especially my senior editor, Wendy Depperschmidt. You're still the best!

I'd also like to thank The City of New Orleans and the people who live in that wonderful city for giving me the inspiration for this book. I fell in love with New Orleans when David and I went there for our honeymoon, and I never get tired of going back. Two years ago, I got the idea for *Rue Toulouse* while sitting on the balcony of our hotel on Toulouse. I hope you enjoy this story as much as I enjoyed writing it.

Debby

About the Author

 Debby Grahl lives on Hilton Head Island, South Carolina, with her husband, David, and their cat, Tigger. When she's not writing, she enjoys biking, walking on the beach, and having a glass of wine at sunset. Her favorite places to visit are the Cotswolds of England, Captiva Island in Florida, New Orleans, New York City, and her home state of Michigan. She is a history buff who also enjoys reading murder mysteries, time travel, and of course, romance. Visually impaired since childhood by Retinitis pigmentosa (RP), she uses screen-reading software to research and write her books. Debby belongs to Romance Writers of America, Florida Romance Writers, Hearts Across History, and Lowcountry Romance Writers. Her first novel, *The Silver Crescent*, was released January 2014.